The Chaplain of the Fleet

Walter Besant

THE CHAPLAIN OF THE FLEET.

THE
CHAPLAIN OF THE FLEET

BY

WALTER BESANT AND JAMES RICE

LIBRARY EDITION

London
CHATTO AND WINDUS, PICCADILLY
1888

CONTENTS.

Part I.

WITHIN THE RULES.

CHAP.
I. HOW KITTY LOST HER FATHER AND HER FRIENDS.

II. HOW KITTY MADE ENGAGEMENTS.

III. HOW WE CAME TO LONDON ON THE COACH.

IV. HOW KITTY FIRST SAW THE DOCTOR.

V. HOW KITTY WITNESSED A FLEET WEDDING.

VI. HOW KITTY BEGAN TO ENJOY THE LIBERTIES OF THE FLEET.

VII. HOW KITTY LEARNED TO KNOW THE DOCTOR.

VIII. HOW KITTY SPENT HER TIME.

IX. HOW THE SOUTH SEA BUBBLE MADE TWO WOMEN PRISONERS.

X. HOW THE DOCTOR WAS AT HOME TO HIS FRIENDS.

XI. HOW THE DOCTOR DISMISSED HIS FRIENDS.

XII. HOW KITTY EXECUTED THE DOCTOR'S REVENGE.

XIII. HOW LORD CHUDLEIGH WOKE OUT OF SLEEP.

XIV. HOW MRS. DEBORAH WAS RELEASED.

XV. HOW MRS. ESTHER WAS DISCHARGED.

I. HOW WE RETURNED TO THE POLITE WORLD.

II. HOW WE WENT TO THE WELLS.

III.	HOW NANCY RECKONED UP THE COMPANY.
IV.	HOW KITTY WENT TO HER FIRST BALL.
V.	HOW KITTY WORE HER CROWN.
VI.	HOW THE DOCTOR WROTE TO KITTY.
VII.	HOW KITTY BROKE HER PROMISE.
VIII.	HOW KITTY HAD LETTERS AND VERSES.
IX.	HOW LORD CHUDLEIGH WENT TO LONDON.
X.	HOW TWO OLD FRIENDS CAME TO EPSOM.
XI.	HOW SIR MILES RENEWED HIS OFFER.
XII.	HOW HARRY TEMPLE PROVED HIS VALOUR.
XIII.	HOW DURDANS WAS ILLUMINATED.
XIV.	HOW MY LORD MADE HIS CONFESSION.
XV.	HOW NANCY HAD A QUICK TONGUE.
XVI.	HOW SPED THE MASQUERADE.
XVII.	HOW KITTY PREVENTED A DUEL.
XVIII.	HOW HARRY GOT RELEASED.
XIX.	HOW WILL LEVETT WAS DISAPPOINTED.
XX.	HOW WILL WOULD NOT BE CROSSED.
XXI.	HOW KITTY WENT TO LONDON.
XXII.	HOW LORD CHUDLEIGH RECEIVED HIS FREEDOM.

Part I.

WITHIN THE RULES.

CHAPTER I.

HOW KITTY LOST HER FATHER AND HER FRIENDS.

My life has been (above any merits of my own) so blessed by Providence, that methinks its history should be begun with the ringing of bells, the singing of psalms, the sound of cornet, flute, harp, sackbut, psaltery, and all kinds of music. For surely the contemplation of a happy course should, even towards its close, be accompanied by a heart full of cheerful piety and gratitude. And though, as often happens to us in the Lord's wisdom, ill fortune, disappointment, troubles of the flesh, and pain of disease may perhaps afflict me in these latter years of fleeting life, they ought not to lessen the glad song of praise for blessings formerly vouchsafed (and still dwelling in my memory) of love, of joy, and of happiness. Truly, the earth is a delightful place; a fair garden, which yields pleasant fruit; and, if it may be so said with becoming reverence, there are yet, outside the gates of Eden, places here and there which for beauty and delight, to those who thither win their way, are comparable with Paradise itself. In such a place it has been my happy lot to dwell.

Yet, just as the newborn babe begins his earthly course with a wail—ah, joyful cry for ear of mother!—so must this book begin with tears and weeping.

The weeping is that of an orphan over her dead father; the tears are those which fall upon a coffin beside an open grave: they are the tears of men and women come to pay this reverence at the burial of a man who was their best friend and their most faithful servant.

The Chaplain of the Fleet

All the morning the funeral knell has been tolling; the people listen, now, to the solemn words of a service which seem spoken by the dead man himself to those who mourn. They admonish and warn, but they bid them be of good cheer, lift up hearts, and trust in the Lord.

When we are in great grief and sorrow, outward things seem to affect us more than in ordinary times, when the heart is in repose, and the mind, perhaps, slower of apprehension. The day, for instance, was late in May; the blackbird, thrush, and chaffinch were singing in the wood beside the church; a lark was carolling in the sky; a cuckoo was calling from the coppice; the hedges were green, and the trees were bright with their first fresh foliage; the white may-blossom, the yellow laburnum, and the laylock were at their best, and the wild roses were just beginning.

To the country girl who had never yet left her native village, this joy of the spring was so natural that it did not jar upon the grief of her soul. When the funeral was over, and the grave filled in and the people all dispersed, she stood for a few moments alone, and then walked away across the long grass of the churchyard, stepping lightly over the graves of the villagers, opened the little wicket gate which led to the vicarage garden, passed in, and sought a sheltered place where, beneath the shade of bushes, she sat upon a bench and folded her hands, looked before her, and fell a-thinking.

She was between sixteen and seventeen, but tall of her age, and looked older; she wore a new black frock; she had thrown her straw hat with black ribbons upon the bench beside her. As for her face, I suppose it was pretty. Alas! I am a hypocrite, because I *know* that it was pretty. As yet, she did not know it, and had never thought about her face. Her eyes were brown (she has ever been thankful to have had brown eyes); her features were regular, and her face rather long; her hair was abundant and soft: it was like the hair of most English maidens, of a dark brown, or chestnut (it is now white); her arms were shapely, and her fingers thin and delicate (they were the fingers of a Pleydell); as for her complexion, it was as good as can be expected in a girl whose blood is pure, who has, as yet, known no late hours, who has been taught to use plenty of cold water and no washes or messes, who has run about without thinking of freckles, and has lived in the open air on homely food. In other words, as fine a show of red and white was in the cheeks of that child as ever Sir Joshua Reynolds tried to copy upon canvas.

She was thinking many things. First, of her father and his death; of the funeral, and the grief shown by people whom she had thought to be hard of heart, insensible to his admonitions, and untouched by his prayers. Yet they stood about the grave and wept, rude women and rough men. Would they ever again find a minister so benevolent, so pious, and so active in all good work? She thought of the house, and how dark and lonely it was, deserted by its former owner. She thought of what she should do, in the time before her, and how she would be received in her new home. One thing comforted her: she looked older than she was, and was tall and strong. She could be helpful.

Then she drew out of her pocket a letter written for her only three days before her father died. She knew it quite by heart, but yet she read it again slowly, as if there might still be something in it which had escaped her.

"MY BELOVED DAUGHTER" (thus it ran),—"Knowing that I am about to die and to appear before my Father and merciful Judge, it is right that I should bestir myself to make thee comprehend the situation in which thou wilt be placed. Of worldly wealth I have, indeed, but little to give thee. Face thy lot with hope, resignation, and a cheerful heart. The righteous man, said one who knew, hath never been found to beg his bread. Indeed, the whole course of this world is so ordered (by Divine wisdom), that he who chooseth the narrow path chooseth also the safest. Therefore, be of good cheer.

"*Imprimis*. When I am buried, search the bedstead, and, in the head thereof, will be found a bag containing the sum of one hundred guineas in gold pieces. I have saved this money during my twenty years of incumbency. I trust that it will not be laid to my charge that I did not give this also to the poor; but I thought of my daughter first. Secondly, Farmer Goodpenny is indebted to me in the sum of twenty-two pounds, four shillings, and eightpence, for which I have his note. I charge thee that he be not asked to pay interest, and since it may be that he hath not the money, let it wait his good time. He is an honest man, who fears God. Thirdly, there is money, some twelve pounds or more, lying in my desk for present use. Fourthly, there are several small sums due to me, money put out and lent (but not at usury), such as five shillings from the widow Coxon, and other amounts the which I will have thee forgive and remit entirely; for these my debtors are poor people. The horse is old, but he will fetch five pounds, and the cow will sell for two. As for the books, they may be sent to Maidstone, where they may be sold. But I doubt they will not bring more than ten guineas, or thereabouts, seeing that the call for works of divinity is small, even among my brethren of the cloth. And when you go to London, forget not to ask of Mr. Longman, publisher, of St. Paul's Churchyard, an account of my 'Sermons,' published by him last year; my essay on 'Philo-Judæus,' issued four years ago; and my 'Reflections on the Christian State,' which he hath by him in manuscript. He will perhaps be able to return a larger sum of money than I was led by him at first to expect.

"My will and plain injunctions are as follows:

"When everything has been paid that is owing, and there are none who can hereafter say that he had a claim upon me which was unsatisfied, get together thy wearing apparel and effects, and under some proper protection, as soon as such can be found, go to London, and there seek out thy uncle and mother's brother, the Reverend Gregory Shovel, Doctor of Divinity, of whom I have spoken to thee of old. I take shame to myself that I have not sent him, for many years, letters of brotherly friendship. Nor do I rightly remember where he is to be found. But I know that he lives, because once a year there comes to me a keg or anker of rum, which I know must be from him, and which I have drunk with my parishioners in a spirit of gratitude. Perhaps it would have been more consistent in a brother clergyman to have sent one of the latest books of our scholars. But he means well, and the rum is, I confess, of the best, and a generous drink, in moderation. He was once Curate and Lecturer of St. Martin's-in-the-Fields; but I would have thee go first to the Coffee-house in St. Paul's Churchyard, where they know all the London clergy, and ask for his present lodging. This found, go to him, tell him that I am dead, give him thy money, entrust thyself to him, and be guided by him as thou hast been by me.

"And now, my daughter, if a father's prayers avail thee, be assured that I die like Jacob the patriarch, blessing thee and commanding thee. For my blessing, I pray that the Lord may have thee in His keeping, and give thee what is good for the eternal life. For my commandment—Be good: for herein is summed up the whole of the Commandments.

"And remember, my child, the Christian who lives in fear of death is foolish: even as he is foolish who will not lay hold of the promise, and so lives in terror of the Judgment. For now I know—yea, I *know*—that the Lord loveth best that man who all the days of his life walks in faith and dies in hope.—Your loving father,

"LAWRENCE PLEYDELL."

Had ever a girl so sweet a message from the dead, to keep and ponder over, to comfort and console her? She knew every word of it already, but the tears came afresh to her eyes in thinking of the dear hand which wrote those words—quiet now, its labours done, in the cold grave. Her father's last Will and Testament gave her more than riches—it gave her strength and consolation. The example of his life, which was so Christian and so good, might be forgotten, because the girl was too young to understand it, and too ignorant to compare; but this letter of true faith and religion would never be forgotten.

The Reverend Lawrence Pleydell, Master of Arts and sometime Fellow of the ancient and learned College or House of Christ, Cambridge, was (which is a thing too rare in these days) a country clergyman who was also a scholar, a divine, a man of pious thought, and a gentleman by descent, though only of a younger branch. It is too often found that if a country clergyman be a gentleman, he continues the habits of his class, such as fox-hunting, card-playing, and wine-drinking, concerning which, although the Bishops seem not yet of one mind upon the matter, I, for my humble part, remembering what kind of man was my good father, venture to think are pursuits unworthy of one who holds a cure of souls. And when a clergyman is a scholar, he is too often devoted entirely to the consideration of his Greek and Latin authors, whereby his power over the hearts of the people is in a measure lost. Or, if he is a divine, he is too often (out of the fulness of his mind) constrained to preach the subtleties and hidden things of theology, which cannot be understood of the common people, so that it is as if he were speaking in an unknown tongue. And sometimes the parson of the parish is but a rude and coarse person, of vulgar birth, who will smoke tobacco with the farmers—yea, even with the labourers—drink with them, and not be ashamed to be seen in beer-houses, tap-rooms, or even at such unseemly diversions as bull-baiting, badger-drawing, and cock-fighting. It were to be wished that the Church were purged of all such.

The parish contained, besides farmers, but one family of gentlefolk, that of Sir Robert Levett, Knight, who with his wife and two children lived at the Hall, and had an estate worth two thousand a year at least. When the vicar's wife died (she was somewhat his inferior in point of family, but had a brother in the Church), and his child was left without a mother, nothing would do for Lady Levett than that the little maid should be taken into the Hall and brought up, having governesses and teaching, with her own daughter, Nancy, who was of about the same age, but a little younger. So the two girls were playfellows and scholars together, being taught those things which it befits a lady to learn, although one of them would be a poor lady indeed. There was one son, Will, who was at first at Eton with his cousin (and Sir Robert's ward), Harry Temple, the young Squire of Wootton Hampstead. It was a fearful joy when they came home for the holidays. For, although they kept the house in activity and bustle, making disorder and noise where there was generally quiet and order, yet after the manner of boys, who rejoice to show and feel their strength, they would play rough tricks upon the two girls, upset and destroy their little sports, and make them understand what feeble things are young maidens compared with boys.

Now just as the two girls were different—for one grew up tall and disposed to be serious, which was Kitty Pleydell, and the other was small and saucy, always with a laugh and a kiss, which was Nancy Levett—so the boys became different: for one, which was Will Levett, a rosy-cheeked lad, with a low forehead and a square chin, grew to dislike learning of all kinds, and was never happy except when he was in the stables with the horses, or training the dogs, or fox-hunting, or shooting, or fishing, or in some way compassing the death of wild creatures, sports to which his father was only moderately addicted; but the other, Harry Temple, was more studiously disposed, always came home with some fresh mark of his master's approbation, and read every book he could find.

There came a change in their behaviour to the girls as they grew older. Will ceased to set a dog to bark at them, and to crack a whip to frighten them, or ride unbroken colts in order to make them cry out for fear; and Harry ceased to tease and torment them with little tricks and devices of mischief at which they were half pleased and half humiliated. When the boys left school they were sent to Pembroke College, Cambridge, a college in which many generations of Levetts had been educated. After two terms, Will came home, looking cheerful though somewhat abashed. He had been rusticated *sine die*, as the phrase runs: which means that he was not to go back again until he had made such ample submission and apology, with promises of future amendment as would satisfy the authorities as to the safety of allowing him back.

It was not known rightly what he had done; there was a story in which a retriever, a horse, a punch-bowl, a badger, a bargee, a pump, and a water-trough were curiously mixed up, and his rustication had somehow to do with the introduction of a proctor (whom one understands to be a learned and reverend magistrate) and a bull-dog, into this inconsistent and discordant company.

Sir Robert looked grave when he received his son, my lady wept, and the girls were ashamed; but all speedily recovered their good spirits, and the whole stable rejoiced exceedingly to see Will back among them. Even the foxes and their cubs, Sir Robert said, which had of late waxed fat and lazy, manifested a lively pleasure, and hastened to get thin so as to afford the greatest sport possible; the trout practised all their tricks in readiness for one who respected a fish of subtlety; the pheasants and young partridges made haste to grow strong on the wing; the snipe and small birds remembered why Nature had taught them to use a devious and uncertain flight; the rabbits left off running straight; the otters remembered the uncertainty of life and the glory of a gallant fight; the ferrets laughed, thinking of the merry days they were going to have; the hares, who never take any solid interest in being hunted, ran away to the neighbouring estates; and the badgers, who were going to be drawn in their holes, turned sulky.

This was what Sir Robert told the girls, who laughed, but believed that it was all true. As for Cambridge, there was no more thought of that.

Will had had enough of lectures, chapels, and dons; henceforth, he said, he should please himself.

"Man," said Sir Robert, "who is ever disappointed, must continually be resigned. What if Will hath refused to get learning? He will not, therefore, gamble away the estate, nor disgrace the name of Levett. Holdfast is a good dog. It is the fortune of this house that if, once in a while, its head prove a fool as regards books, he still sticks to his own."

Will promised to stick fast to his own, and though he gave himself up henceforth altogether to those pursuits which make a man coarse and deaden his sensibility (whereby he loses the best part of his life), he promised, in his father's opinion, to prove a capable manager and just landlord, jealous of his own rights, and careful of those of others.

Will thus remaining at home, the girls saw him every day, and though they had little talk with him, because it could not be expected that they should care to hear how the dogs behaved, and how many rats had been killed that morning, yet he was, in his rough way, thoughtful of them, and would bring them such trifles as pretty eggs, stuffed kingfishers, dressed moleskins, and so forth, which he got in his walks abroad. In the evening he would make his artificial flies, twist his lines, mend his landing-nets, polish his guns; being always full of business, and kindly taking no notice while Nancy or Kitty read aloud, nor seeming to care what they read, whether it was the poetry of Pope, or some dear delightful romance; or the "Spectator," or the plays of Shakespeare. All was one to him.

He seemed in those days a good-natured young man who went his own way and troubled himself not one whit about other people. Women were inferior creatures, of course: they could not shoot, hunt, fish, ride to hounds; they had no strength; they did not like to see things killed; they did not love sport; they did not drink wine; they did not take beer for breakfast; they did not smoke tobacco; they loved tea, chocolate, coffee, and such vanities; they loved to dress fine and stand up making bows to men, which they called dancing; they loved to read a lot of nonsense in rhymes, or to cry over the sorrows of people who never lived. Women, however, had their uses: they kept things in order, looked after the dinner, and took care of the babies.

Will did not say all these things at once; but they were collected together and written down by the girls, who kept a book between them, where they entered all the things they heard which struck their fancy. Nancy even went so far as to try to make up a story about the proctor and the pump, but never dared show it, except to her father, who pinched her ear and laughed. They called the page about the ways of women "Will's Wisdom," and continually added to it without his knowledge; because Will, like all men who love the sports of the field and not the wisdom of the printed page, became quickly angry if he were laughed at. The girls always pictured Esau, for instance, as a grave man, with a square chin, who talked a good deal about his own hunting, took no interest in the occupations of the women, and could never see a joke.

Two years or so after Will's rustication, Harry came of age and left Cambridge without taking a degree. There were bonfires, and oxen roasted whole, and barrels of beer upon the green when he took possession of his own estate and went to live in his own house, which was three miles and a half from the Hall.

He came from Cambridge having no small reputation for learning and wit, being apt at the making of verses in English, Latin, and Italian. He was, moreover, skilled in mathematical science, and especially in astronomy; he had read history, and understood the course of politics. I think that from the beginning he aspired to be considered one of those who by birth and attainments are looked upon as the leaders of the world; he would be a scholar as well as a gentleman; he would be a poet, perhaps to be ranked with Pope or Dryden; he would be a man of fashion; and he would sit in ladies' *salons*, while other men sat over bottles of port, and talked gallantry. As for his appearance, he was tall and slight in figure; his face was long and rather thin; his eyes were grave; his manner was reserved; to the girls he was always courteous, asking their opinion, setting them right when they were wrong, lending them books, and directing them what to read. To Kitty he was a man to be respected, but never, she may truly say, did she allow her thoughts to dwell on the possibility of love: perhaps because love is between opposites, so that the grave may love the gay; perhaps because she knew very early that Lady Levett earnestly desired one thing—that Harry might fall in love with Nancy; and perhaps because to Nancy herself, little, merry Nancy, whose heart was full of sunshine, as her eyes were full of sunlight, and her lips never moved but to say and sing something saucy, or to laugh and smile—to Nancy, I say, this man was an Apollo, and she wondered that all women, not to speak of men (whose stupidity in the matter of reverence for each other is well known) did not fall down before him and do him open worship.

A few months after Harry Temple came of age, the vicar was taken ill with a putrid fever, caught while administering the last rites of the Church to a dying woman, and was carried off in a fortnight. This disaster not only robbed poor Kitty of the best of fathers, but also of the kindest patron and the most loving friend; for it took her away from the Hall, and drove her out, as will be presently seen, to meet dangers as she had never imagined among a people whose wickedness after many years, and even to this day, makes her wonder at the longsuffering of the Lord.

CHAPTER II.

HOW KITTY MADE ENGAGEMENTS.

The day after the funeral, Sir Robert Levett himself walked to the Vicarage in the afternoon, and found the girl still in the garden, on her favourite seat. As soon as she looked into his kind face she burst into fresh tears.

"Cry on, pretty," he said, sitting beside her, and with a tear in his own eye. "Cry on: to cry is natural. Thou hast lost the best and most Christian father that ever girl had; therefore cry on till thou art tired. Let the tears fall. Don't mind me. Out handkerchief. So good a scholar shall we never see again. Cry on, if thou hast only just begun, should it bring thee comfort. Nor ever shall we hear so good a preacher. When thou hast finished let me have my say. But do not hurry."

Even at the very saddest, when tears flow as unceasingly as the fountains in the Land of Canaan, the sight of an elderly gentleman sitting on a bench beneath a mulberry-tree, his hat beside him, his wig in his hands for coolness, his stick between his legs, and his face composed to a decent position, waiting till one had finished, would be enough to make any girl stop crying. Kitty felt immediately inclined to laugh; dried her eyes, restrained her sobs, and pulled out her father's will, which she gave to Sir Robert to read.

He read it through twice, slowly, and then he hummed and coughed before he spoke—

"A good man, Kitty child. See that thou forget not his admonitions. I would he were here still to admonish us all. Sinners that we were, to heed his voice no better. And now he is gone—he is gone. Yet he was a younger man than I, by ten years and more, and I remain." Here he put on his wig, and rose. "As for this money, child, let us lose no time in making that safe, lest some thief should rob thee of it. A hundred guineas! And twenty more with Farmer Goodpenny! And this money waiting at the publishers![A] Verily thou art an heiress indeed!"

In the bedroom, at the head of the great bed, they found beneath the mattress a long narrow box secretly let into the panel close to the great cross-beam. I say secretly, but it was a secret known to all the world. Carpenters always made those secret hiding-places in beds, so that had there been a robber in the house he would have begun by searching in that place. Sir Robert knew where to find the spring, and quickly opened the box.

Within it lay two canvas bags, tied up. Could bags so little hold so great a sum! Sir Robert tossed them into his pockets as carelessly as if they were bags of cherries.

"Now, little maid," said he, sitting on the bed, "that money is safe; and be sure that I shall call on Farmer Goodpenny to-morrow. Let me know what is to be done about thy father's wish that thou shouldst go to London?"

"It is his injunction, sir," said Kitty gravely. "I must obey his will."

"Yet thy father, child, did not know London. And to send a young girl like thyself, with a bag of guineas about thy neck, to ask in a coffee-house for the address of a clergyman is, methinks, a wild-goose sort of business. As for Dr. Shovel, I have heard the name—to be sure, it cannot be the same man——" he stopped, as if he would not tell me what it was he had heard.

"It is my father's command," she repeated.

"Unless nothing better should be found. Now, London is a dangerous place, full of pitfalls and traps, especially for the young and innocent. We are loth to lose thee, Kitty; we are afraid to let thee go. Nothing will do for Lady Levett but that thou remain with us and Nancy."

This was a generous offer, indeed. Kitty's eyes filled with tears again, and while she stood trying to find words of gratitude, and to decline the offer so as not to appear churlish, madam herself came running up the stairs, in her garden hat and plain pinner, and fell to kissing and crying over the girl.

Then she had to be told of the will and last commands.

"To be sure," she said, "thy father's commands must be respected and obeyed. Yet I know not whether it would not be well to disobey them. Kitty, my dear, stay with us and be my daughter, all the same as

Nancy. I do not ask thee to enter my service, or to receive wages, or to do work for me any other than a daughter may."

Kitty shook her head again. She was truly grateful; there was no one so kind as her ladyship; but she must go to London as her father bade her.

"Why," cried Sir Robert, "the child is right. Let her go. But if she is unhappy with her friends, or if she is in any trouble, let her know where to look for help."

"There may be cousins," said madam, "who will find thee too pretty for their own faces, and would keep thee at home with the towels and dusters and napkins. I would not have our Kitty a Cinderella—though house-service is no disgrace to a gentlewoman. Or there may be manners and customs of the house that a young girl should disapprove. Or there may be harsh looks instead of kind words. If that is the case, Kitty, come back to us, who love thee well, and will receive thee with kisses and joy."

Then they left her in the empty house, alone with Deborah, the house servant.

She was looking over her father's books, and taking out one or two which she thought she might keep in memory of him (as if anything were needed) when she heard steps, and Deborah's voice inviting some one to enter.

It was Harry Temple: he stood in the doorway, his hat in his hand, and under his arm a book.

"I was meditating in the fields," he said, "what I should say to Kitty Pleydell, in consolation for her affliction. The learned Boethius——"

"O Harry!" she cried, "do not talk to me of books. What can they say to comfort any one?"

He smiled. Harry's smile showed how much he pitied people not so learned as himself.

"The greatest men," he said, "have been comforted by books. Cicero, for instance... Nay, Kitty, I will not quote Cicero. I came to say that I am sorry indeed to learn that we shall lose thee for a time."

"Alas!" she said, "I must go. It is my father's order."

"I am sure," he replied, "that you would not leave us for a lighter reason. You know our hearts, Kitty, and how we all love you."

"I know——" Kitty began to cry again. Everybody was so full of love and pity. "I know, Harry. And perhaps I shall never n—n—never see you again."

"And does that make this parting harder?" He turned very red, and laid his precious book of consolation on the table.

"Why, of course it does," she replied, wiping her eyes.

"You *shall* see us again," he went on earnestly. "You shall come back with me. Kitty, I will give you one twelvemonth of absence. You know I love you tenderly. But your father's commands must be obeyed. Therefore for a whole year I shall not seek you out. Then, when I come for you, will you return with me, never to go away again?"

"Oh!" she cried, clasping her hands, "how joyfully will I return!"

The young man took her hand and raised it to his lips.

"Divine maid!" he cried. "Fit to grace a coronet, or to make the home of a simple gentleman an Arcadia of pastoral pleasure!"

"Do not mock me, Harry," she said, snatching away her hand, "with idle compliments. But forget not to come and carry me away."

"Alas!" he said; "how shall I exist—how bear this separation for twelve long months? Oh, divine Kitty! Thou will remain an ever-present idea in my heart."

"Harry," she burst out laughing in her tears, "think of the learned Boethius!"

So he left her.

In half an hour another visitor appeared.

This time it was Will. He was in his usual careless disorder; his scarlet coat a good deal stained, his waistcoat unbuttoned, his wig awry, his boots dusty, his neckerchief torn, his hands and cheeks browned by the sun. He carried a horsewhip, and was followed by half-a-dozen dogs, who came crowding into the room after him.

"So," he said, sitting down and leaning his chin upon his whipstock, "thou must go, then?"

"What do you want with me, Will?" she asked, angry that he should show so little sympathy.

"Why," he replied, rubbing his chin with the whipstock, "not much, Kitty. Nancy will come to cry."

"Then you can go away, Will."

"I came to say, Kitty, that though you do be going to go" (Will easily dropped into country talk), "I shanna forget thee. There!"

"Thank you, Will."

"As for the matter of that, I love thee—ah! like I love old Rover here."

"Thank you again, Will."

"And so I've brought along a sixpence—here it is—and we'll break it together." Here he bent and broke the coin with his strong fingers. "My half goes into my pocket—so; and the other half is thine—there." He threw it on the table. "Well, that's done." He stood up, looked at me sorrowfully, and heaved a great sigh. "I doubt I've a done wrong. Hadst been going to stay, a' woulden a' spoke yet awhile. Liberty is sweet—girls are skittish. Well, we'll take a twelvemonth yet. There's no hurry. Plenty time before us. I shall have my liberty for that while. Mayhap I will fetch thee in the spring. Ay, May's the best month to leave the dogs and the birds, though the vermin will begin to swarm—rot 'em! Come, Rover. Good-bye, wench."

He gave her a resounding kiss on the cheek, and turned away.

The girl laughed. She did not pick up the broken sixpence, which, indeed, she hardly noticed, her mind being full of many things.

Presently Nancy came, and the two girls spent a miserable evening together, in great love and friendship.

Now, how could an ignorant country girl, who had never thought over these things at all, guess that she had engaged herself to be married, in one day, in one hour even, to two different men? Yet that was exactly what this foolish Kitty had actually done.

FOOTNOTES

[A]When, some months later, Kitty went to the publisher, that gentleman informed her that there was no money to receive, because he had been a loser by the publication of the books.

CHAPTER III.

HOW WE CAME TO LONDON ON THE COACH.

With the purpose, therefore, of carrying out my father's injunctions, I remained for a few days at the Vicarage alone, having one servant to take care of me. But, had it not been for an accident, I might have remained at the village all my life. "For," said Lady Levett, "it is but right, child, that the instructions of your father should be carried out; I should like to know, however, who is to take charge of thee to London, and how we are to get thee there? A young maid cannot be sent to London on a pack-horse, like a bundle of goods. As for Sir Robert, he goes no more to town, since he has ceased to be a member. I care not for the court, for my own part, and am now too old for the gaieties of London. Nancy will enjoy them, I doubt not, quite soon enough; and as for the boys, I see not very well how they can undertake so great a charge. I doubt, Kitty, that thou must come to the Hall, after all. You can be useful, child, and we will make you happy. There is the still-room, where, Heaven knows, what with the cowslip-wine, the strong waters, the conserving, pickling, drying, candying, and the clove gilliflowers for palleting, there is work enough for you and Nancy, as well as my still-room maid and myself. And just now, Sir Robert calling every day for a summer sallet (which wants a light hand), to cool his blood!"

I would very willingly have gone to the Hall; I asked nothing better, and could think of nothing more happy for myself, if it could so be ordered. My father's wishes must certainly be obeyed; but if no one at the Hall could take charge of me, it seemed, at first, as if there could be no going to London at all, for our farmers and villagers were no great travellers. None of them knew much of this vast round world beyond their own fields, unless it were the nearest market-town, or perhaps Maidstone, or even Canterbury. Now and again one of the rustics would go for a soldier (being crossed in love); but he never came home again to tell of his campaigns. Or one would go for a gentleman's servant (being too lazy to work like his father); then he would return filled with all the wickedness of London, and stay corrupting the minds of the simple folk, till Sir Robert bade him pack and be off, for a pestilent fellow. Or one would go away to the nearest market-town to be apprenticed to a handicraft (being ambitious, as will happen even to simple clods, and aspiring to a shop). But if he succeeded, such an one would seldom come back to the place which gave him birth.

An accident happened which served my purpose. There was a certain farmer on Sir Robert's estate, whose sister had married a London tradesman of respectability and reputed honesty, named Samuel Gambit (he was a builder's foreman, who afterwards became a master builder, and made great sums of money by taking city contracts. His son, after him, rose to be an alderman in the city of London). Whether the young woman was in ill health, or whether she was prompted by affection, I know not, but she left her husband for a space and journeyed into the country to see her friends and people. Now when I heard, by accident, that she was about to return, my heart fell, because I saw that my time was come, and that a proper person to take charge of me during the journey was found in Mrs. Gambit.

Madam sent for her. She was a strong, well-built woman, of about six or seven and twenty, resolute in her bearing, and sturdy of speech. She was not afraid, she said, of any dangers of the road, holding (but that was through ignorance) highwaymen in contempt; but she could not be answerable, she said, and this seemed reasonable, for the safety of the coach, which might upset and break our necks. As for the rest, she would be proud to take the young lady with her to London, and madam might, if she wished, consider the extra trouble worth something; but that she left to her ladyship.

"I know," said Lady Levett, "that it is a great charge for you to conduct a young gentlewoman to town in these bad and dangerous times, when not only the high roads are thronged with robbers, and the streets with footpads, but also the very inns swarm with villains, and gentlemen are not ashamed to insult young persons of respectability in stage-coaches and public places. But Kitty is a good girl, not giddy, and obedient. I will admonish her that she obey you in everything upon the road, and that she keep eyes, ears, and mouth closed all the way."

The good woman undertook to have her eye upon me the whole journey. Then Lady Levett made her promise that she would take me straight to St. Paul's Coffee-house, St. Paul's Churchyard, there to inquire after my uncle's residence, and never leave me until she had seen me deposited safely in Dr. Shovel's hands.

Now was I in a flutter and agitation of spirits indeed, as was natural, considering that I was going to leave my native place for the first time in my life and to seek out new relations.

"Nancy!" I cried, "what will be my lot? What will become of me?"

Nancy said that she would tell my fortune if I would only leave off walking about and wringing my hands and be comfortable.

Then she sat down beside me in her pretty affectionate way, and threw her arms round my waist, and laid her head upon my shoulder.

"You are so tall and so pretty, Kitty, that all the men will lose their hearts. But you must listen to none of them until the right man comes. Oh! I know what he is like. He will be a great nobleman, young and handsome, and oh, so rich! he will kneel at your feet as humble as a lover ought to be, and implore you to accept his title and his hand. And when you are a great lady, riding in your own coach, as happy as the day is long, you will forget—oh no, my dear! sure I am you will never forget your loving Nancy."

Then we kissed and cried over each other in our foolish girls' way, promising not only kind remembrance, but even letters sometimes. And we exchanged tokens of friendship. I gave her a ring, which had been my mother's, made of solid silver with a turquoise and two pearls, very rich and good, and she gave me a silver-gilt locket with chased back, and within it a little curl of her hair, brown and soft.

Lady Levett gave me nothing but her admonition. I was going, she said, to a house where I should meet with strangers who would perhaps, after the manner of strangers, be quicker at seeing a fault than a grace, and this particularly at the outset and very beginning, when people are apt to be suspicious and to notice carefully. Therefore I was to be circumspect in my behaviour, and above all, be careful in my speech, giving soft words in return for hard, and answering railing, if there was any railing, with silence. But perhaps, she said, there would be no railing, but only kindness and love, in the which case I was all the more to preserve sweet speech and sweet thoughts, so as not to trouble love. Then she was good enough to say that I had ever been a good maid and dutiful, and she doubted not that so I would continue in my new world, wherefore she kissed me tenderly, and prayed, with tears in her eyes—for my lady, though quick and sharp, was wondrous kind of heart—that the Lord would have me in His keeping.

I say nothing about Sir Robert, because he was always fond of me, and would almost as soon have parted from his Nancy.

Now it was a week and more since I had, without knowing it, received those overtures of love from Harry Temple and Will, which I took in my innocence for mere overtures of friendship and brotherly affection. They thought, being conceited, like all young men, that I had at once divined their meaning and accepted their proposals; no doubt they gave themselves credit for condescension and me for gratitude. Therefore, when, the evening before I came away, Harry Temple begged me, with many protestations of regret, not to inform Sir Robert or madam of his intentions, I knew not what to say. What intentions? why should I not?

"Reigning star of Beauty!" he cried, laying his hand upon his heart, "I entreat thy patience for a twelvemonth. Alas! such separation! who can bear it!

"'Fond Thyrsis sighs, through mead and vale,
   His absent nymph lamenting——'"

"O Harry!" I cried, "what do I care about Thyrsis and absent nymphs? You have promised to bring me back in a year. Very well, then, I shall expect you. Of course you can tell Sir Robert whatever you please. It is nothing to me what you tell Sir Robert or my lady."

"She is cold as Diana," said Harry, with a prodigious sigh; but I broke from him, and would hear no more such nonsense. Sighing shepherds and cruel nymphs were for ever on Harry Temple's lips.

As for Will, of course he wanted to have an explanation too. He followed Harry, and, in his rustic way, begged to say a word or two.

"Pray go on, Will," I said.

"I promised a twelvemonth," he explained. "I'll not go back upon my word. I *did* say a twelvemonth."

"A twelvemonth? Oh yes. You said the same as Harry, I remember."

"I don't know what Harry said, but I'll swear, whatever Harry said, I said just the clean contrary. Now, then, liberty's sweet, my girl. Come, let us say fifteen months. Lord! when a man is twenty-one he don't want to be tied by the heels all at once. Let's both have our run first. You are but a filly yet—ay—a six months' puppy, so to say."

"You said a twelvemonth, Will," I replied, little thinking of what he meant. How, indeed, could I know? "I shall expect you in a twelvemonth."

"Very good, then. A twelvemonth it must be, I suppose. Shan't tell my father yet, Kitty. Don't you tell un neyther, there's a good girl. Gad! there will be a pretty storm with my lady when she hears it! Ho! ho!"

Then he went off chuckling and shaking himself. How could a courtly gentleman like Sir Robert and a gentlewoman like her ladyship have a son who was so great a clown in his manner and his talk? But the sons do not always take after their parents. A stable and a kennel, when they take the place of a nursery and a school, are apt to breed such bumpkins even out of gentle blood.

In the morning at five I was to start in the cart which would take us across the country to the stage-coach.

Nancy got up with me, and we had a fine farewell kissing. The boys were up too; Harry out of compliment to me, dressed in a nightcap and a flowered morning-gown; and Will out of compliment to his kennel, for whose sake he always rose at daybreak. He was dressed in his old scarlet coat, he carried a whip in one hand, and half-a-dozen dogs followed at his heels.

"Remember, sweet Kitty," whispered Harry, with a ceremonious bow, "it is but for a twelvemonth."

"Only a year," said Will. "Heart up, my pretty!"

They heard what each had said, and they were looking at each other puzzled when I drove away.

The Chaplain of the Fleet

"What did you mean, Will?" asked Harry, when the cart was out of sight, "by saying only a year?"

"I meant what I meant," he replied doggedly. "Perhaps you know, and perhaps you don't."

"Of course I know," said Harry. "The question is, how do you know?"

"Well," replied Will, "that is a pretty odd question, to be sure. How could I help knowing?"

"I think," said Harry, red in the face, "that some one has been injudicious in telling any one."

Will laughed.

"She ought not to have told, that's a fact. But we will keep it secret, Harry; don't tell her ladyship."

So that each thought that the other knew of his engagement with Kitty.

Little heed gave I to them and their promises. It was pleasant, perhaps, though I soon forgot to think about it at all, to remember that Harry and Will after a twelvemonth would come to carry me home again, and that I should never leave the old place again. But just then I was too sad to remember this. I was going away, Heaven knew where, amongst strangers, to people who knew me not; and I mounted the cart in which we were to begin our journey crying as sadly as if it had been the dreadful cart which goes to Tyburn Tree. The best thing to cure a crying fit is a good jolting. It is impossible to weep comfortably when you are shaken and rolled about in a country cart among the deep, hard ruts of last winter. So I presently put up my handkerchief, dried my eyes, and thought of nothing but of clinging to Mrs. Gambit when the wheels sank deeper than usual. The way lay along the lanes which I knew so well, arched over with trees and lofty hedges, then in their beautiful spring dressing. It led past the churchyard, where the sun was striking full upon my father's new-made grave. I tried to think of him, but the cart jolted so terribly that I was fain to remember only how I carried his last admonitions in my bosom, and the money in two bags sewn to my petticoats.

Presently the lane led on to the high-road, which was not quite so rough, and here we came to the roadside inn where the stage-coach changed horses. We waited an hour or so, until at length we saw it coming slowly up the hill, piled with packages and crowded with passengers. But there was room for two more, and we mounted to our places outside. Presently the machine moved slowly along again. It was so heavily-laden and the roads were so rough, that we rolled as if every moment we were going to roll over into the ditch, where we should all be killed. Mrs. Gambit loudly declared that nothing should ever again take her out of London, where a body could ride in a coach without the fear of being upset and the breaking of necks. On this journey, however, no necks were broken, because the coach did not upset. When the rolling was very bad, Mrs. Gambit clutched me with one hand and her right hand neighbour with the other. I, in my turn, seized her with one hand and my right hand neighbour with the other. Then we both shrieked, until presently, finding that we did not actually go over, I began to laugh.

My neighbour was a clergyman of grave and studious aspect. He wore a full wig, which had certainly been a second-hand one when it was bought, so shabby, was it now; his gown was also shabby, and his stockings were of grey worsted. Clearly a country clergyman of humble means. His face, however, looked young. When I caught him by the arm, he laid hold of my hand with both of his, saying gravely, "Now, madam, I hold you so tightly that you cannot fall." This was very kind of him. And, presently, he wanted to lay his arm round my waist for my better protection. But this was taking more trouble than I would consent to.

There was, however, a worse danger than that of upsetting. This year, England suffered from a plague of highway-robbers, the like of which was never before known. The roads were crowded with them. They were mostly disbanded soldiers, who, being either disinclined to return to their old trades, or being unable to find employment, roamed about the country either singly or in pairs, or in bands, rogues and vagabonds, ready to rob, steal, plunder, or even murder as occasion offered. They were sometimes so bold that they would attack a whole coachful of passengers, and take from them whatever they carried, unless, as sometimes happened, there were one or two valiant men on the coach ready to give them a warm reception with guns, pistols, swords, or even stout cudgels. They were said seldom to show much fight (being conscious of the gallows awaiting them if they were wounded or captured), and would generally make off. But it was not always that passengers were found ready to risk the fight, and in most cases they sat still and delivered.

With this danger before us, it was not surprising that the conversation should turn upon highwaymen whenever the road became a little smooth, and I listened with terror to the tales I heard. Most of them were related by a man who sat opposite to me. He wore a scratch wig (probably his second-best), and had his hat flapped and tied about his ears as if it were winter. He was, I suppose, a merchant of some kind, because he talked a great deal about prices, and stocks, and markets, with other things, Greek and Hebrew to me. Also, he looked so uneasy, and kept watching the road with so anxious an air, that I felt sure he must be carrying a great parcel of money like me, and I longed to advise him to imitate my prudence; and at the next town we got down to sew it within his coat. He continually lamented, as we went along, the desperate wickedness of the highway-robbers: he spoke of it as if he were entirely disinterested, and regarded not at all the peril to his own fortune, but only the danger of their own souls, liable to be wretchedly lost and thrown away by their dreadful courses. And he talked so feelingly on this subject that one began to feel as if good words were being spoken to the edification of the soul. As for their suppression, he said that, in their own interests, strong measures would be necessary. Trade would never flourish, and therefore men would not be induced to follow a respectable trade until ships could sail the seas without fear of pirates, and honest merchants carry their property up and down the king's highway without fear of highwaymen. Here we came in sight of a man on horseback, and we all kept silence for an anxious space, till we discovered, by his great wig and black coat, that it was nothing but a country surgeon riding out to see a patient. Then the merchant went on to say that since the gallows did not terrify these evil-doers, he, for one, was for trying how they would like the French wheel.

At this there was a terrible outcry: the clergyman, especially, asking if he wished to introduce French barbarities.

"Such things," he said solemnly, "are the natural accompaniment of Popery. Pray, sir, remember Smithfield."

"Sir," said the merchant, "I hope I am as good a Protestant as my neighbours. I call that, however, not barbarity but justice and mercy which punishes the guilty and deters the weak. As for barbarities, are we Protestants better than our neighbours? Is it not barbarous to flog our soldiers and sailors for insubordination; to flog our rogues at the cart-tail; to lash the backs of women in Bridewell; to cut and scourge the pickpockets so long as the alderman chooses to hold up the hammer? Do we not hack the limbs of our traitors, and stick them up on Temple Bar? Truly the world would come to a pretty pass if we were to ask our cut-throats what punishment would hurt them least."

"I like not the breaking of legs on wheels," cried Mrs. Gambit. "But to call the flogging of Bridewell hussies barbarous! Fie, sir! You might as well call bull-baiting barbarous."

No one wanted to encourage highway-robbers, yet none but this merchant from foreign parts would allow than an Englishman, however wicked, should cruelly have his limbs broken and crushed by a rod of iron.

"As for the gentlemen of the road," said Mrs. Gambit, "I, for one, fear them not. They may take the butter and eggs in my basket, but they won't find my money, for that is in my shoe."

"Nor mine," said I, taking courage and thinking to show my cleverness; "for it is all sewn safe inside my petticoats."

"Hush, silly women!" cried the merchant. "You know not but there is a highwayman sitting in disguise on the coach beside you. I beg pardon, sir," he turned to the clergyman beside me — "no offence, sir — though I have heard of a thief who robbed a coach after travelling in it dressed as a gentleman of your cloth."

"None, sir, none," replied his reverence. "Yet am I not a highwayman, I do assure you for your comfort. Nor have I any money in my pocket or my shoe. I am but a simple clergyman, going to look at a benefice which hath been graciously bestowed upon me."

"That, sir," said the merchant, "is satisfactory, and I hope that no other ears have heard what these ladies have disclosed. Shoes? petticoats? Oh, the things that I have seen and heard!"

The clergyman then told us that he had a wife and six daughters, and that the preferment (two hundred pounds a year!) would make a man of him, who had as yet been little better than a slave with sixty pounds for all his income. The Christian year, he told us, was a long Lent for him, save that sometimes, as at Christmas and Eastertide, he was able to taste meat given to him. Yet he looked fat and hearty.

"My drink," he said, "is from the spring, which costs nothing; and my bread is but oatmeal-porridge, potatoes, or barley-meal."

Then he pressed my hand in his, said I resembled his wife in her younger days, and declared that he already felt to me like a father.

There sat next to the merchant a young gentleman of about seventeen or eighteen, brave in scarlet, for he had just received a commission as ensign in a regiment of the line, and was on his way to join his colours, as he told us with pride. Directly highway robbers were mentioned he assumed, being a young man with rosy and blushing cheek, fitter for a game of cricket on the green than for war's alarms, a fierce and warlike mien, and assured us that we ladies should not want protection while he was on the coach. And he made a great show of loosening his sword in the scabbard to ensure its quick and ready use, should the occasion rise. The merchant received these professions of courage with undisguised contempt; the clergyman smiled; Mrs. Gambit nodded her head and laughed, as if he was a boy whose talk meant nothing. I neither laughed at him nor scowled at him. In fact I was thinking, girl-like, what a handsome boy he was, and hoping that he would some day become a great general. As the country seems at the present juncture sadly in want of great generals, I fear he has been killed in action.

When we stopped for dinner, at one o'clock—I remember that I never before saw so prodigious a piece of roast beef upon the table—our host must needs spoil all enjoyment of the meal by asking us, just as we were sat down, sharp-set by the air, if we had met or seen anything of a certain "Black Will," who seemed to be very well known by all. The very name caused our poor merchant to push back his plate untasted, and the young officer to rise from the table and hasten to assure himself that his sword was loose in the scabbard.

"Because," said the landlord, "it is right for you to know that Black Will is reported in this neighbourhood with all his crew: a bloody lot, gentlemen. I hope you have no valuables to speak of upon you. However, perhaps they will not meet you on the road. They murdered a man last year, a young gentleman like you, sir," nodding to the ensign, "because he offered resistance and drew his sword. What is a little toothpick like that, compared with a quarterstaff in the hands of a sturdy rogue? So they beat his brains out for him. Then they gagged and used most unmercifully, kicking him till he was senseless, an honest gentleman like yourself, sir"—he nodded to our merchant—"who gave them the trouble of taking off his boots, where, for greater safety, as the poor wretch thought, he had bestowed his money——"

"God bless my soul!" cried the merchant, changing colour, so that I for one felt quite certain that his was there too, and that his courage was down in his boots as well, to keep the money company. "Bless my soul! hanging, mere hanging, is too good for such villains."

"It is indeed," replied the landlord, shaking his head. "There was a young lady, too"—I started, because he looked at me—"who had her money sewn in a bag inside her frock." I blushed red, knowing where mine was. "They made her take it off and dance a minuet with one of them in her petticoats. But indeed there is no end to their wickedness. Come, gentlemen, let me carve faster; spare not the beef; don't let Black Will spoil your appetites. Cut and come again. He may be twenty miles away. A noble sirloin, upon my word! To be sure, he may be waiting on the hill there in the wood."

"A glass of brandy, landlord," cried the merchant, who surely was a dreadful coward. "Tell me, would he be alone?"

"Not likely." The landlord, I thought, took a pleasure in making us uneasy. "He would have two or three with him. Perhaps six. With pistols. Do take some more beef. And blunderbusses. Ah! a desperate wicked gang."

In such cheerful discourse we took our dinner, and then, with trepidation, mounted to our places and drove away.

We got up the hill safely, and met no Black Will. During the next stage we all kept an anxious look up and down the road. The coach seemed to crawl, and the way was rough. The sight of a man on horseback made our hearts beat; if we saw two, we gave ourselves up for lost. But I was pleased all the time to mark the gallant and resolute behaviour of the boy, who, with his hand upon the hilt of his sword, sat pale but determined; and when he caught my eye, smiled with the courage of one who would defend us to the death, as I am sure he would, like the gallant young knight he was.

Towards the evening we caught sight of the tower of Canterbury Cathedral, and soon afterwards we rolled through the streets of that ancient city, and got down at the Crown Inn, where we were to rest for the night.

I pass over, as unworthy of record, my own wonder at so great and beautiful a city. This was the first town I had ever seen; these the first shops; and this the first, and still the grandest, to my mind, of great cathedral churches. We walked through the great church at sunset, where there was something truly awful in the lofty arches mounting heavenwards, and the gloom of the roof. Outside there were Gothic ruins; rooks were calling to each other in the trees, and swifts were flying about the tower.

At supper we had more talk about highway-robbers, but we were assured that there was less danger now, because between Canterbury and London the road is more frequented, and therefore robbers, who are by nature a timorous folk, hesitate to attack a coach. Moreover, the landlord told us that we should have with us two or three honest citizens of Canterbury, substantial tradesmen, who travelled to London together for mutual protection, taking money with them, and pistols with which to defend themselves.

"One of them," he added, "is a lieutenant in the train-band, and a draper in the city: a more resolute fellow never handled a yard-measure."

The gentlemen ordered a bowl of punch after supper, and we retired. As we left the room, the clergyman followed us. Outside the door, Mrs. Gambit having already begun to go upstairs, he said he would give me his benediction, which he did, kissing me on the cheeks and lips with much (and undeserved) affection. He was good enough to say that I greatly resembled his youngest sister, the beautiful one, and he desired closer acquaintance. Nor could I understand why Mrs.

Gambit spoke scornfully of this act of kindness, which was entirely unexpected by me. "Kindness, quotha!" she cried. "A pious man indeed, to love to kiss a pretty maid! I like not such piety."

In the morning the train-band lieutenant, with his two friends, came swaggering to the inn. He carried his pistols openly, and made more display of them, I thought, than was necessary, considering his character for resolution and desperate bravery. Then we started, our little soldier still ready with his sword.

The road was smoother; it ran for the most part along enclosures and gentlemen's parks. It was broad and straight, having been made, we were told by the draper, in the time of the Romans; and as we drew near to London, the villages became more frequent, and the road was covered with carts, waggons, and carriages of every kind, all moving towards London. Was London bigger than Canterbury? I asked. They laughed at my innocence, and began to tell me that you might take the whole of Canterbury out of London and not miss it much: also that he or she who had not seen London had not seen the greatest marvel and wonder of the world.

"There are fine buildings," said the merchant, "in Paris, though the streets are foul; but in London there are buildings as fine, with streets that are broader: and there is the trade. Aha!"—he smacked his lips—"Paris hath no trade. One has to see the ships in the Pool, and the Custom House, and the wharves, before one can understand how great and rich a city is London. And one should also—but that, young lady, you cannot ever do, live as long as you will, being only a woman—feast at one of the great City Companies to understand how nobly they can use their wealth."

We were still anxious about highwaymen, but our fears were greatly lessened by the presence of the brave draper of Canterbury. The clergyman kept up a flow of anecdotes, which showed strange acquaintance with the wickedness of the world, on highwaymen, footpads, robbers of all kinds, deceivers of strangers, and practisers on innocence. The merchant listened eagerly, and together they bemoaned the credulity of the ignorant, and the subtlety of the designing.

The Chaplain of the Fleet

Our spirits grew higher as we neared the end of our journey. Now, indeed, there was but little fear. The coach travels from Canterbury to London in a single day; we should arrive before nightfall.

"Ha! ha!" said the merchant, rubbing his hands, "we who travel encounter many dangers. In London one can go to bed without fearing to be murdered in one's sleep, and walk abroad without looking to be brained and murderously treated for the sake of a purse and a watch. There may be pickpockets, shoplifters, and such petty rogues: there may be footpads about St. Pancras or Lincoln's Inn Fields, but small villains all compared with these desperate rogues of highwaymen."

"Desperate indeed," said the clergyman. "Dear sir, we should be grateful for our preservation."

It was already past seven when we arrived at the Talbot Inn. The merchant fetched a deep sigh, and thanked Providence aloud for keeping us safe from the danger of "Stand and deliver!" The clergyman said, "Amen," but gently reproved the merchant for not allowing him, as an ordained minister, to take the lead in every devotional exercise. When they got down they entered the house together. The young ensign pulled off his hat to me, and said that no doubt the rogues had got wind of an officer's presence on the stage. Then he tapped his sword-hilt significantly, and got down, and I saw him no more. The gallant draper, getting down slowly, lamented that he must still be carrying loaded pistols, with never an opportunity for using them upon the road, and uncocked his weapons with as much ostentatious care as he had shown in loading them. For my own part, I had no taste for fighting, or for seeing fights, and was only too glad to escape the hands of men who, if tales were true, did not even respect a girl's frocks. The clergyman bestowed a final benediction upon me, saying that he craved my name with a view to a closer friendship; and would have kissed me again had not Mrs. Gambit pushed him away with great roughness.

The thing I am now about to relate will doubtless seem incredible. Yet it is true. I learned it some time after, when Black Will was hanged, and his last Dying Speech and Confession was cried in the streets.

The merchant and the clergyman entered the Talbot Inn to drink together a bowl of punch at the former's expense before separating.

The latter, out of respect for his cloth, called for a private room, whither the punch was presently brought.

Now, when they had taken a glass or two each, both being very merry, they were disturbed by the entrance of two tall and ill-favoured fellows, who walked into the room and sat down, one on each side of the merchant.

"Gentlemen!" he cried, "this is a private room, ordered by his reverence here and myself for the peaceful drinking of a thanksgiving glass."

"No," replied the clergyman, rising and locking the door; "I find, dear sir, that this room had been already bespoke by these gentlemen, who are friends of mine own, and that we have very urgent business which particularly concerns yourself."

At these words the merchant turned pale, being, as you may imagine, horribly frightened, and perceiving that he had fallen into a nest of hornets. Whereupon he sprang to his feet, and would have rushed to the door, but that two of the villains seized him and pushed him back into the chair, while the third drew a knife and held it at his throat, informing him that his weasand would most certainly be cut across did he but move a finger or utter a sigh. At this dreadful threat the poor man gave himself up for lost, and said no more, only the tears of despair rolled down his face as he thought of what was going to happen to him.

The good clergyman then, with smiles and a polite bow, informed him that in this world things are not always what they seemed to be. "Honest tradesmen," he said, "often turn out to be common cheats, and substantial citizens become bankrupts. Therefore, it is not surprising if a reverend minister of the Established Church should occasionally bear a hand in a little scheme in which good acting and dexterity are essentials necessary for success. In fact," he went on, drinking up all the punch meanwhile, "though to you and to many good friends I am a pious divine, among my particular intimates and these gentlemen of the road"—here he pointed to the two villains—"I am no other than Black Will, at your service! Nay, do not faint, dear sir. Although you would break me on the wheel, had you the power,

I assure you I shall do you no harm in the world. Wherefore, kick off your boots!"

Alas! in his boots was the money which the poor man was bringing home from France. They took it all. They tied him to his chair, and that to the table. They gagged him; they put his wig on the table, tied a handkerchief over his head, so that he should seem to be asleep; and then they left him, telling the waiter that the gentleman in the blue room was tired after his journey, and would like to be undisturbed for an hour or two.

To think that this villain (who was but twenty-four when he was hanged, a year or so later) should dare to feel towards me like a father, and to give me his blessing—on the lips!

CHAPTER IV.

HOW KITTY FIRST SAW THE DOCTOR.

It was past seven in the evening when we arrived at the Talbot Inn of Southwark, and too late to begin our search after my uncle that evening. Mrs. Gambit, therefore, after conference with a young man of eight-and-twenty or so, dressed in broadcloth, very kindly offered me a bed at her own lodging for the night. This, she told me, was in a quiet and most respectable neighbourhood, viz., Fore Street, which she begged me not to confound with Houndsditch. I readily assured her that I would preserve separate the ideas of the two streets, which was easy to one who knew neither.

She then informed me that the young man was no other than her husband, foreman of works to a builder, and that, to save the expense of a porter, he would himself carry my box. Mr. Gambit upon this touched his hat respectfully, grinned, shouldered the box, and led the way, pushing through the crowd around us, and elbowing them to right and left without a word of excuse, as if they were so many ninepins.

I learned afterwards that it is customary with the mechanical tradesmen of London thus to assert their right of passage, and as it is not every one who gives way, the porter's burden is not unfrequently lowered while he stops to fight one who disputes his path. In evidence of these street fights, most of the London carters, coachmen, chairmen, porters, and labourers, bear continually upon their faces the scars, recent or ancient, of many such encounters. As for the gentlemen, it seems right that they should not disdain to strip and take a turn with their fists against some burly ruffian who would thrust his unmannerly body past his betters, confident in his superior strength.

Mr. Gambit looked round from time to time to see if we were following, and it gave me pain to observe how my box, which was long in shape, became the constant cause of sad accidents; for with it Mr. Gambit either knocked off a hat, or deranged a wig, or struck violently some peaceful person on the back of his head, or gave an inoffensive citizen a black eye, or caused profane passengers to swear.

He was, however, so big, strong, and careless about these reproaches, that no one cared to stop him or offered to fight him until he was well on ahead.

"It's a royal supper," he turned and nodded pleasantly, shouting these words to his wife: the box thus brought at right angles to the road, barred the way while he spoke, except to the very short. "Tripe—fried tripe!—with onions and carrots and potatoes. Will be done to a turn at eight. Make haste!"

What crowds! what rushing to and fro! what jostling, pushing, and crowding! What hurrying, and what wicked language! Sure something dreadful must have happened, nor could I believe Mrs. Gambit when she assured me that this was the usual crowd of London.

Then we came to London Bridge: and I saw the ships in the river and the Tower of London. Oh, the forests of masts! And beyond the river, the steeples of the great city shining bright in the evening sunshine. Which of them was my uncle's church?

We crossed the bridge; we walked up Gracechurch Street to Cornhill; we passed through a labyrinth of narrow and winding lanes, crowded like the wider streets. Mr. Gambit hurried along, thinking, I suppose, of his supper, and using my box as a kind of battering-ram with which to force a way. Presently we came to a broad street, which was, in fact, Fore Street, where was Mrs. Gambit's lodging.

"Eight o'clock," said Mr. Gambit, as we reached the top of the stairs. "Now for supper."

There was such a noise in the street below that we could hardly hear the church bells as they struck the hour. Yet there were churches all round us. But their bells clanging together only added somewhat to the general tumult.

"Eight o'clock, wife—good time!"

He dropped my box upon the floor, and hastened down the stairs.

It was a comfortable lodging of two rooms, in one of which a cloth was laid for supper, which Mr. Gambit speedily brought from a cookshop, and we had a royal supper indeed, with two quarts at least of the nauseous black beer of London, to which such men are extravagantly addicted.

Supper ended, Mr. Gambit lit a pipe of tobacco and began to smoke, begging me not to mind him. His wife told him of the farm and her brother, and I tried to listen through the dreadful noise of the street below. It was a warm evening and our window was thrown open; people were passing up and down, talking, singing, whistling, shouting, and swearing. I could hear nothing else; but the good man seemed as if he was deaf to the roar of the street, and listened to his wife as quietly as if we were in the fields. I asked him presently, with a shout, what was the cause of a dreadful riot and tumult? He laughed, and said that it was always the same. It was a pity, I said, that London being so rich, could not keep the streets quiet.

"Ay, but," said he, "there are plenty of poor people as well, and you must first ask what they think about having their mouth shut."

The strangeness of the place and the noise in the streets kept me awake nearly all that night, so that, when Mrs. Gambit called me in the morning, I was still tired. But it was time to be up and seeking for my uncle.

We got everything ready: my father's last will and testament; my bags of money, which Mrs. Gambit carried for me in her basket, and tied the basket to her arm; and my box of clothes. Then, because Mrs. Gambit said that a young lady should not walk with her box carried by a porter, like a servant wench, we hired a coach and told him to drive us to St. Paul's Coffee-house.

It is not far from Fore Street to St. Paul's Churchyard, but the crowd in the streets, the waggons and carts, and the dreadful practice of London drivers to quarrel and then to stop while they abuse each other, delayed us a great deal, so that it was already half-past nine when we came to the Coffee-house.

We got down, leaving the coach at the door.

It was a place the like of which I had never dreamed of. To be sure, everything was new to me just then, and my poor rustic brain was turning with the novelty. There was a long room which smelt of tobacco, rum-punch, coffee, chocolate, and tea; it was already filled with gentlemen, sitting on the benches before small tables, at which some were taking pipes of tobacco, some were talking, some were writing, and some were reading the newspapers. Running along one side of the room was a counter covered with coffee-pots, bottles of Nantz, Jamaica rum, Hollands, and Geneva: there were also chocolate-dishes, sugar, lemons, spices, and punch-bowls. Behind the counter sat a young woman, of grave aspect, knitting, but holding herself in readiness to serve the customers.

The gentlemen raised their heads and stared at me; some of them whispered and laughed; all gazed as if a woman had no more business there than in the inner precincts of the Temple. That was what occurred to me instantly, because they were, I observed, all of them clergymen.

They were not, certainly, clergymen who appeared to have risen in the world, nor did their appearance speak so much in their favour as their calling. They were mostly, in fact, clad in tattered gowns, with disordered or shabby wigs, and bands whose whiteness might have been restored by the laundress, but had changed long since into a crumpled yellow. I heard afterwards that the house was the resort of those "tattered crapes," as they are irreverently called, who come to be hired by the rectors, vicars, and beneficed clergy of London, for an occasional sermon, burial, or christening, and have no regular cure of souls.

On such chance employment and odd jobs these reverend ministers contrive to live. They even vie with each other and underbid their neighbours for such work; and some, who have not the means to spend a sixpence at the Coffee-house, will, it is said, walk up and down the street, ready to catch a customer outside. One fears that there must be other reasons besides lack of interest for the ill success of these men. Surely, a godly life and zeal for religion should be, even in this country of patronage, better rewarded than by this old age of penury and dependence. Surely, too, those tattered gowns speak a tale of improvidence, and those red noses tell of a mistaken calling.

This, however, I did not then know, and I naturally thought there must be some great ecclesiastical function in preparation, a confirming on a large scale, about to be celebrated in the great cathedral close beside, whose vastness was such as amazed and confounded me. These clergymen, whose poverty was no doubt dignified by their virtues, were probably preparing for the sacred function after the manner practised by my father, namely, by an hour's meditation. Perhaps my uncle would be among them.

Seeing me standing there helpless, and I daresay showing, by my face, what I immediately manifested in speech, my rusticity, the young woman behind the counter came to my assistance, and asked me, very civilly, what I lacked.

"I was told," I stammered, "to inquire at the St. Paul's Coffee-house for the present lodging of my uncle." As if there was but one uncle in all London!

"Certainly, madam," said the woman, "if you will tell me your uncle's name."

"I was told that you knew, at this house, the residence of every London clergyman."

"Yes, madam, that is true; and of a good many country clergymen. If you will let me know his name, we will do what we can to assist you."

"He is named" (I said this with a little pride, because I thought that perhaps, from my own rusticity and the homeliness of my companion, she might not have thought me so highly connected), "he is the Reverend Gregory Shovel, Doctor of Divinity."

"Lord save us!" she cried, starting back and holding up her hands, while she dropped her knitting-needle. Why did she stare, smile, and then look upon me with a sort of pity and wonder? "Dr. Shovel is your uncle, madam?"

"Yes," I said. "My father, who was also a clergyman, and is but lately dead, bade me come to London and seek him out."

She shook her head at this news, and called for one William. There came from the other end of the room a short-legged man, with the palest cheeks and the reddest nose I had ever seen. They spoke together for a few minutes. William grinned as she spoke, and scratched his head, under the scantiest wig I had ever seen.

"Can you tell me?" I began, when she returned. I observed that William, when he left her, ran quickly up the room, whispering to the gentlemen, who had ceased to stare at me, and that, as soon as he had whispered, they all, with one consent, put down their pipes, or their papers, or their coffee, stayed their conversation, and turned their clerical faces to gaze upon me, with a universal grin, which seemed ill-bred, if one might so speak of the clergy. "Can you tell me?"

"I can, madam; and will," she replied. "What, did your father not know the present residence of Dr. Shovel? I fear it will not be quite such as a young lady of your breeding, madam, had a right to expect. But doubtless you have other and better friends."

"She has, indeed," said Miss Gambit, "if his honour Sir Robert Levett, Justice of the Peace, is to be called a good friend. But if you please, tell us quickly, madam, because our coach waits at the door, and waiting is money in London. The country for me, where a man will sit on a stile the whole day long, and do nothing, content with his daily wage. And the sooner we get away from these reverend gentlemen, who stare as if they had never seen a young lady from the country before, the better."

"Then," the young woman went on, "tell your man to drive you down Ludgate Hill and up the Fleet Market on the prison side; he may stop at the next house to the third Pen and Hand. You will find the doctor's name written on a card in the window."

We thanked her, and got into the coach. When we told the coachman where to go, he smacked his leg with his hand, and burst out laughing.

"I thought as much," cried the impudent rascal. "Ah, Mother Slylips! wouldn't the doctor serve your turn, but you must needs look out for one in the Coffee-house? I warrant the doctor is good enough for the likes of you!"

He cracked his whip, and we drove off slowly.

Now, which was really extraordinary, all the reverend gentlemen of the coffee-room had left their places and were crowded round the door, some of them almost pushing their wigs into the coach windows in their eagerness to look at us. This seemed most unseemly conduct on the part of a collection of divines; nor did I imagine that curiosity so undignified, and so unworthy a sacred profession, could be called forth by the simple appearance of a young girl in the coffee-room.

The faces formed a curious picture. Some of the clergymen were stooping, some standing, some mounting on chairs, the better to see, so that the doorway of the Coffee-house seemed a pyramid of faces. They were old, young, fat, thin, red, pale, of every appearance and every age; they were mostly disagreeable to look at, because their possessors were men who had been unsuccessful, either through misfortune or through fault; and they all wore, as they stared, a look of delighted curiosity, as if here was something, indeed, to make Londoners talk—nothing less, if you please, than a girl of seventeen, just come up from the country.

"Bless us!" cried Mrs. Gambit, "are the men gone mad? London is a wicked place indeed, when even clergymen come trooping out merely to see a pretty girl! Fie for shame, sir, and be off with you!"

These last words were addressed to one old clergyman with an immense wig, who was actually thrusting his face through the coach window. He drew it back on this reprimand, and we went on our way.

I looked round once more. The young woman of the counter was still in the doorway, and with her William, with the scrubby wig and the red nose; round them were the clergymen, and they were all talking about me, and looking after me. Some of them wagged their heads, some shook theirs, some nodded, some were holding their heads on one side, and some were hanging theirs. Some were laughing, some smiling, some were grave. What did it mean?

"If," said Mrs. Gambit, "they were not clergymen, I should say they were all tomfools. And this for a pretty girl—for you are pretty, Miss Kitty, with your rosy cheeks and the bright eyes which were never yet spoiled by the London smoke. But there must be plenty other pretty girls in London. And them to call themselves clergymen!"

"Perhaps they were looking at you, Mrs. Gambit."

The idea did not seem to displease her. She smiled, smoothed the folds of her gown, and pulled down the ends of her neckerchief.

"Five years ago, child, they might. But I doubt it is too late. Set them up, indeed! As if nothing would suit them to look at but the wife of a respectable builder's foreman. They must go into the country, must they, after the pretty faces?"

The Chaplain of the Fleet

But oh, the noise and tumult of the streets! For as we came to the west front of St. Paul's, we found Ludgate Hill crowded with such a throng as I had never before believed possible. The chairmen jostled each other up and down the way. The carts, coaches, drays, barrows, waggons, trucks, going up the hill, met those going down, and there was such a crush of carriages, as, it seemed, would never be cleared. All the drivers were swearing at each other at the top of their voices.

"Shut your ears, child!" cried Mrs. Gambit. But, immediately afterwards: "There! it's no use; they could be heard through my grandfather's nightcap! Oh, this London wickedness!"

There are many kinds of wickedness in London; but the worst, as I have always thought, because I have seen and heard so much of it, is the great and terrible vice of blasphemy and profane swearing, so that, if you listen to the ragamuffin boys or to the porters, or to the chair and coach men, it would seem as if it were impossible for them to utter three words without two, at least, being part of an oath.

Then some of the drivers fought with each other; the people in the coaches looked out of the windows—swore, if they were men; if they were ladies, they shrieked. Most of those who were walking up and down the hill took no manner of notice of the confusion; they pushed on their way, bearing parcels and bundles, looking neither to the right nor to the left, but straight in front, as if they had not a moment to spare, and must push on or lose their chance of fortune. Some there were, it is true, who lingered, looking at the crush in the road and the men fighting; or, if they were women, stopping before the shops, in the windows of which were hoods, cardinals, sashes, pinners, and shawls, would make the mouth of any girl to water only to look at them. At the doors stood shopmen, bravely habited in full-dressed wigs with broad ribbon ties behind, who bowed and invited the gazers to enter. And there were a few who loitered as they went. These carried their hats beneath their arms, and dangled canes in their right hands.

There was plenty of time for us to notice all that passed, because the block in the way took fully half an hour to clear away. We were delayed ten minutes of this time through the obstinacy of a drayman, who, after exchanging with a carter oaths which clashed, and clanged, and echoed in the air like the bombshells at the siege of Mans, declared that he could not possibly go away satisfied until he had fought his man. The mob willingly met his views, applauding so delicate a sense of honour. They made a ring, and we presently heard the shouts of those who encouraged the combatants, but happily could not see them, by reason of the press. Mrs. Gambit would fain have witnessed the fight; and, indeed, few country people there are who do not love to see two sturdy fellows thwack and belabour each other with quarterstaff, singlestick, or fists. But I was glad that we could not see the battle, being, I hope, better taught. My father, indeed, and Lady Levett were agreed that in these things we English were little better than the poor pagan Romans, who crowded to see gladiators do battle to the death, or prisoners fight till they fell, cruelly torn and mangled by the lions; and no better at all than the poor Spanish papists who flock to a circus where men fight with bulls. It is hard to think that Roman gentlewomen and Spanish ladies would go to see such sights, whatever men may do. Yet in this eighteenth century, when we have left behind us, as we flatter ourselves, the Gothic barbarisms of our ancestors, we still run after such cruelties and cruel sports as fights with fists, sticks, or swords, baitings of bull, bear, and badger, throwing stones at cocks, killing of rats by dogs and ferrets, fights of cocks, dogs, cats, and whatever other animals can be persuaded to fight and kill each other.

When the fight was over, and one man defeated—I know not which, but both were horribly bruised and stained with blood—the carts cleared away rapidly, and we were able to go on. Is it not strange to think that the honour of such a common fellow should be "satisfied" when he hath gotten black eyes, bloody nose, and teeth knocked down his throat?

We got to the bottom of the hill, and passed without further adventure through the old gate of Lud, with its narrow arch and the stately effigy of Queen Elizabeth looking across the Fleet Bridge. Pity it is that the old gate has since been removed. For my own part, I think the monuments of old times should be carefully guarded, and kept, not taken away to suit the convenience of draymen and coaches. What would Fleet Street be without its bar? or the Thames without its river-gates? Outside, there was a broad space before us. The Fleet river ran, filthy and muddy, to the left, the road crossing it by a broad and handsome stone bridge, where the way was impeded by the stalls of those who sold hot furmety and medicines warranted to cure every disease. On the right, the Fleet had been recently covered in, and was now built over with a long row of booths and stalls. On either side the market were rows of houses.

"Fleet Market," said the driver, looking round. "Patience, young lady. Five minutes, and we are there."

There was another delay here of two or three minutes. The crowd was denser, and I saw among them two or three men with eager faces, who wore white aprons, and ran about whispering in the ears of the people, especially of young people. I saw one couple, a young man and a girl, whom they all, one after the other, addressed, whispering, pointing, and inviting. The girl blushed and turned away her head, and the young man, though he marched on stoutly, seemed not ill pleased with their proposals. Presently one of them came to our coach, and put his head in at the window. It was as impudent and ugly a head as ever I saw. He squinted, one eye rolling about by itself, as if having quarrelled with the other; he had had the bridge of his nose crushed in some fight; some of his teeth stuck out like fangs, but most were broken; his chin was bristly with a three days' beard; his voice was thick and hoarse; and when he began to speak, his hearers began to think of rum.

"Pity it is," he said, "that so pretty a pair cannot find gallant husbands. Now, ladies, if you will come with me I warrant that in half an hour the doctor will bestow you upon a couple of the young noblemen whom he most always keeps in readiness."

Here the driver roughly bade him begone about his business for an ass, for the young lady was on her way to the doctor's. At this the fellow laughed and nodded his head.

"Aha!" he said, "no doubt we shall find the gentleman waiting. Your ladyship will remember that I spoke to you first. The fees of us messengers are but half-a-crown, even at the doctor's, where alone the work is secure."

"What means the fellow?" cried Mrs. Gambit. "What have we to do with gentlemen?"

"All right, mother," he replied, with another laugh. Then he mounted the door-step, and continued to talk while the coach slowly made its way.

We were now driving along the city side of the Fleet Market, that side on which stands the prison. The market was crowded with buyers and sellers, the smell of the meat, the poultry, and the fruit, all together, being strong rather than delicate.

"This," said Mrs. Gambit, "is not quite like the smell of the honeysuckle in the Kentish hedges."

The houses on our right seemed to consist of nothing but taverns, where signs where hoisted up before the doors. At the corner, close to the ditch was the Rainbow, and four doors higher up was the Hand and Pen, next to that the Bull and Garter, then another Hand and Pen, then the Bishop Blaize, a third Hand and Pen, the Fighting Cocks, and the Naked Boy. One called the White Horse had a verse written up under the sign:

> "My White Horse shall beat the Bear,
> And make the Angel fly;
> Turn the Ship with its bottom up,
> And drink the Three Cups dry."

But what was more remarkable was that of the repetition in every window of a singular announcement. Two hands were painted, or drawn rudely, clasping each other, and below them was written, printed, or scrawled, some such remarkable legend as the following:

"Weddings Performed Here."
"A Church of England Clergyman always on the Premises."
"Weddings performed Cheap."
"The Only Safe House."
"The Old and True Register."
"Marriage by Church Service and Ordained Clergymen."
"Safety and Cheapness."
"The Licensed Clergyman of the Fleet."
"Weddings by a late Chaplain to a Nobleman — one familiar with the Quality."

The Chaplain of the Fleet

"No Imposition."
"Not a Common Fleet Parson;"

with other statements which puzzled me exceedingly.

"You do well, ladies," the man with us went on, talking with his head thrust into the coach, "you do well to come to Doctor Shovel, whose humble servant, or clerk, I am. The Doctor is no ordinary Fleet parson. He does not belong to the beggarly gentry—not regular clergymen at all who live in a tavern, and do odd jobs as they come, for a guinea a week and the run of the landlord's rum. Not he, madam. The Doctor is a gentleman and a scholar: Master of Arts of the University of Cambridge he was, where, by reason of their great respect for his learning and piety, they have made him Doctor of Divinity. There is the Rev. Mr. Arkwell, who will read the service for you for half-a-crown; he was fined five shillings last week for drunkenness and profane swearing. Would it be agreeable to your ladyship to be turned off by such an impious rogue? There is the Rev. Mr. Wigmore will do it for less, if you promise to lay out your wedding money afterwards on what he calls his Nantz: he hath twice been fined for selling spirituous drinks without a license. Who would trust herself to a man so regardless of his profession? Or the Rev. John Mottram—but there, your ladyship would not like to have it read in a prison. Now, at the Doctor's is a snug room with hassocks. There is, forsooth, the Rev. Walter Wyatt, brother of him who keeps the first Pen and Hand after you turn the corner; but sure, such a sweet young lady would scorn to look for drink after the service; or the Rev. John Grierson, or Mr. Walker, or Mr. Alexander Keith, will do it for what they can get, ay! even—it is reported—down to eighteenpence or a shilling, with a sixpennyworth of Geneva. But your ladyship must think of your lines; and where is your security against treachery? No, ladies. The Doctor is the only man; a gentleman enjoying the liberties of the Fleet, for which he hath given security; a Cambridge scholar; who receives at his lodging none but the quality; no less a fee than a guinea, with half-a-crown for the clerk, ever enters his house. The guinea, ladies, includes the five-shilling stamp, with the blessing of the Archbishop of Canterbury, which binds the happy pair like an act of parliament or a piece of cobbler's wax. This cheapness is certainly due to the benevolence and piety of the Doctor, who would be loth indeed to place obstacles in the way of so Christian and religious a ceremony."

"We have certainly," cried Mrs. Gambit, in dismay at such a flow of words, "got into Tom Fool's Land. This man is worse than the parsons at the Coffee-house."

"Now, ladies," the fellow went on, throwing the door wide open with a fling, and letting down the steps, "this is the house. Look at it, ladies!"

We got down and stood looking at it.

It was a low house of mean appearance, built in two stories of brick and timber, the first floor overhanging the lower, as was the fashion until the present comfortable and handsome mode of using stucco and flat front was adopted. The brick had been once covered with a coat of yellow wash, which had crumbled away over most of the front; the timber had once been painted, but the paint had fallen off. The roof was gabled; like the rest of the house, it looked decaying and neglected. The window of the room which looked out upon the street was broad, but it was set with leaden frames of the kind called diamond, provided with the common greenish glass, every other pane being those thick bull's-eye panes, which would stand a blow with a club without being broken. Little light would enter at that window but for the bright sun which shone full upon it; the casement, however, was set open to catch the air.

As for the air, that was hardly worth catching, so foul was it with the fumes of the market. Right in front of the door stood a great heap of cabbage leaves, stalks, and vegetable refuse, which sometimes was collected, put in barrows, and carted into the Fleet Ditch, but sometimes remained for months.

Mrs. Gambit sniffed disdainfully.

"Give me Fore Street," she said. "There's noise, if you like, but no cabbage-stalks."

"This, ladies," said the man after a pause, so that we might be overpowered with the grandeur of the house; "this is no other than the great Dr. Shovel's house. Here shall you find a service as regular and as truly read as if you were in the cathedral itself. Not so much as an amen dropped. They do say that the Doctor is a private friend of the dean, and hand-in-glove with the bishop. This way. Your ladyship's box? I will carry it. This is the good Doctor's door. The clerk's fee half-a-crown; your ladyship will not forget, unless the young gentleman, which is most likely, should like to make it half-a-guinea. I follow your ladyships. Doubt not that, early as it is, his reverence will be found up and ready for good works."

"I believe," said Mrs. Gambit, "that this man would talk the hind legs off a donkey. Keep close to me, Miss Kitty. Here may be villainy; and if there is, there's one at least that shall feel the weight of my ten nails. Young man," she addressed the fellow with sharpness, "you let that box alone, or if you carry it, go before; I trust Londoners as far as I can see them, and no farther."

"Pray, ladies," cried the man, "have no suspicion."

"It's all right," said the coachman, grinning. "Lord! I've brought them here by dozens. Go in, madam. Go in, young lady."

"This way, ladies," cried the man. "The Doctor will see you within."

"A clergyman," continued Mrs. Gambit, taking no manner of notice of these interruptions, "may not always, no more than a builder's foreman, choose where he would live. And if his parish is the Fleet Market, among the cabbages, as I suppose the Doctor's is, or about the Fleet Prison, among the miserable debtors, as I suppose it may be, why he must fain live here with the cabbage-stalks beneath his nose, and make the best of it."

"Your ladyship," the messenger went on, addressing himself to me, "will shortly, no doubt, be made happy. The gentleman, however, hath not yet come. Pray step within, ladies."

"You see, Miss Kitty," said Mrs. Gambit, pointing to the window, with a disdainful look at this impertinent fellow, "this is certainly the house. So far, therefore, we are safe."

In the window there hung a card, on which was written in large characters, so that all might read:

> REVEREND GREGORY SHOVEL,
>
> DOCTOR OF DIVINITY,
>
> FORMERLY OF CAMBRIDGE UNIVERSITY.

Now, without any reason, I immediately connected this announcement with those curious advertisements I had seen in the tavern windows. And yet, what could my uncle have to do with marrying? And what did the man mean by his long rigmarole and nonsense about the Reverend This and the Reverend That?

However, Mrs. Gambit led the way, and I followed.

The messenger pushed a door open, and we found ourselves in a low room lit by the broad window with the diamond panes, of which I have spoken. The air in the room was close, and smelt of tobacco and rum: the floor was sanded: the wainscoting of the walls was broken in places; walls, floors, and ceiling were all alike unwashed and dirty: the only furniture was a table, half-a-dozen cushions or hassocks, and one great chair with arms and back of carved wood. On the table was a large volume. It was the Prayer-book of the Established Church of England and Ireland, and it was lying open, I could plainly see, at the Marriage Service.

At the head of the table, a reflection of the sunlight from the window falling full upon his face, sat a man of middle age, about fifty-five years or so, who rose when we came in, and bowed with great gravity. Could this be my uncle?

He was a very big and stout man—one of the biggest men I have ever seen. He was clad in a rich silk gown, flowing loosely and freely about him, white bands, clean and freshly starched, and a very full wig. He had the reddest face possible: it was of a deep crimson colour, tinged with purple, and the colour extended even to the ears, and the neck— so much of it as could be seen—was as crimson as the cheeks. He had a full nose, long and broad, a nose of great strength and very deep in colour; but his eyes, which were large, reminded me of that verse in the Psalms, wherein the divine poet speaks of those whose eyes swell out with fatness: his lips were gross and protruded; he had a large square forehead and a great amplitude of cheek. He was broad in the shoulders, deep-chested and portly—a man of great presence; when he stood upright he not only seemed almost to touch the ceiling, but also to fill up the breadth of the room. My heart sank as I looked at him; for he was not the manner of man I expected, and I was afraid. Where were the outward signs and tokens of that piety which my father had led me to expect in my uncle? I had looked for a gentle scholar, a grave and thoughtful bearing. But, even to my inexperienced eyes, the confident carriage of the Doctor appeared braggart: the roll of his eyes when we entered the room could not be taken even by a simple country girl for the grave contemplation of a humble and fervent Christian: the smell of the room was inconsistent with the thought of religious meditation: there were no books or papers, or any other outward signs of scholarship; and even the presence of the Prayer-book on the table, with the hassocks, seemed a mockery of sacred things.

"So, good Roger," he said, in a voice loud and sonorous, yet musical as the great bell of St. Paul's, so deep was it and full—"So, good Roger, whom have we here?"

"A young lady, sir, whom I had the good fortune to meet on Ludgate Hill. She was on her way to your reverence's, to ask your good offices. She is—ahem!—fully acquainted with the customary fees of the Establishment."

"That is well," he replied. "My dear young lady, I am fortunate in being the humble instrument of making so sweet a creature happy. But I do not see … in fact … the other party."

"The young lady expects the gentleman every minute," said the excellent Roger.

"Oh!" cried Mrs. Gambit, "the man is stark mad—staring mad!"

"Sir," I faltered—"there is, I fear, some mistake."

He waved both of his hands with a gesture reassuring and grand.

"No mistake, madam, at all. I am that Dr. Shovel before whom the smaller pretenders in these Liberties give place and hide diminished heads. If by any unlucky accident your lover has fallen a prey to some of those (self-styled) clerical gentry, who are in fact impostors and sharpers, we will speedily rescue him from their talons. Describe the gentleman, madam, and my messenger shall go and seek him at the Pen and Hand, or at some other notorious place."

The clerk, meanwhile, had placed himself beside his master, and now produced a greasy Prayer-book, with the aid of which, I suppose, he meant to give the responses of the Church. At the mention of the word "mistake" a look of doubt and anxiety crossed his face.

"There is, indeed, some mistake, sir," I repeated. "My errand here is not of the kind you think."

"Then, madam, your business with me must be strange indeed. Sirrah!" he addressed his clerk, in a voice of thunder, "hast thou been playing the fool? What was it this young lady sought of you?"

"Oh, sir! this good person is not to blame, perhaps. Are you indeed the Rev. Gregory Shovel, Doctor of Divinity?"

"No other, madam." He spread out both his arms, proudly lifting his gown, so that he really seemed to cover the whole of the end of the room. "No other: I assure you I am Dr. Gregory Shovel, known and beloved by many a happy pair."

"And the brother-in-law of the late Reverend Lawrence Pleydell, late vicar of——"

He interrupted me. "Late vicar? Is, then, my brother-in-law dead? or have they, which is a thing incredible, conferred preferment upon sheer piety?"

"Alas! sir," I cried, with tears, "my father is dead."

"Thy father, child!"

"Yes, sir; I am Kitty Pleydell, at your service."

"Kitty Pleydell!" He bent over me across the table, and looked into my face not unkindly. "My sister's child! then how——" He turned upon his clerk, who now stood with staring eyes and open mouth, chapfallen and terrified. "FOOL!" he thundered. "Get thee packing, lest I do thee a mischief!"

CHAPTER V.

HOW KITTY WITNESSED A FLEET WEDDING.

Then I pulled out my father's letter, and gave it to him to read.

He took it, read it carefully, nodding gravely over each sentence, and then returned it to me.

"Lawrence, then," he said softly, "Lawrence is dead! Lawrence Pleydell is dead! And I am living. Lawrence! He hath, without reasonable doubt, passed away in full assurance. He hath exchanged this world for a better. He hath gone to happiness. Nay, if such as he die not in faith, what hope remains for such sinners as ourselves? Then would it be better for those who dwell in the Liberties of the Fleet if they had never been born. So. My sister's child. Hold up thy face, my dear." He kissed me as he spoke, and held his hand under my chin so that he could look at me well. "There is more Pleydell than Shovel here. That is well, because the Pleydells are of gentle blood. And the daughter doth ever favour the father more than the mother. Favour him in thy life, child, as well as in thy features.

"Lawrence is dead!" he went on. "The gentlest soul, the most pious and religious creature that the world has ever seen. He, for one, could think upon his Maker without the terror of a rebellious and prodigal son. The world and the flesh had no temptations for him. A good man, indeed. It is long since I saw him, and he knew not where I live, nor how. Yet he, who knew me when I was young, trusted still in me — whom no one else will trust. This it is to start in life with goodly promise of virtue, scholarship, and religion."

He cleared his throat, and was silent awhile.

"Thy father did well, child. I will treat thee as my own daughter. Yet I know not, indeed, where to bestow thee, for this house is not fit for girls, and I have none other. Still, I would fain take thy father's place, so far as in me lies. He, good man, lived in the country, where virtue, like fresh butter and new-laid eggs, flourishes easily and at the cost of a little husbandry in the way of prayer and meditation. As for us who live in great cities, and especially in the Rules or Liberties of the Fleet, we may say with the Psalmist, having examples to the contrary continually before us, with temptations such as dwellers in the fields wot not of, 'He that keepeth the Law, happy is he!' I have neither wife nor child to greet thee, Kitty. I must bestow thee somewhere. What shall we do?"

He paused to think.

"I might find a lodging——but no, that would not do. Or in——but the house is full of men. There is the clerk of St. Sepulchre's, whose wife would take thee; but the rector bears me a heavy grudge. Ho! ho!" he laughed low down in his chest. "There is not a parish round London, from Limehouse to Westminster, and from Southwark to Highgate, where the niece of Dr. Shovel would not find herself flouted, out of the singular hatred which the clergy bear to me. For I undersell them all. And if they pass an Act to prevent my marrying, then will I bury for nothing and undersell them still. Well, I must take order in this matter. And who are you, my good woman?" He asked this of Mrs. Gambit.

"Jane Gambit, sir," she replied, "at your service, and the wife of Samuel Gambit, foreman of works. And my charge is not to leave Miss Kitty until she is safe in your reverence's hands. There are the hands, to be sure; but as for safety——"

She paused, and sniffed violently, looking round the room with a meaning air.

"Why, woman, you would not think the child in danger with me?"

"I know not, sir. But Miss Kitty has been brought up among gentlefolk, and the room is not one to which she has been accustomed to live in, or to eat in, or to sleep in, either at the Vicarage or the Hall. Tobacco and the smell of rum may be very well—in their place, which, I humbly submit, is in a tavern, not a gentlewoman's parlour."

"The woman speaks reason," he growled, laying his great hand upon the table. "See, my dear, my brother-in-law thought me holding a rich benefice in the Church. Those get rich benefices who have rich friends and patrons. I had none; therefore I hold no benefice. And as for my residence, why, truly, I have little choice except between this place and the Fleet Prison, or perhaps the King's Bench. Else might I welcome thee in a better and more convenient lodging. Know, therefore, Kitty, without any concealment, that I live here secluded in the Liberties of the Fleet in order that my creditors, of whom I have as many as most men and more importunate, may no longer molest me when I take my walks abroad; that I am in this place outside the authority of the bishop; and that my occupation is to marry, with all safety and despatch without license, or asking of banns, or any of the usual delays, those good people who wish to be married secretly and quickly, and can afford at least one guinea fee for the ceremony."

I stared in amazement. To be sure, every clergyman can marry, but for a clergyman to do naught else seemed strange indeed.

He saw my amazement; and, drawing his tall and burly figure upright, he began to deliver an oration—I call it an oration, because he so puffed his cheeks, rolled his sentences, and swelled himself out while he spoke, that it was more like a sermon or oration than a mere speech. In it he seemed to be trying at once to justify himself in my eyes, to assert his own self-respect, and to magnify his office.

"It is not likely, child," he said, "that thou hast been told of these marriages in the Fleet. Know, therefore, that in this asylum, called the Rules of the Fleet, where debtors find some semblance of freedom and creditors cease to dun, there has grown up a custom of late years by which marriages are here rapidly performed (for the good of the country), which the beneficed clergy would not undertake without great expense, trouble, delay, and the vexation of getting parents' and guardians' consent, to say nothing of the prodigality and wasteful expense of feasting which follows what is called a regular marriage. Therefore, finding myself some years ago comfortably settled in the place, after contracting a greater debt than is usually possible for an unbeneficed clergyman, I undertook this trade, which is lucrative, honourable, and easy. There are indeed," he added, "both in the Prison and the Rules, but more especially the latter, many Fleet parsons"—here he rolled his great head with complacency—"but none, my child, so great and celebrated as myself. Some, indeed, are mere common cheats, whose marriages—call them, rather, sacrilegious impostures—are not worth the paper of their pretended certificates. Some are perhaps what they profess to be, regularly ordained clergymen of the Church of England and Ireland as by law established, the supreme head of which is his gracious Majesty. But even these are tipplers, and beggars, and paupers—men who drink gin of an evening and small beer in the morning, whose gowns are as ragged as their reputations, and who take their fees in shillings, with a dram thrown in, and herd with the common offscourings of the town, whom they marry. Illiterate, too: not a Greek verse or a Latin hexameter among them all. Go not into the company of such, lest thou be corrupted by their talk. In the words of King Lemuel: 'Let them drink and forget their poverty, and remember their misery no more.'" Here he paused and adjusted his gown, as if he were in a pulpit. Indeed, for the moment, he imagined, perhaps, that he was preaching. "As for me, Gregory Shovel, my marriages are what they pretend to be, as tight as any of the archbishop's own tying, conducted with due decorum by a member of the University of Cambridge, a man whose orders are beyond dispute, whose history is known to all, an approved and honoured scholar. Yes, my niece, behold in me one who has borne off University and College medals for Latin verse. My Latin verses, wherein I have been said to touch Horace, and even to excel Ovid, whether in the tender elegiac, the stately alcaic, the melting sapphic, or the easy-flowing hendecasyllabic loved of Martial, have conferred upon my head the bays of fame. Other Fleet parsons? Let them hide their ignorant heads in their second-hand peruques! By the thunders of Jupiter!"—his powerful voice rose and rolled about the room like the thunder by which he swore—"By the thunders of Jupiter, I am their Bishop! Let them acknowledge that I, and I alone, am THE CHAPLAIN OF THE FLEET!"

During this speech he swelled himself out so enormously, and so flourished his long gown, that he seemed to fill the whole room. I shrank into a corner, and clasped Mrs. Gambit's hand.

This kind of terror I have always felt since, whenever, which is rare, I have heard a man speak in such a full, rich, manliness of voice. It was a voice with which he might have led thousands to follow him and do his bidding. When I read of any great orator at whose speeches the people went mad, so that they did what he told them were it but to rush along the road to certain death, I think of the Reverend Dr. Shovel. I am sure that Peter the Hermit, or St. Bernard, must have had such a voice. While he spoke, though the words were not noble, the air was such, the voice was such, the eloquence was such, that my senses were carried away, and I felt that in the hands of such a man no one was master of himself. His demeanour was so majestic, that even the shabby, dirty room in which he spoke became for the time a temple fit for the sacred rites conducted by so great and good a man: the noise of carts, the voices of men and women, were drowned and stilled beneath the rolling music of his voice. I was rapt and astonished and terrified.

Mrs. Gambit was so far impressed when the Doctor began this oration, that she instantly assumed that attitude of mind and body in which country people always listen to a sermon: that is to say, she stood with her chin up, her eyes fixed on the ceiling (fie! how black it was!), her hands crossed, and her thoughts wandering freely whithersoever they listed. It is a practice which sometimes produces good effects, save when the preacher, which is seldom, hath in his own mind a clear message to deliver from the Revealed Word. For it prevents a congregation from discerning the poverty of the discourse; and in these latter days of Whitfield, Wesley, and the sad schisms which daily we witness, it checks the progress of Dissent.

The Doctor, after a short pause, swept back his flowing gown with a significant gesture of his left hand, and resumed the defence or apology for his profession. It was remarkable that he spoke as earnestly, and with as much force, eloquence, and justness in this address to two women—or to one and a half, because Mrs. Gambit, thinking herself in church, was only half a listener—as if he had been addressing a great congregation beneath the vast dome of St. Paul's. The Doctor, I afterwards found, was always great; no mean or little ways were his: he lived, he spoke, he moved, he thought like a bishop. Had he been actually a bishop, I am sure that his stateliness, dignity, and pomp would have been worthy of that exalted position, and that he would have graced the bench by the exhibition of every Christian virtue, except perhaps that of meekness. For the Doctor was never meek.

"Let us," said the Doctor, "argue the question. What is there contrary to the Rubric in my calling? The Church hath wisely ordered that marriage is a state to be entered upon only after sanctification by her ministers or priests; I am one of those ministers. She hath provided and strictly enjoined a rule of service; I read that service. She hath recommended the faithful to marry as if to enter a holy and blessed condition of life; I encourage and exhort the people to come to me with the design of obeying the Church and entering upon that condition. She hath, in deference to the laws of the land, required a stamped certificate (at five shillings); I find that certificate in obedience to the law. Further, for the credit of the cloth, and because people must not think the ministers of the Church to be, like common hackney coachmen, messengers, running lackeys, and such varlets, at the beck and call of every prentice boy and ragamuffin wench with a yard-measure and a dishclout for all their fortune; and because, further, it is well to remind people of thrift, especially this common people of London, who are grievously given to waste, prodigality, gluttony, fine clothes, drinking, and all such extravagances—nay, how except by thrift will they find money to pay their lawful tithes to Mother Church?—wherefore it is my custom—nay, my undeviating rule—to charge a fee of one guinea at least for every pair, with half-a-crown for the services of the clerk. More may be given; more, I say, is generally given by those who have money in pocket, and generous, grateful hearts. What, indeed, is a present of ten guineas in return for such services as mine? Child, know that I am a public benefactor; behold in me one who promotes the happiness of his species; but for me maids would languish, lovers groan, and cruel guardians triumph. I ask not if there be any impediment; I inquire not if there be some to forbid the banns; I do not concern myself with the lover's rent-roll; I care not what his profession—I have even married a lady to her footman, since she desired it, and a nobleman to his cook, since that was his lordship's will. I ask not for consent of parents; the maiden leaves my doors a wife: when she goes home, no parents or guardians can undo the knot that I have tied. Doctors, learned in theology, casuistry, science, and philosophy, have been called by divers names; there have been the Subtle Doctor, the Golden Doctor, the Eloquent Doctor. For me there has been reserved the title of the Benevolent Doctor; of me let it be said that he loved even beyond his respect towards his diocesan, even beyond obedience to his ecclesiastical superiors, even beyond consideration to the parish clergy, who by his means were deprived of their fees, the happiness of his fellow men and women."

The Chaplain of the Fleet

His voice had dropped to the lower notes, and his last words were spoken in deep but gentle thunder. When he had finished, Mrs. Gambit dropped her chin and returned to practical business.

"And pray, sir, what will Miss Kitty do?"

Recalled to the facts of the case, the Doctor paused. His cheeks retracted, his breadth and height became perceptibly smaller.

"What will she do? That is, indeed, a difficulty."

"If," said Mrs. Gambit, "your honour is a prisoner — — "

"Woman!" he roared, "I enjoy the Liberties of the Fleet — the Liberties, do you hear? Prate not to me of prisoners. Is Dr. Shovel a man, think ye, to clap in a prison?"

"Well, then, is Miss Kitty to live here?" She looked round in disgust. "Why, what a place is this for a young lady virtuously and godlily reared! Your ceiling is black with smoke; the windows are black with dirt; the walls are streaked with dirt; the floor is as thick with mud as the road — faugh! If your honour is a bishop, as you say you are, you can doubtless put the poor young lady, who is used to sweet air and clean floors, where she will get such — and that without profane swearing."

The last remark was caused by language used at that moment outside the window by a man wheeling a barrow full of cabbages, which upset. While picking up the vegetables, he swore loudly, administering rebuke in a couple of oaths at least, and in some cases more, to every head of cabbage in turn. An unreflecting wretch indeed, to break a commandment upon a senseless vegetable!

"Nay," I said, "my uncle will do what is best for me."

"I will do for thee," he said, "what I can. This place is not fit for a young girl. All the morning it is wanted for my occupation. In the evening I am visited by gentlemen who seek me for certain merits, graces, or beauties of conversation in which I am said (although I boast not) to be endowed with gifts beyond those allotted to most men. No, child, thou must not stay here."

While we stood waiting for his decision, we became aware of a most dreadful noise outside. Men were shouting, women were screaming;

of course bad language and cursing formed a large part of what was said. The air about the Fleet was always heavy with oaths, so that at last the ear grew accustomed to them, and we noticed them no more than in the quiet fields one notices the buzzing of the insects. But these people, whoever they were, congregated outside the door of the house; and after more oaths and loud talk, the door was opened and they all tramped noisily into the room—a party of men and women, twelve in all—and drew up in some sort of order, every man leading a woman by the hand. As for the men, though I had never seen the sea, I knew at once that monsters so uncouth and rough could be none other than sailors. They were all dressed alike, and wore blue jackets with flannel shirts and coloured silk neckties: every man carried round his waist a rope, at the end of which was a knife; they wore three-cornered hats without lace or any kind of trimming; they had no wigs, but wore their own hair plastered with tallow, rolled up tightly and tied behind; and one bore a great and grisly beard most terrible to behold. Great boots covered their feet; their hands were smeared with tar; their faces were weather-beaten, being burnt by the sun and blown by the breeze; their eyes were clear and bright, but their cheeks were bruised as if they had been fighting: they were all laughing, and their countenances betokened the greatest satisfaction with everything. As for the women, they were young, and some of them, I suppose, were handsome, but they looked bold and rough. They were very finely dressed, their frocks being of silk and satin, with flowered shawls, and hats of a grandeur I had never before seen; immense hoops and great patches. But the fight outside had torn their finery, and more than one nymph had a black eye. However, these accidents had not diminished the general joy, and they were laughing with the men.

"Why—why!" roared the Doctor, as he called them to attention by banging the table with his fist, so that the windows rattled, the women shrieked, and the plaster fell from the wall. "What is this? Who are ye?"

The impudent fellow with the white apron who had brought us to the place, here stepped in, bringing with him another couple. He, too, had been fighting, for his face was bleeding and bruised. Fighting, I presently found, was too common in Fleet Market to call for any notice.

"What is this, Roger?" repeated the Doctor. "These tarpaulins are no cattle for my handling. Let them go to the Pen and Hand, or some other pigsty where they can be irregularly and illegally married for eighteenpence and a glass of rum."

"Please your reverence," said Roger, handling his nose, which was swollen, tenderly, "they are honest gentlemen of the sea, paid off at Wapping but yesternight, still in their sea-going clothes by reason of their having as yet no time to buy long-shore rigging; not common sailors, but mates by rating in the ship's books, and anxious to be married by none other than your reverence."

"Ay—ay! honest Roger." The Doctor's voice dropped and became soft and encouraging. "Ay—ay! this is as it should be. Know they of the fee?"

"They wish me to offer your reverence," said the clerk, "a guinea apiece, and five guineas extra for your honour's trouble, if so be so small a gift is worth your acceptance; with half-a-crown apiece for the clerk, and a guinea for his nose, which I verily believe is broken in the bridge. I have had great trouble, your reverence, in conveying so large a party safe. And indeed I thought, at one time, the Rev. Mr. Arkwell would have had them all. But the gallant gentlemen knew what was best for them; and so, your honour, with a nose——"

The Doctor shook his head and interrupted any further explanation.

"That would indeed have been a misfortune for these brave fellows. Come, Roger, collect the fees, and to business with what speed we may."

"Now then," said Roger roughly, "money first, business afterwards. No fee, no marriage. Pay up, my lads!"

The men lugged out handfuls of gold from their pockets, and paid without hesitation what they were told. But the women grumbled, saying that for half-a-crown and a dram they would have been married quite as well, and so much more to spend. When the Doctor had put the fees in his pocket, he advanced to the table and took up the Prayer-book. What would my father have said had he witnessed this sight?

Then Roger pulled out his greasy book, and put himself in place ready to say the responses. All being ready, the Doctor again banged the table with his fist so that they all jumped, and the women screamed again, and more plaster fell off the wall.

"Now, all of you!" he roared, "listen to me. The first man who interrupts, the first woman who laughs, the first who giggles, the first who dares to misbehave or to bring contempt on this religious ceremony, I will with my own clerical hands pitch headforemost into the street. And *he shall remain unmarried!*"

Whether they were awed by his great voice and terrible aspect, the men being short of stature as all sailors seem to be, or whether they feared to be pitched through the window, or whether they trembled at the prospect of remaining unmarried (perhaps for life) if the Doctor refused to perform the ceremony, I know not. What is quite certain is that they one and all, men and women, became suddenly as mute as mice, and perfectly obedient to the commands of Roger the clerk, who told them where to stand, when to kneel, what to say, and what to do. A curtain ring acted as wedding-ring for all.

The Doctor would omit nothing from the service, which he read from beginning to end in his loud musical voice. When he had married the whole six, he shut the Prayer-book, produced six stamped certificates, rapidly filled in the names and dates, which he also entered in his "Register," a great book with parchment cover. Roger acted as witness. Then the brides were presented by the Doctor with the certificates of their marriage. The ceremony lasted altogether about half-an-hour.

"You are now, ladies and gentlemen," he said, smiling pleasantly, "married fast and firm, one to the other. I congratulate you. Marriage in the case of sailors and sailors' wives is a condition of peculiar happiness, as you will all of you presently discover. The husband, at the outset, is liable for the debts of his wife"—here the men looked sheepishly at each other—"this no doubt will be brought home to all of you. There are several brave gentlemen of the sea now languishing in the Fleet Prison through inability to pay off these encumbrances.

They will continue to lie there for the whole term of their lives, these unfortunate men. Husbands are also liable for the debts incurred by their wives while they are abroad"—here one or two of the men murmured something about London Port and giving it a wide berth, which I did not understand. "As for the wives of seafaring men, their blessings and privileges are also peculiar and numerous. They will have to remain at home and pray for the safety of the husbands whom they will see perhaps once every five years or so: they will, in this widowed state, be able to practise many Christian virtues which those who enjoy the constant presence of a husband are less often called upon to illustrate: such are patience under privation, resignation, and hope. Most of them will find the allowance made to them by their husbands insufficient or irregularly paid. If any of them marry again, or be already married, it is, let me tell you, a hanging matter. Yea, there are already in Newgate hard by, several unfortunate women cast for execution who have married again while their husbands were at sea. Lying in the cells they are, waiting for the cart and the gallows!" Here the women looked at one another and trembled, while their cheeks grew pale. "It is too late now. Should there be any woman here who has committed the crime of bigamy, let that woman know that it is too late for aught but repentance. The gallows awaits her. You are now therefore, my friends, bound to each other. I trust and hope that these marriages have not been hastily or lightly entered upon. You have heard the duties of husband to wife and wife to husband, in the words of the service duly read to you by a clergyman of the Church of England. Go now, perform those duties: be bright and shining examples of temperance, fidelity, and virtue. Should any man among you find that his marriage hath led him, through such a cause as I have indicated, to the King's Bench, or the Fleet, or the Compter; should he have to exchange, against his will, the free air of the sea for the confinement of a gaol, and the rolling deck for the narrow courtyard; should he see himself reduced (having never learned any handicraft or trade) to starvation through these liabilities of his wife, or should any woman among you have hereafter to stand her trial for bigamy either for this work newly accomplished or for any future crime of the same nature, it will then be your comfort to reflect that you were not married by an irregular, self-constituted, self-styled Fleet parson, but by an ordained clergyman and a Doctor of Divinity. Wherefore, I wish you well. Now go, less noisily than you came. But the noise I impute to your ignorance, as not knowing the quality of the man into whose presence you so rudely pushed. As for the marriage feast, see that you enjoy it in moderation. Above all, let your liquors be good. To which end—I speak it purely out of my benevolence and for the good of head and stomach—you will find the rum at the Bishop Blaize cheap and wholesome. Be not tempted to prefer the Rainbow or the Naked Boy, where the liquor is deplorable; and perhaps, in an hour or so, I may look in and drink your healths. Roger, turn them out."

They went away sheepish and crestfallen, who had come noisy and triumphant. I was ashamed, thinking of my father, and yet lost in wonder, looking at my uncle who had so easily tamed this savage crew.

"I am glad," said the Doctor, when they had gone, "that this chance did not become the windfall of an irregular and unlicensed practitioner. They cannot say that I warned them not. Well, let them have their way. A few days more and the men will be afloat again, all their money gone; and the women— —"

"Will they starve, sir?" I asked.

"I doubt it much," he replied. "Come, child, I have a thought of a plan for thee. Follow me. And you, good woman, come with us that you may see your charge in safety."

The thing that I had seen was like a dream—the appearance of the disorderly sailors and the women whom they married; the words of the service read solemnly in this unhallowed room; the exaction of the money beforehand; the bleeding faces and marks of the recent fight; the exhortation of the Doctor; the disappearance of the actors; the swollen nose, black eye, and the importance of the clerk reading the responses—what strange place was this whereunto I had been led? One pitied, too, the poor fellows on whom Fate had bestowed such wives. I thought, child as I was, how terrible must be life encumbered with such women! Womanlike, I was harder on the women than the men. Yet truly, women are what men make them.

"Follow me, child."

He led us out of the house, turning to the right. In the market was a lot of country people who were standing about a stall. And we heard a voice: "There's the Doctor—there goes the great Dr. Shovel."

My uncle drew himself up to his full height, and stalked grandly along with the eyes of the people upon him. "See," he seemed to say, by the swelling folds of his gown, "see my fame, how widespread it is—my reputation, how great!"

He stopped at the corner of Fleet Lane, where the houses were no longer taverns, and announcements of marriages were no longer to be seen. It was a house of three stories high, with a door which, like all the doors in that neighbourhood, stood ever open.

Here the Doctor stopped and addressed Mrs. Gambit—

"You spoke of safety. I am about to confide this child to the care of two gentlewomen, poor, but of good birth and character, whom unjust laws and the wickedness of men have condemned to imprisonment. I know of no better guardians; but you shall satisfy yourself before you go away. Wait a moment while I confer with the ladies."

We stayed below for ten minutes. Then my uncle came down the stairs, and bade me return with him to be presented to the ladies, who had kindly accepted the charge, on condition, he said, of my good conduct.

I followed him, Mrs. Gambit keeping close to me. We stopped at a door on the first floor. The room was poor and shabby: the furniture, of which there was not much, was old and worn: there was no carpet: a white blind was half drawn over the window: the place, to judge by the presence of a saucepan, a kettle, and a gridiron, was apparently a kitchen as well as a sitting-room: all, except a great portrait of a gentleman, in majestic wig and splendid gown, which hung over the fireplace, was mean and pinched. Two ladies, of fifty or thereabouts, stood before me, holding out hands of welcome.

They were both exactly alike, being small and thin, with hollow cheeks, bright eyes, and pointed features like a pair of birds: they wore white caps, a sort of grey frock in cheap stuff: their hair was white: their hands were thin, with delicate fingers, transparent like the fingers of those who have been long in bed with sickness: they were of the same height, and appeared to be of the same age—namely, fifty or thereabouts. My first thought, as I looked at them, was that they had not enough to eat—which, indeed, like all first thoughts, was correct, because that had generally been the case with these poor creatures.

"Kitty," said the Doctor, taking me by the hand, "I present you to Mrs. Esther Pimpernel"—here the lady on the left dipped and curtsied, and I also, mighty grave—"and to Mrs. Deborah Pimpernel"—here the same ceremony with the lady on the right. "Ladies, this is my niece Kitty Pleydell, daughter of my deceased sister Barbara and her husband Lawrence Pleydell of pious memory. I trust that in consenting thus generously to receive this child in your ward and keeping, you will find a reward for your benevolence in her obedience, docility, and gratitude."

"Doctor," murmured Mrs. Esther, in a voice like a turtledove's for softness, "I am sure that a niece of yours must be all sensibility and goodness."

"Goodness at least," said her sister, in sharper tones.

I saw that the difference between the sisters lay chiefly in their voices.

"She will, I trust, be serviceable to you," said the Doctor, waving his hand. "She hath been well and piously brought up to obedient ways. Under your care, ladies, I look for a good account of her."

"Dear and reverend sir," Mrs. Esther cooed, "we are pleased and happy to be of use to you in this matter. No doubt little miss, who is well grown of her years, will repay your kindness with her prayers. As for us, the memory of your past and present goodness——"

"Tut, tut!" he replied, shaking his great head till his cheeks waggled, "let us hear no more of that. In this place"—here he laid his right hand upon his heart, elevating his left, and leaning his head to one side—"in this place, where infamy and well-deserved misery attend most of those who dwell in it, it is yours, as it should be mine, to keep burning continually the pure flame of a Christian life."

"How sweet! how noble!" murmured the sisters.

The Chaplain of the Fleet

Was it possible? The man whom we had just seen reading the service of Mother Church, which my father had taught me to regard as little less sacred than the words of the Bible itself, in a squalid room, reeking with the fumes of rum and stale tobacco, before a gang of half-drunken sailors, assumed naturally and easily, as if *it belonged to him,* the attitude and language of one devoted entirely to the contemplation and practice of virtue and good works. Why, his face glowed with goodness like the sun at noonday, or the sun after a shower, or, say, the sun after a good action. The Doctor, indeed, as I learned later, could assume almost any character he pleased. It pleased him, not out of hypocrisy, but because for a time it was a return to the promise of his youth, to be with these ladies the devout Christian priest. In that character he felt, I am convinced, the words which came spontaneously to his lips: for the moment he *was* that character. Outside, in the Fleet Market, he was the great Dr. Shovel—great, because among the Fleet parsons he was the most successful, the most learned, the most eloquent, the most important. In his own room he married all comers, after the manner we have seen; and it raised the envy of his rivals to see how the crowd flocked to him. But in the evening he received his friends, and drank and talked with them in such fashion as I never saw, but of which I have heard. Again, it raised their envy to witness how men came from all quarters to drink with the Doctor. At that time he was no longer the Christian advocate, nor the clergyman; he was a rollicking, jovial, boon companion, who delighted to tell better stories, sing better songs, and hold better talk—meaning more witty, not more spiritual talk—than any of those who sat with him. I have never been able to comprehend what pleasure men, especially men of mature years, can find in telling stories, and laughing, drinking, smoking tobacco, and singing with one another. Women find their pleasures in more sober guise: they may lie in small things, but they are innocent. Think what this world would be were the women to live like the men, as disorderly, as wastefully, as noisily!

"Now, good woman," said my uncle to Mrs. Gambit, "are you satisfied that my niece is in safe hands?"

"The hands are good enough," replied the woman, looking round her; "but the place——"

"The place is what it is," said the Doctor sharply; "we cannot alter the place."

"Then I will go, sir."

With that she gave me my parcel of money, kissed me and bade me farewell, curtsied to the ladies, and left us.

"I shall send up, ladies," said the Doctor, "a few trifles of additional furniture: a couple of chairs, one of them an arm-chair—but not for this great, strong girl, if you please—a bed, a shelf for books; some cups and saucers we shall provide for you. And now, ladies, I wish you good-morning. And for your present wants—I mean the wants of this hungry country maid, who looks as if mutton hung in toothsome legs on every verdant hedge—this will, I think, suffice;" he placed money in Mrs. Esther's hand—I could not but think how he had earned that money—and left us.

When he was gone the two ladies looked at each other with a strange, sad, and wistful expression, and Mrs. Esther, with the guineas in her hand, burst into tears.

CHAPTER VI.

HOW KITTY BEGAN TO ENJOY THE LIBERTIES OF THE FLEET.

Her tears disconcerted me extremely. What did she cry for? But she presently recovered and dried her eyes. Then she looked at me thoughtfully, and said—

"Sister, I suppose this child has been accustomed to have a dinner every day?"

"Surely," replied Mrs. Deborah. "And to-day we shall dine."

To-day we should all dine? Were there, then, days when we should all go hungry?

"You must know, my dear," Mrs. Esther explained in a soft, sad voice, "that we are very poor. We have, therefore, on many days in a week to go without meat. Otherwise we should have to do worse"—she looked round the room and shuddered—"we should have to give up the independence of our solitude. Hunger, my child, is not the worst thing to bear."

"A piece of roasting-beef, sister," said Mrs. Deborah, who had now assumed a hat and a cloak, "with a summer cabbage, and a pudding in the gravy."

"And I think, sister," said Mrs. Esther, her eyes lighting up eagerly, "that we might take our dinner—the child might like to take her dinner—at twelve to-day."

While Mrs. Deborah went into the market, I learned that the two sisters had taken no food except bread and water for a week, and that their whole stock now amounted to two shillings in money and part of a loaf. What a strange world was this of London, in which gentlewomen had their lodging in so foul a place and starved on bread and water!

"But," she repeated with a wan smile, "there are worse things than hunger. First, we must pay our rent. And here we are at least alone; here we may continue to remember our breeding."

Before Mrs. Deborah returned, I also learned that they were chiefly dependent on a cousin for supplies of money, which were made to them grudgingly (and indeed he was not rich), and that the Doctor had provided for my maintenance with the offer of so large a weekly sum that it promised to suffice for the wants of all.

"We are," said Mrs. Esther, "but small eaters; a little will suffice for us. But you, child, are young; eat without fear, eat your fill; the money is for you, and we shall grudge you nothing."

While the beef was roasting I noticed how their eyes from time to time, in spite of themselves, would be fixed upon the meat with a hungry and eager look. Nor had I any enjoyment of the meal till I had seen their pangs appeased. After the plenty of the Vicarage and the Hall, to think of bread and water, and not too much bread, for days together! Yet, hungry as they were, they ate but little; it shamed me to go on eating, being always a girl of a vigorous appetite and hard-set about the hour of noon; it shamed me at first, also, to observe their ways of thrift, so that not the least crumb should be wasted. Mrs. Deborah read my thoughts.

"In this place," she said, "we learn to value what it takes money to procure. Yet there are some here poorer than ourselves. Eat, child, eat. For us this has been, indeed, a feast of Belteshazzar."

Dinner over, we unpacked my box, and they asked me questions. I found that they were proud of their birth and breeding; the portrait over the fire was, they told me, that of their father, once Lord Mayor of London, and they congratulated me upon being myself a Pleydell, which, they said, was a name very well known in the country, although many great city families might be ignorant of it.

"No gift, my dear," said Mrs. Esther, "is so precious as gentle blood. Everything else may be won, but birth never."

All day long there went on the same dreadful noise of shouting, crying, calling, bawling, rolling of carts, cracking of whips, and trampling of horses' feet. In the evening I asked, when the sun went down, but the noise decreased not, if it was always thus.

"Always," they replied. "There is no cessation, day or night. It is part," said Mrs. Deborah, "of our punishment. We are condemned, child; for the sin of having a negligent trustee, we go in captivity, shame, and degradation all our lives."

"Nay," said her sister, "not degradation, sister. No one but herself can degrade a gentlewoman."

Truly, the noise was terrible. When I read in the "Paradise Lost," of fallen angels in their dark abode, I think of Fleet Market and the Fleet Rules. It began in the early morning with the rolling of the carts: all day long in the market there was a continual crying of the butchers: "Buy, buy, ladies—buy! Rally up, ladies—rally up!" There were quarrels unceasing and ever beginning, with fights, shouting and cursing: the fish-women quarrelled at their stalls; the poultry-wives quarrelled over their baskets; the porters quarrelled over their burdens; the carters over the right of way; the ragamuffin boys over stolen fruit. There was nothing pleasant, nothing quiet, nothing to refresh; nothing but noise, brawling, and contention. And if any signs of joy, these only drunken laughter from open tavern-doors.

Thus I began to live, being then a maid of sixteen years and seven months, in the Rules and Liberties of the Fleet Prison; surely as bad a place, outside Newgate Prison, as could be found for a girl brought up in innocence and virtue. For, let one consider the situation of the Rules. They include all those houses which lie between the ditch, or rather the market, on the west, and the Old Bailey on the east—fit boundaries for such a place, the filthy, turbid ditch and the criminal's gaol—and Fleet Lane on the north to Ludgate Hill on the south. These streets are beyond and between the abodes of respectability and industry. On the east was the great and wealthy City with the merchants' houses; on the west the streets and squares where the families of the country had their town residence; on the south, the river; on the north, the dark and gloomy streets of Clerkenwell, where thieves lay in hiding and the robbers of the road had their customary quarters. Why, Jonathan Wyld himself, the greatest of villains, lived hard by in Ship Court. Is there, anywhere, in any town, an acre more thickly covered with infamy, misery, starvation, and wretchedness?

If we walked abroad, we could not go north because of Clerkenwell, where no honest woman may trust herself: if we went south we had to walk the whole length of the market, past the marrying taverns, so that shame fell upon my heart to think how my uncle was one of those who thus disgraced his cloth: when we got to the end, we might walk over the Fleet Bridge, among the noisy sellers of quack medicines, pills, powders, hot furmety, pies, flounders, mackerel, and oysters; or on Ludgate Hill, where the touts of the Fleet parsons ran up and down, inviting couples to be married, and the Morocco men went about, book in hand, to sell their lottery shares. The most quiet way when we took the air was to cross Holborn Bridge, and so up the hill past St. Andrew's Church, where, if the weather were fine, we might go as far as the gardens of Gray's Inn, and there sit down among the trees and feel for a little the joy of silence.

Said Mrs. Deborah, one day, when we two had sat there, under the trees, for half an hour, listening to the cawing of the rooks—

"Child, the place"—meaning the Rules—"is the City of Destruction after Christian and Christiana, and the boys, and Mercy, were all gone away."

We lived in one room, which was both kitchen and parlour. We had no servant; the Doctor's provision kept us in simple plenty; we cleaned and dusted the place for ourselves; we cooked our dinners, and washed our dishes; we made our dresses; we did for ourselves all those things which are generally done by a servant. Mrs. Esther said that there was no shame in doing things which, if left undone, would cause a gentlewoman to lose her self-respect. 'Twas all, except the portrait of her father, that she had left of her former life, and to this she would cling as something dearer than life.

There were other lodgers in the house. All who lodged there were, of course, prisoners "enjoying" the Rules—who else would live in the place? On the ground-floor was Sir Miles Lackington, Baronet. He was not yet thirty, yet he had already got rid of a great and noble estate by means of gambling, and now was compelled to hide his head in this refuge, and to live upon an allowance of two guineas made weekly to him by a cousin. This, one would have thought, was a disgrace enough to overwhelm a gentleman of his rank and age with shame. But it touched him not, for he was ever gay, cheerful, and ready to laugh. He was kind to my ladies and to me; his manners, when he was sober, were gentle; though his face was always flushed and cheeks swollen by reason of his midnight potations, he was still a handsome fellow; he was careless of his appearance as of his fortune; he would go with waistcoat unbuttoned, wig awry, neckcloth loose, ruffles limp; but however he went it was with a laugh. When he received his two guineas he generally gave away the half among his friends. In the evening they used to carry him home to his room on the ground-floor, too drunk to stand.

I soon got to know him, and we had frequent talks. He seemed to be ever meeting me on the stairs when I went a-marketing; he called upon us often, and would sit with me during the warm summer afternoons, when the sisters dropped off to sleep. I grew to like him, and he encouraged me to say freely what I thought, even to the extent of rating him for his profligate practices.

"Why," he would say, laughing, "I am at the lowest—I can go no lower; yet I have my two guineas a week. I have enough to eat, I drink freely: what more can I want?"

I told him what his life seemed to me.

He laughed again at this, but perhaps uneasily.

"Does it seem so terrible a thing," he said, leaning against the window with his hands in his pockets, "to have no cares? Believe me, Kitty, Fortune has brought me into a harbour where winds and tempests never blow. While I had my estate, my conscience plagued me night and morning. And yet I knew that all this must fly. Hazard doth always serve her children so, and leaves them naked. Well—it is gone. So can I play no more. But he who plays should keep sober if he would win. Now that I cannot play, I may drink. And again, when, formerly, I was rich and a prodigal, friend and enemy came to me with advice. I believe they thought the Book of Proverbs had been written specially to meet my case, so much did they quote the words of Solomon, Agar, and Lemuel. But, no doubt, there have been fools before, and truly it helpeth a fool no whit to show him his folly. 'As a thorn goeth up into the hand of a drunkard, so is a parable in the mouth of fools.' I remember that proverb. Now that Hazard hath taken all, there is no longer occasion for advice. Child, you look upon one who hath thrown away his life, and yet is happier in his fall and repents not. For I make no doubt but that, had I my fortune back, 'twould fly away again in the same fashion."

He concluded with an allusion to the Enemy of Mankind, for which I rebuked him, and he laughed, saying—

"Pretty Puritan, I will offend no more."

Had I been older and more experienced, I should have known or suspected why he came so often and met me daily. Kitty had found favour in the sight of this dethroned king. He loved the maid: her freshness, her rosy cheeks, her youth, her innocence pleased him, I suppose. We know not, we women, for what qualities there are in us that we are loved by men, so that they will commit so many follies for our sake.

"Thou art such a girl, sweet Kitty," he said to me, one day, "so pretty and so good, as would tempt a man wallowing contentedly in the pigsties of the world, to get up, wash himself, and go cleanly, for thy sake. Yet what a miserable wretch should I be did I thus learn to feel my own downfall!"

And again he told me once that he was too far gone to love me; and not far enough gone to do me an injury.

"Wherefore," he added, "I must worship at thy shrine in silent admiration."

It was kindly done of Sir Miles to spare an ignorant girl. For so ignorant was Kitty, and so brotherly did he seem, that had he asked her to become his wife, I think she would have consented. Oh, the fine state, to be my Lady Lackington, and to live in the Rules of the Fleet!

Another lodger in our house, a man whose face inspired me with horror, so full of selfish passion was it, was a Captain Dunquerque. With him were his wife and children. It was of the children, poor things, that our Esther spoke when she said there were some in the place poorer than themselves; for the wife and children starved, while the captain, their father, ate and drank his fill. A gloomy man, as well as selfish, who reviled the fate which he had brought upon himself. Yet for all his reviling, he spared himself nothing so that his children might have something. I am glad that this bad man has little to do with my history. Another lodger, who had the garret at the top, was Solomon Stallabras, the poet.

It is very well known that the profession of letters, of all the trades, callings, and conditions of men, is the most precarious and the most miserable. I doubt, indeed, whether that ought to be called a profession which requires no training, no colleges or schools, no degree, and no diploma. Other professions are, in a way, independent: the barrister doth not court, though he may depend upon, the favour of attorneys; the rector of the parish doth not ask the farmers to support him, but takes the tithes to which he is entitled; the poor author, however, is obliged to receive of his publisher whatever is offered, nor is there any corporate body or guild of authors by whom the situation of the poet may be considered and his condition improved. Alone among learned men, the author is doomed to perpetual dependence and poverty. Indeed, when one considers it, scarce anything else is to be expected, for, in becoming an author, a man is so vain as to expect that to him will be granted what has been given to no man except Shakespeare—a continual flow of strength, spirits, ingenuity, wit, and dexterity, so as to sustain, without diminution or relaxation, the rapid production of works for the delight of the world. I say rapid, because the books are bought by publishers at a low rate, though they are sold to the public at large sums. And, if we think of it, scarce any author produces more than one or two books which please the world. Therefore, when the fountain runs dry, whither is that poor author to turn? The public will have none of him; his publisher will have none of him; there remains, it is true, one hope, and that unworthy, to get subscriptions for a volume which he will never produce, because he will have eaten up beforehand the money paid for it before it is written.

The Fleet Prison and its Rules have always been a favourite resort and refuge for poets and men of letters. Robert Lloyd died there, but long after I went away; Richard Savage died there; Churchill was married in the place, and would have died there, had he not anticipated his certain fate by dying early; Samuel Boyce died there; Sir Richard Baker died there; William Oldys, who died, to be sure, outside the Rules, yet drank every night within them; lastly, within a stone's throw of the Rules, though he was never a prisoner, died the great John Bunyan himself.

I heard my ladies, from time to time, talk of a certain Mr. Stallabras. They wondered why he did not call as usual, and laid the blame upon me; little madam had made him shy. One day, however, Mrs. Esther being called out by one of Captain Dunquerque's children, came back presently, saying that Mr. Stallabras was starving to death in his room.

Mrs. Deborah made no reply, but instantly hurried to the cupboard, when she took down the cold beef which was to be our dinner, and cut off three or four goodly slices; these she laid on a plate, with bread and salt, and put the whole upon a napkin, and then she disappeared swiftly.

"The poor young man! the dear young man!" cried Mrs. Esther, wringing her hands. "What can we do? My dear, the sweetest and most mellifluous of poets! The pride and glory of his age! It was he who wrote 'Hours of the Night,' the 'Pleasures of Solitude,' the 'Loves of Amoret and Amoretta,' and other delightful verses; yet they let him languish in the Fleet! What are my countrymen thinking of? Would it not be better to rescue (while still living) so ingenious and charming a writer from his poverty, than to give him (as they must), after his death, a grave in Westminster Abbey?"

I asked her if we should read together these delightful poems.

"We have no copy," she said. "Mr. Stallabras, who is all sensibility, insists, from time to time, upon our having copies, so that we may read them aloud to him. Yet his necessities are such that he is fain to take them away again and sell them. As for his manners, my dear, they are very fine, being such as to confer distinction upon the Rules. He has not the easy bearing of Sir Miles Lackington, of course, which one would not expect save in a man born to good breeding; but he possesses in full measure the courtesy which comes from study and self-dignity. Yet he is but a hosier's son."

Mrs. Deborah here returned, bearing an empty plate.

She had trouble at first, she said, to persuade him to eat. His prejudices as a gentleman and a scholar were offended by the absence of horse-radish; but, as he had eaten nothing for two days, he was induced to waive this scruple, and presently made a hearty meal. She had also persuaded him to come downstairs in the evening, and take a dish of tea.

Thanks to the Doctor's liberality in the matter of my weekly board, tea was now a luxury in which we could sometimes indulge. Nothing gave Mrs. Esther more gratification than the return, after long deprivation, to that polite beverage.

At about five o'clock the poet made his appearance. He was short of stature, with a turned-up nose, and was dressed in a drab-coloured coat, with bag-wig, and shoes with steel buckles. Everything that he wore had once been fine, but their splendour was faded now; his linen was in rags, his shoes in holes; but he carried himself with pride. His dignity did not depend upon his purse; he bore his head high, because he thought of his fame. It inflicted no wound to his pride to remember that he had that day been on the eve of starvation, and was still without a farthing.

"Miss Kitty," he said, bowing very low, "you see before you one who, though a favourite of the Muses, is no favourite of Fortune:

"'Gainst hostile fate his heart is calm the while,
Though Fortune frown, the tuneful sisters smile.'

Poetry, ladies, brings with it the truest consolation."

"And religion," said Mrs. Esther.

"There lives not—be sure—the wretch," cried the poet, "who would dissociate religion and the Muse."

This was very grand, and pleased us all. We had our dish of tea, with bread and butter. I went on cutting it for the poet till the loaf was quite gone.

During the evening he gave utterance to many noble sentiments—so noble, indeed, that they seemed to me taken out of books. And before he went away he laid down his views as to the profession of letters, of which I have already spoken, perhaps, too severely.

"It is the mission of the poet and author," he said, "to delight, and to improve while delighting. The man of science may instruct; the poet embodies the knowledge, and dresses it up in a captivating way to attract the people: the divine teaches the dogmas of the Church; the poet conveys, in more pleasing form, the lessons and instructions of religion: the philosopher and moralist lay down the laws of our being;

the author, by tropes and figures, by fiction, by poetry, shows the proper conduct of life, and teaches how the way of virtue leads to happiness. Is not this a noble and elevating career? Does not a man do well who says to himself, 'This shall be my life; this my lot?'"

He paused, and we murmured assent to his enthusiasm.

"It is true," he went on, "that the ungrateful world thinks little of its best friends; that it allows me—*me*, Solomon Stallabras, to languish in the Rules of the Fleet. Even that, however, has its consolation; because, ladies, it has brought me the honour and happiness of your friendship."

He rose, saluted us all three in turn, and sat down again.

"Art," he went on, "so inspires a man with great thoughts, that it makes more than a gentleman—it makes a nobleman—of him. Who, I would ask, when he reads the sorrows of Clarissa, thinks of the trade—the mere mechanical trade—in which the author's money was earned? I cannot but believe that the time will come when the Court itself, unfriendly as it now is to men of letters, will confer titles and place upon that poor poet whose very name cannot now reach the walls of the palace."

My ladies' good fortune (I mean in receiving the weekly stipend for my maintenance) was thus shared by the starving poet, whom they no longer saw, helpless to relieve him, suffering the privation of hunger. Often have I observed one or other of the sisters willingly go without her dinner, pleading a headache, in order that her portion might be reserved for Mr. Stallabras.

"For sensibility," said Mrs. Esther, "is like walking up a hill: it promotes appetite."

"So does youth," said Mrs. Deborah, more practical. "Mr. Stallabras is still a young man, Kitty; though you think thirty old."

That he was a very great poet we all agreed, and the more so when, after a lucky letter, he secured a subscriber or two for his next volume, and was able to present us once more with a book of his own poetry. I do not know whether he more enjoyed hearing me read them aloud (for then he bowed, spread his hands, and inclined his head this way and that, in appreciation of the melody and delicacy of the sentiments), or whether he preferred to read them himself; for then he could stop when he pleased, with, "This idea, ladies, was conceived while wandering amid the fields near Bagnigge Wells;" "This came to me while watching the gay throng in the Mall;" "This, I confess, was an inspiration caught in church."

"Kitty should enter these confessions in a book," said Mrs. Esther. "Surely they will become valuable in the day—far distant, I trust—when your life has to be written, Mr. Stallabras."

"Oh, madam!" He bowed again, and lifted his hands in deprecation. But he was pleased. "Perhaps," he said, "meaner bards have found a place in the Abbey, and a volume dedicated to their lives. If Miss Kitty will condescend to thus preserve recollections of me, I shall be greatly flattered."

I did keep a book, and entered in it all that dropped from his lips about himself, his opinions, his maxims, his thoughts, and so forth. He gradually got possessed of the idea that I would myself some day write his life, and he began insensibly to direct his conversation mainly to me.

Sometimes he met me in the market, or on the stairs, when he would tell me more.

"I always knew," he said, "from the very first, that I was born to greatness. It was in me as a child, when, like Pope, I lisped in numbers. My station, originally, was not lofty, Miss Kitty." He spoke as if he had risen to a dazzling height. "I was but the son of a hosier, born in Fetter Lane, and taught at the school, or academy, kept by one Jacob Crooks, who was handier with the rod than with the Gradus ad Parnassum. But I read, and taught myself; became at first the hack of Mr. Dodsley, and gradually rose to eminence."

He had, indeed, risen; he was the occupant of a garret; his fame lay in his own imagination; and he had not a guinea in the world.

"Miss Kitty," he said, one day, "there is only one thing that disqualifies you from being my biographer."

I asked him what that was.

"You are not, as you should be, my wife. If virtue and beauty fitted you for the station of a poet's wife, the thing were easy. Alas, child! the poet is poor, and his mistress would be poorer. Nevertheless, believe that the means, and not the will, are wanting to make thee my Laura, my Stella, and me thy Petrarch, or thy Sidney."

It was not till later that I understood how this starveling poet, as well as the broken baronet, had both expressed their desire (under more favourable circumstances) to make love to me. Grand would have been my lot as Lady Lackington, but grander still as Mistress Stallabras, wife of the illustrious poet, who lived, like the sparrows, from hand to mouth.

CHAPTER VII.

HOW KITTY LEARNED TO KNOW THE DOCTOR.

Those evenings of riot from which Sir Miles was so often carried home speechless, were spent in no other place than that very room where I had seen the marriage of the sailors; and the president of the rabble rout was no other than the Doctor himself.

I learned this of Sir Miles. If my ladies knew it, of which I am not certain, they were content to shut their eyes to it, and to think of the thing as one of the faults which women, in contempt and pity, ascribe to the strange nature of man. I cannot, being now of ripe years, believe that Heaven hath created in man a special aptitude for debauchery, sin, and profligacy, while women have been designed for the illustration of virtues which are the opposite to them. So that, when I hear it said that it is the way of men, I am apt to think that way sinful.

It was Sir Miles himself who told me of it one morning. I found him leaning against the doorpost with a tankard of ale in his hand.

"Fie, Sir Miles!" I said. "Is it not shameful for a gentleman to be carried home at night, like a pig?"

"It is," he replied. "Kitty, the morning is the time for repentance. I repent until I have cleared my brain with this draught of cool October."

"It is as if a man should drag a napkin in the mud of the Fleet Ditch to clean it," I said.

He drank off his tankard, and said he felt better.

"Pretty Miss Kitty," he said, "it is a fine morning; shall we abroad? Will you trust yourself with me to view the shops in Cheapside or the beaux in the Mall? I am at thy service, though, for a Norfolk baronet, my ruffles are of the shabbiest."

I told him that I would ask Mrs. Esther for permission. He said he wanted first a second pint, as the evening had been long and the drink abundant, after which his brain would be perfectly clear and his hand steady.

I told him it was a shame that a gentleman of his rank should mate with men whose proper place was among the thieves of Turnmill Street, or the porters of Chick Lane, and that I would not walk with a man whose brain required a quart of strong ale in the morning to clear it.

"As for my companions," he said, taking the second pint which the boy brought him and turning it about in his hands, "we have very good company in the Liberties—quite as good as your friend Christian, in that story you love so much, might have had in Vanity Fair, had he been a lad of mettle and a toper. There are gentlemen of good family, like myself; poets like Solomon Stallabras; merchants, half-pay captains and broke lieutenants; clerks, tradesmen, lawyers, parsons, farmers, men of all degrees. It is like the outside world, except that here all are equal who can pay their shot. Why, with the Doctor at the head of the table, and a bowl of punch just begun, hang me if I know any place where a man may feel more comfortable or drink more at his ease."

"The Doctor," I asked. Now I had seen so little of my uncle that I had almost forgotten the marriage of the sailors, and was beginning again to think of him as the pious and serious minister who spoke of sacred things to my guardians. "The Doctor?"

"Ay;" Sir Miles drank off the whole of his second pint. "Who else?" His voice became suddenly thick, and his eyes fixed, with a strange light in them. "Who else but the Doctor? Why, what would the Rules be without the Doctor? He is our prince, our bishop, our chaplain—what you will—the right reverend his most gracious majesty the King of the Rules." Sir Miles waved his hand dramatically. "He keeps us sweet; he polishes our wits; but for him we should be wallowing swine: he brings strangers and visitors to enliven us; drinks with us, sings with us, makes wit for us from the treasures of his learning; condescends to call us his friends; pays our shot for us; lends us money; gives food to the starving, and drink—yes, drink, by gad! to the thirsty, and clothes to the naked. Ah, poor girl! you can never see the Doctor in his glory, with all his admirers round him, and every man a glass of punch in his hand and a clean tobacco-pipe in his mouth. The Doctor? he is our boast; a most complete and perfect doctor; the pride of Cambridge; the crown and sum of all doctors in divinity!"

He had forgotten, I suppose, his invitation to take me for a walk, for he left me here, staggering off in the direction of the Hand and Pen, where, I doubt not, he spent the rest of his idle and wasted day.

It would have been useless and cruel to talk to my guardian about this discovery. It was another thing to be ashamed of. Sir Miles told me less than the truth. In fact the Doctor's house was the nightly resort of all those residents in the Rules whom he would admit to his society. Hither, too, came, attracted by his reputation for eloquence, wit, and curious knowledge, gentlemen from the Temple, Lincoln's Inn, and other places, who were expected, as a contribution to the evening, to send for bowls of punch. But of this presently.

I saw my uncle seldom. He visited the sisters from time to time, and never failed to ask particularly after my progress in knowledge, and especially in the doctrines of the Church of England. On these occasions he generally left behind him, as a present, some maxim or precept tending to virtue, which we could repeat after his departure and turn over in our minds at leisure. Once he found me alone, Mrs. Deborah being indisposed and confined to her room, where her sister was nursing her. He took advantage of their absence to impress upon me the necessity of circumspection in my manner of life.

"Heaven knows, child," he said, "what thy future will be. Hither come none but profligates and spendthrifts. Yet what else can I do with thee? Where bestow thee?"

"Oh, sir!" I said, "let me not be taken from my dear ladies."

"Thou shalt not, child; at least for the present. But it is bad for thee to live here; it is bad for thee to have as an uncle one whose life is sadly inconsistent with his Christian profession, and who might despair, were it not for the example of Solomon (methinks from his history may be sucked consolation by all elderly and reverend sinners). Like him, what I lack in practice I partly make up with precept. He who, like me, is a Fleet parson, should be judged differently from his fellows: he is without the license, and therefore hath forfeited paternal affection of his bishop; he is exposed to temptations which beset not other folk; among those who flock to him for marriage are some who would fain commute their fees for brandy and strong drinks, or even bilk the clergyman altogether—a sin which it is difficult to believe can be forgiven. Hence arise strifes and wraths, unseemly for one who wears a cassock. Hither come those who seek good fellowship and think to find it in the Rules; Templars, young bloods, and wits. Hence arise drinking and brawling; and as one is outside the law, so to speak, so one is tempted to neglect the law. I say nothing of the temptations of an empty purse. These I felt, with many prickings and instigations of the Evil One, while I was yet curate of St. Martin's-in-the-Fields, before I escaped my creditors by coming here. Then I was poor, and found, as the Wise Man says, that 'The poor is hated even of his own neighbour.'"

He went on, half preaching, half talking.

A man who sinned greatly, yet preached much; who daily fell, yet daily exhorted his neighbour to stand upright; who knew and loved, as one loves a thing impossible to attain, the life of virtue; who drank, laughed, and bawled songs of an evening with his boon companions; who married all comers, no questions asked, without scruple and without remorse; a priest whose life was a disgrace to his profession; who did kind and generous things, and paid that homage to Virtue which becomes one who knows her loveliness.

It pleased him to talk, but only with me, about himself. He was always excusing himself to me, ashamed of his life, yet boasting of it and glorying in it; conscious of his infamy, and yet proud of his success; always thinking by what plea he could justify himself, and maintain his self-respect.

"I am a man," he said, "who is the best of a bad profession. My work is inglorious, but I am glorious; my rivals, who would rob me of my very practice, do not hate me, but esteem and envy me. I have, yea, outside these Rules, friends who love me still; some of them pity me, and some would see me (which is impossible) restored to the fold and bosom of the Church; some who drink with me, talk with me, borrow of me, walk with me, smoke with me, and are honoured by my friendship. There is no man living who would wish me harm. Surely, I am one of those who do good to themselves, whom, therefore, their fellow-men respect."

I have said that he was generous. Sir Miles spoke the truth when he declared that the Doctor fed the starving and clothed the naked. Truly it seems to me natural to believe that these good deeds of his must be a set-off to the great wickedness of his life. There were no occupants of the prison and its Liberties who were rich. Some there were who would have starved but for the charity of their friends. The poor prisoners were allowed to beg, but how could poor gentlewomen like my guardians bear to beg for daily bread? Rather would they starve. As for the prison, I know nothing of it; I never saw the inside; it was enough for me to see its long and dreary wall. I used to think at night of the poor creatures shut up there in hopeless misery, as I thought, though Sir Miles declared that most of them were happier in the prison than out; and beside the latticed gate there stood every day a man behind bars begging with a plate and crying: "Pity the poor prisoners."

Is it not sad that the same punishment of imprisonment must be meted out to the rogue and the debtor, save that we let the rogue go free while we keep the debtor locked up? Truly, the Vicar of St Bride's or even the Dean of St. Paul's himself could preach no better sermon, could use no words more fitted to arrest the profligate and bring the thoughtless to reason, than that doleful cry behind the bars. Nor could any more salutary lesson be impressed upon young spendthrifts than to take them from house to house in the Rules and show them the end of graceless ways.

CHAPTER VIII.

HOW KITTY SPENT HER TIME.

As soon as they were settled together, and the ladies had decided in their own minds that the girl would lighten their lives, they resolved that Kitty's education must not be neglected, and for this end began to devise such a comprehensive scheme as would have required the staff of a whole university to carry it through. Everything was set down (upon a slate) which it behoved a girl to know. Unfortunately the means at their disposal did not allow of this great scheme. Thus it was fitting that music should be taught: Mrs. Deborah had once been a proficient on the spinnet, but there was no spinnet to be had; the French tongue forms part of polite education, but though both ladies had learned it of old, their memory was defective, and they had neither dictionary nor grammar nor any book in the language; limning, both with pencil and in water-colours, should be taught, but the sisters could neither of them draw, and hardly knew a curve from a straight line. Calligraphy is almost a necessary, but the handwriting of both ladies was tremulous, and of antiquated fashion; they knew not the modern Italian hand. There was in the Rules a professor in the art, and an attempt was made to get lessons from him. But he was already old and hastening to the grave, which speedily closed over him; his hand shook, because he drank strong waters; his coat was stained with beer and punch; his wig smelt always of tobacco.

Mrs. Deborah undertook, as a beginning, to teach the girl book-keeping by single and double entry. How or why she ever came to learn this science has never been understood. Yet she knew it, and was proud of it.

"It is a science," she said, "which controls the commerce of the world. By its means are we made rich: by the aid of book-keeping we apportion the profit and the loss which are the rewards of the prudent or the punishment of the thriftless. Without book-keeping, my dear, the mysteries and methods of which I am about to impart to you, neither a Whittington, nor a Gresham, nor even a Pimpernel, would have risen to be Lord Mayor of London."

Kitty only imperfectly grasped the rudiments of this science. No doubt, had she been placed in a position of life where it was required, she would have found it eminently useful. Mrs. Esther, for her part, taught her embroidery and sampler work. As for preserving, pickling, making of pastry and home-made wines, cookery, distilling, and so forth, although the sisters had been in their younger days notable, it was impossible to teach these arts, because, even if there had been anything to pickle or preserve, there was only one sitting-room in which to do it. Therefore, to her present sorrow, Kitty speedily forgot all that she had formerly learned in the still-room at Lady Levett's. For there is no station so exalted in which a lady is not the better for knowing the way in which such things should be done, if it is only that she may keep her maids in order. And if, as the learned Dr. Johnson hath informed us, a lady means one who dispenses gifts of hospitality and kindness, there is another reason why she should know the value of her gifts. There is something divine in the contemplation of the allotment of duty to the two sexes; man must work, build up, invent, and acquire, for woman to distribute, administer, and divide.

As for reading, they had a book on the history of England, with the cover off, and wanting the title-page with several chapters. There was one of those still remaining in which the author exhorted his readers (her teachers told the girl that the admonition belonged to women as well as men) never to grow faint or to weary in the defence of their Liberties. She ignorantly confounded the Liberties of the country with the Liberties of the Fleet, and could not avoid the reflection that a woman would certainly put more heart into her defence of the Liberties if these were cleaner, and if there were fewer men who swore and got drunk. There were also a Bible and a Church Prayer-book; there were three odd volumes of "Sermons;" and there were besides odd volumes of romances, poems, and other works which Mr. Solomon Stallabras was able to lend.

Mrs. Deborah added to her knowledge of book-keeping some mastery over the sublime science of astronomy. By standing on chairs at the window when the west wind blew the fogs away and the sky was clear, it was possible to learn nearly everything that she had to teach. The moon was sometimes visible, and a great many of the stars, because, looking over the market, the space was wide. Among them were the Pole Star, the Great Bear, Orion's belt, and Cassiopeia's chair. It was elevating to the soul on such occasions to watch the heavenly bodies, and to listen while Mrs. Deborah discoursed on the motions of the planets and the courses of the stars.

"The moon, my dear," she would say, "originally hung in the heavens by the hand of the Creator, goes regularly every four weeks round the sun, while the sun goeth daily round the earth: when the sun is between the earth and the moon (which happens accidentally once a month or thereabouts), part of the latter body is eclipsed: wherefore it is then of a crescent-shape: the earth itself goes round something—I forget what—every year: while the planets, according to Addison's hymn, go once a year, or perhaps he meant once a month, round the moon. This is the reason why they are seen in different positions in the sky. And I believe I am right in saying that if you look steadily at the Great Bear, you may plainly see that every night it travels once about the earth at least, or it may be oftener at different seasons. When we reflect"—here she quoted from recollection—"that these bodies are so far distant from us, that we cannot measure the space between; that some of them are supposed to be actually greater than our own world; that they are probably inhabited by men and women like ourselves; that all their movements round each other are regular, uniform, never intermittent—how ought we to admire the wisdom and strength of the Almighty Hand which placed them there!"

Then she repeated, with becoming reverence, the words of Mr. Addison, the Christian poet, beginning:

> "Soon as the evening shades prevail
> The moon takes up the wondrous tale,
> And nightly to the listening earth
> Repeats the story of her birth.
> While all the stars that round her burn,
> And all the planets in their turn,
> Confirm the tidings as they roll,
> And spread the truth from pole to pole."

In such meditations and exercises did these imprisoned ladies seek to raise their souls above the miseries of their lot. Indeed, one may think there is nothing which more tends to make the mind contented and to prevent repining, than to feel the vastness of nature, the depth and height of knowledge open to man's intellect, the smallness of one's self, and the wisdom of God. And although poor Mrs. Deborah's astronomy was, as has been seen, a jumble; although she knew so little, indeed, of constellations or of planets, that the child did not learn to distinguish Jupiter from the Pole Star, and never could understand (until that ingenious gentleman, who lately exhibited an orrery in Piccadilly, taught her) how the planets and stars could go round the moon, and the moon round the sun, and the sun round the earth, without knocking against and destroying one another, she must be, and is, deeply grateful for the thoughts which the good lady awakened.

In all things the sisters endeavoured to keep up the habits and manners of gentlefolk. The dinner was at times scanty, yet was it served on a fair white cloth, with plates and knives orderly placed: a grace before the meat, and a grace after.

In the afternoon, when the dinner was eaten, the cloth removed, and the plates washed, they were able sometimes to sally forth and take a walk. In the summer afternoons it was, it has been said, pleasant to walk to the gardens of Gray's Inn. But when they ventured to pass through the market there was great choice for them. The daily service in the afternoons at St. Paul's was close at hand: here, while the body was refreshed with the coolness of the air, the mind was calmed with the peace of the church, and the soul elevated by the chanting of the white-robed choristers and the canons, while the organ echoed in the roof. After the service they would linger among the tombs, of which there are not many; and read the famous Latin inscription over the door of the cathedral, "*Si monumentum requiris, circumspice.*"

"I knew him," Mrs. Esther would whisper, standing before the great man's monument. "He was a friend of my father's, and he often came and talked, my sister and myself being then but little, on the greatness of astronomy, geometry, and architecture. In the latter years of his life he would sit in the sunshine, gazing on the noble cathedral he had built. Yet, grand as he is, he would still lament that his earlier plans, which were grander still, had not been accepted."

Then out into the noisy street again: back to the shouts of chairmen, waggon-drivers, coachmen, the bawling of those who cried up and down pavements, the cries of flying piemen, newsmen, boys with broadsheets, dying confessions, and ballads—back to the clamour of Fleet Market.

Another excursion, which could only be undertaken when the days were long, was that to Westminster Abbey.

The way lay along the Strand, which, when the crowded houses behind St. Clement's and St. Mary's were passed, was a wide and pleasant thoroughfare, convenient for walking, occupied by stately palaces like Northumberland and Somerset Houses, and by great shops. At Charing Cross one might cross over into Spring Gardens, where, Mrs. Esther said, there was much idle talk among young people, with drinking of Rhenish wine. Beyond the gardens was St. James's Park: Kitty saw it once in those days, being taken by Sir Miles Lackington; but so crowded was it with gallant gentlemen, whose wigs and silken coats were a proper set-off to the hoops and satins of the ladies, that she was ashamed of her poor stuff frock, and bade Sir Miles lead her away, which he did, being that day sorrowful and in a repentant mood.

"I have myself worn those silk waistcoats and that silver lace," he said with a sigh. "My place should be amongst them now, were it not for Hazard. Thy own fit station, pretty pauper, is with those ladies. But Heaven forbid you should learn what they know! Alas! I knew not when I ought to stop in the path of pleasure."

"Fie!" said she. "Young men ought not to find their pleasure in gambling."

"Humanity," said Sir Miles, becoming more cheerful when the Park was left, "has with one consent resolved to follow pleasure. The reverend divines bid us (on Sunday) be content to forego pleasure; in the week they, too, get what pleasure they can out of a punch-bowl. I am content to follow with other men. Come, little Puritan, what is thy idea of pleasure?"

That seemed simple enough to answer.

"I would live in the country," said she readily, "away from this dreadful town; I would have enough money to drink tea every day (of course I would have a good dinner, too), and to buy books, to visit and be visited, and make my ladies happy, and all be gentlewomen together."

"And never a man among you all?"

"No—we should want no man. You men do but eat, drink, devour, and waste. The Rules are full of unhappy women, ruined by your extravagances. Go live all together and carry each other home at night, where no woman can see or hear."

He shook his head with a laugh, and answered nothing. That same night, however, he was led home at midnight, bawling some drinking song at the top of his voice; so that the girl's admonition had no effect upon him. Perhaps profligate men feel a pleasure not only in their intemperance but also in repentance. It always seemed to me as if Sir Miles enjoyed the lamentations of a sinner the morning after a debauch.

On the few occasions when their journey was prolonged beyond Charing Cross, the ladies were generally attended and protected by Mr. Solomon Stallabras, who, though little in stature, was brave, and would have cudgelled a porter, or cuffed a guardsman, in the defence of ladies, as well as the strongest and biggest gentleman.

There are many other things to see in Westminster Abbey—the coronation throne, Henry the Seventh's Chapel, the monuments of kings, queens, great lords, and noble generals—but Mr. Stallabras had an eye to one spot only.

"There," he said, "is the Poet's Corner: with Dryden, Ben Jonson, and the glorious dead of this spot, shall, perhaps, my ashes be mixed. Ladies, immortality is the poet's meed."

The poor man needed some solace in these days, when his poverty was excessive. Later on he found a little success: obtained an order for a volume of "Travels in Cashmere" (whither he had never been), which brought him in eight guineas. He afterwards added "A Romantic Tale," the scene of which was laid in the same sweet abode of Sensibility. It was interspersed with verses, as full of delicacy as the tale itself. But the publisher, who gave him five guineas for it, complained afterwards that he had lost by his bargain. Mr. Stallabras often boasted of the great things he could do were there no publishers, and regretted the invention of printing, which rendered this class, who prey upon the very vitals of poor poets, a necessity.

These holidays, these after-hours of rest in the tranquil aisles of St. Paul's, or the awful Gothic shades of Westminster, were far between. Mostly the three sat together over their work, while the tumult raged below.

"Patience, child," said Mrs. Deborah. "Patience, awhile. We have borne it for nigh thirty years. Can you, who have hope, not bear it a little longer?"

Said Mrs. Esther: "Providence wisely orders every event, so that each year or each day shall add something to the education of the soul. It is doubtless for some wise purpose we have been kept in scarceness among runagates and spendthrifts."

On Sundays they generally went to the church of St. Giles, Cripplegate. It was a long way from the Rules, but the ladies liked it because it was the church where their father lay buried. From the place where they sat in the seats of the poor, which have neither cushions nor backs, they could read the tablet to the memory of the late Joshua Pimpernel, once Lord Mayor of London, and Alderman of Portsoken Ward. The great church was full of City memories, dear to them from their childhood: when they were girls they used to sit in a stately pew with red serge seats and hassocks; now, they worshipped in the same church, but on the benches among the poor women and the children. Yet there was the same service, with the rector and the clerk in their desks, the schoolboys of the Charity along the left, and the schoolgirls of the Charity along the right; the beadles and vergers, the old women who swept the church, opened the pew doors, curtsied to the quality and remained behind for doles—all brought back their childhood. They were as poor themselves as these old trots, but they could not stay for doles. It is a large and handsome church, filled with grave citizens, responsible men, whose ventures are abroad on many seas, respected for wealth and upright conduct, good men and true, such as was, in his day, my Lord Mayor Pimpernel himself; with the citizens sit their wives bravely attired, and their daughters making gallant show in hoops, patches, lace, sarsnet, and muslin. Outside the church a graveyard, piled and full, still with a tree or two upon it, whose boughs in June are covered with bright green leaves, among which the sparrows twitter and fly about. There is also a great round tower of antique look, which once had been part of the Roman wall of London.

Here they went to worship. When the minister came to the words in the Litany —

"Lord have mercy upon all prisoners and captives,"

the sisters would catch each other by the hand, and audibly follow the reader in prayer as well as response. For thirty years, for fifty-two Sundays in each year, they had made that prayer in the same words, for most of the time in the same church. Yet what answer?

Kitty took the prayer, presently, for herself as well. If these ladies were prisoners, why, what was she? If they might not sleep abroad, and only walk in the streets by permission and licence of the law, how was she different from them, since she could not, being but a maid, and young and penniless, go abroad at all without them or some other protection?

The sight of the leaves on the trees outside; the fluttering and flying of the sparrows, now and then the buzzing of a foolish bee who had found his way into the church, carried the girl's thoughts away to the quiet place in the country where, between Hall and Vicarage, she had been brought up. Would the sweet country never more be seen? Was her life to be, like that of these poor ladies, one long prison among reprobates and profligates?

The summer came on apace: it grew hot in June; in July it was so hot that they were fain to sit all day and to sleep all night, with open windows. The air was cooler, perhaps, at night, but it was laden with the odours of decaying cabbages, trodden peas and beans, rotten strawberries, bruised cherries, broken gooseberries, with the nauseous breath of the butcher's stall, and the pestilential smell of the poulterer's shop. Moreover, they could not but hear the oaths and ribaldries of those who sat and lounged about the market, staying in the open air because it was warm and because it was cheap. The bulkheads, bunks, booths, stalls, and counters of the market were free and open to the world: a log of wood for a pillow, a hard plank for a bed; this was the reward of a free and lawless life. On most nights it seemed best to lie with windows closed and endure the heat. Yet closed windows could not altogether keep out the noise, for on these summer nights all the knaves and thieves unhung in this great town seemed to be gathered here, pleased to be all together, a Parliament of rogues, under the pent-houses and on the stalls of the market. And as in some Roman Catholic countries nuns and monks maintain a perpetual adoration to the Blessed Virgin, whom they ignorantly worship, so did these reprobates maintain a perpetual litany of ribaldry and foul conversation. It never ceased. When one grew tired he lay down and slept: his friends carried on the talk; the drinking booths were open all night long, so that those who talked might slake their thirst, and if any waked and felt thirsty he too might have a drain and so lie down again. Day and night there was a never-ending riot: the ladies, as the hot days continued, grew thinner and paler, but they bore it patiently; they had borne it for thirty years.

Between two and three in the morning there generally came a little respite; most of the brawlers were then asleep, drunk, or tired out; only at corners, where there was drink to be had, men and women still gathered together, talking and joking. At four, or thereabouts, the market-carts began to arrive, and noise of another kind began.

One morning in July Kitty awoke—it was a hot and close night—just when all the City clocks were striking three; it was broad daylight; she sprang from bed, and drawing the blind aside a little, looked out upon the market below and the City around. In the clear and cloudless air, before the new day had charged it with a fresh covering or headpiece of smoke, she saw the beautiful spires of St. Bride's, St. Dunstan's, St. Andrew's, St. Mary's, and St. Clement's rising one beyond the other into the clear blue sky, their weather-cocks touched by the morning sun; on the south, over the river, were visible the green hills of Surrey, the sun shining on their hanging woods, as plain as if they were half a mile away. On the north there were the low hills of Highgate, Hampstead, and Hornsey, the paradise of cits, and yet places most beautiful, wooded and retired. Everywhere, north, west, and south, spires of churches rising up to the heavens, as if praying for the folk beneath. And under her eyes, the folk themselves!

They were human ruins of the past, the present, and the future.

Old men were among them who lay with curled up limbs, shaking with cold, warm though the night was, and old women, huddled up in scanty petticoats, lying with tremulous lips and clasped hands. The cheeks both of the old men and the old women were swollen with drink. What was the record of their lives? Some of them had been rogues and vagabonds from the very first, though how they managed to scape the gallows would be hard to tell. Doubtless their backs were well scarred with the fustigations of the alderman's whip, and they could remember the slow tread of the cart behind which they had marched from Newgate to Tyburn, the cruel cat falling at every step upon their naked and bleeding shoulders. Yet what help? They must starve or they must steal; and, being taken, they must be hanged or must be flogged.

Why, these poor old men and poor old women should, had they not missed the meaning of their lives, have been sitting in high places, with the state and reverence due to honoured age, with the memory of a life well fought, hung with chains of gold, draped with cloth of silver and lace. Yet they were here, crouched in this filthy, evil-smelling place, eyes shut, backs bent, lips trembling, cheeks twitching, and minds hardened to iniquity. Did any of them, perchance, remember how one who knew declared that never had he seen the righteous forsaken or the good man beg his bread?

A dreadful shivering seized the girl. What plank of safety, what harbour of refuge was open to her that she too might escape this fate? What assurance had she that her end might not be like unto the end of these? Truly none, save that faith by which, as Paul hath taught, the only way to heaven itself is opened.

Then there were young men with red and swollen faces, thieves and vagabonds by profession, who found the air of the market more pleasant than that of Turnmill or Chick Street. Yet it was an ominous and suspicious place to sleep in; a place full of bad dreams for thieves, criminals, and debtors, since close at hand was the Fleet Prison, its wards crowded with the careless, who lounged and jested, and the hopeless, who sat in despair; since but a hundred yards from them stood the black and gloomy Newgate, its condemned cells full of wretches, no worse than themselves, waiting to be hanged, its courts full of other wretches, no worse than themselves, waiting to be tried, sentenced, and cast for execution, and its gaol-fever hanging over all alike, delivering the wards from their prisoners, cheating the hangman, hurrying to death judge, jury, counsel, prisoner, and warders together. But they never think upon such things, these poor rogues; each hopes that while his neighbour is hanged, he will escape. They cannot stop to think, they cannot turn back: behind them is the devil driving them downwards; before them, if they dare to lift their eyes, the horrid machinery of justice with pillory, whip, and gallows. Among them, here and there, pretty boys and girls, lying asleep side by side upon the hard wooden stalls; boys with curly hair and rosy faces, girls with long eyelashes, parted lips, and ruddy cheeks—pity, pity, that when they woke they should begin again the only trade they knew: to thieve, filch, and pick pockets, with the reward of ducking, pumping, flogging, and hanging.

So clear was the air, so bright the morning, that what she saw was impressed upon her memory clearly, so that she can never forget it. The old men and old women are dead; the young men and women are, one supposes, hanged; what else could be their fate? And as for the boys and girls, the little rogues and thieves, who had no conscience and took all, except the whippings, for frolic, are any left still to sleep on hot nights in that foul place, or are all hanged, whipped at the cart-tail, burnt in the hand, or at best, transported to labour under the lash in the plantations?

Sinner succeeds unto sinner as the year follows year; the crop of gallows fruit increases day by day; but the criminals do not seem to become fewer.

CHAPTER IX.

HOW THE SOUTH SEA BUBBLE MADE TWO WOMEN PRISONERS.

One Sunday evening in the autumn, the market being then quiet, the two ladies and the girl sat round a fire of coal, talking together by its light. The memories of the sisters, by some accident, were carried back to the past, and they told the child the story, of which she already knew a part, how by a great and crying injustice of the law, they had been shut up in prison, for no fault of their own, for nearly thirty years.

"My father's eyes," said Mrs. Deborah, looking at the portrait over the fireplace, "seem to rest upon me to-night."

Mrs. Esther shuddered.

"It is a sign, sister," she said, "that something will happen to us."

Mrs. Deborah laughed a little bitterly. I thought afterwards that the laugh was like that of Sarai, because a thing did happen to her, as will presently be seen.

"Nothing," she said, "will happen to you and to me any more, Esther, except more pain and more starvation."

"Patience, Deborah," sighed Mrs. Esther. "We who have borne our captivity for nine-and-twenty years——"

"And seven months," said her sister.

"Can surely bear it a little longer."

"We were girls when we came here," said Mrs. Deborah; "girls who might have had lovers and become mothers of brave sons—not that you, Kitty, should let your thoughts run on such matters. But there are no honest lovers for honest girls in the Rules of the Fleet."

"Lovers!" echoed Mrs. Esther, with a heavy sigh. "Mothers! with sons! Ah, no! not for us."

"We are old women now, sister. Well, everything is short that hath an end. Let us take comfort. To earthly prison is a certain end appointed."

"We came to the gaol, sister," continued Mrs. Esther, "two girls, weeping, hand-in-hand. Poor girls! poor girls! My heart bleeds to think of them, so young and so innocent."

"We shall go out of it," said her sister, "with tears of joy. They shall write upon our tombstones, 'These sisters thank God for death.'"

"What fault, we asked—ah! Deborah, how often we asked it!—what fault had we committed? For what sin or crime of ours did this ruin fall upon us?"

"I ask it still," said Deborah the impatient, "I ask it every day. How can they call this a land of justice, when two innocent women can be locked up for life?"

"My sister, we may not kick against the pricks. If laws are unjust they must be changed, not disobeyed."

Mrs. Deborah replied by a gesture of impatience.

"We were blessed with parents," said Mrs. Esther, half talking to herself, half to me, "whose worth and piety were as eminent as their lofty positions in the City. Our respected father was Lord Mayor in the year 1716, when, with our esteemed mother, who was by birth a Balchin, and the granddaughter of Sir Rowland Balchin, also once Lord Mayor, he had the honour of entertaining his Highness Prince George of Denmark. We were present at that royal banquet in the gallery. Our father was also, of course, an alderman——"

"Of Portsoken Ward," said Mrs. Deborah.

"And Worshipful Master of the Company of Armour Scourers."

"And churchwarden of St. Dionis Backchurch," said Mrs. Deborah.

"Which he beautified, adding a gallery at his own expense."

"And where, in 1718, a tablet was placed in the wall to his memory," added Mrs. Deborah.

"And one to the memory of Esther, his wife," continued the elder sister, "who died in the year 1719, so that we, being still minors, unfortunately became wards of a merchant, an old and trusted friend of our father."

"A costly friend he proved to us," said Mrs. Deborah.

"Nay, sister, blame him not. Perhaps he thought to multiply our fortunes tenfold. Then came the year of 1720, when, by visitation of the Lord, all orders and conditions of men went mad, and we, like thousands of others, lost our little all, and from rich heiresses of twenty thousand pounds apiece—such, Kitty, was then our enviable condition—became mere beggar-girls."

"Worse," said Mrs. Deborah grimly. "Beggar-wenches are not in debt; they may go and lay their heads where they please."

"We were debtors, but to whom I know not; we owed a large sum of money, but how much I know not; nor have ever been able to understand how our guardian ruined us, with himself. I was twenty-two, and my sister twenty-one; we were of age; no one could do anything for us; needs must we come to the Fleet and be lodged in prison."

"Esther!" cried her sister, shuddering; "must we tell her all?"

"My child," continued Mrs. Esther, "we suffered at first more than we dare to tell you. There was then in charge of the prison a wretch, a murderer, a man whose sins towards me I have, I hope, forgiven, as is my Christian duty. But his sins towards my sister I can never forgive; no, never. It is not, I believe," she said with more asperity than I had ever before remarked in her—"it cannot be expected of any Christian woman that she should forgive in a wicked man his wickedness to others."

"That is my case," said Mrs. Deborah. "The dreadful cruelties of Bambridge, so far as I am concerned, are forgiven. I cannot, however, forgive those he inflicted upon you, Esther. And I never mean to."

This seemed at the moment an edifying example of obedience to the divine law. Afterwards the girl wondered whether any person was justified in nourishing hatred against another. And as to that, Bambridge was dead; he had committed suicide; he had gone where no human hate could harm him.

Every one knows that this man must have been a most dreadful monster. He was the tenant, so to speak, of the prison, and paid so much a year for the privilege of extorting what money he could from the unfortunate debtors. He made them pay commitment fees, lodging fees, and fees of all kinds, so that the very entrance to the prison cost a poor wretch sometimes more than forty pounds. He took from the two ladies all the money they had, to the last guinea; he threatened them with the same punishment which he (illegally) inflicted on the unfortunate men; he would, he said, clap them in irons, set them in tubs, put them in the strong-room, which was a damp and dark and filthy dungeon, not fit for a Turk; he kept their lives in continual terror of some new misery: they had ever before their eyes the spectacle of his cruelties to Captain MacPheadrid, whom he lamed; Captain Sinclair, whom he confined until his memory was lost and the use of his limbs; Jacob Mendez, whom he kept locked up till he gave up his uttermost farthing; and Sir William Rich, whom he slashed with a hanger and beat with sticks because he could not pay his lodging.

And as every one knows, Bambridge was at last turned out through the exertions of General Oglethorpe.

> "And how can I forget the generous band,
> Who, touched with human woe, redressive searched
> Into the horrors of the gloomy gaol!"

"We endured these miseries," continued Mrs. Esther, "for four years, when our cousin was able to go security and pay the fees for us to leave the dreadful place and enjoy the Rules. Here, at least, we have some liberty, though we must live among scenes of rudeness, and see and hear daily a thousand things which a gentlewoman should be able to escape and forget. Our cousin," she went on, after a pause, "is not rich, and is able to do little for us: he sends us from time to time, out of his poverty, something for our necessities: out of this we have paid our rent, and being able sometimes to do some sewing work, we have lived, though but poorly. Two women want but little: a penny will purchase a dish of broth."

"It is not the poverty we lament," said Mrs. Deborah, "it is the place wherein we live."

"Then," Mrs. Esther went on, "Heaven sent us a friend. My dear, be it known to you, that had it not been for the Doctor, we had, ere now, been starved. He it was who found us in hunger and cold; he fed us, clothed us, and warmed us."

"To us, at least, he will always be the best of men," said Mrs. Deborah.

"More than that, sister; he hath brought us this child to be our joy and comfort: though God in His mercy forbid that your young days should all be wasted in this wicked place, which surely is the very mouth——"

Here they were interrupted by an uproar in the street below us: a bawling and bellowing of many men: they were bringing home the baronet, who was already drunk. Among the voices Kitty heard, and hung her head with shame, the tones of her uncle, as clear and sonorous as the great bell of St. Paul's.

They said nothing for a space. When all was quiet again, and the brawlers had withdrawn, Mrs. Esther spoke in her gentle way.

"A man's life doth, doubtless, seem to himself different from what he seems to the women who know him. We know not his moments of repentance, his secret prayers, or his temptations. Men are stronger than women, and they are also weaker: their virtues are nobler: their vices are more conspicuous. We must not judge, but continue to think the best. I was saying, my dear, when we were interrupted by the brawling of Sabbath-breakers, that your uncle, the worthy Doctor, is the most kind-hearted and generous of men. For all that he has done to us, three poor and defenceless women, we have nothing to give in return but our prayers. Let us give him these, at least. May the Lord of all goodness and mercy reward him, strengthen him, and forgive him whatever frailties do beset him!"

CHAPTER X.

HOW THE DOCTOR WAS AT HOME TO HIS FRIENDS.

If it be true (which doubtless will be denied by no one) that women are fond of changing their fashions and of pranking themselves continually in some new finery, it is certainly no less true that men—I mean young ones—are for ever changing their follies as well as their fashions. The follies of old men—who ought to be grave, in contemplation of the next world—seem to remain the same: some of them practise gluttony: some love the bottle: some of them the green table: some, even more foolish, pretend to renew their youth and counterfeit a passion for our sex. As for the fashions of the young men, one year it is the cocking of a hat, the next it is the colour of a waistcoat, the cut of a skirt, the dressing of a wig; the ribbon behind must be lengthened or reduced, the foretop must stick up like a horn one year and lie flat the next, the curls must be amplified till a man looks like a monstrous ram, or reduced till he resembles a monkey who has been shaved; the sword must have hilt and scabbard of the fashionable shape which changes every year; it must be worn at a certain angle; the rule about the breadth of the ruffle or the length of the skirt must be observed. So that, even as regards their fashions, the men are even with the women. Where we cannot vie with them is in the fashion of their amusements, in which they change for ever, and more rapidly than we change the colour of a ribbon. One season Ranelagh is the vogue, the next Vauxhall; the men were, for a year or two, bitten by that strange madness of scouring the streets by night, upsetting constables, throwing pence against window-panes, chasing belated and peaceful passengers, shouting and bellowing, waking from sleep timid and helpless women and children. Could one devise a braver and more noble amusement? Another time there was the mischievous practice of man-hunting. It was thought the work of a fine fellow, a lad of spirit, to lie hidden, with other lads of spirit, in Lincoln's Inn Fields, or some such quiet place, behind the bushes, until there might pass by some unfortunate wretch, alone and unprotected. Then would they spring to their feet, shouting, "That's he! that's he! after him, boys!" and pursue the poor man through the streets with drawn swords and horrid cries, until, half dead, he rushed into some tavern or place of refuge. As for actors, singers, or dancers, they take them up for a season, and then abandon them for no merit or fault in them whatever; one day they are all for Church, and the next they applaud Orator Henley; one day they shout for Nancy Dawson, and the next for Garrick; one day they are Whig, and the next Tory; one year they brandish thick clubs, wear heavy greatcoats with triple capes, swear, drink porter, and go like common coachmen; the next, with amber canes, scented gloves, lace ruffles, flowered silk waistcoats, skirts, extended like a woman's hooped petticoat, they amble along as if the common air was too coarse for them, mince their words, are shocked at coarse language, and can drink nothing less fine than Rhenish or Champagne, though the latter be seven shillings and sixpence a flask; and as for their walk, they go on tip-toe like a city madam trying to look like a gentlewoman. The next year, again, they are all for Hockley-in-the-Hole and bear-baiting. This year, the fashion was for a short space, and among such as could get taken there, to spend the evenings in the Rules of the Fleet, where, the bloods of the town had discovered, was to be found excellent company for such as liked to pay for it, among those who had been spent and ruined in the service of fashion, gaming, and gallantry.

There are plenty of taverns and houses of call in London where a gentleman may not only call for what he pleases to order, but may also be diverted by the jests and songs of some debauched, idle fellow who lies and lops about all day, doing no work and earning no money, but in the evening is ready to sing and make merriment for a bowl of punch. This rollicking, roaring blade, the lad of mettle, was once a gentleman, perhaps, or a companion to gentlemen. To him nature, intending her worst, hath given a reckless temperament, an improvident brain, a merry laugh, a musical voice, a genius for mimicry, of which gifts he makes such excellent use that they generally lead him to end his days in such a position. Men need not, for certain, go to Fleet Market to find these buffoons.

Yet, within the Rules, there was an extraordinary number of these careless vagabonds always ready to enjoy the present hour could some friend be found to pay the shot. In the morning they roamed the place, leaned against bulkheads, sat in doorways, or hid themselves within doors, dejected, repentant, full of gloomy anticipations; in the evening their old courage came back to them, they were again jocund, light-hearted, the oracle of the tavern, the jester and Jack-pudding of the feast, pouring out songs from the collections of Tom D'Urfey, and jokes from Browne and Ned Ward.

Many of the taverns, the Bishop Blaize, for example, and the Rainbow, kept one or two of these fellows in their regular employ. They gave them dinner, with, as soon as the guests arrived in the evening, liberty to call for what they pleased. If the visitors treated them, so much the better for the house; but there were, however, conditions, unwritten but understood: they were never to be sad, never grave, never to show the least signs of repentance, reflection or shame; and they were not to get drunk early in the evening, or before the better sort of visitors, whose entertainment they were to provide. Shameful condition! shameful servitude, for man (who hath a soul to think of) to obey!

One has to confess with shame that among the tavern buffoons, the Professional Tom Fools of the Fleet, were several of those clergymen whose trade it was to make rash couples wretched for life. This peculiarity, not to be found elsewhere, provided, perhaps, a novelty in vice which for a time made the Rules a favourite resort of men about town: the knowledge that the man who, without a rag left of the gravity belonging to his profession, laughed, sang and acted for the amusement of all comers, should have borne himself as a grave and reverend divine, gave point to his jest and added music to his song. It is not every day that one sees a merry-andrew in full-bottomed wig, bands, and flowing gown; it is not in every tavern that one finds the Reverend James Lands dancing a hornpipe in clogs, or the Reverend William Flood bawling a comic song while he grins through a horse-collar. Nor could the wits find at the coffee-houses of St. James's or Covent Garden, or at any ordinary place of amusement, a clergyman at the head of the table ruffling it with the best—albeit with tattered gown and shabby wig—ready with jest more profane, wit more irreverent, song and story more profligate, than any of the rest.

As for Doctor Shovel, it must not be supposed that he was to be found in any of these places.

"What!" he was wont to cry, "should a man of reputation, a scholar, whose Latin verses have been the delight of bishops and the pride of his college, a clergyman of dignity and eloquence, condescend to take the pay of a common vintner, make merriment for the company of a mug-house, hobnob with a tradesmen's club, play buffoon for a troop of Templars, and crack jests for any ragamuffin prentice with half-a-crown to call for a bottle? No, sir! The man who would know Doctor Gregory Shovel must seek him in his own house, where, as a gentleman and a scholar, he receives such as may be properly introduced on every night of the year—Sundays excepted, when he takes his drink, for the most part, alone."

In fact, his house was the chief attraction of the Rules; but access was only granted to those who were brought by his friends. Once introduced, however, a man was free of the house, and might not only come again as often as he pleased, but bring other friends. Now, as men prize most that which is least easy to procure, whether they want it or not, it became a distinction to have this right of spending the evening in the Fleet Market. A fine distinction, truly!

Those, however, who went there were not unlikely to find themselves among a goodly assemblage of wits and men of fashion. The Doctor played the host with the dignity of a bishop, and the hospitality of a nobleman; chairs were set around the table, in that room where he performed his daily marriages; those who came late could stand or send for a bench from the market; Roger and William, the two clerks, were in attendance to go and fetch the punch which the Doctor or his guests provided for the entertainment of all. Tobacco was on the table; the Doctor was in the chair, his long pipe in his mouth, his great head leaning back, his eyes rolling as he talked, before him his glass of punch. He was no buffoon; he did not cut capers, nor did he dance, nor did he sing Tom D'Urfey's songs, nor did he quote Ned Ward's jokes. If the company laughed, it was at one of his own stories, and when he sang, the words were such as might have been heard in any gentlewoman's parlour, and the music was Arne's, Bull's, Lilly's, or Carey's. Round him were poets, authors, scholars, lawyers, country gentlemen, and even grave merchants; some of them were out at elbows, threadbare, and sometimes hungry, but they were as welcome as the richer sort who paid for the punch. The younger men came to listen to one who was notorious for his impudent defiance of the law, and was reported to possess excellent gifts of conversation and of manner. The elder men came to look upon a man unabashed in his disgrace, whom they had known the favourite of the town.

"All the world," Sir Miles Lackington told me, "ran after Doctor Shovel when he was a young man and evening lecturer at St. Martin's-in-the-Fields; never was clergyman more popular in the world or in the pulpit; what was to be looked for when such a young man spent his morning with great ladies, who cried, 'Oh, sweet sir! oh, reverend sir! how eloquent, how gracious are your words!' but that he should see within reach promise of preferment, and run into debt to maintain a fine appearance and a fine lodging?"

The fine ladies had gone off after other favourite divines; their promises were forgotten; they had listened to other voices as musical, and bowed their heads before other divines as pious. The debts were unpaid—the Doctor in the Rules. He possessed no longer the wonderful comeliness with which he had stolen away the hearts of women, he preached no more in any pulpit; but his old dignity was left, with his eloquence and his wit. He who had charmed women now attracted men.

"Fie!" he would say; "remind me not of that time. I was once the pet and plaything of ladies, a sort of lapdog to be carried in their coaches: a lackey in a cassock, with my little store of compliments, pretty sayings, and polite maxims: my advice on patches, powder, and Eau de Chypre: my family prayers: my grace before meat: my sermons on divine right and the authority of the Church; and my anecdotes to make my lady laugh and take the cross looks out of little miss's dimpled cheeks. And, gentlemen, withal a needy curate, a poor starveling, a pauper with never a guinea, and a troop of debts which would not disgrace a peer.

"Whereas," he would continue, "here I live free of duns and debt: the countesses may go hang: I look for no more patrons: I expect no beggarly preferment; I laugh at my ease, while my creditors bark but cannot bite."

To those who objected that in former times he preached to the flock, and that his eloquence was now as good as lost to the Church, he replied that, as Chaplain of the Fleet, he preached daily, whereas formerly he had preached but once a week, which was a clear gain for righteousness.

"What! would you have me send forth my newly married lambs without a word of exhortation beyond the rubric? Nay, sir; that were to throw away the gift of speech, and to lose a golden occasion. None leave my chapel-of-ease unless fortified and exhorted to virtue by such an admonition as they have never before enjoyed."

One evening in October, when the summer was over and the autumn already set in, the Doctor sat as usual in his arm-chair. Before him stood his tobacco-box, and beside it lay his pipe. As yet, for it was but eight o'clock, there was no punch. Four great wax candles stood lighted on the table, and in the doorway were the two impudent varlets, whom he called his clerks, leaning against the posts, one on either hand.

There was but one visitor as yet. He was a young Templar, almost a boy, pale and thin because of his late hours and his excesses. And the Doctor was admonishing him, being at the time in a mood of repentance, or rather of virtue.

"Young man," he said, "I have observed thee, and made inquiry among thy friends regarding thy conduct, which resembles, at present, that of the prodigal son while revelling in his prodigality. Learn from this place and the wretches who are condemned to live in it, the end of profligacy. What the words of Solomon have hitherto been powerless to teach, let the Chaplain of the Fleet enforce. The wellspring of wisdom is as a flowing brook, says the Wise Man. Yet ye drink not of that stream. Also he saith that Wisdom crieth at the gates, at the entry of the city. But ye regard not. He hath told ye how the young man, void of understanding, falls continually into the pit of destruction. But ye heed not. The drunkard and the glutton, he hath declared, shall come to poverty. Ye listen not, but continue to eat and to drink. Wherefore, young man, look around thee and behold this place. We who are here sit among wine-bibbers and spendthrifts: we have not in our comings and goings—but, alas! we never go—any gracious paths of pleasantness: we go never among the meadows to breathe the air of buttercups and to ponder on the divine wisdom: we listen perpetually to the cackle of fools, the braying of asses, whom we could indeed wish to be wild and on their native Asiatic plains; and the merriment of madmen, which is like unto the crackling of thorns beneath the pot: we have—though our sins are multitudinous as the moments—no time nor opportunity for repentance: and even if we did repent, there is no way out for us, no escape at all, but still we must remain among the wicked until we die. Even the Christian priest, who finds himself (through thoughtlessness over money matters, being continually occupied with higher things) brought hither, must leave the ways which are right, and cleave unto those which are wrong. It is only by lying, bullying, and swearing, that money (by which we live) is drawn here out of the purses of silly and unwary people. Granted that we draw it. What boots it if one's rogues bring in a hundred couples in a month? The guineas melt away like snow in the sunshine, and nothing remains but the evil memory of the sins by which they were gotten."

The Templar, astonished at such a sermon from such a man, hung his head abashed. He came to drink and be merry, and lo! an exhortation to virtue. While the Doctor was yet speaking, there came a second visitor—no other than Mr. Stallabras, the poet, who came, his head erect, his hand thrust in his bosom, as if fresh from an interview with the Muses. The Doctor regarded him for a moment, as one in a pulpit might regard a late-comer who disturbed his sermon, and went on with his discourse:

"This is a place, young man, where gnashing of teeth may be heard day and night by him who has ears to hear, and who knows that the sound of riot and merriment are but raised to drown despair: to him every song is a throb of agony, every jest rings in his ears like a cry of remorse: we are in a prison, though we seem to be free; we are laid by the heels, though we are said to enjoy the Liberties of the Fleet; we live and breathe like our fellows, but we have no hope for the rest of our lives; we go not forth, though the doors are open; we are living monuments, that foolish youth may learn by our luckless fate to avoid the courses which have brought us hither. Wherefore, young man, beware! *Discite justitiam moniti.*"

He paused awhile, and then continued:

"Yet we should not be pitied, because, forsooth, we do but lie in the beds that we have chosen. No other paradise save a heaven of gluttony would serve our turn. In the Garden of Eden, should we

The Chaplain of the Fleet

peradventure and by some singular grace win thither, we should instantly take to wallowing in the mud and enjoying the sunshine: some of us would sit among the pigsties in happy conversation and friendship with the swine: some would creep downstairs and bask among the saucepans before the kitchen fire: some would lie among the bottles and casks in the cellar. Not for such as have come here are the gardens, the streams, the meadows, and the hilltops."

Then came two more guests, whom he saluted gravely. These were accustomed to the Doctor's moods, and sat down to the table, waiting in silence. He, too, became silent, sitting with his head upon his hand. Then came others, who also found the Doctor indisposed for mirth. Presently, however, he banged the table with his fist, and cried out in those deep tones which he could use so well:

"Come, life is short. Lamenting lengthens not our days. Brothers, let us drink and sing. Roger, go bring the bowl. Gentlemen all, be welcome to this poor house. Here is tobacco. Punch is coming. The night is young. Let every man be merry."

The room was half full: there were, besides the residents and lodgers of the place, young lawyers from the Temple, Gray's Inn, and Lincoln's Inn; poets not yet in limbo; authors who were still able to pay for their lodgings; young fellows whose creditors were still forbearing; and a few whose rich coats and lace betokened their rank and wealth.

The evening began, the Doctor's voice loud above all the rest. Half an hour afterwards, when the air of the room was already heavy with tobacco-smoke, Sir Miles Lackington who usually came with the earliest, arrived, bringing with him a young gentleman of twenty-two years or thereabouts, who was bravely dressed in a crimson coat, lined with white silk: he had also a flowered silk waistcoat, and the hilt of his sword was set with jewels. He was, in fact, one of those gentlemen who were curious to see this jovial priest, self-styled Chaplain of the place where there were so many parsons, who set the laws of the country at defiance with an audacity so splendid. He looked surprised, as if he had not expected so large an assembly.

"Follow me, my lord," said the baronet, whose jolly face was already flushed, and his voice already thick with wine. "Come, my lord, let us get nearer the Doctor. Gentlemen, by your leave: will you make place for his lordship? Doctor, this gentleman is none other than the young Lord Chudleigh, who hath heard of your eloquence and your learning, and greatly desires your better acquaintance. Rascal Roger, chairs for my lord and myself!"

He pushed his way through the crowd, followed by his guest. The doctor turned his head, half rose; his melancholy mood had passed away: he was in happy vein: he had sung one or two songs in a voice which might have been heard at Temple Bar: he had taken two or three glasses of punch, and smoked a pipe and a half of the best Virginian; he was in the paradise which he loved. Yet when Sir Miles Lackington spoke, when he named his guest, the Doctor's face became suddenly pale, he seemed to totter, his eyes glared, and he caught at the arm of his chair, as if about to be stricken with some kind of fit. His friends, who had never seen those ample and rubicund cheeks other than of a glowing ruddiness, were greatly terrified at this phenomenon.

"The Doctor is ill," cried Solomon Stallabras, starting to his feet. "Give air—open the windows—let us carry the Doctor into the street!"

But he recovered.

"It is nothing," he said. "A sudden faintness. The day has been close. Let no one move." He drank off his glass of punch: the colour came back to his face and the firmness to his legs. "I am well again. Sir Miles, you are always welcome. Were the Liberties peopled with such as you, we should be well sped indeed. Quick with the chairs, Roger. I rejoice to see your lordship in this poor house of mine. Had other noblemen of your lordship's rank but kept their word, I should this day have welcomed you in the palace of a bishop. Forget, my lord, that I am not a bishop: be assured that if I cannot bestow the episcopal absolution and benediction which he of London hath ever ready for a nobleman, my welcome is worthy of a prelate, and the punch not to be surpassed even at Lambeth Palace. Sir Miles, you forgot, I think, to make me acquainted with his lordship's noble name."

"I am the Lord Chudleigh," said the young man doubtfully, and with a pleasing blush.

"Again, your lordship is welcome," said the Doctor. "In the old days when I was young and able to stir abroad in the world, without a creditor in every street and a vindictive dun in every shop (whose revenge in this my confinement has only brought lamentation on every mother's son, because they remain all unpaid), it was my privilege to be much with your noble father. In truth, I knew not that he was dead."

"My father died two years ago at his country house."

"Indeed!" The Doctor gravely gazed in his guest's face, both still standing. "Is that really so? But we who live in this retirement hear little news. So Lord Chudleigh is dead! I went upon the Grand Tour with him. I was his tutor, his companion, his friend, as he was kind enough to call me; he was two years younger than myself, but our tastes were common, and what he bought I enjoyed and often chose. There came a time when—but your lordship is young—you know not yet how rank and class separate friends, how the man of low birth may trust his noble friend too much, and he of rank may think the decalogue written for the vulgar. Your father is dead! I had hoped to see him if but once more, before he died: it was not to be. I would have written to him upon his deathbed had I known: I owed him much—very much more than I could hope to repay, yet would I have repaid something. Your father died suddenly, my lord, or after painful illness?"

"He died, Doctor Shovel, after a long and very painful illness."

"Why, there," cried the Doctor, as if disappointed. "Had I only known there would have been time for half-a-dozen letters. I would I had been with him myself."

"It is kind of you, sir," said his lordship, "thus to speak of my father."

"Did he—but I suppose he had forgotten—did he condescend to speak of me?"

"Never," replied Lord Chudleigh; "at least not to me."

"There were certain passages in his life," the Doctor went on thoughtfully, "of such a kind as recur to the memory of sick and dying men, when the good and evil deeds of our lives stand arrayed before us like ministering spirits and threatening demons. Certain passages,

I say, which were intimately associated with myself. Indeed, it cannot be that they entirely perished from his lordship's memory. Since he spoke not of them, let me not speak. I am sorry, my lord, to have saddened you by thus recalling the thought of your dead father."

"Nay, sir," said Lord Chudleigh, "to have met so old a friend of my father's is a pleasure I did not expect. I humbly desire, sir, your better acquaintance."

The company during this long talk were mostly standing. It was no new thing to meet a man of rank at the Doctor's, but altogether new to have the conversation assume so serious a tone. Every one felt, however, that the dignity of the Doctor was greatly increased by this event.

Then the Doctor waved his hand, and resumed his cheerful expression.

"Gentlemen," he said, "be seated all, I pray. My lord, your chair is at my right. Enough of the past. We are here to enjoy the present hour, which is always with us and always flying from us. We crown it with flowers and honour it with libations: we sing its presence with us: we welcome its coming, and speed its parting with wine and song. So far are we pagans: join with us in these heathen rites wherein we rejoice in our life and forget our mortality. None but poets are immortal. Solomon—Solomon Stallabras, the modern Apollo, the favourite of the Nine, we drink your health and wish the long deferring of your immortality. Let us drink, let us talk, let us be merry, let us while away the rosy hours." He banged the table with his fist and set the glasses clinking. Then he filled a glass with punch and handed it to Lord Chudleigh. "As for you, Sir Miles," he said, "you may help yourself. Ah, tippler! the blush of the bottle is already on thy cheeks and its light is in thy eyes. Wherefore, be moderate at the outset. Roger, thou villain, go order another bowl, and after that more bowls, and still more bowls. I am athirst: I shall drink continually: I shall become this night a mere hogshead of punch. So will all this honourable company; bid the vintner beware the lemon and be sparing of the sugar, but liberal with the clove and the nutmeg. This night shall be such a night as the Rules have never before seen. Run, rogue, run!" Roger vanished. "Let me sing you, my lord, a song of my youth when nymphs and shepherdesses ran in my head more than Hebrew and theology."

He sang in his rich, full, and musical voice, the following ditty:

> "Cried the nymph, while her swain
> Sought for phrases in vain,
> 'Ah, Corydon, let me a shy lover teach;
> Your flowers and rings,
> Your verses and things,
> Are pretty, but dumb, and I love a bold speech.
>
> "'To dangle and sigh,
> To stammer and cry,
> Such foolishness angers us maidens in time:
> And if you would please,
> Neither tremble nor tease,
> But remember to woo us with laughter and rhyme.
>
> "'Go, hang up thy crook,
> Change that sorrowful look
> And seek merry rhymes and glad sayings in verse:
> Remember that Kitty
> Rhymes still unto pity,
> And Polly takes folly for better or worse.
>
> "'Come jocund and gay,
> As the roses in May,
> With a rolling leg and a conquering smile:
> Forget not that mirth
> Ever rhymes unto worth,
> And lucky the lover who laughs all the while.'"

"I wrote the song," said the Doctor, "when it was the fashion to be sighing at the feet of Chloe. Not that my song produced any impression on the fashion. Pray, my lord, is it the custom, nowadays, to woo with a long face and a mournful sigh?"

Lord Chudleigh laughed and put the question by.

"What do women care for lovers' sighs? I believe, gentlemen, they like to be carried by assault. Who can resist a brave fellow, all fire and passion, who marches to the attack with a confident laugh and a gallant bearing? It is the nature of the sex to admire gallantry. Therefore, gentlemen, put on your best ruffles, cock your hats, tie your wigs, settle the angle of your swords, and on with a hearty countenance.

"I remember, being then in Constantinople, and at a slave-market where Circassians were to be bought, there came into the place as handsome a young Turk as ever you might wish to set eyes upon. Perhaps he was a poet, because when he had the slaves brought out for his inspection, at sight of the prettiest and youngest of them all, he fell to sighing just like an English gentleman in love. Presently there came in an old ruffler of fifty, who, without any sighs or protestations, tugged out his purse and bought the slave, and she went off delighted at having fetched so good a price and pleased so resolute a fellow."

The Doctor continued to pour forth stories of adventure and experience, interspersed with philosophical maxims. He told of courts and cities as he saw them in the year 1720, which was the year in which he made the Grand Tour with the late Lord Chudleigh. He told old tales of Cambridge life. While he talked the company listened, drank, and smoked; no one interrupted him. Meanwhile he sent the punch about, gave toasts—with every glass a toast, with every toast a full glass—and swore that on such a night no one should pay but himself, wherefore let every man fill up.

"Come, gentlemen, we let the glasses flag. I will sing you another song, written for the good old days of Tom D'Urfey, when men were giants, and such humble topers as ourselves would have met with scant respect.

"Come, all ye honest topers, lend an ear, lend an ear,
While we drain the bowl and push the bottle round, bottle round;
We are merry lads, and cosy, cosy here, cosy here;
Though outside the toil and moil may resound, may resound.

"Let us drink reformation to mankind, to mankind;
Example may they follow from our ways, from our ways:
And whereas to their follies they are blind, they are blind,

Their eyes may they open to their craze, to their craze.

"For the miser all day long hugs his gold, hugs his gold;
And the lover for his mistress ever sighs, ever sighs:
And the parson wastes his words upon his fold, upon his fold;
And the merchant to the ledger glues his eyes, glues his eyes.

"But we wrangle not, but laugh, while we drink, while we drink;
And we envy no man's happiness or wealth, or his wealth;
We rest from toil and cease from pen and ink, pen and ink;
And we only pray for liquor and for health, and for health.

"Then the miser shall, like us, call for wine, call for wine:
And the lover cry for lemon and the bowl, and the bowl:
And the merchant send his clerks for brandy fine, brandy fine;
And the parson with a bottle soothe his soul, soothe his soul.

"And the rogue shall honest grow, o'er a glass, o'er a glass;
And the thief shall repent beside a keg, beside a keg:
And enmity to friendship quickly pass, quickly pass;
While good fellows each to others drink a peg, drink a peg.

"All kill-joy envies then shall disappear, disappear;
Contented shall we push the bottle round, bottle round;
For 'tis cosy, topers all, cosy here, cosy here;
Though outside the toil and moil may resound, may resound."

Thus did the Doctor stimulate his guests to drink. As the night wore on, one by one dropped away: some, among whom were Sir Miles, dropped asleep; a few lay upon the floor. As for Lord Chudleigh, the fiery liquor and the fumes of the tobacco were mounting to his brain, but he was not, like the rest, overpowered. He would have got up and gone away, but that the Doctor's voice, or his eyes, held him to his place.

"I am thinking," said the Doctor with a strange smile, "how your father at one time might have rejoiced to think that you should come here. The recollection of his services to me must have soothed his last moments. Would that I could repay them!"

Lord Chudleigh assured him that, so far as he knew, there was nothing to repay, and that, if there had been, his father's wish would certainly have been to forgive the debt.

"He could not forgive the debt," said the Doctor, laughing. "It was not in his power. He would have owned the debt. It was not money, however, but a kindness of quite another sort."

"Then," said Lord Chudleigh, prettily bowing, "let me thank you beforehand, and assure you that I shall be proud to receive any kindness in return that you may have an opportunity to show me."

"Believe me, my lord," said the Doctor, "I have the will if not the power: and I shall not forget the will, at least."

"It is strange," he continued, "that he never spoke about his younger days. Lord Chudleigh attracted to himself, between the age of five-and-twenty and thirty, the friendship and respect of many men, like myself, of scholarship and taste, without fortune. He with his friends was going to supply that defect, a promise which circumstances prevented him from fulfilling. The earthen vessel swims merrily, in smooth water, beside the vessel of brass; when a storm rises it breaks to atoms. We were the earthen vessels, he the brazen; we are all broken to atoms and ground beneath the heel. I, who almost alone survive, though sunk as low as any, am yet not the least miserable, and can yet enjoy the three great blessings of humanity in this age—I mean tobacco, punch, and the Protestant religion. Yet one or two of the earthenware pots survive: Judge Tester, for instance, a fellow whose impudence has carried him upwards. He began by being a clown born and bred. First he was sent to the Inns of Court, where he fell into a red waistcoat and velvet breeches, and so into vanity. Impudence, I take it, is the daughter of vanity. As for the rest, a few found their way to this classic region, on which Queen Elizabeth from the Gate of Lud looks down with royal benignity; but these are gone and dead. One, I know, took to the road, and is now engaged in healthful work upon a Plantation of Maryland; two were said to have joined the Waltham Blacks, and lived like Robin Hood, on venison shot in the forest, and other luxuries demanded of wayfarers pistol in hand; one I saw not long ago equipped as a smallcoal man in blue surplice, his shoulder laden with his wooden tinder, and his measure twisted into the mouth of his sack; another, a light-weight and a younger son, became a jockey, and wore the leathern cap, the cut bob, the buff breeches, and the fustian frock, till he was thrown and broke his neck. I laugh when I think of what an end hath come to all the greatness of those days. To be sure, my lord paid for all and promised future favours; but we were fine gentlemen on nothing, connoisseurs with never a guinea, dilettanti who could not pay for the very eye-glasses we carried. In the province of love and gallantry every man, beggar as he was, thought himself a perfect Oroondates. We sang with taste; we were charming men, nonpareils. We had the tastes of men of fortune; we talked as if the things we loved were within our reach; we dreamed of pictures, bronzes, busts, intaglios, old china, or Etruscan pateræ. And we had the vices of the great as well as their tastes. Like them we drank; like them we diced; like them we played all night at brag, all-fours, teetotum, hussle-cup, chuck-farthing, hazard, lansquenet. So we lived, and so we presently found the fate of earthen vessels. Heaven hath been kinder to some of us than we deserve. Wherefore, gentlemen, drink about." Here the Doctor looked round him. "Gentlemen, I perceive that I have been for some time talking to a sleeping audience. Roger, pour me out another glass. Swine of Circe, I drink to your headaches in the morning. Now, lads, turn all out."

CHAPTER XI.

HOW THE DOCTOR DISMISSED HIS FRIENDS.

Those of the guests who had not already departed, were sitting or lying asleep upon the floor or on the chairs. The last to succumb had been Lord Chudleigh, not because his was the strongest head, but because he had drunk the least and struggled the hardest not to fall a victim to the punch. Sir Miles had long since sunk peacefully upon the floor, where he lay in oblivion, one of the men having loosened his cravat to prevent the danger of apoplexy. Solomon Stallabras, among whose vices was not included the love of strong drink, was one of the earliest to depart; the young Templar whom the Doctor exhorted to virtue early in the evening, was now lying curled up like a child in the corner, his virtuous resolutions, if he had ever formed any, forgotten. Others there were, but all were crapulous, stupid, senseless, or asleep.

The Doctor stood over his victims, victorious. He had taken, singly, more punch than any three of them together; yet there they all lay helpless, while he was steady of head and speech; it was past two o'clock in the morning; the candles, low now, and nearly spent, burned dim in the thick, tobacco-laden air; the walls were streaming with the heat generated by the presence of so many men and so much drink. Roger, with the red nose and pale cheeks, still stood stolidly at the door, waiting for the half-finished bowl and the last orders; beside him, his fellow-lackey and clerk William.

"Turn all out, Roger," said the Doctor.

"Aye, sir," said Roger.

Both men addressed themselves to the task. They were accustomed to turn out their master's guests in this fashion. First, they lifted the fallen form of Sir Miles, and bore him carefully to his lodging; then they carried out the young Templar and the others who lay snoring upon the floor, and deposited them upon the stalls of the market outside, where the fresh air of the night might be expected to restore them speedily.

Meanwhile, Roger and William, for their better protection, would themselves watch over them until such time as they should awake, rise, and be ready to be led home with tottering step and rolling gait, for such reward as the varlets might demand.

The Doctor's clerks had a hard life. They began to tout on Ludgate Hill and the Fleet Bridge at eight; they fought for their couples all the morning with other touts; in the evening, they waited on the Doctor's guests; at midnight, they bore them into the market; there they watched over them till they could be taken home. A hard and difficult service. But there were few of the men about the Fleet who did not envy a situation so well paid; indeed, one cannot but admire the hardness of men to whom a daily fight, with constant black eyes, broken teeth, and bleeding nose, appears of such slight importance in the day's work, as not to be taken into account.

There remained Lord Chudleigh, who had fallen asleep in his chair, and was the last.

"As for this young gentleman, Roger," said the Doctor, "carry him upstairs and lay him upon my bed; he is of different stuff. Do not wake him, if you can help it."

Nothing but an earthquake or an explosion of gunpowder could have awakened the young man, so senseless and heavy was he. They bore him up the stairs, the Doctor following; they took off his boots, his coat, and waistcoat, put on him the Doctor's nightcap, and laid him in the bed.

All finished, the Doctor bade them drink off the rest of the punch, and begone.

The Doctor, left quite alone, opened the windows and doors, and stepped out into the market. At two o'clock on a cold October morning, even that noisy place is quiet; a west wind had driven away the smoke, and the sky was clear, glittering with innumerable stars. The Doctor threw open his arms and took a deep breath of the cold air, standing with his wig off, so that the wind might freshen his brain. Before him he saw, but he took no heed, the helpless forms of his guests, lying on the stalls; beside them sat, wrapped in heavy coats, his two serving-men, looking like vultures ready to devour their prey, but for fear of their master, who would infallibly cause them to be hanged.

After a few minutes in the open air, the Doctor returned to his room; he was sober, although he had taken enough punch to make ten men drunk; and steady of hand, although he had smoked so much tobacco; but the veins on his face stood out like purple cords, his eyes were bloodshot, his great lips were trembling.

He did not go to bed, but lit a fresh pair of candles, and sat in his chair thinking.

His thoughts carried him back to some time of trouble, for he presently reached out his hand, seized his tobacco-pipe, and crushed it in fragments; then he took the glass from which he had been drinking, and crushed that, too, in his great strong fingers.

"I knew not," he murmured, "that the villain was dead. If I had known that he was ill, I should have gone to see him, if only to remind him, with a curse, of the past. He is dead; I can never curse him face to face, as I hoped to do. I did not think that he would die before me; he seemed stronger, and he was younger. I looked to seek him out at any time, when I wanted a holiday, or when I wanted a diversion. I thought I would take him in his own house, and show him, in such words as only I can command, how mean a creature he was, and what a treacherous cur. Now he is dead. He actually never will be punished at all."

This reflection caused him the greatest sadness. He shook his head as he thought it over.

"It is not," he said to himself, "that I wished to be revenged on him (though doubtless, as men are but frail, that desire entered somewhat into my hopes), so much as that I saw in him a man who, above most men, deserved to be punished. I break the law daily, incurring thereby the penalty of a hundred pounds, which I never pay, for each offence. Yet truly am I less burdened in my conscience than should have been this Lord Chudleigh. And he hath died in honour. In this world one man steals a pig, and receives the approbation of his kind; another looks over a wall, and is clapped in gaol for it; one man slaughters a thousand, and is made a duke; another kills one, and is hanged. I am in prison, who never did anything against the law until I came here, nor harmed any except my creditors. My lord, who thought the ten commandments made for creatures of baser blood, and the round world, with all that therein is, only created for his own insatiable appetite, lives in honour and dies—what can I tell?—perhaps in grace; fortified, at least, with the consolations of the Church and the benedictions of his chaplain. So all things seem matter of chance. As Solomon Stallabras says, in one of his fables:

> "'We little flies who buzz and die,
> Should never ask the reason why.'"

He yawned; then, struck with a sudden thought, he took one of the candles and softly mounted the stairs. Shading the light with his hand, he looked upon the face of the young man sleeping on his bed. A handsome young man, with regular features strongly marked, delicate lips, and pointed chin.

"Truly," said the Doctor, "a youth of great beauty. Another David. He is more handsome than his father, even in those young days when he caressed me to my ruin, and led me on with promises to my undoing. Yet he hath the trick of the Chudleigh lip, and he hath his father's nose. Would that his father were alive, and that it was he and not his son lying here at my mercy! The son is something; out of regard to his father's memory, he shall not get off scot-free. But what is to be done? There is nothing, I think, that I would not do"—his red face grew purple as he thought of his wrongs—"were his father living, and could I make him feel through his son. Nothing, I believe. As I am a Christian man, if my lord were alive this day, I think I could tie a stone round the boy's neck and chuck him into the Fleet Ditch at Holborn Bridge. And yet, what a poor and miserable thing to do! A moment of brutal satisfaction in thinking of the father's agony—an eternity of remorse. But his father is dead; he cannot feel at all any more, whatever I do. If I could"—his face grew dark again, and he ground his teeth—"I believe I could drag the boy downwards, little by little, and destroy his very soul, to make his father suffer the more."

He gasped and caught his breath.

"Why," he murmured, "what is this? It is well for men that they are not led into temptation. This young lord hath fallen into my hands. Good. What shall I do with him? He knows nothing. Yet he must suffer something. It is the law. We are all under the law. For the third and fourth generation—and he is only the first generation. His children and his grandchildren will have to suffer after him. It is not my fault. I am clearly carrying out the law. He is providentially led here, not that I may take revenge upon the son of my enemy for his father's wrong, but that he might receive chastisement at my hands, being those of the fittest person, even as Solomon was chosen to slay both Joab and Shimei. What then shall I do? The Reverend Gregory Shovel cannot murder the boy; that would be the common, vulgar thought of a Fleet Market butcher or a hodman. Murder? A nauseous thought."

He took up the candle and stole noiselessly down the stairs, as if the thought had driven him from the place.

When he was back in his own room he began to walk up and down, thinking.

"He is but a boy," he said, "a handsome boy; 'twould be a sin to harm him. Yet, being sent here as he is, in a way that can be no other than providential, 'twould be a sin to let him go. How if I make him pay all my debts, and so leave the Liberties and live respectably ever after? Respectably!" he laughed a little. "Why, who would believe that the great Doctor Shovel could be respectable? The mud of this place, this dwelling beside a ditch, hath entered into my soul as the iron of the chains entereth into the soul of the prisoner. My name is too deeply daubed with the Fleet mud; it cannot be cleansed. And should I give up my place? Should I leave to another the honour I have won and the income I make therefrom? Shall there be another Chaplain of the Fleet while I survive? No; that will never do. How could I live away from this room wherein I wallow day and night? Here am I at mine ease; here I get wealth; I cannot leave this place."

He was in great perplexity. He wandered up and down; he was torn between his wrath against the father and his consciousness that it would be a mean and dreadful villainy to take revenge upon the son.

"I must have taken too much punch," he said, "thus to be agitated. Punch, like wine, 'is a mocker, strong drink is raging.' The Christian should forgive; the father is dead; the lad is a handsome lad and may be good. Besides, whatever I do to the boy, his sire will neither know nor feel. I might as well suppose that the legs and heads on Temple Bar feel what is said about them below. I am a fool; yet am I but a man. For such a crime even a saint would feel a righteous wrath. Yet it is cowardly to take revenge upon the son, the committer of the crime having gone to his own place. Yet he *is* that man's son. What then to do?"

He turned the question over a thousand times, yet found no answer. At last a thought came to him. He nodded his head and laughed aloud. Then he sought his arm-chair, adjusted his ample gown so as to get the greatest amount of comfort out of it, placed his feet upon a stool, and folded his arms.

"I have taken at least a quart of punch more than is good for me. That is most certain. Otherwise I should have known at once what I should do. I have actually forgotten the peculiarities of my own position. Which shows that I am neither so young nor so strong as I have been. Perhaps the system wants a fillip. I will take a dose of Norway tar-water to-morrow. But first, my lord, you shall find out, early in the morning, why I am called the Chaplain of the Fleet."

CHAPTER XII.

HOW KITTY EXECUTED THE DOCTOR'S REVENGE.

The Doctor seldom transacted business before nine o'clock in the morning, unless, as sometimes happened, a spirited apprentice, a lad of mettle, came with his master's daughter, both stealing away at seven, before the master and mistress were up, when she was supposed to be attending morning prayers at church, or helping Molly the maid with the mop, and he was expected to be cleaning out the shop and dressing the window. The ceremony over, they would go home again, but separately, young miss carrying her Prayer-book before her as demure as a kitten, looking as if she had never heard of a Fleet marriage, and was ignorant of the great Doctor Shovel, chaplain, yea, bishop of that place; while the boy, with brush and broom and watering-can, would be zealously about his master's work when that poor man—his morning dish of chocolate or pint of small ale despatched—appeared in the shop for the conduct of the day's affairs. Afterwards they could choose their own time for declaring what had been done. Thus did the Doctor make or mar the fortunes of many a bold prentice-boy.

This morning the Doctor awoke from sleep at seven or thereabouts, having in four hours slept off the punch and tobacco in his arm-chair. His face became almost benign in its thoughtful kindliness as he remembered the guest lying asleep upstairs, and what he was about to do for him. He rose, shook himself, opened the windows and doors, and went out into the market, still in his nightcap, carrying his wig in one hand and his silk handkerchief in the other.

The market was already crowded with purchasers, principally those who buy a barrowful of fruit and vegetables, and bawl through the streets until all is sold. But there was a good sprinkling of maids and housewives buying provisions for the day. The morning was fresh, with a little autumn fog, and the sun shining through it like a great yellow disk; the waggons stood about with their loads of cabbages, carrots, parsnips, potatoes, apples, plums, and sloes, waiting till they could be discharged; on the heaped-up pile of fruits and vegetables you could see hanging still the slender threads and cobwebs which are spun every night in autumn time by invisible spiders, and appear in the morning strung with beads of dew.

"Stand aside!" cried the stall-keepers, one and all. "Make way for the Doctor! Don't you see the Doctor? Room for the Doctor!"

He walked magisterially to the pump, under which he held his bare head for a few moments while a boy pumped the cold water over him. This done, he shook his head, mopped his poll with his silk handkerchief, clapped on his wig, and returned to his own house, his robes majestically floating around him.

The market, proud of its Doctor, made way for him with salutations and inquiries after his reverence's health.

At the house he found his two runners waiting for him, as fresh—if pale cheeks and red noses can look fresh—as if they had not been up until two o'clock in the morning.

He sent for a pint of small ale, and began to consider what next.

"Roger," he said, "canst thou, at the present moment, lay thy hand upon a woman willing to be a bride, either in the prison or elsewhere?"

Roger hesitated.

"It depends, your reverence, on the bridegroom. About Tower steps, for instance, and down Wapping way, there are brides in plenty to be picked up for the asking."

"Not brides for me, Roger. Think again. I want a bride who wants a husband, and not a sailor's money; who will stick to her husband and make him as happy in his wedded life as you and the rest of mankind are or have been."

Roger grinned. He was himself a widower, and could be tickled with the joke.

"I think I know the very woman," he said. "A young widow——"

"Good," said the Doctor.

"She has been extravagant, and is in debt——"

"Very good," said the Doctor.

"A prisoner in the Fleet; but I can fetch her out in a twinkling, for half-a-crown."

"Ay—ay," said the Doctor. "Go on, honest Roger. A widow, extravagant, and in debt. That promises well."

"Her husband was an honest draper in Gracechurch Street, who lately died of smallpox, leaving her a good business and a thousand pounds in money. She hath already squandered the thousand, wasted the business, and brought herself to ruin. She is comely, and is but thirty years of age; to get out of the Fleet, I think she would marry the——"

"She shall marry better than that, Roger. Go fetch her here: tell her to come and talk with me, and that if she pleases me in her conversation and appearance, she may shortly marry a gentleman."

"This," said the Doctor, when his man was gone, "will be a good stroke of business. This shall be his punishment. My lord shall marry this extravagant slut. No paltry common revenge this. Just punishment for the first generation. He will gain a pocketful of debts and a wife who will stick to him like a leech. Aha!—a city wench—none of your proud city madams, grand enough to be a countess—but a plain tradesman's widow, with no ideas beyond a dish of tea, Bagnigge Wells, strawberries at Bayswater, cakes at Chelsea, or at the best, a night of wonder-gaping at the quality at Vauxhall; a wife of whom he will be ashamed from the very first. This is good business. What a pity! what a thousand pities that his noble father is no more!"

The Doctor laughed and rubbed his hands. Then he mounted the stairs again, and entered his bedroom. The lad was still sound asleep; his cheeks less red, and his breathing lighter.

"His head will ache," said the Doctor. "I fear he is unaccustomed to punch. When he wakes his limbs will feel like lead: his throat will feel like a limekiln; his tongue will be furred like the back of a squirrel; his eyes will be hot and heavy, as if he had a fever; his hand will shake like the hand of a palsied man; he will totter when he tries to walk. Ah! cursed drink! Time was when I, who am now as seasoned as a port-wine cask, or a keg of Nantz, would feel the same when I awoke after such a night. Age brings its consolations." He rubbed his hands, thinking that he could now drink without these symptoms. "I will marry him," he continued, "while he is yet half drunk. When he recovers, it will be time to explain the position of things. Should I explain, or should his wife? Ho! ho! A draper's widow, of Gracechurch Street, to marry the heir of all the Chudleighs!"

He stood over the bed again, and passed his hand lightly over the sleeping boy's cheeks. Something in his looks touched the Doctor, and his eyes softened.

"Poor lad! I never had a son. Perhaps, if there had been one, things would have been different. He is a very handsome boy. Pity, after all, that he must marry this jade, this extravagant wench who will waste and scatter his patrimony, and likely bring him to shame, when, being so young, so handsome, and so rich, he might have had the prettiest girl in the country"—here he started—"might have had—might have had—can he not have? Is there a prettier girl or a better-bred girl anywhere in the land than Kitty Pleydell? What more can any man want? she is of gentle blood—on one side at least, for the Shovels, it is very certain, do somewhat smack of the soil. Never a Shovel, except the Reverend Gregory Shovel, Doctor of Divinity, who hath risen to greatness. Clods all. Here is a great chance for such a revenge as would have driven the old lord mad, and will be a blessing and a boon to the young lord. Ho! ho! my Lord Breaker of Promises, my Lord Trampler of Dependents, my Lord Villain and Rogue, how likes your lordship that your son should marry my niece? As for you, young spark, I will give you a bride so sweet, so fair, so fresh, that by heavens! you ought to woo her for a twelvemonth, and then go and hang your foolish neck by a garter because she would not say yea. Well, well! let us return good for evil—let us still be Christians. Yet no Lord Chudleigh hath deserved to have any benefit at my hands."

He rubbed his hands: he laughed to himself, his shoulders rolling from side to side: he nodded his head pleasantly at his victim, then he went downstairs again, with grave and thoughtful mien. He was thinking how best to bring about his purpose.

He found, however, waiting below, Roger, his man. With him there came a woman dressed in shabby finery. She was a woman of about thirty-two years of age, stout, and still comely; she looked about the room as if in search of some one; her face was eager and anxious. When she saw the Doctor, she put her handkerchief to her eyes and burst, or pretended to burst, into tears.

"Alas, Doctor!" she cried, "I am truly ashamed to come in such a plight. But I have nothing else to put on. And Roger, good man, says that the gentleman will not wait. Who is the gentleman? Surely not Thomas Humpage, the mercer, who always promised to marry me when my husband should die, and now refuses because, although a warm man, he will not take upon him the burden of my poor debts. Alas! men are ever thus towards us poor women. Pray, Doctor, who is the gentleman? Far be it from me to keep the poor man waiting; and indeed, I was ever a pitiful woman, and — —"

"You are under a little mistake, madam," said the Doctor, interrupting her. "There is no gentleman here asking for you. Roger is an ass, and a pig."

Roger made no reply. Excess of zeal frequently led him into mistakes. He stared straight before him, and modestly edged away in the direction of the door, so as to be out of reach both of the Doctor's fist, the weight of which he knew already, and the lady's nails.

The poor woman's face fell, and real tears crowded into her eyes. Now the Doctor was a man who could not bear the sight of a woman crying, so he hastened to soothe her.

"Your case, madam," he said, "hath awakened my commiseration. I have sent for you to know whether, should Roger be able to find a suitable husband, you would be willing to take him."

"O Doctor!" she sobbed; "best of men! If only you can find me a husband, I should be grateful to the end of my days. I would marry any one — any one — even Roger."

Roger swiftly vanished through the door.

"He may be as old as Methusalem, and as ugly as a foreign Frenchman, but I would marry him — to take my place in the prison and go free once more."

"Roger," said the Doctor, "is a great match-maker. He hath persuaded many couples into this room that never thought, when they went out to take the air and see the shops, of coming here. See, now, would the skipper of a merchantman serve your turn?"

The Chaplain of the Fleet

"Doctor, I love a sailor. They make confiding husbands, and they bring home money."

"Once married, you are free. And then your creditors would have to catch your husband, who, if he is the handy tarpaulin that deserves you, will show them a clean pair of heels off the Nore. Madam, I will do my best. Meanwhile, perhaps a guinea would be of use to you."

She cried in earnest as she took it.

"O Doctor! the debts are not much altogether; a poor two hundred pounds. And a man may always be happy in the prison. There are skittles and beer. But a woman never can. And I would go to see him sometimes—say twice a year."

She went away weeping. But she stopped when she saw Roger outside the door, and held a few minutes' eager conversation with him before she returned to her prison. Perhaps he found some simple country lad or sailor who was beguiled into marrying her, only to take upon him her debts, and to lie within four walls instead of her. But indeed I know not.

We had finished our breakfast and were tidying the room: my thoughts were full of the country that morning, because I had dreamed of the old place and the garden with its yellow leaves, the trailing cobwebs, banks covered with branches of mignonette, nasturtium eight feet long, pinks now mostly over, bending their faded heads, and the larkspur, foxglove, Venus's looking-glass, bachelors' buttons, mournful widow, boys' love, stocks, their glory over now, their leaves withering and all run to seed. I was talking about these sweet things with my ladies, when I heard the Doctor's voice at the bottom of the stairs, bidding me quickly take my hat and hood and run down to him, for that he needed me for half an hour.

I obeyed, little thinking what was to follow. He said nothing, but, by a gesture, bade me follow him.

When we came to his house, Roger and William, his two runners, were waiting outside the door, and the room was set out in the usual fashion, in readiness for any who might chance to call.

"You," said the Doctor to the men, "wait outside until I call you. Stay, fetch a quart of ale at once."

The Chaplain of the Fleet

The ale brought, the men retired and shut the door.

"Kitty," said my uncle, "I have long intended to bestow upon thee the greatest good fortune which it is in my power to procure. Thou art a good girl: thou art my sister's child: thou hast shown a spirit of obedience. I have reflected that it is not well for thee to remain much longer in the Rules, and the only way to provide thee with a home elsewhere, is to provide thee with a husband."

"But, sir," I said, beginning to be extremely terrified, "I do not want a husband."

"So say all young maids. We, child, know what is best for them. I could have found thee a husband among my friends. Sir Miles Lackington, indeed, spoke to me concerning the matter; he is a baronet. The Lackingtons are an old family; but he hath squandered his fortune, and I cannot learn that any more money will come to him. Besides, he drinks more than is befitting even in a gentleman of title."

"Oh, sir!" I cried, "not Sir Miles."

"No, Kitty"—the Doctor smiled benevolently upon me—"I regard thy happiness first. No drunkard shall marry my niece. Mr. Stallabras hath also opened his mind upon thee; he is an ingenious man, with a pretty wit, and if verses were guineas, would be a great catch for thee. But alas! he hath no money, so I dismissed him."

Poor Solomon! That, then, was the reason of a late melancholy which we had remarked in him. Mrs. Esther took it as caused by the wrestling of genius, and said that the soul within him was too great for the bodily strength.

"But, Kitty," here the Doctor beamed upon me like the sun in splendour, "I have here—yea, even in this house, the husband of my choice, the man who will make thee happy. Start not—it is resolved. Child, *obey me.*"

I declare that I was so terrified by the Doctor's words, so amazed by his announcement, so spellbound by his words and manner, that I did not dare resist. Had he told me that I was to be hanged, I could not have made an effort to save myself.

"Obey me," he repeated, bending his eyebrows, and looking upon me no longer as a sun in splendour, but as an angry judge might look upon a criminal. "Stand here—so—do not move; keep thy face covered with thy hood, all but thine eyes. Give me your hand when I ask it, and be silent, save when I bid thee speak. Be not afraid, girl; I do this for thine own good. I give thee a gentleman for thy husband. Thou shalt not leave this place yet awhile, but needs must that thou be married. I return in five minutes."

He took the jug of beer and climbed the stairs. I meanwhile stood where he had placed me, my hood over my head, in the most dreadful terror that ever assailed the heart of any girl.

Upstairs the Doctor awakened Lord Chudleigh with some difficulty. He sat up on the bed and looked round him, wondering where he was.

"I know now," he murmured, "you are Doctor Shovel, and this is——"

"Your lordship is in the Liberties of the Fleet."

"My head is like a lump of lead," said the young man.

"Your lordship was very merry last night, as, indeed, befits the happy occasion."

"Was I merry? Indeed, I think I was very drunk. What occasion?"

"Drink a little small ale," said the Doctor; "it will revive you."

He took a long drink of the beer, and tried to stand.

"So," he said, "I am better already; but my head reels, Doctor, and my legs are unsteady. It serves me right. It is the first time, and it shall be the last."

"I hope so, since your lordship is about to undertake so important a charge."

"What charge?" asked Lord Chudleigh, still dazed and unsteady.

"Is it possible that your lordship hath forgotten your mistress of whom you would still be talking last night? 'The sweetest girl in England—the prettiest girl in all the world—the fairest, kindest nymph'—I quote your lordship."

The Chaplain of the Fleet

Lord Chudleigh stared in amazement.

"The sweetest girl? — what girl?"

"Oh, your lordship is pleased to jest with me."

"I remember you, Doctor Shovel, whom I came to see last night with Sir Miles Lackington; I remember the punch and the songs; but I remember nothing about any girl."

"Why, she is downstairs now, waiting for your lordship. You will come downstairs and keep your appointment."

He spoke in a peremptory manner, as if ordering and expecting obedience.

"My appointment? Have I gone mad? It is this cursed punch of yours. My appointment?"

The Doctor gave him his coat and wig, and helped him to put them on.

"I attend your lordship. She is downstairs. Take a little more ale to clear your head: you will remember then."

The young man drank again. The beer mounted to his brain, I suppose, because he laughed and straightened himself.

"Why, I am a man again. An appointment? No, Doctor, hang me if all the beer in your cellar will make me remember any appointment! Where is Sir Miles? He might tell me something about it. Curse all punch, I say. Yet, if the lady be downstairs, as you say, I suppose I must have made some sort of appointment. Let me see her, at any rate. It will be easy to—to— —" here he reeled, and caught hold of the Doctor's hand.

What a crime! What a terrible wicked thing was this which we did — my uncle and I! I heard the steps on the stairs; I might have run away; the door was before me; but I was afraid. Yes, I was afraid. My uncle had made me fear him more than I feared the laws of my God; or, since that is hardly true, he made me fear him so much that I forgot the laws of my God, I did not run away, but I waited with a dreadful fluttering of my heart.

I held my hood, drawn over my head, with my left hand, so that only my eyes were visible, and so I kept it all the time.

I saw in the door the most splendid young man I had ever seen; he was richly dressed, though his coat and ruffles showed some disorder, in crimson coat and sash, with flowered silk waistcoat, and sword whose hilt gleamed with jewels. His cheek was flushed and his eyes had a fixed and glassy look; the Doctor led him, or rather half supported him. Was this young man to be my husband?

Roger must have been watching outside, for now he came in and locked the door behind him. Then he drew out his greasy Prayer-book, standing by his lordship, ready to support him if necessary.

"So," he said, "this is the sweetest girl in all England—hang me if I remember! Look up, my girl: let me see thy face. How can I tell unless I see thy face?"

"Silence!" said the Doctor in a voice of command.

I know not what strange power he possessed, but at the sound of his voice the young man became suddenly silent and looked about the room, as if wondering. For myself, I knew that I was to be married to him; but why? what did it mean?

The Doctor had begun the service. My bridegroom seemed to understand nothing, looking stupidly before him.

Roger read the responses.

The Doctor did not hurry; he read the exhortation, the prayers, the Psalms, through slowly and with reverence; other Fleet parsons scrambled through the service; the Doctor alone knew what was due to the Church; he read the service as a clergyman who respects the service ought to read.

"Wilt thou have this woman to thy wedded wife?"

The man Roger gave the dazed bridegroom a jog in the ribs.

"Say 'I will,'" he whispered loudly.

"I will," said the young man.

"Wilt thou," the Doctor turned to me, "have this man to thy wedded husband?"

The Chaplain of the Fleet

Roger nodded to me. "Say 'I will,'" he admonished me.

I obeyed; yet I knew not what I said, so frightened was I.

"Who giveth," the Doctor went on, "this woman to be married to this man?"

The dirty, battered rogue, the clerk, took my hand and laid it in that of the Doctor. I was given away by the villain Roger. Then the service went on.

"With this ring"—the man's hand was holding mine, and it was dry and hot; his face was red and his eyes were staring—"with this ring I thee wed; with my body I thee worship; with all my worldly goods I thee endow."

Consider—pray consider—that when I took part in this great wickedness, I was but a young girl, not yet seventeen years old; that the thing came upon me so suddenly that I had not the sense to remember what it meant; that my uncle was a man of whom any girl would have been afraid. Yet I knew that I ought to have fled.

When my bridegroom held my hand in his I observed that it was hot and trembling; his eyes did not meet mine; he gazed upon the Doctor as if asking what all this meant. I took him, in my innocence, for a madman, and wondered all the more what this freak of the Doctor's could mean.

For ring, the Doctor drew from his guest's little finger a diamond ring, which was full large for my third finger.

When the service was finished, bride and bridegroom stood stupidly staring at each other (only that still I wore my hood drawn over my face), while Roger placed upon the table a great volume bound in parchment with brass clasps.

"This, my lord, is our Register," said the Doctor, opening it at a clean page. "Sign there, if you please, in your usual hand. I will fill in the page afterwards."

He took the pen and signed, still looking with wondering eyes.

"Now, child," said the Doctor, "do you sign here, after your husband. The certificate you shall have later. For the present, I will take care of it. Other practitioners of the Fleet, my lord," he said, with professional pride, as he looked at his great volume, "would enter your name in a greasy pocket-book and give your wife a certificate on unstamped paper. Here you have a register fit for a cathedral, and a certificate stamped with no less illustrious a name than the Archbishop of Canterbury. Your lordship hath signed your name in a steady and workmanlike fashion, so that none henceforth shall be able to malign your conduct on this day; they shall not say that you were terrified, or bribed, or were in a state of liquor on the day of your marriage; all is free and above suspicion. I congratulate your lordship on this auspicious occasion. Roger, your mark here as witness. So. It is customary, my lord, to present the officiating clergyman, myself, with a fee, from a guinea upwards, proportionate to the rank and station of the happy bridegroom. From your lordship will I take nothing for myself; for the witness I will take a guinea."

Here the bridegroom pulled out his purse and threw it on the table. He spoke not a word, however; I think his brain was wandering, and he knew not what he did. Yet he obeyed the voice of the Doctor, and fell into the trap that was set for him, like a silly bird allured by the whistle of the fowler. I am certain that he knew not what he did.

The Doctor pulled one guinea from the purse, and handed it back to the owner.

"Roger," he said, "go drink his lordship's health; and hark ye—silence. If I hear that you have told of this morning's doings, it shall be the worst day in all your life. I threaten not in vain. Go!"

Then the Doctor took up the tankard of ale which stood in the window-seat.

"Your health, my lord;" he drank a little and passed it to his lordship, who drained it; and then, with a strange, wild look, he reeled to the Doctor's arm-chair and instantly fell fast asleep.

"Your husband is not a drunkard, Kitty, though this morning he appears in that light."

"But am I married?" I asked.

The Chaplain of the Fleet

"You are really married. You are no longer Kitty Pleydell; you are Catherine, Lady Chudleigh. I wish your ladyship joy."

I stared at him.

"But he does not know me; he never saw me," I remonstrated.

"That he does not know you yet is very true," replied the Doctor. "When the fitting time comes for him to know you, be sure that I will remind him. For the present he shall not know whom he has married.

"I perceive," he went on, seeing that I made no reply, "that thou art a good and obedient child. Ask no questions of me. Say not one word to any one of this day's work. Be silent, and thou shalt have thy reward. Remember—*be silent*. Now go, child. Go, Lady Chudleigh."

CHAPTER XIII.

HOW LORD CHUDLEIGH WOKE OUT OF SLEEP.

Alas! there was small pride in that thought. What joy of being Lady Chudleigh, when I had to pick my way home through the dirty and crowded market, thinking of the pain and grief this wicked thing would cause my ladies when they learned it, of the shame with which my father's soul would have been filled had he known it, and the wrath of Lady Levett when she should hear it! "Oh, Kitty!" I thought, "how miserably art thou changed in four short months! In the happy fields at home, everything (save when the rustics swore at their cattle) breathed of religion and virtue; in this dreadful place, everything leads to profligacy and crime. And what a crime! And the poor young gentleman! Did ever any one hear the like, that a young girl, not yet quite seventeen, should thus consent to marry a man whom she had never seen! Oh, shame and disgrace! And that young man, so handsome and so gallant, albeit so tipsy that he could scarcely stand. Who would have thought, four months ago, that Kitty would be that wicked creature?" Afterwards, I thought of the dreadful wickedness of marrying while still in mourning for a father not yet six months dead. But I confess that at first, so confused was I, that this thought did not oppress me. Indeed, there was almost too much to think about. Suppose I was, by a careless word, to reveal the secret! Suppose the rascal Roger were to tell it abroad in the market! Suppose the young man (whose name I did not dare to pronounce) were to see me, and find my name! Suppose the Doctor were at once to reveal to my—husband, I suppose I ought to call him—who and what I was! All these thoughts, I say, crowded into my mind together, and filled me with repentant terrors.

I went straight home, because there was no other place to go to. Mrs. Deborah reminded me, when I had taken off my hood, that we were still engaged upon the long-outstanding account between Richard Roe, gentleman, and Robert Doe, draper. It was one of the problems of the Book-keeping Treatise, how rightly to state this account to the satisfaction both of Doe (who wanted all he could get), and of Roe (who wanted to pay as little as possible). I remember that Richard Roe had not only bought extraordinary things (for a gentleman), such as ladies' hoops and paniers, but had bought them in immense quantities, to be explained, perhaps, by the supposition that he was a benefactor to the female sex, or perhaps that he was shipping things to Madagascar, where I believe a sarsnet pinner, if in scarlet, is considered worth a diamond as big as a pigeon's egg; and a few bottles of eau de Chypre are thought a bargain, if purchased by a ruby weighing a pound or so.

We had been engaged for a month upon a statement of the account showing the exact liabilities of Richard Roe (who used to pay in odd sums, with pence and farthings, at unexpected times); we never got it right, and then we began again. Fortunately, it costs nothing to clean a slate.

I sat down to this task with listless brain. What girl, after being so suddenly hurled into matrimony, with the possession of so great a secret, could take any interest in the debts of Richard Roe? The figures got mixed; presently, I was fain to lay the slate aside, and to declare that I could do no more that day.

Nor, indeed, could I do anything—not even hear what was said, so that my ladies thought I was sickening for some fever; which was not improbable, fever being rife at this time, owing to the smell from the vegetables, and one of the little Dunquerques in our own house down with it. Ah! could they only have guessed the truth, what sorrow and pity would have been theirs, with what righteous wrath at the sin.

When I was gone, the Doctor called back Roger, and they carried the unhappy bridegroom again to the bedroom, where they laid him on the bed and then left him to himself.

"He will sleep," said the Doctor, experienced in these cases, "until the afternoon. Have a cup of mutton-broth for him when he wakes, with a pint of small ale."

Then he returned, and the ordinary business of the day began. The couples came in—half-a-dozen of them. One pair gave him five guineas. They were an Irishman, who thought he was marrying a rich widow; and a woman head over ears in debt, who thought she was marrying a wealthy squire. A week afterwards the unhappy bridegroom came to the Doctor to undo the match, which was impossible. He escaped his wife's creditors, however, and took to the road, where, after many gallant exploits, he was caught, tried, and hanged at Tyburn, making a gallant and edifying end, and ruffling it bravely to the very foot of the ladder. The day, therefore, was profitable to the Doctor.

"Well begun, Roger," he said, "is well done. The morning's work is worth ten guineas. I would rest this afternoon; wherefore, bring no more couples. Yet one would fain not disappoint the poor creatures. Let them come, then, Roger. We may not weary in well-doing. And, hark ye, take this guinea to Mistress Dunquerque—not the captain, mind—and bid her spend it for the children; and inquire whether Mr. Stallabras hath paid his rent lately; if not, pay it; and buy me, on Ludgate Hill, a hat and feathers for Miss Kitty; and, varlet! if thou so much as breathe of what was done here this morning—I threaten not, but I know the history of thy life. Think of the past; think of Newgate, close by; and be silent as the grave."

At three o'clock in the afternoon, when the Doctor, after his dinner, sat over a cool pipe of Virginia, Lord Chudleigh came downstairs. He was dressed and in his right mind, although somewhat flushed of cheek and his hand shaky.

"Doctor Shovel," he said, "I thank you for your hospitality, and am sorry that I have abused it. I am ashamed to have fallen into so drunken and helpless a condition."

"Your lordship," said the Doctor, rising and bowing, "is welcome to such hospitality as this poor house of a prisoner in the Liberties of the Fleet can show a nobleman of your rank. I am the more bound to show this welcome to your lordship, because, for such as is my condition, I am beholden to the late Lord Chudleigh."

This was a speech which might have more than one meaning. His lordship made no answer, staring in some perplexity, and fearful that the punch might still be in his head.

"It was in this room," he said presently, "that we drank last night. I remember your chair, and these walls; but I remember little more. Fie, Doctor! your way of treating guests is too generous. Yet I have had a curious and uneasy dream. Those books"—he pointed to the Register and the Prayer-book—"were those upon the table last night? They were in my dream—a very vivid and real dream. I thought I was standing here. Your man was beside me. Opposite to me was a girl, or woman, her face and figure covered with a hood, so that I knew not what she was like. Then you read the marriage-service, drew the ring from off my finger, and placed it upon hers. And you pronounced us man and wife. A strange and interesting dream!"

"What was the ring, my lord?"

"A diamond ring, set round with seven pearls; within, the crest of my house, and my initials."

"Let me see the ring, my lord."

He changed colour.

"I cannot find it."

"My lord, I know where is that ring."

The Doctor spoke gravely, bending his great eyebrows. Lord Chudleigh was a man of fine presence, being at least five feet ten inches in height, without counting the heels of his boots and the foretop of his wig. Yet the Doctor, whose heels were thicker and his toupee higher, was six feet two without those advantages. Therefore he towered over his guest as he repeated—

"I know where to find that ring!"

"You cannot mean, Doctor——" cried Lord Chudleigh, all the blood flying to his face.

"I mean, my lord, simply this, that at eight o'clock this morning, or thereabouts, you rose, came downstairs, met a young lady who was waiting for you, and were by me, in presence of trustworthy witnesses, duly and properly married."

"But it was a dream!" he cried, catching at the table.

"No dream at all, my lord. A fact, which you will find it difficult to contradict. Your marriage is entered in my Register; I have the lines on a five-shilling stamp. I am an ordained minister of the Church of England; the hours were canonical. It is true that I may be fined a hundred pounds for consenting to perform the ceremony; but it will be hard to collect that money. Meanwhile, those who would inflict the fine would be the last to maintain that sacerdotal powers, conferred upon me at ordination, can suffer any loss by residence in the Rules of the Fleet. Ponder this, my lord."

"Married!" cried Lord Chudleigh. "Married? It is impossible."

"Your dream, my lord, was no dream at all, but sober truth, believe me."

"Married?" he repeated.

"Married," said Doctor Shovel. "I fear that your state of mind, during the performance of the ceremony, was not such as a clergyman could altogether wish to see. Still who am I, to decide when a gentleman is too drunk to marry?"

"Married! Oh, this is some dreadful dream! Where is my bride? Show me my wife!"

"She is gone, Lord Chudleigh."

"Gone! Where is she gone?"

The Doctor shook his head for an answer.

"Who is she? What is her name? How came she here?"

"I am sorry that I cannot answer your lordship in these particulars. She came—she was married—she went away! In her own good time she will doubtless appear again."

"But who is she?" he repeated. "What is she like? Why did she marry me?"

"Why did your lordship marry her? That, methinks, would be the proper question."

"Show me your Register, man!" Lord Chudleigh was sober enough now, and brought his fist down upon the table in peremptory fashion. "Show me your Register and your certificate!"

"Ta! ta! ta!" cried the Doctor. "Softly, young man, softly! We are not used to threats in this chapel-of-ease, where I am archbishop, bishop, and chaplain, all in one. For the Register, it is securely locked up; for the certificate, it is perhaps in the hands of Lady Chudleigh."

"Lady Chudleigh!"

"Perhaps her ladyship hath consigned it to my keeping. In either case, you shall not see it."

"This is a conspiracy," cried Lord Chudleigh. "I have been deceived by rogues and knaves! This is no true marriage."

"You would say that I am lying. Say so, but, at your peril, *think* so. You are as truly married as if you had been united in your own parish church, by your own bishop. Believe that, for your own safety, if you believe nothing else. At the right time, her ladyship will be revealed to you. And remember, my lord"—here the Doctor, towering over him, shook his great forefinger in warning or menace—"should you attempt another marriage in the lifetime of your present wife, you shall be brought to your trial for bigamy as sure as my name is Gregory Shovel. Laws, in this country, are not altogether made for the punishment of the poor, and even a peer may not marry more than one woman."

"I will have this wickedness exposed," cried his lordship hotly.

"Alas! my lord," said the Doctor, "the name of Gregory Shovel is already well known. I am but what your father caused me to be."

"My father! Then there is revenge… The benefits which my father conferred upon you——"

"They were greater than any I can confer upon you. He kept me with him as his private jester. I found him wit: he fed me upon promises. He turned me forth, to be flung into a debtor's prison. That, however, was nothing. Your lordship will own"—here the Doctor laughed, but without merriment—"that I have returned good for evil; for, whereas your father robbed me of a wife, I have presented you with one."

"O villain!" cried my lord. "To revenge the wrongs of the father upon the son—and this wretch continues to wear the gown of a clergyman!"

"Say what you please. So rejoiced am I with this day's work that I allow you to cast at me what names come readiest to your tongue. But remember that curses sometimes come home."

"Where is my wife, then?" he demanded furiously.

"I shall not tell you. Meantime, choose. Either let this matter be known to all the world, or let it remain, for the present, a secret between you and me. As for the lady, she will be silent. As for the rogue, my clerk, if he so much as breathes the secret to the cabbage-stalks, I have that which will hang him."

"I want to see the woman who calls herself my wife," he persisted.

"That shall you not. But perhaps, my lord, you would like to go home to St. James's Square with such a wedding-party as we could provide for you: a dozen of Fleet parsons fuddled; the bride's friends, who might be called from their stalls in the market; the music of the butchers, with salt-boxes, marrow-bones, and cleavers; the bride herself. Look out of the window, my lord. Which of the ragged baggages and trollops among the market-women most takes your lordship's fancy?"

Lord Chudleigh looked and shuddered.

"Go your way," the Doctor went on, "and always remember you have a spouse. Some day, for the better glorifying of your noble name, I will produce her. But not yet. Be under no immediate apprehension. Not yet. At some future time, when you are happy in the applause of a nation and the honours of a sovereign, when your way is clear before you and your conscience gives you the sweet balm of approbation, when you have forgotten this morning, we shall come, your wife and I, with 'Room for my Lady Chudleigh! Way there for her ladyship and Doctor Gregory Shovel from the Rules of the Fleet!'"

"Man," replied Lord Chudleigh, "I believe you are a devil. Do what you will; do your worst. Yet know that the woman may proclaim her infamy and your own; as for me, I will not speak to her, nor listen to her, nor own her."

"Good!" said the Doctor, rubbing his hands. "We talk in vain. I now bid farewell to your lordship. Those convivial evenings which you desired to witness will still continue. Let me hope to welcome your lordship again on the scene of your unexpected triumphs. Many, indeed, is the man who hath come to this house single and gone out of it double; but none for whom awaits a future of such golden promise. My most hearty congratulations on this auspicious and joyful event! What can come out of this place but youth, beauty, birth, and virtue? And yet, my lord, there is one singularity in the case. One moment, I pray"—for Lord Chudleigh was already outside the door—"you are the only man I ever knew who spent his honeymoon—alone!"

CHAPTER XIV.

HOW MRS. DEBORAH WAS RELEASED.

No one would be interested to read more of my shame and repentance at that time; nor does it help to tell how the Doctor was asked by my ladies if I was subject to any kind of illness for which I might be sickening. The reply of the Doctor to them, and his private admonitions to myself, may be partly passed over; it was true, no doubt, as he said while I trembled before him, that a young girl, ignorant and untaught, would do well to trust her conscience into the spiritual direction of a regularly-ordained clergyman of the Church of England like himself. As for the marriage, I was to remember that it was done and could not be undone. He hung round my neck by a black ribbon the diamond ring, my wedding-ring, by which to keep my condition ever before myself; to be sure it was not likely that I should forget it, without the glitter and sparkle of the brilliants, which I used to look at night and morning in secret. What did he think of me, this husband of mine, the young man with the handsome face, the white hands, and the fixed, strange eyes? Did he, night and morning, every day curse his unknown wife?

"Let him curse," said the Doctor. "Words break no bones; curses go home again; deeds cannot be undone. Patience, Kitty! before long thou shalt be confessed by all the world, the Lady Chudleigh. Come, cheer up, child!" he concluded kindly. "As for what is done, it is done. Partly I did it to clear off an old score, whereof I may perhaps tell thee at another time, and partly for thy honour and glory. Thy father, Kitty, was proud of his name and family, though he married my sister, the daughter of a tenant farmer; but never a Pleydell yet has been lifted up so high as thou shalt be: while as to the Shovels, I am myself the only great man they have yet sent into the world, and they are not likely to go beyond the Chaplain of the Fleet."

Then he held up his great forefinger, as long and thick as a school ruler, bent his shaggy eyebrows, and pushed out his lips.

"Remember, child, silence! And go no more moping and sorrowful, because thou shalt soon sit in thine own coach, with the world at thy feet, singing the praises of the beautiful Lady Chudleigh. Such a girl as my Kitty for Sir Miles Lackington? Why, he hath eyes for the beauty of a glass of Bordeaux—he hath sense to rejoice over a bowl of punch; but from Helen of Troy or Cleopatra of Egypt he would turn away for a bottle of port. Or Stallabras, now—should such a creature as he presume to think of such a woman? Let poets sing of women at a distance—the farther off the better they sing—that is right. Why, child, such curls as thine, such roses of red and white, such brown eyes, such lips and cheek and chin, such a figure as thou canst show to dazzle the eyes of foolish boys—Lord Chudleigh should go on his knees before me in gratitude and transport. And, believe me, some day he will."

We are all alike, we women. Call us beautiful, and you please us. It was almost the first time that any one had called me beautiful save Sir Miles Lackington when in his cups, or Solomon Stallabras in his poetic way. Yet every pretty girl knows that she is pretty. There are a thousand things to tell her: the whispers of the women, the sidelong looks of the folk in the streets, the envy of envious girls, the praise of kindly girls, her glass, the deference paid by men of all classes and all ages to beauty, the warnings of teachers, nurses, governesses, and matrons that beauty is but skin-deep, virtue is better than looks, handsome is as handsome does, 'tis better to be good than pretty, comeliness lasts but a year, while goodness lasts for ever, and so on—all these things make a girl on whom heaven has bestowed this most excellent gift of beauty know quite as well as other people what she possesses, though she knows not yet the power of the gift.

"You are pretty, child," said Mrs. Esther to me on the very same day as the Doctor. "You will be a beautiful woman."

"Which is no good to a girl in the Rules," said Mrs. Deborah, "but rather a snare and a danger."

"Nay, sister," said Mrs. Esther, "it is a consolation to be beautiful. You, dear, when we were thirty years younger, were beautiful enough to melt the heart even of the monster Bambridge."

"A beautiful face and person," Mrs. Deborah added with a smile on her poor face as she thought of the past, "should belong to a good and virtuous soul. In the better world I have no doubt that the spirits of the just will arise in such beauty of face and form as shall be unto themselves and their friends an abiding joy."

Let us think so: when I die it may be a consolation to me that a return to the beauty of my youth is nigh at hand. I am but a woman, and there is nothing in the world—except the love of my husband and my children—that I think more precious than my past beauty.

Soothed, then, by my uncle's flatteries, comforted by his promises, and terrified by his admonitions, I fell in a very few days into the dreams by which youth beguiles the cares of the present. My husband, Lord Chudleigh, would go his own way and never ask after me; I should go mine as if he did not exist; some time or other we should leave the Liberties of the Fleet, and go to live near Lady Levett and my dear Nancy. As for the coronet and the rank, I was too ignorant to think much about them. They were so high above me, I knew so little what they meant, that I no more thought of getting them than of getting David's harp and crown. I waited, therefore, being a wife and yet no wife, married and yet never seen by my husband; sacrificed to the wrath of the Doctor, as that poor Greek maiden in the story told me by my father, murdered at Aulis to appease the wrath of a goddess.

Two events happened which, between them, quite drove the marriage out of my mind, and for awhile made me forget it altogether.

The first of these was the illness of Mrs. Deborah.

There was fever about the market, as I have said; one of the little girls of Mrs. Dunquerque, in our house, was laid down with it. In autumn there was always fever in the place, caused, my ladies said, by the chill and fog of the season, by the stench of the vegetables and fruit of the market, and perhaps by the proximity of Newgate, where gaol fever was always cheating the gallows. One day, therefore, Mrs. Deborah lay down, and said she would rather not get up again any more. She would not eat, nor would she have any medicine except a little tarwater which seemed to do her no good. When she got very ill indeed, she consented to see an apothecary; he prescribed blood-letting, which, contrary to expectation, made her only weaker. Then we went to the old woman who kept a herb shop at the other end of Fleet Lane, and was more skilful than any physician. She gave us feverfew, camomile, and dandelion, of which we made hot drinks. As the patient grew worse instead of better, she made an infusion of shepherd's-purse, pennycress, and pepperwort, to stimulate the system; she brought a tansy-pudding, which poor Mrs. Deborah refused to eat; and when gentian water failed, the old woman could do no more.

On the fifth day, Mrs. Deborah gave herself up, and contemplated her end in a becoming spirit of cheerfulness. She comforted her sister with the hope that she, too, would before long join her in a world "where there is no noise, my dear, no fighting, no profane swearing, no dirt, no confusion, no bawling, no starving, no humiliation. There shall we sit in peace and quiet, enjoying the dignity and respect which will be no doubt paid to two Christian gentlewomen."

"I might have known it," sighed poor Mrs. Esther in her tears. "Only a week ago a strange dog howled all night below our window. I should have known it for a warning, sent for you, my dear, or me, or for Kitty. It cannot have been meant for Sir Miles, for the poor gentleman, being in his cups, would not notice it: nor to Mr. Stallabras, for he sets no store by such warnings."

"It was for me," said Mrs. Deborah with resignation, while Mrs. Esther went on recollecting omens.

"Last night I heard the death-watch. Then, indeed, sister, I gave you up."

"It was a message for me," said the sick woman, as if she had been Christiana in the story.

"And this morning I heard a hen crow in the market—a hen in a basket. Alas! who can have any doubt?"

"It is but six weeks," said Mrs. Deborah, feebly, "since a hearse on its way to a funeral stopped before our door. I remember now, but we little thought then, what *that* meant."

"I saw, only a fortnight ago," continued Mrs. Esther, "a winding-sheet in the tallow. I thought it pointed at Kitty, but would not frighten the child. Sister, we are but purblind mortals."

Far be it from me to laugh at beliefs which have so deep a root in Englishwomen's hearts: nor is it incredible to those who believe in the divine interference, that signs and warnings of death should be sent beforehand, if only to turn the thoughts heavenward and lead sinners to repent. But this I think, that if poor Mrs. Deborah had not accepted these warnings for herself, she might have lived on to a green old age, as did her sister. Being, therefore, convinced in her mind that her time was come, she was only anxious to make due preparation. She would have been disappointed at getting well, as one who has packed her boxes for a long journey, but is told at the last moment that she must wait.

As she grew weaker, her brain began to wander. She talked of Bagnigge Wells, of Cupid's Garden, the entertainments of her father's company, and the childish days when everything was hopeful. While she talked, Mrs. Esther wept and whispered to me—

"She was so pretty and merry! Oh! child, if you could have seen us both in our young days—if you could have seen my Deborah with her pretty saucy ways; her roguish smile, her ready wit made all to love her! Ah! me—me—those happy days! and now! My dear Deborah, it is well that thou shouldst go."

This was on the morning of Mrs. Deborah's last day in life. In the afternoon her senses returned to her, and we propped her up, pale and weak, and listened while she spoke words of love and farewell to be kept sacred in the memory of those who had to go on living.

"For thirty years, dear sister," she murmured, while their two thin hands were held in each other's clasp—"for thirty years we have prayed daily unto the Lord to have pity upon all prisoners and captives, meaning more especially, ourselves. Now, unto me hath He shown this most excellent mercy, and calleth me away to a much better place than we can imagine or deserve. I had thought it would be well if He would lead us out of this ward to some place where, in green lanes and fields, we might meditate for a space in quiet before we died. I should like to have heard the song of the lark and seen the daisies. But God thinks otherwise."

"Oh, sister—sister!" cried Mrs. Esther.

The Chaplain of the Fleet

"'There shall be no more death, neither sorrow, nor crying, neither shall there be any more pain,'" said Mrs. Deborah. "Kitty, child," she turned her pale face to me, "be kind to my sister."

We wept together. Outside there was the usual tumult of the market—men buying and selling, with shouts and cries; within, three women weeping, and one dying.

"Go, dear," said she who was dying; "call the Doctor. He hath been very generous to us. Tell him I would receive the last offices from his hands."

The Doctor came. He read the appointed service in that deep voice of his, which was surely given him for the conversion of the wicked. The tears streamed down his face as he bent over the bed, saying in the words of the Epistle appointed—"'My daughter, despise not thou the chastening of the Lord, nor faint when thou art rebuked of Him. For whom the Lord loveth He chasteneth; and scourgeth every child whom He receiveth.'"

In the evening the poor lady died, being released from her long imprisonment by that Royal Mandate, the Will of God.

We buried her in the green and pleasant churchyard of Islington. It is a sweet spot, far removed from the noise of London; and though her poor remains feel nothing, nor can hear any more the tumult of crowds, it is good to think that round her are no streets, only the few houses of the village. She lies surrounded by fields and trees; the daisies grow over her grave, the lark sings above the church; she is at rest and in peace.

CHAPTER XV.

HOW MRS. ESTHER WAS DISCHARGED.

After poor Mrs. Deborah's death my lessons came to a sudden stop, and have never been resumed. Some of that perspicacity of style which I have often admired in our modern divines might have fallen to my lot, to enrich this narrative, had I continued in my course of single and double book-keeping.

"I am not clever," said Mrs. Esther, "like Deborah. She was always the clever one as well as the beauty. That gave her a right to her little temper, poor dear. I cannot teach astronomy, because one star is to me exactly like another. Nor do I know aught about book-keeping, except that it is a very useful and necessary science. Therefore, Kitty, thou must go untaught. For that matter, I think you know as much as a woman need ever know, which is to read, to write—but one ought not to expect of a woman such exactness in spelling as of a scholar—and to cipher to such a moderate degree as may enable her to add up her bills. But it grieves me to think you are growing up so tall and straight without learning how to make so much as a single cordial, or any strong waters. And with our means, what chance of teaching you to toss a pancake, fold an omelette, or dish a Yorkshire pudding?"

It was then that we began to console ourselves for my ignorance, our troubles, and even, I bear mind, for our late loss, by reading "Clarissa," a book which the Doctor, ever watchful in the interests of virtue, presented to Mrs. Esther with a speech of condolence. He said that it was a work whose perusal could not fail most strongly to console her spirit and to dispose her for resignation; while for purity of morals, for justice of observation, and for knowledge of the human heart, it was unequalled in any language. He then made a digression, and compared the work with the ancient Greek romances. Adventure, he said, was to be found in Heliodorus, and the story told by Apuleius of Cupid and Psyche was exquisitely pathetic; yet none of the earlier writers could be compared, or even named in the same breath, with Mr. Richardson, who reminded him especially of Sophocles, in the tenderness with which he prepared the minds of his audience for the impending tragedy which he could not alter or abate, seeing that it was the will of Necessity. There was nothing, he went on to say, more calculated to inspire or to strengthen sentiments of virtue in the breasts of the young—and especially in the young of the feminine sex—than a contemplation of Clarissa's virtue and Lovelace's wickedness. We were greatly edified by these praises, coming from so great a scholar and one so eminently fitted to discourse on virtue. We received the work, prepared (so far as I was concerned) to partake of food for reflection of the satisfying kind (so that the reader quickly lays aside the work while he meditates for a few days on what he has read) which is supplied by the pious "Drelincourt on Death." Hervey's "Meditations among the Tombs," or Young's "Night Thoughts."

"After dinner, my dear," said Mrs. Esther, "you shall read it aloud to me. Do not stop if I shut my eyes in order to hear the better. These good books should be carefully listened to, and read very slowly. Otherwise their lessons may be overlooked, and this would be a sad pity after all the good Doctor's trouble in first reading the book for us. What scholarship, Kitty! and what a passion, nay, what an ardour, for virtue animates that reverend heart!"

I cannot but pause here to ask whether if Mr. Richardson had chosen to depict to the life the character of a clergyman, who had fallen into such ways as my uncle, with his sins, his follies, his degradation, the Doctor would himself have laid it to heart? Alas! I fear not. We know not ourselves as we are: we still go dreaming we are something better than we seem to others: we have a second and unreal self: the shafts of the satirist seem to pierce the hearts of others. I am sure that many a Lovelace, fresh from the ruin of another Clarissa (if, indeed, there could be another creature so incomparable), must have read this great romance with tears of pity and indignation. Otherwise the race of Lovelaces would long since have become extinct.

We received, therefore, "Clarissa," expecting edification, but not joy. We even put it aside for a week, because Mrs. Esther hardly felt herself, at first, strong enough to begin a new book, which might flood her mind with new ideas and make her unsettled. At last, however, she felt that we must no longer postpone obeying the Doctor.

"Only a short chapter, my dear, to begin with. Heavens! how shall we struggle through eight long volumes?"

I shall be ever thankful that it was my duty to read these dear delightful pages of this great romance. You may judge of our joy when we read on, day after day, hurrying over household work in the morning, neglecting our walks abroad, and wasting candlelight in the evening the more to enjoy it. We laid aside the book from time to time while we wept over the author's pathetic scenes. Oh, the horrid usage of poor Clarissa! Was ever girl more barbarously served? Was ever man so wicked as her lover? Were parents ever so blinded by prejudice? Had girl ever so unkind a brother—ever so perverse a sister? I thought of her all day long, and at night I dreamed of her: the image of Clarissa was never absent from my brain.

Everything in the book was as real to me as the adventures of Robinson Crusoe, or those of Christian on his pilgrimage from the City of Destruction. So long as the reading of this immortal book lasted—we read page after page twice, thrice, or four times over, to get out of them the fullest measure of sympathy, sorrow, and delight—we loved with Clarissa: her sorrows were ours: we breathed and talked Clarissa: Mrs. Esther even prayed, I believe—though the book was already printed, and therefore it was too late for prayer—that the poor, sweet innocent, might escape the clutches of her wicked lover, who, sure, was more a demon than a man: we carried the thought of Clarissa even to church with us.

We invited our friends to share with us this new-found joy. Solomon Stallabras was always ready to weep with us over a dish of tea. Never any man had a heart more formed for the tenderest sensibility. Pity that his nose was so broad and so much turned up, otherwise this natural tenderness might have been manifested in his countenance. While I read he gazed upon my face, and was fain, from time to time, to draw forth his handkerchief and wipe the tears from his streaming eyes.

"Stop, Miss Kitty!" he would say: "let us pause awhile: let us come back to virtue and ourselves. It is too much: the spectacle of so much youth and beauty, so much innocence—the fate of our poor Clarissa—read by a nymph whose lot is so below her merits—it is too much, Mrs. Pimpernel—it is indeed!"

In some way, while I read, this poet, whose imagination, as became his profession, was strong, mixed up Clarissa with myself, and imagined that my ending might be in some way similar to that of the heroine. Now, with Solomon Stallabras, to think was to believe. Nothing was wanting but a Lovelace. I believe that he waited about the market in hopes of finding him lurking in some corner. Perhaps he even suspected poor Sir Miles. Had he found him, he assured Mrs. Esther, he fully intended to pierce him to the heart with a spit or skewer from one of the butcher's stalls; adding that it would be sweet for him to die, even from the cart at Tyburn, for my sake. But no Lovelace was trying to make me leave my shelter with Mrs. Esther.

Sometimes Sir Miles Lackington came to join in the reading, but we found him wanting in sensibility. Without that quality, Richardson's novels cannot be enjoyed. He inclined rather to the low humour which makes men enjoy Fielding's "Tom Jones," or Smollett's "Peregrine Pickle"—works full, no doubt, of a coarse vitality which some men like, but quite wanting in the delicate shades of feeling that commend an author to the delicacy of gentlewomen. And to think that old Samuel Richardson was nothing but a printer by trade! Heaven, which denied this most precious gift of creation to such tender and poetic souls as that of Solomon Stallabras, vouchsafed to bestow it upon a printer—a mechanical printer, who, if he was not paid for setting up type himself, yet employed common workmen, superintended their labours, paid them their wages, and put profits into his purse. It seems incredible, but then Shakespeare was only an actor.

"The sunshine of genius," said Solomon, "falls upon the children of the lowly as well as those of the rich. I am myself a scion of Fetter Lane."

Sometimes, indeed, Sir Miles Lackington was so wanting in delicacy and so rude as to laugh at us for our tears.

"You cry over Richardson," he said; "but if I were to bring you 'Tom Jones' I warrant you would laugh."

"'Tom Jones,'" said Mrs. Esther, "is clearly a work of coarseness. Ladies do not wish to laugh. The laws of decorum forbid unrestrained mirth to females of good breeding. Fielding may suit the pewter pots of the tavern; Richardson goes best with the silver service of the mansion."

We looked about us as if our room was the mansion and our cupboard was lined with silver dishes.

Sir Miles laughed again.

"Give me a pewter mug well filled and often filled," he said, "with 'Tom Jones' to bear it company, and I ask no more. 'Clarissa,' and the silver service may remain with you, ladies. Strange, however, that folk should prefer a printer to a gentleman. Why, Fielding comes of an honourable house."

"Gentle blood," replied Mrs. Esther, "does not, unfortunately, always bring the gifts of poetry and sensibility. You are yourself of gentle birth, Sir Miles, yet you own that you love not Richardson. Many great authors have been of lowly extraction, and Mr. Stallabras was saying finely but yesterday, that the sunshine of genius falls upon the children of the poor as often as upon those of the rich."

Solomon inclined his head and coloured; Sir Miles laughed again in his easy fashion.

"But," he said, "Mr. Richardson knows nothing about the polite *ton*. His men are master tradesmen disguised in swords and scarlet coats; they are religious tradesmen, wicked tradesmen, and so forth; but they are not gentlemen; they cannot talk, think, or walk, write, or act like gentlemen. If we want to read about polite society, let us at least ask gentlemen to write for us."

Sir Miles read little, yet his judgment was generally right, and since I have seen the society of which Richardson wrote, I have learned that he was right in this case; for Richardson, pathetic and powerful as he is, had certainly never been among the class whose manners and conversation he attempted to portray.

Presently we finished "Clarissa," with floods of tears. I believe that no book was ever written which has caused so many tears as this work. Just then it was about the end of the year: we had already eaten our Christmas plum porridge in the darkest and deadest time of the year, the time when fogs fall over the town by day and stop all work: when nights are long and days short: when the market was quiet at night because it was too cold to stand about or to lie in the open: when all the fighting and brawling were over before five o'clock, and the evenings were tranquil though they were long. It was just after we ended our book, and were still tearful under its influence, that our deliverance came to us.

I think it was on the 31st of December in that same year of grace, seventeen hundred and fifty, in which I had come to the Liberties, and twenty-nine full years with some eleven months since the poor ladies had been incarcerated. I well remember the day, though not certain of the date. It was evening: we had finished work: supper was on the table when we should care to take it—bread and an excellent Dutch cheese; the candle was extinguished, and we were sitting before the fire. Mrs. Esther was talking, as women love sometimes to talk, about the little things they remember: she was telling me—not for the first time—of the great frost of 1714, when she was a young girl, and of the fair which they held upon the ice; of the dreadful scare there was in 1718 from the number of highwaymen and footpads, for whose apprehension the Government offered as much as £100 a head; of Orator Henley, who began to preach in Clare Market shortly after the ladies came to the Fleet; of the dreadful storm in 1739, which killed the famous colony of sparrows in the Mile End Road; of the long frost of 1739, when from Christmas unto February the poor watermen and fishermen could not earn a single penny; of the fever of 1741; of the banishment of papists before the Pretender's landing, in 1744; of the great Rebellion of 1745, when the city so nobly did its duty.

"My dear," she said, "we, that is the citizens, because the prisoners of the Fleet and the persons who enjoy the Liberties could hardly be expected to contribute money or aught but prayers—and most of the poor creatures but little used to praying!—raised twelve thousand shirts with as many garments to correspond, ten thousand woollen caps (to serve, I suppose, as nightcaps for our brave fellows when they slept in the open air), ten thousand pairs of stockings, twelve thousand gloves, a thousand blankets—which only makes one blanket for twelve men, but I hope they took turns about—and nine thousand spatterdashes. There was a camp on Finchley Common, of which we heard but did not visit; the militia were kept in readiness—a double watch was set at every one of the city gates; there were some in the Liberties, who thought that a successful invasion of England might lead to the burning of account-books, registers, ledgers, and warrants, in which case we might all get out and keep out. For my own part, my dear, and for my sister Deborah's part, I am happy to say that we preferred the Protestant succession even to our own freedom, and wished for no such lawless ending to a captivity however unjust, but prayed night and day for the confusion of the young Pretender. Happily our prayers were answered, and great George preserved."

Then we talked of the past year, how it had brought Mrs. Esther a daughter—as she was good enough to say—and taken away a sister. She cried a little over her loss, but presently recovered, and taking my hand in hers, said many kind and undeserved things to me, who had been often petulant and troublesome: as that we must not part, who had been so strangely brought together, unless my happiness should take me away from the Fleet (I thought, then, of my husband, and wondered if he would ever come to take me away), and then said that as we were at New Year's Eve, we should make good resolutions for the next year, which were to be kept resolutely, not broken and thrown away; that for her part, she designed, if I agreed and consented to the change, to call me niece, and I should call her aunt, by which mutual adoption of each other our affection and duty one towards the other would be strengthened and founded, as it were, on a sure and stable basis.

"Not, my dear," she added, "that you can ever call yourself a Pimpernel—an honour granted to few—or that you should ever wish to change your name; but in all other respects you shall be the same as if you were indeed my own niece, the daughter of my brother (but I never had one) or sister (but I had only one, and she was as myself). Truly the Pleydells are a worthy family, of whom we have no need to be ashamed."

I was assuring her that nothing could alter my love and gratitude for her exceeding kindness, when we heard footsteps and voices on the stairs, and presently a knock at the door, and the Doctor stood before us. Behind him were Sir Miles Lackington and Solomon Stallabras.

"Madam," said the Doctor, "I wish you a good evening, with the compliments of the season. Merry as well as happy may you be next year."

I declare that directly I saw his face, my heart leaped into my mouth. I *knew* that he was come with great and glorious news. For his eyes glowed with the light of some suppressed knowledge, and a capacious smile began with his lips and glowed over the vast expanse of his ruddy cheeks.

"Merry, Doctor—no. But happy if God will."

"Ta! ta! ta! we shall see," he replied. "Now, madam, I have a thing to say which will take some time to say. I have taken the liberty of bringing with me a bottle of good old port, the best to be procured, which strengthens the nerves and acts as a sovereign cordial in cases of sudden excitement. Besides, it is to-night New Year's Eve, when all should rejoice." He produced the bottle from under his gown and placed it on the table. "I have also taken the liberty to bring with me our friends and well-wishers, Sir Miles Lackington and Mr. Stallabras, partly to—to—" here he remembered that a corkscrew was not likely to be among our possessions—"to draw the cork of the bottle, a thing which Sir Miles does with zeal and propriety." The Baronet with great gravity advanced and performed the operation by a dexterous handling of the poker, which detached the upper part of the neck. "So," continued the Doctor; "and partly that they too, who have been so long our true and faithful friends, may hear what I have to say, and so that we may all rejoice together, and if need be, sing psalms with merry hearts."

Merry hearts? Were we to sing psalms with merry hearts in the place where for thirty years every day had brought with it its own suffering and disgrace to this poor lady?

Yet, what news could the Doctor have which made his purple face so glad, as if the sunlight instead of our fire of cannel coal was shining full upon it?

"Kitty child," he went on, "light candles: not one candle—two candles, three candles, four candles—all the candles you have in the place; we will have an illumination. Sir Miles, will you please to sit? Mr. Stallabras, will you take Kitty's chair? She will be occupied in serving. Glasses, child, for this honourable company. Why"—he banged his fist upon the table, but with consideration, for it was not so strong as his own great table—"why, I am happier this night than ever I have been before, I think, in all my life. Such a story as I have to tell!"

I placed on the table the three candlesticks which formed all our stock, and set candles in them and lit them. I put out such glasses as we had, and then I stood beside Mrs. Esther's chair and took her hand in mine. I knew not what to expect, yet I was certain that it was something very good for Mrs. Esther. Had it been for me, the Doctor would have sent for me; or for himself, he would have told it without this prodigality of joy. Surely it must be for my good patron and protector! My pulses were bounding, and I could see that Mrs. Esther, too, was rapidly rising to the same excitement.

"Certain I am," said Sir Miles, "that something has happened. Doctor, let us quickly congratulate you. Let us drink your health. I burn to drink some one's health."

"Should something have happened," said the poet, "I would it were something good for ladies who shall be nameless."

"Stay," said the Doctor. He stood while the rest were sitting. He thus increased the natural advantage of his great proportions. "We are not yet come to the drinking of healths. But, Mrs. Pimpernel, I must first invite you, before I go on with what I have to say, to take a glass of this most generous vintage. The grapes which produced it grew fat and strong in thinking of the noble part they were about to fulfil: the sunshine of Spain passed into their juices and filled them with the spirit of strength and confidence: that spirit lies imprisoned in the bottle before us——"

"It does—it does!" murmured Sir Miles, gazing thoughtfully at the bottle.

"He ought to have been a poet!" whispered Solomon.

The Doctor looked round impatiently, and swept the folds of his gown behind him with a large gesture.

"For what did the grapes rejoice? Why was the vintage more than commonly rich? Because in the fulness of time it was destined to comfort the heart and to strengthen the courage of a most worthy and cruelly tried lady. Indeed, Mrs. Pimpernel, wonderful are the decrees of heaven! Drink, madam."

He poured out a glass of wine and handed it to her. She stared in his face almost stupidly: she was trying to repress a wild thought which seized her: her lips were parted, her gaze fixed, her hands trembling.

"Drink it, madam," ordered the Doctor.

"What is it? oh! what is it?" she cried.

"Drink the wine, madam," said Sir Miles kindly. "Believe me, the wine will give you courage."

I took the glass and held it to her lips, while she drank submissively.

"With a bottle of port before him," said Sir Miles encouragingly, "a man may have patience for anything. With the help of such a friend, would I receive with resignation and joy, good fortune for myself or disasters to all my cousins, male and female. Go on, Doctor. The lady hath taken one glass to prepare her palate for the next."

"Patience, now," said the Doctor, "and silence, all of you. Solomon Stallabras, if you liken me again to a poet, you shall leave this room, and lose the joy of hearing what I have to tell."

"It is now some three months that the thought came into my mind of investigating the case of certain prisoners lying forgotten in the prison or dragging along a wretched existence in the Rules. It matters not what these cases were, or how I have sped in my search. One case, however, has filled me with gratitude and joy because — madam," he turned suddenly on poor Mrs. Esther, "you will please to listen patiently. This case concerns the unhappy fate of two poor ladies. Their history, gentlemen" — oh! why could he not get on faster? — "is partly known to you. They were daughters of a most worthy and respected city merchant who, in his time, served many civic offices with dignity and usefulness, including the highest. He was a benefactor to his parish, beautified his church, and died leaving behind him two young daughters, the youngest of whom came of age in the year 1720. To each of them he left a large fortune, no less than twenty thousand pounds. Alas! gentlemen, this money, placed in the hands of their guardian and trustee, a friend as honourable as the late Lord Mayor himself, the ladies' father, namely, Alderman Medlicott, was in the year 1720 shamefully pillaged and stolen by the alderman's clerk, one Christopher March, insomuch that (the alderman having gone mad by reason of his losses) the poor girls had no longer any fortune or any friends to help, for in that bad time most all the merchants were hit, and every one had to look after himself as best he could. Also this plundering villain had so invested part of their money, in their own name by forgeries, as to make them liable for large sums which they had not the means of paying. They were therefore arrested and confined in the prison hard by, where under the rule of the rogue Bambridge they suffered many things which it is painful to recall or to think about. Presently, however, that tormentor and plague of the human race—*captivorum flagellum*—scourge of innocent captives and languishing debtors, having been mercifully removed and having hung himself like Judas and so gone to his own place, these ladies found the necessary security which ensures for all of us this partial liberty, with the opportunity, should we embrace it, of improving the golden hours. In other words, gentlemen, they came out of the prison, and have ever since dwelt amongst us in this place.

"Gentlemen, we have with us here many improvident and foolish persons who have mostly by their own misconduct reduced themselves to our unhappy condition. It needs not that in this place, which is not a pulpit, I should speak of those who have gambled away their property"—Sir Miles shook his head—"or drank it away"—Sir Miles stared straight at the ceiling—"or have missed their chances, or been forgotten by Fortune"—Mr. Stallabras groaned. "Of these things I will not speak. But it is a thing notorious to all of us that the Liberties are not the chosen home of virtue. Here temperance, sobriety, morality, gentle words, courteous bearing, truth, honour, kindness of thought, and charity—which seeketh not her own—are rarely illustrated and discourteously entreated. Wherefore, I say, that for two ladies to have steadfastly resisted all the temptations of this place, and to have exhibited, so that all might copy, the exemplar of a perfect Christian life during thirty years, is a fact which calls for the gratitude as well as the astonishment of the wondering Rules."

"He *ought* to have been a——" began Solomon Stallabras, wiping a sympathetic tear, but caught the Doctor's frowning eye and stopped; "an—an Archbishop," he added presently, with a little hesitation.

"Sir," said the Doctor, "you are right. I ought to have been an archbishop. Many an archbishop's Latin verses have been poor indeed

The Chaplain of the Fleet

compared with mine. But to proceed. Madam, I would fain not be tedious."

"Oh, sir," said Mrs. Esther, whose brain seemed confused with this strange exordium.

"After thirty years or thereabouts of most undeserved captivity and forced retirement from the polite world—which they were born to adorn—these ladies found themselves by the will of Providence forced to separate. One of them winged her glad flight to heaven, the other was permitted to remain awhile below. It was then that I began to investigate the conditions of their imprisonment. Madam," he turned suddenly to Mrs. Esther, so that she started in her chair and trembled violently, "think of what you would most wish: name no trifling matter; it is not a gift of a guinea or two, the bettering of a meal, the purchase of a blanket, the helping of a poor family; no boon or benefit of a day or two. Let your imagination rove, set her free, think boldly, aim high, think of the best and most desirable thing of all."

She tried to speak, her lips parted; she half rose, catching at my hand: but her words were refused utterance; her cheek grew so pale and white that I thought she would have swooned and seized her in my arms, being so much stronger and bigger. Then I ventured to speak, being moved myself to a flood of tears.

"Oh, madam! dear madam! the Doctor is not jesting with you; he hath in his hands the thing that we desire most of all. He brings you, I am sure, great news—the greatest. Oh, sir"—I spoke now for her who was struck dumb with hope, fear, and astonishment—"what can this poor lady want but her release from this dreadful place? What can she pray for, what can she ask, morning and night, after all these years of companionship with profligates, spendthrifts, rogues, and villains, the noisy market people, the poor suffering women and children of this den of infamy, but her deliverance? Sir, if you have brought her that, tell her so at once, to ease her mind."

"Well said, Kitty," cried Sir Miles. "Doctor, speak out."

"No poet—not even Alexander Pope—could have spoken more eloquently," cried Solomon Stallabras.

As for Mrs. Esther, she drew herself gently from me, and stood with her handkerchief in her hand, and tears in her eyes, her poor thin figure trembling.

"I have brought with me," said the Doctor, taking her hand and kissing it, "the release of the most innocent prisoner in the world."

She steadied herself for a few moments. Then she spoke clearly and calmly.

"That," she said, "has ever been the utmost of my desire. I have desired it so long and so vehemently (with my sister Deborah, to whom it has been granted) that it has become part of my very being. I have desired it, I think, even more than my sister. Thirty years have I been a prisoner in the Fleet, though for twenty-six in the enjoyment of these (so-called) Liberties. Gentlemen, you know full well what manner of life has been ours; you know the sights, the sounds, the wickednesses of this place." Here Sir Miles hung his head. "I am, as the Doctor most kindly hath told you, a gentlewoman born; my father, besides being a great and honourable merchant of this most noble city of London, once Lord Mayor, an Alderman of Portsoken Ward, and Worshipful Master of the Company of Armour Scourers, was also a true Christian man, and taught us early the doctrines and virtues of the true faith. We were educated as heiresses; we were delicately brought up in the love of duty and religion; too delicately for women fated to herd with the worst and bear the worst. It is, therefore, no merit of ours if we have behaved, according to our lights, as Christian gentlewomen. Yet, sirs, kind friends, it has been great unhappiness to us; bear with me a little, for when I think of my sister's sufferings, and my own, I fain must weep. It has been, believe me, great, great unhappiness."

I think we all wept with her. Yet it was astonishing to see with what quiet dignity she spoke, resuming, at a moment's notice, the air not only of a gentlewoman, which she had never lost, but of one who is no longer troubled by being in a false position, and can command, as well as receive, respect. I saw before me a great city lady, as she had been trained and brought up to be. Small though she was, her dignity made her tall—as her unmerited sufferings and patience made her great.

Sir Miles laid his hand on the poet's shoulder.

"Great heaven!" he cried. "Canst thou weep any more over the misfortunes of Clarissa, with this poor lady's sorrows in thy recollection?"

The Doctor wiped his eyes. But for those backslidings which we have already lamented, what an admirable character, how full of generosity, how full of sympathy, how kind of heart, was my uncle!

"Pray, madam," he said, "be seated again. Will you take another glass of wine?"

"No, Doctor," she replied. "This is now no case for the help of wine. Pray finish the story of your benevolent care."

"Why, madam, as for benevolence," he said, "I have but done what Sir Miles Lackington or Solomon Stallabras"—the poet spread his arms and tapped his breast—"would have done, had they possessed the power of doing; what, indeed, this crying slip of a girl would have done had she known how. Benevolence! Are we, then, Old Bailey prisoners, chained by the leg until the time comes for us to go forth to Tyburn Tree? Are we common rogues and vagabonds, that have no bowels? Can such a life as yours be contemplated with unmoved eyes? Is Sir Miles a Lovelace for hardness of heart? or Solomon Stallabras a salamander? Am I a Nero? Nay, madam, speak no more of benevolence. Know, then, that of all the people whom the conduct of the villain Christopher March with regard to your affairs injured, but two are left alive. The heirs of the rest are scattered and dispersed. These two have prospered, and are generous as well as old; their hearts melted at the tale of suffering; they have agreed together to give back to you, not only the security which keeps you here, but also a formal release of your debt to them; you can go whenever you please."

"Why, then," shouted Sir Miles, grasping the bottle, "we can drink her——"

"Stay," said the Doctor. "There is one thing more. This generous gift restores to you, not only liberty, but also your father's country estate in Hertfordshire, worth six hundred pounds a year. And here, madam, are the papers which vouch for all. You have now your own estate, and are once more a gentlewoman of fortune and position."

She took the papers, and held them grasped tightly in her lap.

"And now, gentlemen," said the Doctor, gently taking the bottle from the baronet's hand, "we will drink—you, too, Kitty, my dear, must join—a happy new year to Mrs. Esther Pimpernel."

They drank it with no more words; and Sir Miles fell on his knees and kissed her hand, but without speaking aught.

Mrs. Esther sat still and quiet, trying to recover herself; but the first eloquence would not return, and she could not speak for crying and sobbing. In broken words she said, while she caught the Doctor's great hand and held it, that he had been, in very sooth, her guardian angel; that it was he who had rescued her sister and herself from the monster Bambridge and the horrors of the prison; that, but for him, they would long ago have starved: that, but for him, she should have languished for the rest of her days in the Rules. Then she prayed that God would reward the protector and defender of the poor.

The Doctor drew away his hand, and, without a word, walked out of the room with hanging head, followed by Sir Miles and Mr. Stallabras.

"We shall go, my sweet Kitty; together we shall leave this dreadful place," she murmured when we were alone. "What is mine is yours, my child. Let us humbly to our knees."

Part II.

THE QUEEN OF THE WELLS.

CHAPTER I.

HOW WE RETURNED TO THE POLITE WORLD.

We love those places most where we lived when we were young, and where we were wooed and won, and where we had those sweet dreams, which can only come to the very young, of a happy future, impossible in this transitory and fleeting life. Dear to me and romantic are the scenes which to many are associated with disease and infirmity, or at best with the mad riot of the race, the assembly, and the ball.

Truly there is no time, for a woman, like the time when she is young and beautiful, and is courted by a troop of lovers. She feels her power, though she does not understand it; she remembers it long after the power has gone, with the witchery of bright eyes, soft cheeks, and blooming youth. I think there can never be any faith or hope in the future so strong as to resist the sigh over the past, the feeling that it is better to be young than to be old: to blossom than to wither.

When we went to Epsom Wells we had managed between us, by silence as to the past and a tacit understanding, to forget the Rules altogether. Forgetting, indeed, is easy. Surely the butterfly forgets the days when it was a mere crawling grub; Cophetua's queen no doubt soon learned to believe that she had royal blood, or blue blood at least, in her peasant veins (for my own part, I think the king should have mated with one nearer his own rank). There is little difficulty in putting out of sight what we wish forgotten. There was a man, for instance, about the Fleet market, running odd jobs, who actually had forgotten that he was once hanged. The people used to go there on purpose to see the wretch, who was, I remember, bow-legged and long-armed, with broad shoulders; his face was marked with smallpox; he squinted; he had a great scar upon his cheek; the bridge of his nose was broken; he had no forehead visible; his ears projected on either side, and were long, like the ears of a mule; his eye-teeth were like tusks; and as for his expression, it was that which John Bunyan may have had in his mind when he wrote about the mob in Vanity Fair, or the ill-favoured ones who got over the wall and accosted Christiana—an expression which one may briefly describe as indicating a mind not set upon spiritual things. Now this man had actually once been hanged, but being taken away after the hanging to Barber Surgeons' Hall, near St. Giles's Church, Cripplegate, was then restored to life by one who thought to dissect him. That was why everybody looked after him, and would have asked him questions if they had dared accost such a ruffian. For it seemed to the unthinking as if he, alone among living men, had, like Dante and Virgil, gone into the regions of the dead, conversed with the spirits of the unjust (being himself a monstrous criminal), and, after witnessing their tortures, had returned to the living. To those who bribed him with rum and then put questions, he replied that as for the hanging, it might be as the gentleman said, but he had forgotten it. As for what he saw between his hanging and his restoration to life, he had forgotten that too. Now if a man can forget having been hung, it stands to reason that he can forget anything.

At all events, without the insensibility of this wretch, we speedily agreed to forget the Fleet Rules, and in all our conversations to make as if we had never been there at all, and knew of the place, if at all, then only by hearsay and common bruit and rumour. As for the Chaplain of the Fleet, the great promoter of those marriages which made the place infamous and the chief performer of them notorious, we agreed that we were only to think of him as our benefactor.

Not that we put these resolutions into words, but we arrived at them in the manner common among women, with whom a smile or a glance is as intelligible as many words (with a bottle of wine) among men.

It was due to this desire to forget the past that we never even read through the "Farewell to the Fleet," presented to us by Mr. Solomon Stallabras on the morning of our departure. The first four lines, which was as far as I got, ran as follows:

"With easy air of conscious worth expressed,
Fair Pimpernel her sorrows oft addressed;
The listening echoes poured her sighs abroad,
Which all unheard by men, were heard by God."

He handed the verses to us with a low bow as we stepped into the coach, leaving him behind still—poor wretch!—"enjoying" the Liberties.

We first repaired, with the view of spending a period of retirement, to a convenient lodging in Red Lion Street, where Mrs. Esther set herself seriously to resume the dress, manner, language, and feelings of a gentlewoman.

"We have been," she said, "like the sun in eclipse. It is true that one does not cease to enjoy, under all circumstances, the pride of gentle birth, which has been my chief consolation during all our troubles. But if one cannot illustrate to the eyes of the world the dignified deportment and genteel appearance due to that position, the possession of the privilege is a mere private grace, like the gift of good temper, patience, or hope."

At first and for some weeks we held daily conversations and consultations on the subject of dress. We were, as may be guessed, somewhat like Pocahontas, of Virginia, when she left the savages and came into the polite world—because we had to begin from the very first, having hardly anything in which a lady could go abroad, and very little in which she could sit at home. Truly delightful was it to receive every day the packages of brocades, lace, satins, silks, sarsnets, besides chintzes, muslins, woollen things, and fine linen wherewith to deck ourselves, and to talk with the dressmaker over the latest fashion, the most proper style for madam, a lady no longer young, and for me, who, as a girl, should be dressed modestly and yet fashionably.

"We must go fine, child," said Mrs. Esther. "I, for my part, because a fine appearance is due to my position: you, because you are young and beautiful. The gallants, to do them justice, are never slow in running after a pretty face; but they are only fixed by a pretty face in a pretty setting."

Alas! to think that my face, pretty or not, already belonged, willy-nilly, to a man who had never run after it.

Mrs. Esther found that not only the fashions of dress, but those of furniture, of language, of manners, and of thought, were changed since her long imprisonment began. We therefore made it our endeavour by reading papers, by watching people, and by going to such places as the Mall, the Park, and even the fashionable churches, to catch as far as possible, the mode. Mrs. Esther never quite succeeded, retaining to the last a touch of antiquated manners, an old-fashioned bearing and trick of speech, which greatly became her, though she knew it not. Meanwhile we held long and serious talk about the rust of thirty years, and the best way to wear it off.

In one of the sermons of the Reverend Melchior Smallbrook, a divine now forgotten, but formerly much read, the learned clergyman states that the sunshine of prosperity is only dangerous to that soul in which tares are as ready to spring as wheat: adducing as a remarkable example and proof of this opinion, the modern prelates of the Church of England, whose lives (he said) are always models to less fortunate Christians, although their fortunes are so great. Now in Mrs. Esther's soul were no tares at all, so that the sunshine of prosperity caused no decrease or diminution of her virtues. She only changed for the better, and especially in point of cheerfulness and confidence. For instance, whereas we were formerly wont, being poorly clad, to creep humbly to church, sit in the seats reserved for the poor (which have no backs to them, because the bishops consider the backs of the poor to be specially strengthened by Providence, which hath laid such heavy burdens upon them), and afterwards spend the day sadly over Hervey's "Meditations among the Tombs," we now went in hoops, laces, mantles, or cardinals, with faces patched, to the new church in Queen Square, where we had front seats in the gallery, and after church we dined off roast meat, with pudding, and after dinner read such discourses as presented, instead of penitential meditations, a thankful, nay, a cheerful view of life. I am sure, for my own part, I found the change greatly for the better. But we made no new friends, because Mrs. Esther wished to remain in strict retirement until she had recovered what she called the Pimpernel Manner.

"It is a Manner, my dear, as you will perceive when I recover it, at once dignified and modest. My father and my grandfather, both Lord Mayors, possessed it to an eminent degree, and were justly celebrated for it. My poor sister would never have acquired it, being by nature too sprightly. I was gradually learning it when our misfortunes came. Naturally afterwards it would have been absurd to cultivate its further development. The Pimpernel Manner would have been thrown away in——such a place as that to which we retired."

I am so stupid that I never clearly understood the Pimpernel Manner, even when Mrs. Esther afterwards assured me that she had now fully recovered it.

Meantime, my education was resumed in the lighter departments. No girl who had once tackled book-keeping, by single and double entry, could want any more solid instruction. My guardian played the harpsichord for me, while my dancing-master gave me lessons in the minuet; or she personated a duchess, a countess, or even the most exalted lady in the land, while the master, a pink of courtesy, who had once danced on the boards of Drury Lane, presented me dressed in hoops and a train. I was so diligent in dancing that I was soon ready, he assured me, to make a figure at any assembly, whether at Bath, Epsom, Tunbridge Wells, Vauxhall, or Ranelagh. But for the present these gaieties had to be postponed, partly because the Pimpernel Manner was slow in developing, and without it my guardian would not stir abroad, partly because we had no gentleman to go with us. Sir Miles Lackington would, I am sure, have gone with us, had we asked him to take us. But he was not to be depended upon if a bottle of wine came in the way. Solomon Stallabras would have gone, but the poor poet had no clothes fit for a polite assembly. Moreover, there was an objection, Mrs. Esther said, to both those gentlemen, that the fact of their being in the enjoyment of the Liberties of the Fleet might have been thrown in our teeth at a polite assembly.

It seemed to me then, being ignorant of the extreme wickedness of men, a grievous thing that gentlewomen cannot go whithersoever they please without the protection of a man. What sort of an age, I asked, is this, which pretends to have cast aside Gothic barbarism, yet cannot suffer its ladies to go unprotected for fear of insult or damage to their reputation? Scourers and Mohocks, I said, no longer infest the streets, which are for the most part secure even from footpads and purse-cutters. I was as yet, however, unacquainted with that class of man which loves to follow a woman, to stare at her, and to make her tremble with fear, being no better, but rather worse, than so many highwaymen, common bullies, and professed rogues.

Sir Miles Lackington did not desert us. Neither my cruelty, he said, nor his own unworthiness could persuade him to do that; he must needs follow and worship at the shrine of his unattainable sun and shining star—with such nonsense as men will still be talking even when they know that the woman is not for them.

On the occasion of the first visit I privately informed him that we wished to have no mention made of the place where we were once residing. He very kindly agreed to silence on this point, and we sustained between us a conversation after the manner of polite circles. Sir Miles would ask us, with a pinch of snuff, if we liked our present lodging—which was, as I have said, in Red Lion Street, not far from the fields and the Foundling Hospital—better than those to be obtained in Hill Street and Bruton Street, or some other place frequented by the best families. Madam, with a fashionable bow, would reply that we were favourably placed as regards air, that of Bloomsbury being good for persons like herself, of delicate chests; and that concerning educational conveniences for miss, she found the quarter superior to that mentioned by Sir Miles. Then the honest baronet would relate, without yawning or showing any signs of fatigue, such stories of fashionable life as he had learned from those who had lately come to the Fleet, or remembered from his short career among the world of fashion. We agreed, always without unnecessary waste of words, to consider him as a gentleman about town, familiar with the Great.

The Doctor came but rarely. He brought wise counsel. He was a miracle of wisdom. No one is ever so wise in the conduct of his friends' affairs as he who has wrecked his own. Have we not seen far-seeing and prudent ministers of state, who have conducted the business of the nation with skill and success, yet cannot manage their own far more simple business?

Mrs. Esther talked to no one but to him about the past. She had no secrets from him. She even wished him, if possible, to share in her good fortune, and wanted him to appease his creditors with half of all that was hers. But he refused.

"My imprisonment," he said, "is also my freedom. While I am lying in the Fleet I can go abroad as I please; I fear no arrest: my conscience does not reproach me when I pass a shop and think of what I owe the tradesman who keeps it, because my creditors have paid themselves by capture of my body. Your purse, dear madam, were it ten times as long, would not appease the hungry maw of all my creditors and lawyers. Of old, before I took refuge among the offal and off-scouring of humanity, the prodigal sons, and the swine, there was no street west of Temple Bar where I did not fear the voice of a creditor or expect the unfriendly shoulder-tap of a bailiff. Besides, were I free, what course would be open to me? Now I live in state, with the income of a dean: outside I should live in meanness, with the income of a curate. I will retire from my present position—call it cure of souls, madam—when the Church recognises merit by translating me from the Fleet market to a fat prebendal stall. And, believe me, Virtue may find a home even beside those stalls, and among those grunting swine."

I understand now, being much older and abler to take a just view of things, that if my uncle could have obtained his discharge he would have been unwilling to take it. For, granted that he was a learned and eloquent man, that he would have attracted multitudes to hear him, learning and eloquence, in the Church, do not always obtain for a clergyman the highest preferment; the Doctor, who was no longer young, might have had to languish as a curate on forty or perhaps sixty pounds *per annum*, even though it became the fashion to attend his sermons. And, besides, his character was for ever gone, among his brethren of the cloth. A man who has been a Fleet parson is like one who has passed a morning in hedging and ditching. He must needs wash all over. Truly, I think that the Doctor was right. To exercise the functions of his sacred calling all the morning for profit, to drink with his friends all the evening, to spend a large portion of his gains in deeds of charity and generosity among a poor, necessitous, prodigal, greedy, spendthrift, hungry, thirsty, and shameful folk, who rewarded his liberality by a profusion of thanks, blessings, and good wishes, was more in accordance with the Doctor's habits of thought.

He persuaded himself, or tried to persuade others, that he was doing a good work in the morning; in the afternoon he performed works of charity; in the evening he abandoned himself to the tempter who led him to sing, drink, and jest among the rabble rout of Comus.

One morning he bade me put on my hat and walk with him, because he had a thing to say. I obeyed with fear, being certain he was going to speak about my unknown husband.

"Girl!" he said, as we walked past the last house in Red Lion Street and along the pathway which leads to the Foundling Hospital. "Girl, I have to remind you and to warn you."

I knew well what was to be the warning.

"Remember, you are now seventeen and more; you are no longer a young and silly girl, you are a young woman; thanks to your friends, you have taken the position of a young gentlewoman, even an heiress. You will soon leave this quiet lodging and go where you will meet society and the great world; you are pretty and well-mannered; you will have beaux and gallants dangling their clouded canes at your heels and asking your favours. But you are married. Remember that: you are married. You must be careful not to let a single stain rest upon your reputation."

"Oh, sir!" I cried, "I have endeavoured to forget that morning. Was that marriage real? The poor young gentleman was tipsy. Can a tipsy man be married?"

"Real?" The Doctor stood and gazed at me with angry eyes and puffed cheeks, so that the old terror seized me in spite of my fine frock and hoop. "Real? Is the girl mad? Am I not Gregory Shovel, Doctor of Divinity of Christ's College, Cambridge? Not even the King's most sacred Majesty is married in more workmanlike fashion. Let your husband try to escape the bond. Know that he shall be watched: let him try to set it aside: he shall learn by the intervention of learned lawyers, if he do not trust my word, that he is as much married as St. Peter himself."

"Alas!" I said. "But how shall my husband love me?"

"Tut! tut! what is love? You young people think of nothing but love—the fond inclination of one person for another. Are you a pin the worse, supposing he never loves you? Love or no love, make up thy mind, child, that happy shall be thy lot. Be contented, patient, and silent. When the right day comes, thou shalt step forth to the world as Catherine, Lady Chudleigh."

That day he said no more to me. But he showed that the subject was not out of his thoughts by inquiries into the direction and progress of my studies, which, he hinted, should be such as would befit my rank and position. Madam thought he meant my rank as her heiress, a position which could not be illustrated with too much assiduity.

Soon after we went to Red Lion Street, my uncle gave madam my bag of guineas.

"Here is the child's fortune," he said. "Let her spend it, but with moderation, in buying the frocks, fal-lals, and trifles which a young gentlewoman of fortune should wear. Grudge not the spending. Should more be wanting, more shall be found. In everything, my dear lady, make my niece an accomplished woman, a woman of *ton*, a woman who can hold her own, a woman who can go into any society, a woman fit to become the wife—well—the wife of a lord."

It was on New Year's Day that we left the Fleet; it was in the summer, at the end of June, when we decided that enough had been done to rub off the rust of that unfashionable place.

"You, my dear," said Mrs. Esther, "have the sprightly graces of a well-born and well-bred young woman: I can present you in any society. I, for my part, have recovered the Pimpernel Manner. I can now make an appearance worthy of my father."

I assured my kind lady that although, to be sure, I had never been able to witness the great original and model from which the Pimpernel Manner was derived, yet that no lady had so fine an air as herself; which was certainly true, madam being at once dignified and gifted with a formal condescension very pretty and uncommon.

CHAPTER II.

HOW WE WENT TO THE WELLS.

Access to the polite world is more readily gained (by those who have no friends) at one of the watering-places than in London. Considering this, we counselled whether it would not be better to visit one, or all, of the English Spas, rather than to climb slowly and painfully up the ladder of London fashion.

Mrs. Esther at first inclined to Bath, which certainly (though it is a long journey thither), is a most stately city, provided with every requisite for comfort, possessing the finest Assembly Rooms and the most convenient lodgings. It also affords opportunities for making the acquaintance and studying the manners of the Great. Moreover, there can be no doubt that its waters are efficient in the cure of almost all disorders; and the social enjoyment of the hot bath, taken in the company of the wits and toasts who go to be parboiled together in that liquid Court of scandal, chocolate, and sweets, is surely a thing without a rival.

On the other hand, Tunbridge Wells is nearer London; the roads are good; a coach reaches the place in one day; and, so amazing is the rapidity of communication (in which we so far excel our ancestors), that the London morning papers reach the Wells in the evening, and a letter posted from the Wells in the morning can be answered in the following evening. Also the air is fine at Tunbridge, the waters wholesome, and the amusements are said to be varied. Add to this that it is greatly frequented by the better sort of London citizens, those substantial merchants with their proud and richly dressed wives and daughters, whom Mrs. Esther always looked upon as forming the most desirable company in the world. So that it was at first resolved to go to Tunbridge.

But while we were making our preparations to go there, a curious longing came upon Mrs. Esther to revisit the scenes of her youth.

"My dear," she said, "I should like to see once more the Wells of Epsom, whither my father carried us every year when we were children. The last summer I spent there was after his death, in the dreadful year of 1720, when the place was crowded with Germans, Jews, and the people who flocked to London with schemes which were to have made all our fortunes, but which only ruined us, filled the prisons and madhouses, drove honest men upon the road, and their children to the gutters. Let us go to Epsom."

Epsom Wells, to be sure, was no longer what it had been. Indeed, for a time, the place had fallen into decay. Yet of late, with their horse-racing in April and June, and the strange repute of the bone-setter Sally Wallin, the salubrity of the air on the Downs, the easy access to the town, which lieth but sixteen miles or thereabouts from Paul's, and the goodness of the lodgings, the fame of the place had revived. The gentry of the country-side came to the Monday breakfasts and assemblies, when there was music, card-playing, and dancing; the old buildings were again repaired, and Epsom Wells for a few years was once more crowded. To me, as will presently be very well understood, the place will ever remain a dear romantic spot, sacred to the memory of the sweetest time in a woman's life, when her heart goes out of her keeping, and she listens with fear and delight to the wooing of the man she loves.

We went there in the coach, which took about three hours. We arrived in the afternoon of a sunny day — it was a Friday, which is an unlucky day to begin a journey upon — in the middle of July. We were presently taken to a neat and clean lodging in Church Parade, where we engaged rooms at a moderate charge. The landlady, one Mrs. Crump, was the widow, she told us, of a respectable hosier of Cheapside, who had left her with but a slender stock. Her children, however, were in good service and thriving; and, with her youngest daughter, Cicely, she kept this lodging-house, a poor but genteel mode of earning a livelihood.

The first evening we sat at home until sunset, when we put on our hoods and walked under the trees which everywhere at Epsom afford a delightful shade during the heat of the day, and a romantic obscurity in the twilight. A lane or avenue of noble lime-trees was planted in the Church Parade. Small avenues of trees led to the houses, and formed porches with rich canopies of green leaves. There was a good deal of company abroad, and we could hear, not far off, the strains of the music to which they were dancing in the Assembly Rooms.

"We have done well, Kitty," said Mrs. Esther, "to come to this place, which is far less changed than since last I came here. I trust it is not sinful to look back with pleasure and regret on the time of youth." Here she sighed. "The good woman of the house, I perceive with pleasure, remembers the name of Pimpernel, and made me a becoming courtesy when I informed her of my father's rank. She remembers seeing his Lord Mayor's Show. There are, it appears, many families of the highest distinction here, with several nabobs, rich Turkey and Russian merchants, great lawyers, and county gentry. She assures me that all are made welcome, and that the assemblies are open to the whole company. And she paid a tribute to thy pretty face, my dear."

In the morning we were awakened, to our surprise and delight, by a delectable concert of music, performed for us, by way of salutation or greeting, by the band belonging to the place. They played, in succession, a number of the most delightful airs, such as, "A-hunting we will go," "Fain I would," "Spring's a-coming," "Sweet Nelly, my heart's delight," and "The girl I left behind me." The morning was bright, and a breeze came into my open window from the Surrey Downs, fresh and fragrant with the scent of wild flowers. My brain was filled with the most ravishing ideas, though I knew not of what.

"My dear," said Mrs. Esther, at breakfast, "the compliment of the music shows the discernment of the people. They have learned already that we have pretensions to rank, and are no ordinary visitors, not haberdashers' daughters or grocers'."

(It is, we afterwards discovered, the rule of the place thus to salute new comers, without inquiry at all into their rank or fortune. We rewarded the players with half-a-crown from madam, and two shillings from myself.)

It is, surely, a delightful thing to dress one's self in the morning to the accompaniment of sweet music. If I were a queen, I would have a concert of music every day, to begin when I put foot out of bed: to sing in tune while putting on one's stockings: to dance before the glass while lacing one's stays: to handle a comb as if it was a fan, and to brush one's hair with a swimming grace, as if one was doing a minuet, while the fiddles and the flutes and the hautboys are playing for you. Before I had finished dressing, however, Cicely Crump, who was a lively, sprightly girl, with bright eyes, and little nose, about my own age, came to help me, and told me that those ladies who went abroad to take the air before breakfast wore in the morning an easy dishabille, and advised me to tie a hood beneath the chin.

"But not," she said with a laugh, "not to hide too much of your face. What will they say to such a face at the ball?"

We followed her advice, and presently sallied forth. Although it was but seven o'clock, we found a goodly assemblage already gathered together upon the Terrace, where, early as it was, the shade of the trees was agreeable as well as beautiful. The ladies, who looked at us with curiosity, were dressed much like ourselves, and the gentlemen wore morning-gowns, without swords: some of the elder men even wore nightcaps, which seemed to me an excessive simplicity. Everybody talked to his neighbour, and there was a cheerful buzz of conversation.

"Nothing is changed, my dear," said Mrs. Esther, looking about her with great satisfaction; "nothing except the dresses, and these not so much as we might have expected. I have been asleep, dear, like the beauty in the story, for thirty years. But she kept her youth, that lucky girl, while I—heigh-ho!"

Cicely came with us to show us the way. We went first along the Terrace and then to the New Parade, which was also beautifully shaded with elms and limes. Between them lies the pond, with gold and silver fish, very pretty to look at, and the tumble-down watch-house at one end. Then she showed us the pump-room.

"Here is the spring," she said, "which cures all disorders: the best medicine in the world."

There was in the room a dipper, as they call the women who hand the water to those who go to drink it. We were told that it was customary to pay our footing with half-a-crown; but we drank none of the water, which is not, like that of Tunbridge Wells, sweet and pleasant to the taste. Then Cicely led us to another building hard by, a handsome place, having a broad porch with columns, very elegant. This, it appeared, was the Assembly Room, where were held the public balls, concerts, and breakfasts. We entered and looked about us. Mrs. Esther recalled her triumphs in this very room, and shed a tear over the past. Then a girl accosted us, and begged permission to enter our names in a great book. This (with five shillings each by way of fees) made us free of all the entertainments of the season.

Near the Assembly Rooms was the coffee-house, used only by the gentlemen.

"They pretend," said Cicely, "to come here for letter-writing and to read the news. I do not know how many letters they write, but I do know what they talk about, because I had it of the girl who pours out their coffee, and it is not about religion, nor politics, but all about the toast of the day."

"What is the toast of the day?" I asked.

Cicely smiled, like a saucy baggage as she was, and said that no doubt Miss Kitty would soon find out.

"Already," she said, "Mr. Walsingham is looking at you."

I saw an old gentleman already dressed for the morning, with lace ruffles and a handkerchief for the neck of rich crimson silk, who sat on one of the benches beneath the trees, his hand upon a stick, looking at me with a sort of earnestness.

"Hush!" cried Cicely, whispering; "he is more than eighty years of age: he goes every year to Epsom, Bath, and Tunbridge—all three—and he can tell you the name of the toast in every place for fifty years, and describe her face."

A "toast," then, was another word for a young lady.

As we passed his bench, the old gentleman rose and bowed with great ceremony to madam.

"Your most obedient servant, madam," he said, still looking at me. "I trust that the Wells will be honoured by your ladyship with a long stay. My name is Walsingham, madam, and I am not unknown here. Permit me to offer my services to you and to your lovely daughter."

"My niece, sir." Madam returned the bow with a curtsey as deep. "My niece, Miss Kitty Pleydell. We arrived last night, and we expect to find our stay so agreeable as to prolong it."

"The Wells, madam, will be delighted." He bowed again. "I hope to be of assistance—some little assistance—in making your visit pleasant. I have known Epsom Wells, and, indeed, Bath and Tunbridge as well, for fifty years. Every year has been made remarkable in one of these places by the appearance of at least one beautiful face: sometimes there have been even three or four, so that gentlemen have been divided in opinion. In 1731, for instance, a duel was fought at Tunbridge Wells, between my Lord Tangueray and Sir Humphrey Lydgate, about two rival beauties. Generally, however, the Wells acknowledge but one queen. Yesterday I was publicly lamenting that we had as yet no one at Epsom whom we could hope to call Queen of the Wells. Miss Kitty Pleydell"—again he bowed low—"I can make that complaint no longer. I salute your Majesty."

"Oh, sir," I said, abashed and confused, "you are jesting with me!"

He replied gravely, that he never jested on so serious a subject as the beauty of a woman. Then he hoped to see us again upon the Terrace or on the Downs in the course of the day, and left us with a low bow.

"I told you, miss," said Cicely, "that it would not be long before you found out what is meant by a toast."

She next took us to a book-shop, where we learned that for a crown we could carry home any book we pleased from the shop and read it at our ease; only that we must return it in as good condition as we took it out, which seems reasonable. The people in the shop, as are all the people at Epsom, were mighty civil; and madam, partly with a view of showing the seriousness of her reading, took down a volume of sermons, which I carried home for her.

Next day, however, she exchanged this for a volume of "Pamela," which now began to occupy our attention almost as much as "Clarissa" had done, but caused fewer tears to flow. Now is it not a convenient thing for people who cannot afford to buy all they would read, thus to pay a subscription and to borrow books as many as they wish? I think that nothing has ever yet been invented so excellent for the spread of knowledge and the cultivation of taste. Yet it must not go too far either; for should none but the libraries buy new novels, poems, and other works of imagination, where would be the reward of the ingenious gentlemen who write them? No; let those who can afford buy books: let those who cannot buy all they can, and join the library for those they cannot afford to buy. What room looks more comfortably furnished than one which has its books in goodly rows upon the shelves? They are better than pictures, better than vases, better than plates, better than china monkeys; for the house that is so furnished need never feel the dulness of a rainy day.

There remained but two subscriptions to pay before our footing was fairly established.

The leader of the music presented himself, bowing, with his subscription-book in his hand. The usual amount was half a guinea. Madam gave a guinea, being half for herself, and half for me, writing down our names in the book. I saw, as we came away, that a little group of gentlemen quickly gathered round the leader and almost tore the book from his hand.

"They are anxious to find out your name, miss," said Cicely. "Then they will go away and talk in the coffee-house, and wonder who you are and whence you came and what fortune you have. Yet they call us women gossips!"

Lastly, there was the clergyman's book.

"Heaven forbid," said madam, "that we pay for the music and let the prayers go starving!"

This done, we could return home, having fairly paid our way for everything, and we found at our lodgings an excellent country breakfast of cream, new-laid eggs, fresh wild strawberries from Durdans Park, delicate cakes of Mrs. Crump's own baking, and chocolate, with Cicely to wait upon us.

It was the godly custom of the place to attend public worship after breakfast, and at the ringing of the bell we put on our hats and went to the parish church, where we found most of the ladies assembled. They were escorted to the doors of the sacred house by the gentlemen, who left them there. Why men (who are certainly greater sinners, or sinners in a bolder and more desperate fashion, than women) should have less need of prayers than we, I know not; nor why a man should be ashamed of doing what a woman glories in doing. After their drinkings, their duels, their prodigalities, and wastefulness, men should methinks crowd into the doors of every church they can find, women leading them thereto. But let us not forget that men, when they live outside the fashion and are natural, are by the bent of their mind generally more religiously disposed than women: and, as they make greater sinners, so also do they make more illustrious saints.

When we came out of the church (I forgot to say that we were now dressed and ready to make as brave a show as the rest) we found outside the doors a lane of gentlemen, who, as we passed, bowed low, hat in hand. At the end stood old Mr. Walsingham.

He stood with his hat raised high in air, and a smile upon his lined and crowsfooted face.

"What did I say, Miss Kitty?" he whispered. "Hath not the Queen of the Wells arrived?"

I do not know what I might have said, but I heard a cry of "Kitty! Kitty!" and, looking round, saw—oh, the joy!—none other than my Nancy, prettier than ever, though still but a little thing, who ran up to me and threw herself in my arms.

CHAPTER III.

HOW NANCY RECKONED UP THE COMPANY.

Nancy Levett herself, pretty and merry, prattling, rattling Nancy, not grown a bit, and hardly taller than my shoulder. I held her out at arm's length.

"You here, Nancy?"

Then we kissed again.

"And not a bit changed, Nancy?"

"And oh! so changed, Kitty. So tall and grand. Come to my mother."

Lady Levett was standing close by with Sir Robert, who took me by the shoulders and kissed my cheeks, forehead and lips in fatherly fashion.

"Gadso!" he cried. "This is brave indeed. Things are likely to go well at Epsom. We have got back our Kitty, wife."

Lady Levett was colder. Perhaps she had misgivings on what had been done with me for the last twelvemonth. And then I, who had gone away a simple, rustic maid, was now in hoops, patches and powder.

"Kitty will tell us presently," she said, "I doubt not what she has done, and under whose protection she is travelling."

Then I hastened to present Mrs. Esther, who stood aside, somewhat embarrassed.

"Madam," I said, "I present to you my benefactress and guardian, Mrs. Esther, to whose care I was entrusted by my uncle. Dear aunt, this is my Lady Levett. Mrs. Esther Pimpernel, madam, hath done me the singular kindness of calling me her niece."

"My niece and daughter by adoption," said that kind lady. "Your ladyship will be pleased, out of your goodness of heart, to hear the best report of this dear child's health and conduct. The good principles, my lady, which she learned of you and of her lamented father, have borne fruit in virtues of obedience and duty."

Both ladies made a deep reverence. Then said Lady Levett—"I assure you, my dear madam, I looked for nothing less in this dear child. From such a father as was hers, could aught but good descend? Madam, I desire your better acquaintance. For Kitty's sake, I hope we may be friends."

"Why," said Sir Robert, "we are friends already. Kitty, thou art grown: thou art a fine girl. I warrant we shall have breaking of hearts before all is done. Epsom Wells was never so full of gallants. Well, breaking of hearts is rare sport, and seldom hurts the men, though they make so great a coil about it in their rhymes and nonsense. But have a care, both of you: sometimes the girls get their own little cockleshells of hearts broken in earnest."

"I should like to see the man among them all who could break my heart," said Nancy pertly, laughing.

"Yours?" her father asked, tapping her pretty rosy cheek. "It is such a little one, no one can find it: nevertheless, lass, it is big enough to carry all thy father's in it, big as he is."

Then we began to ask questions all together. I to inquire after the village and the hall, the church, the ponies, the garden, the hounds, the fruit, all the things we used to think about: and Will, they told me, was at home, but was coming to the Wells for certain races in which he would himself ride. Harry Temple was gone to London, but would perhaps come to Epsom as soon as he knew who was there. Why had I written not one single letter?

I blushed and hung my head. I could not tell the truth, for the sake of Mrs. Esther, how I was ashamed at first to speak of the place in which I found myself, and afterwards was afraid; but I should have to explain my silence.

"It was not," I stammered, "that I was ungrateful to your ladyship for all your kindness. But things were strange at first, and there was nothing that I could take any pleasure in telling your ladyship. And a London letter from a simple girl, who can send no news of the great world, is a worthless thing to deliver by the post."

"Nay, child," said Lady Levett, "we should not have grudged the charge for good tidings of thy welfare."

"Our Kitty," said Mrs. Esther, colouring a little, for it is never pleasant to help at concealing, dissembling, or falsifying things, "has had a busy time of late. Your ladyship knows, doubtless, that her education was not completed. We have had masters and teachers of dancing, music, deportment, and the like during the last few months, and I trust that we shall find she will do credit to the instruction she has received. Meanwhile I have, for reasons which it would not interest your ladyship to learn, been living in great retirement. We had a lodging lately in Red Lion Street, not far from the Foundling Hospital, where the air is good and the situation quiet."

We fell, presently, into a sort of procession. First went Lady Levett and Mrs. Esther (I overheard the latter speaking at length of her father, the Lord Mayor, of her grandfather, also the Lord Mayor, and of her last visit to Epsom), then came Nancy, Sir Robert, who held my hand, and myself. The music, which had stopped during prayers, began again now. The Terrace was crowded with the visitors, and Nancy began to point them out to me as we walked along.

"Look, child—oh! how beautiful you have grown!—there is Mr. Pagoda Tree—it is really Samuel Tree, or Obadiah Tree, or, I think, Crabapple Tree, but they all call him Pagoda Tree: he has made a quarter of a million in Bengal, and is come running to Bath, Epsom and Tunbridge, in search of a wife. With all his money I, for one, would not have him, the yellow little Nabob! He has five-and-twenty blacks at his lodgings, and they say he sticks dinner-knives into them if his curry be not hot enough. There goes the Dean of St. Sepulchre's. He is come to drink the waters, which are good for a stomach enfeebled by great dinners; there is no better fox-hunter in the county, and no finer judge of port. Pity to be seventy years old when one has all the will and the power to go on doing good to the Christian Church by fox-hunting and drinking"—he was certainly a very red-faced divine, who looked as if this world was more in his thoughts than the next, where, so far as we know, fox-hunting will not be practised and port will not be held in esteem. "You see yonder little fribble, my dear—do not look at him, or it will make him think the better of himself: he is a haberdasher from town, who pretends to be a Templar. A fribble, Kitty—oh! you innocent, tall, beautiful creature!—a fribble is a thing made up of rags, wig, ruffles, wind, froth, amber cane, paint, powder, coat-skirts and sword. Nothing else, I assure you. No brains, no heart, no ears, no taste, nothing. There are many fribbles at the Wells, who will dance with you, talk to you, and—if you have enough money—would like to run away with you. Don't throw yourself away on a fribble, Kitty. And don't run away with anybody. Nothing so uncomfortable.

"That gallant youth in the red-coat is an officer, who had better be with his colours in America than showing his scarlet at the Wells. Yet he is a pretty fellow, is he not? Here are more clergymen——" One of them somewhat reminded me of my uncle, for he wore, like him, a full wig, a cassock of silk, and a flowing gown; also, he carried his head with the assurance which belongs to one who is a teacher of men, and respects his own wisdom. But he differed from my uncle in being sleek, which the famous Chaplain of the Fleet certainly was not. He dropped his eyes as he went, inwardly rapt, no doubt, by heavenly thoughts.

"That," Nancy went on, "is the great Court preacher, the Reverend Bellamour Parolles, Master of Arts. The shabby divine beside him is the Vicar of Sissinghurst, in Kent, who is here to drink the waters for a complaint that troubles the poor man. What a difference!"

The country parson went dressed in a grey-striped calamanco nightgown; he wore a wig which had once been white, but was now, by the influence of this uncertain climate, turned to a pale orange; his brown hat was encompassed by a black hatband; his bands, which might have been cleaner, decently retired under the shadow of his chin; his grey stockings were darned with blue worsted. As they walked together it seemed to me that the country parson was saying to the crowd: "You see—I am in rags; I go in darns, patches, and poverty; yet by my sacred profession and my learning, I am the equal of my brother in silk." While the more prosperous one might have been thought to say: "Behold the brotherhood and equality of the Church, when I, the great and fashionable, know no difference between myself and my humble brethren!"

In the afternoon and evening there was, however, this difference, that the town parson was seen at the Assembly Rooms among the ladies, while his country brother might have been seen at the Crown, over a pipe and a brown George full of strong October.

Then Nancy went on to point out more of the visitors. There were merchants, well known on the Royal Exchange; courtiers from St. James's; country gentlemen, with their madams, brave in muslin pinners and sarsnet hoods, from estates remote from the great town, where they had never ceased to consider themselves the feudal lords of the people as well as the land: there were younger sons full of talk about horses and hounds: there were doctors in black, with bag-wigs: there were lawyers in vacation, their faces as full of sharpness as is the face of a fox: there were young fellows not yet launched upon the fashionable world, who looked on with the shyness and impudence of youth, trying to catch the trick of dress, manner and carriage which marks the perfect beau; there were old fellows, like Mr. Walsingham, who sat on the benches, or ran about, proud of their activity, in attendance on the ladies. It was indeed a motley crew.

"They say that Epsom has come into fashion again," Nancy went on. "I know not. Tunbridge is a dangerous rival. Yet this year the place is full. That young man coming to speak to me you may distinguish by your acquaintance, my dear."

What a distinction! "He is—I hope your lordship is well this morning—he is the young Lord Eardesley, whose father is but just dead. He is a Virginian by birth, and all his fortune, with which the family estates have been recovered, was made by tobacco on his plantations. He has hundreds of negro slaves, besides convicts. Yet he is of grave and serious disposition, and abhors the smell of a pipe. Peggy Baker thinks to catch his lordship. Yet coronets are not so easily won."

She stopped again to speak to some ladies of her acquaintance.

"Well, my dear, as for our manner of life here, it is the same as at all watering-places. We dress and undress: we meet at church, and on the Terrace and the New Parade, and the Assembly Rooms: we go to the Downs to see races before dinner and after dinner: we talk scandal: we say wicked things about each other: we try to catch the eyes of the men: we hate each other with malice and uncharitableness: we raffle: we gamble: we listen to the music: we exchange pretty nothings with the beaux: we find out all the stories about everybody here: and we dance at the Assembly."

She stopped to breathe.

"This is a rattle," said Sir Robert, "which never stops—like the clack of the water-wheel. Go on, Nan."

"One of our amusements," she went on, tossing her little head, "is to buy strawberries, cherries, vegetables, salad, fowls and ducks of the higglers who bring them to the market, or carry them round to the houses of the town. The gentlemen, I observe, derive a peculiar satisfaction in chucking those of the higglers who are young and good-looking under the chin. This, I confess, is a pleasure which I cannot for my own part understand."

"Saucy baggage!" said her father.

"You and I, Kitty," she continued, "who do not want to chuck farmers' daughters under the chin, may, when we are tired of the races or the promenade, take an airing in a coach, or watch the raffling, or the card-players. Here they play cards all day long, except on Sunday. Or we may go to the book-shop and hear the latest scandal: or we may go home and trim our own things and talk about frocks, and patches, and poetry, and lace, and lovers. But, for Heaven's sake, Kitty, do not, in this censorious place, make that pretty face too cheap, and let no one follow you on the Terrace but the best of the company."

"Good advice," said Sir Robert. "This girl of mine has got her father's head."

"As for cards," Nancy went on, taking no notice of her father's interruption, "the tables are always laid in the Assembly Room: the ladies mostly play at quadrille, and the gentlemen at whist; but there are tables for hazard, lansquenet, faro, and baccarat, where all comers are welcome, provided they have got money to lose and can lose it without also losing their temper, a thing we women throw away daily, and lose without regarding it, so cheap and abundant a commodity it is. My dear, so long as I value my face, I will never touch the odious delightful things. Yet the joy of winning your enemy's money! Oh! oh! And the dreadful grief to lose your own!

"There is a concert this evening. I would not advise you to attend it, but to wait for Monday's ball—there to make your first appearance. I shall go, because some of my swains are going to play with the paid musicians; and of course I look to see them break down and spoil the whole music, to their great confusion.

"But Monday—Monday is our day of days. All Sunday we think about it, and cannot say our prayers for thinking of the dear delightful day. And what the clergyman preaches about none of us know, for wishing the day was here. On Monday we have a great public breakfast to begin with: the gentry come to it from all the country-side, with the great people from Durdans: in fine weather we breakfast under the trees upon the Terrace while the music plays. You will find it pleasant to take your chocolate to the strains of flute and clarinet, French horn and hautboy; the sunshine raises the spirits, and the music fills the head with pretty fancies. Besides, every girl likes to be surrounded by tall fellows who, though we care not a pin for one of them, are useful for providing conversation, cakes, and creams, telling stories, saying gallant things, fetching, carrying, and making Peggy Baker jealous. On Monday, too, there are always matches on the Downs: we pretend to be interested in the horses: we come back to dinner and a concert: in the afternoon some of the gentlemen give tea and chocolate; and at six o'clock, the fiddles tune up—oh, the delicious scraping!—we all take our places: and then begins—oh! oh! oh!—the dear, delightful ball! My child, let Miss Peggy Baker dress her best, put on her finest airs, and swim about with her most languishing sprawl, I know who shall outshine her, and be the Queen of the Wells."

"Yourself, dear Nancy?"

"No; not myself, dear Nancy," she replied, imitating. "Oh! you well may blush for shame, pretty hypocrite! 'Tis yourself, dear Kitty, that I mean. You shall burst upon their astonished gaze like Venus rising from the sea in our picture at home, only better dressed than that poor creature!"

Just then a young lady, with the largest hoop I had ever seen, with patches and powder, and accompanied by three or four gentlemen, came slowly along the walk. As she drew near she looked at me with curiosity. She was a tall girl—nearly as tall as myself—with features rather larger than ordinary, and as she moved I understood what Nancy meant by languishing and swimming.

Nancy ran to meet her, taking her by both hands, and affecting a mighty joy.

"Dear Miss Peggy," she began, "I am charmed to see you looking so well and lovely. How that dress becomes your shape! with what an air sits that hat!"

"Oh, Miss Nancy!" Miss Peggy swam and languished, agitating her fan and half shutting her eyes, which were very large and limpid. "Praise from such a judge of beauty and dress as yourself is rare indeed. What should we poor women do without the discrimination of our own sex. Men have no discernment. A well-dressed woman and a draggletail are all one to them."

"Not all men, dear Miss Peggy," continued Nancy, her eyes sparkling. "Mr. Walsingham was only saying this morning that you are, like himself, a proof of the salubrity of the Wells, since it is now the fifth season——"

"The third, dear child," Miss Peggy interrupted, with a tap of her fan on Nancy's knuckles—indeed she deserved it. "I am very much obliged to Mr. Walsingham, whose tongue is free with all the ladies at the Wells. It is but yesterday since he said of you——"

"This is my friend, Miss Kitty Pleydell," said Nancy quickly, rubbing her knuckles. "Kitty, my dear, you have heard of the beautiful Peggy Baker, last year the Toast of Tunbridge Wells, and the year before the Toast of Bath. Up to the present she has been our pride. On Monday evening you shall see her in her bravest attire, the centre of attraction, envied by us poor homely creatures, who have to content ourselves with the rustic beaux, the parsons, the lawyers, and the half-pay officers."

Now, whether this artful girl did it on purpose, or whether it was by accident, I know not: but every word of this speech contained an innuendo against poor Miss Peggy. For it was true that she had been for two years following a Toast, but she was still unmarried, and without a lover, though she had so many men for ever in her train; and it was also true that among her courtiers at Epsom, the little band who held back while the ladies talked, there were, as I afterwards learned, at least three rustic beaux, two lawyers, a fashionable parson, and six half-pay officers. However, she disguised whatever resentment she might have felt, very kindly bade me welcome to the Wells, hoped that I should enjoy the place, told Nancy that her tongue run away with her, and that she was a saucy little baggage, tapped her knuckles for the second time with her fan, and moved away.

When Nancy had finished telling me of the amusements of the place and the people—I omit most of what she said as to the people because, although doubtless true, the stories did not redound to their credit, and may now very well be forgotten—we left the Terrace, Sir Robert now joining madam, and looked at the stalls and booths which were ranged along the side. They were full of pretty things exhibited for sale, and instead of rude prentice boys for salesmen they were good-looking girls, with whom some of the gentlemen were talking and laughing.

"More chin-chucking, my dear," said Nancy.

It was the fashion to have a lottery at almost every stall, so that when you bought anything you received a ticket with your purchase, which entitled you to a chance of the prize. When you chose a bottle of scent, the girl who gave it you handed with it a ticket which gave you the chance of winning five guineas: with a pair of stockings came a ticket for a ten-guinea lottery. It was the same thing with all the shops. A leg of mutton bought at the butcher's might procure for the purchaser the sum of twenty guineas; the barber who dressed your hair presented you with a chance for his five-guinea draw; the very taverns and ordinaries had their lotteries, so that for every sixpenny plate of boiled beef a 'prentice had his chance with the rest, and might win a guinea; you ordered a dozen oysters, and they came with the fishmonger's compliments and a ticket for his lottery, the first prize of which would be two guineas, the drawing to take place on such a day, with auditors appointed to see all fair, and school children named to pull out the tickets; even the woman who sold apples and cherries in a basket loudly bellowed along the street that she had a half-crown draw, a five-shilling draw, and so on. Every one of us treasured up the tickets, but I never met any who won. Yet we had the pleasure of attending the drawing, dreaming of lucky numbers, and spending our prizes beforehand. I am sure that Nancy must have spent in this way many hundreds of pounds during the season, and by talking over all the fine things she would buy, the way in which their exhibition upon her little figure would excite the passion of envy in the breast of Peggy Baker and others, and her own importance thus bedecked, she had quite as much pleasure out of her imaginary winnings as if they had been real ones. It is a happy circumstance for mankind that they are able to enjoy what they never can possess, and to be, in imagination, the great, the glorious, the rich, the powerful personages which they can never, in the situation wherein Providence has placed them, hope to become.

Presently we went home to dinner, which was served for us by Cicely Crump. After dinner, while Mrs. Esther dozed, Cicely told me her history. Her father, she said, had been a substantial tradesman in Cheapside, and though little of stature, was in his youth a man of the most determined courage and resolution. When only just out of his apprenticeship he fell in love with a beautiful young lady named Jenny Medlicott (daughter of the same Alderman Medlicott whose ruin brought poor Mrs. Esther to destruction): as he knew that he could never get the consent of the alderman, being poor and of obscure birth, and knowing besides that all is fair in love, this lad of mettle represented himself to his nymph as a young gentleman of the Temple, son of a country squire. In this disguise he persuaded her to run away with him, and they were married. But when they returned to London they found that the alderman was ruined, and gone off his head. Therefore they separated, the lady going to Virginia with Lady Eardesley, mother of the young lord now at Epsom, and the husband going back to the shop. After the death of poor Jenny he married again. "And," said Cicely, "though my mother is no gentlewoman, one cannot but feel that she might have been Miss Jenny Medlicott herself had things turned out differently. And that makes all of us hold up our heads. And as for poor father, he never forgot his first wife, and was always pleased to relate how he ran away with her all the way to Scotland, armed to the teeth, and ready, for her sake, to fight a dozen highwaymen. Such a resolute spirit he had!"

Then Nancy Levett came, bringing with her a milliner, Mrs. Bergamot.

"Kitty," she cried, "I cannot rest for thinking of your first ball, and I have brought you Mrs. Bergamot to advise. My dear, you *must* be well dressed." Then she whispered: "Do you want money, dear? I have some."

I told her I had as much as a hundred and twenty guineas, at which she screamed with delight.

"Kitty!" she cried again, clasping my hands. "A hundred guineas! a hundred guineas! and twenty more! My dear, that odd twenty, that poor overflowing of thy rich measure, is the utmost I could get for this season at the Wells. Oh! happy, happy girl, to have such a face, such a shape, such eyes, such hair, such hands and feet, and a hundred and twenty guineas to set all off!"

She sat down, clasped her hands, and raised her eyes to Heaven as if in thankfulness. I think I see her now, the little dainty merry maid, so arch, so apt, sitting before me with a look which might be of envy or of joy. She had eyes so bright, a mouth so little, dimples so cunning, a cheek so rosy and a chin so rounded, that one could not choose but love her.

"Miss Pleydell," she said to the milliner, "has not brought all her things from London. You must get what she wants at once, for Monday's ball. Now, let us see."

Then we held a parliament of four, counting Cicely, over the great question of my frocks. Nancy was prime minister, and did all the talking, turning over the things.

"Let me see, Mrs. Bergamot. Fetch us, if you have them—what you have—in flowered brocades—all colours—violet, pink, Italian posies, rose, myrtle, jessamine, anything; a watered tabby would become you, Kitty; any painted lawns,—silks and satins would be almost too old for you: do not forget the patches *à la grecque*—Kitty, be very careful of the patches; gauzes, what you have, Mrs. Bergamot; we want more hoods, a feathered muff, stomacher, Paris nets, *eau de Chypre* or *eau de luce*, whichever you have; ear-rings are no use to you, my poor child. Pity that they did not pierce your ears: see the little drops dangling at mine. At any rate, thank Heaven that we neither of us want vermilion for the cheeks. Poor Peggy! she paints these two years and more. Ruffs, Mrs. Bergamot, and tippets, cardinals, any pretty thing in sarsnets, and what you have in purple. Kitty, purple is your colour. You shall have a dress all purple for the next ball. Ah! if I could carry purple! But you, Kitty, with your height and figure—stand up, child—why, she will be Juno herself!"

"Truly," said the dressmaker, "as for Miss Pleydell, purple has come into fashion in pudding-time, as folk say."

"A pretty woman," Nancy went on, examining me as if I had been a dummy, "not a pretty 'little thing' like me, is as rare in Epsom as a black swan or a white blackbird, or green yellow-hammer, or a red blue tit."

When the dressmaker was gone, and we were left alone, Nancy began again, out of her great experience, to talk of the place we were in.

"My dear," she said, "before one's father one cannot say all that one would wish"—could such wisdom be possible at seventeen-and-a-half? "This is a very shocking and wicked place; we used to be taught that girls ought to sit in a corner, after they had put on their best things, and wait to be spoken to, and not to think about attracting the men; and not, indeed, to think about the men at all, save in their own room, where they might perhaps pray that if there were any men in the world not addicted to gambling, drinking, cursing, hunting, fighting, and striking, those men might be led by Heaven to cast eyes of love upon them. Oh!"—here she held up her hands and shook her head just like a woman four times her age, and steeped in experience—"in this place it is not long that the girls sit in a corner, and, indeed, I do not greatly love corners myself; but the very wives, the matrons, the married women, my dear,"—her voice rose with each word till it had mounted nearly to the top of the possible scale,—"are coquettes, who interfere with the girls, and would have the gallants dangling at their heels. As for their husbands, they are the last persons considered worthy of their notice; they put on their dresses and deck themselves out to please anybody rather than the persons whom it should be their only study to please."

"Nancy," I whispered, "when you are married, will you never, never dress to please anybody but your husband?"

"Why," she replied, "my father, my mother, my children (if I have any), my friends will be pleased to see me go fine. But not for lovers—oh!"

We agreed that would-be lovers should be received and properly dealt with before marriage.

"Bashfulness, here," continued the pretty moralist, "is—Heaven help us!—lack of breeding; what goes down is defiance of manners and modesty. Propriety is laughed at; noise is wit; laughter is repartee; most of the women gamble; nearly all are in debt; nobody reads anything serious; and we backbite each other perpetually."

I know not what had put her in so strange a mood for moralising.

"However," she said, "now that you are come, we shall get on better. I have made up my mind that you are to be the Toast of the season. I shall set you off, because you are brown and I am fair; you are tall, and I am short; you are grave, and I am merry; you are thoughtful, and I am silly; you have brown eyes, and I have blue. We will have none but the best men about us; we will set such an example as will shame the hoydens of girls and tame the Mohocks among the men. Miss Lamb of Hackney, who thinks herself a beauty, will then be ashamed to jump about and scream at the Assembly with nothing over her skinny shoulders. Peggy Baker shall have after her none but the married men (who are of no possible use except to spoil a girl's reputation), although she sighs and swims and sprawls with her eyes half shut. Do you know that she sat for her portrait to Zincke, at Marylebone Gardens, as Anne Boleyn, and was painted with eyelashes down to the corners of her mouth?"

"Nancy," I cried, "you are jealous of Miss Peggy Baker."

She laughed, and talked of something else. From this I conjectured that Peggy had said or reported something which offended her. What had really been said, I learned afterwards, was that Nancy was running after Lord Eardesley, which was unkind as well as untrue.

"Last year," she said, "after you went away, nothing would serve my mother but a visit to Bath. It is not so gay as Tunbridge Wells, because the company are mostly country folk, like ourselves, who stand upon their dignity; but it is better than this place, where there are so many London cits that it passes one's patience, sometimes, to see their manners"—really, Nancy must have been seriously put out. "However, I dare say Bath is as wicked as any of the watering towns, when you come to know it. I liked the bathing. What do you think, Kitty, of everybody promenading in the water up to their chins—that is to say, the little people, like me, up to their noses (only I wore pattens to make myself higher), and the tall men up to their shoulders, in hot water? Everybody frolicking, flirting, and chattering, while japanned trays float about covered with confectionery, tea, oils, and perfumes for the ladies; and when you go away, your chair is nothing but a tub full of hot water, in which you are carried home. We stayed there all July and August, though my mother would have kept me, if she could, from the baths till I was bigger. Harry Temple was there, too, part of the time."

"And how doth Harry?"

"He is a good honest fellow," said Nancy, "though conceited and a prig; his mouth full of learned words, and his head full of books. He seemed to pine after your departure, Kitty, but soon recovered himself, and now eats and drinks again as before. He found some congenial spirits from Oxford at Bath, and they used to talk of Art, and pictures (when any one was listening), and bronzes, and all sorts of things that we poor people know nothing of."

Then she told me how Harry had made a poem upon me, after my departure, which he turned into Latin, Greek, and Italian, and had given Nancy a copy. And how Will had christened one pup Kitty, and another Pleydell, and a third Kitty Pleydell, and was casting around how to give a fourth puppy my name as well.

It seemed so long ago that I had almost forgotten poor rustic Will, with his red face, his short sturdy figure, and his determination.

"Dear Kitty," said Nancy, "if thou couldst take a fancy for our Will—he is a brave lad, though dull of parts and slow of apprehension. As for Harry"—here she stopped, and blushed.

I remembered my secret, and blushed as well (but for guilt and shame); while poor Nancy blushed in maiden modesty.

"Dear Nancy," I replied, kissing her, "believe me, but I could never marry your brother Will. And as for Harry——"

"As for Harry," she echoed, with downcast eyes.

It was easy to read her secret, though she could not guess mine.

"As for Harry," I said, "where could he be better bestowed than——"

Here I kissed her again, and said no more, because between two women what more need be said?

Alas! I had quite forgotten—indeed, I never suspected—that I was actually engaged to become the wife of both Harry and Will, who was at this same time the wife of Lord Chudleigh. And both men were on their way to Epsom to claim the promise.

CHAPTER IV.

HOW KITTY WENT TO HER FIRST BALL.

If I were to write all that Nancy said on Saturday afternoon it would fill a volume; and if I were to write down all that we four said about my dress for the Monday ball, it would take four volumes at least, so nimbly ran our tongues. It was determined, however, that the purple frock should be put in hand at once, with ribbons and everything to correspond; but that for this occasion, as time pressed, we would take my best frock, a new white satin, never before worn. Mrs. Bergamot would dress me, and the hairdresser was engaged for two o'clock.

"Everything," said Nancy, "depends upon the first impression. Already the world is agog to see the beautiful Miss Pleydell dressed. As for me, my dear, nobody noticed my first appearance at all. And yet I thought I looked very nice. To be sure, a person of my inches cannot expect to command attention. I am feeling my way, however, and though I am little, my tongue is sharp. After Monday we will have our court, you and I, to ourselves. The men will be at our feet, and Peggy may lie all on a rock deploring."

I asked her afterwards how she could speak so openly before this milliner, who would probably tell all the town what she had said.

"My dear," she replied sharply, "your Nancy is not altogether a goose, and she knows what she is doing. Mrs. Bergamot is a most trustworthy person. I quite rely upon her. I have never known her fail in her duties as town-crier. She will spread it abroad that you have brought a hundred guineas and more to spend in frocks and things; she will tell everybody that you have ordered a purple velvet in the first fashion; she will not fail to repeat that you and I together mean to lead the company at the Wells; she will probably tell Peggy that she may go and sit on a rock deploring; and she will inform Miss Lamb of Hackney that her shoulders are skinny. They cannot hate us worse than they do, therefore we will make them fear us."

What a little spitfire was this Nancy of mine!

To the religious and the sober, Sunday is a day of serious meditation as well as of rest: to me, the Sunday before the ball was a day of such worldly tumult as should afford ample room for repentance in these later years. Unhappily, we repent but seldom of these youthful sins. Yet, when we went to church, the organ seemed to play a minuet, the hymns they sang might have been a hey or a jig in a country dance, and the sermon of the preacher might have been a discourse on the pleasures and enjoyments of the world, so rapt was my mind in contemplation of these vanities.

The service over, we walked out through a lane of the godless men who had not gone to church. Nancy came after me very demure, carrying her Prayer-book, her eyes cast down as if rapt in heavenly meditation. But her thoughts were as worldly as my own, and she presently found an opportunity of whispering that Peggy Baker had thrown glances of the greatest ferocity from her pew at herself and me, that Mrs. Bergamot had already spread the news about, and that the concourse of men at the door of the sacred place was entirely on my account. "If it was not Sunday," she added, "and if it were not for the crowd around us, I should dance and sing."

The time for opening the ball was six, at which time dancing began, and was continued until eleven, according to the laws wisely laid down by that public benefactor and accomplished Amphitryon, Mr. Nash, who effected so much improvement for Bath and Tunbridge that his rules were adopted for all other watering-places. Before his time there were no fixed hours or fixed prices, the laws of precedence were badly observed, the gentlemen wore their swords, and disputes, which sometimes ended in duels, were frequent and unseemly. Now, however, nothing could be more orderly than the manner of conducting the entertainment. The charge for admission was half-a-crown for gentlemen, and one shilling for ladies; no swords were permitted, and the ball was opened by the gentleman of the highest rank in the room. At Epsom, a country squire or a city knight was generally the best that could be procured, whereas at Bath an earl was not uncommon, and even a duke was sometimes seen.

My hairdresser, who was, on these occasions, engaged from six o'clock in the morning until six in the evening, was fortunately able to give me half an hour at two o'clock, so that I had not more than four hours or so to sit without moving my head. This was a very happy circumstance, many ladies having to be dressed early in the morning, so that for the whole day they could neither walk about nor move for fear of the structure toppling over altogether. Mrs. Bergamot herself dressed me. I wore my white satin frock over a great hoop with fine new point-lace for tuckers; my kerchief and ruffles were in lace, and I had on a pearl and coral necklace, presented to me by Mrs. Esther, who was contented to wear a black ribbon round her neck in order that I might go the finer. As for herself, she wore a rich brocade, which greatly became her and made her look like a countess.

"Nay, child," she said, "not a countess, but like a gentlewoman, as hath ever been my simple ambition, and the daughter of a great London merchant."

But to think that in every house in Epsom there was one girl, at least, or perhaps two, who were spending as much time and thought as myself upon the decoration of our persons for this ball! And what chance had I of distinction among so many fine women of less rustic breeding?

"She will do, Mrs. Bergamot, I think," said Mrs. Esther.

"Madam," replied the dressmaker, who no doubt considered it part of her business to flatter her customers, "Madam, I dare swear that there hath not appeared—I do not say at Epsom alone, but at Tunbridge and at Bath—so beautiful a creature in the memory of man. Mr. Walsingham, who remembers all the beauties for fifty years, declares that Miss Kitty surpasses all. Straight as a lance, madam, and shapely as a statue, with such a face as will deal havoc and destruction among the men."

Mrs. Esther nodded her head and laughed. Then she shook her head and looked grave.

"We must not become vain, Kitty," she said. "Beauty is but skin-deep; it fades like the flowers: think only of virtue and goodness, which never fade. And yet, child, thou art young: thou art beautiful: be happy in the sunshine, as is meet. Thank Heaven for sunshine!"

She pressed my hand in hers, and the tears rose to her eyes. Was she thinking of her own youth, which had been so unhappy?

When Mrs. Bergamot left us, she confessed to me that, like me, she had been in a strange agitation of spirit at the contemplation of this assembly.

"It is thirty years," she said, "since I have been in a gay crowd. I thought that such a thing as the sight of youth and happiness would never come to me again. And to think that, after all these years, I should go back to the very room where, in 1720, amid a crowd of adventurers, speculators, and gamblers, who were going to ruin us all, I attended my last ball!"

This was while we were waiting for the chairs.

"I think," she went on, in her soft voice, which was like the rippling of a stream, "that my child will do credit to herself. I am glad that you have kept your neck covered, my dear. I would rather see you go modest than fine. I hope that Lady Levett will be there before us. In such cases as this the sight of a friend gives us, as it were, an encouragement: it is like a prop to lean against. I hope the chairs will not be late. On the other hand, one would not, surely, arrive too early. My dear, I am trembling all over. Are you sure you have forgotten none of your steps? Ah! if no one were to ask you to dance, I should die of shame and mortification! But they will—oh! they will. My Kitty is too beautiful to sit among the crowd of lookers-on."

Here came Cicely, running to tell us that the chairs were below, and that the men swore they could not wait.

"A minute—one minute only. Dear, dear, how quick the girl is! Cicely, take one last look at Miss Kitty. Do you think, child, she has got everything, and is properly dressed?"

"Quite properly, madam. No lady in the assembly will shine like Miss Pleydell."

"Good girl. And, Cicely, if you see that anything is wanting in my dress, do not scruple to tell me. Young eyes are sometimes quicker than old ones."

"Nothing, madam. Your ladyship is dressed in the fashion."

Then the chairmen, who, like all their tribe, were unmannerly fellows, bellowed that they would wait no longer, and we descended the stairs. One would have been ashamed to confess the fact, but it actually was the very first time I had ever sat in a chair. The shaking was extremely disagreeable, and one could not, at the beginning, feel anything but pity for the poor men who made their living by carrying about the heavy bodies of people too fine or too lazy to walk. However, that feeling soon wore off: just as the West Indian and Virginian planters learn by degrees to believe that their negro slaves like to work in the fields, are thankful for the lash, and prefer digging under a hot sun to sleeping in the shade.

We arrived at the Assembly Rooms a few minutes before six. The rooms were already crowded: the curtains were drawn, and the light of day excluded. But in its place there was a ravishing display of wax candles, arranged upon the walls on sconces, or hanging from the ceiling. The musicians in the gallery were already beginning, as is their wont, to tune their instruments, twanging and blowing, just as a preacher begins with a preliminary hem.

My eyes swam as I surveyed the brilliant gathering; for a moment I held Mrs. Esther by the wrist, and could say nothing nor move. I felt like an actress making her appearance for the first time upon the stage, and terrified, for the moment, by the faces looking up, curious and critical, from the crowded pit and glittering boxes.

At that moment Lady Levett arrived with her party. I think Sir Robert saw our distress and my guardian's anxiety to appear at her ease, for he kindly took Mrs. Esther by the hand, and led her, as if she were the greatest lady in the assembly, to the upper end, while Nancy and I followed after.

"O Kitty!" she whispered; "there is no one half so beautiful as you—no one in all the room! How the men stare! Did they never see a pretty woman before? Wait in patience for a little, ye would-be lovers, till your betters are served. Peggy Baker, my dear, you will burst with envy. Look! Here she comes with her courtiers."

In fact, Miss Baker herself here appeared with her mother, surrounded by three or four gentlemen, who hovered about her, and she languidly advanced up the room.

The Chaplain of the Fleet

She came straight to us, and, after saluting Lady Levett and Mrs. Esther, held out her hand to Nancy and curtseyed to me.

"You look charming to-night, dear Miss Nancy. That frock of yours—one is never tired of it."

"And you—oh, dear Miss Peggy!"

Nancy turned white, because her frock was really rather an old one.

"It is good wearing stuff," said Miss Peggy. "Yet I had thought that mode gone out."

"So it had, my dear," said Nancy sharply; "and I believe it went out five seasons ago. That is longer than I can recollect. But it has come back again. Fashions do revive, sometimes."

This was a very ill-natured thing to say, and made poor Miss Peggy wince and colour, and she did not retaliate, because, I suppose, she could think of nothing to say.

Then old Mr. Walsingham, who had constituted himself the director of the ceremonies, appeared. He was dressed in the most beautiful crimson silk coat, lined with white, and purple waistcoat, and he came slowly up the hall, with a gentleman whose bearing was as great as his own, but whose years were less.

"It is young Lord Chudleigh," whispered Peggy Baker, fanning herself anxiously. "He has come from Durdans with his party."

Lord Chudleigh!

Heavens! To meet in such a manner, in such a place, my own husband!

"What is the matter, Kitty dear?" asked Nancy. "You turned quite pale. Bite your lips, my dear, to get the colour back."

"It is nothing. I am faint with the heat and the lights, I suppose. Do not take notice of me."

Peggy Baker assumed an air of languor and sensibility, which, though extremely fine, was perhaps over-acted.

"Lord Chudleigh," she said, "is of course the person of the highest distinction in the room. He will invite, I presume, Lady Levett to open the ball with the first minuet. If Lady Levett declines, he will be free to select another partner."

In fact, Mr. Walsingham conducted Lord Chudleigh to Lady Levett, and presented him to her. Her ladyship excused herself on the ground that her dancing days were over, which was of course expected. His lordship then said a few words to Mr. Walsingham, who nodded, smiled, and conducted him to the little group composed of Nancy, Peggy Baker, and myself. But he presented his lordship—to me!

"Since," he said, while the room went round with me, "since Lady Levett will not condescend to open the ball with your lordship, I beg to present you to Miss Kitty Pleydell, who appears to-night, for the first time, at our assembly; and, I am assured, for the first time in any assembly. My lord, the sun, when he rises in splendour, dims the light of the moon and stars. Miss Kitty, I would I were fifty years younger, that I might challenge this happy young gentleman for the honour of the dance."

Then Lord Chudleigh spoke. I remembered his voice: a deep shame fell upon my soul, thinking where and how I had heard that voice before.

"Miss Pleydell," he said, bowing low, "I humbly desire the honour of opening the ball with you."

It was time to rally my spirits, for the eyes of all the company were upon us. There was only one thing to do—to forget for the moment what was past, and address myself to the future.

I can look back upon the evening with pride, because I remember how I was able to push away shame and remembrance, and to think, for the moment, about my steps and my partner.

Twang, twang, twang, went the fiddles. The conductor raised his wand. The music crashed and rang about the room.

"Courage, Kitty!" whispered Nancy. "Courage! Think you are at home."

The hall was cleared now, and the people stood round in a triple circle, watching, while my lord, his hat beneath his arm, offered me his hand, and led me into the middle of the room.

The last things I observed as I went with him were Mrs. Esther, wiping away what looked like a little tear of pride, and Peggy Baker, with red face, fanning herself violently. Poor Peggy! Last year it was she who would have taken the place of the most distinguished lady in the company!

They told me afterwards that I acquitted myself creditably. I *would* not permit myself to think under what different circumstances that hand had once before held mine. I would not break down before the eyes of so many people, and with Peggy Baker standing by, ready to condole with me on my discomfiture. But I could not bring myself to look in the face of my partner: and that dance was accomplished with eyes down-dropped.

Oh! it was over at last; the dance which was to me the most anxious, the most delightful, the most painful, that ever girl danced in all this world! And what do you think strengthened my heart the while? It was the strangest thing: but I thought of a certain verse in a certain old history, and I repeated to myself, as one says things when one is troubled:

"Now the king loved Esther above all the women, and she obtained grace and favour in his sight: so that he set the royal crown upon her head."

"Child," whispered Mrs. Esther, her face aglow with pleasure and pride, "we are all proud of you."

"Kitty," said Lady Levett, who was more critical, because she knew more of the polite world, "you acquitted yourself creditably. Next time, do not be afraid to look your partner in the face. My lord, I trust that Miss Pleydell's performance has made you congratulate yourself on my declining the honour of the minuet?"

"Your ladyship," said Lord Chudleigh, "may be assured that, if anything could compensate for that disappointment, the grace and beauty of my fair partner have effected that object."

"Gadzooks!" cried Sir Robert. "Here is a beating about the bush! Kitty, my pretty maid, no duchess could have danced better, and never a queen in Christendom is more beautiful! Say I well, my lord?"

"Excellently well, Sir Robert. You have said more than I dared; not more than I thought."

Then Mr. Walsingham came bustling to congratulate me.

"But one opinion—only one opinion, Miss Pleydell! Lady Levett, your obedient servant. Mrs. Pimpernel, I offer my congratulations on this young lady's success. I would it had been Bath, or even Tunbridge, whence the rumour of such beauty and such grace would have been more quickly carried about the country. But it will be spread abroad. There are three hundred tongues here to-night, who will talk, and three hundred pens who will write. Miss Kitty, once more I salute your Majesty—Queen of the Wells!"

Then Lord Chudleigh, and Sir Robert Levett, and the gentlemen standing round sank on one knee and bowed almost to the ground, crying—

"Queen of the Wells! Queen of the Wells!"

And Nancy, in her pretty, saucy way, ran and stood beside me laughing.

"And I am her Majesty's maid of honour. Remember that, gentlemen all!"

"The saucy baggage!" cried Sir Robert.

And Peggy Baker, for whom in this hour of triumph one felt a little pity, came too, with a curtsey and a smile which looked more like a frown.

"Miss Pleydell must accept my homage, too," she said. "We are fortunate in having one so inimitably lovely for our Queen. It makes one wonder where so much beauty could have been hidden."

I suppose she meant this as an innuendo that I was not, therefore, accustomed to such good company. I thought of Fleet Lane and the Market, and I laughed aloud.

But Lord Chudleigh was expected to dance with another lady before the ball was opened; and here was another disappointment for poor Peggy, for he led out Nancy, who took his hand with a pride and joy which did one's heart good to look at.

If I had been afraid to raise my eyes, Nancy was not; she looked in my lord's face and laughed; she talked and prattled all the time she was dancing; and she danced as if the music was too slow for her, as if she would fain have been spinning round like a school-girl when she makes cheeses, as if her limbs were springs, as if she would gladly have taken her partner by both hands and run round and round with him as she had so often done with me when we were children together, playing in the meadows beside the Hall. All the people looked on and laughed and clapped their hands; never was so merry a minuet, if that stately dance could ever be made merry. As for me, I was able to look at his face again, though that was only to begin the punishment of my crime.

What did I remember of him? A tall young man of slender figure; with cheeks red and puffed, a forehead on which the veins stood out ready to burst, a hand that shook, eyes that looked wildly round him; a dreadful, terrible, and shameful memory. But now, how changed! As for his features, I hardly recognised them at all. Yet I knew him for the same man.

Go get a cunning limner and painter. Make him draw you a face stamped with some degrading vice, or taken at the moment of committing some grievous sin against the conscience. Suppose, for instance, that the cheeks swell out with gluttony; or let the lips tremble with intemperance; or let the eyes grow keen and hawk-like with gambling: let any vice he pleases be stamped upon that face. Then let him go away and draw that face (which before was dark with sin and marked with the seal of the Devil) as it should be, pure, wise, and noble as God, who hath somewhere laid by the model and type of every created face, intended it to be. You will know it and you will know it not.

The face which I had seen was not the face of a drunkard, but of a drunken man, of a man heavy and stupid with unaccustomed drink. I had always thought of him as of a creature of whose violence (in his cups) I should go in daily terror, when it should please the Doctor to take me to my husband. Now that I saw the face again, the spirit of drunkenness gone out of it, it seemed as if the man could never stoop to weakness or folly, so strong were the features, so noble were the eyes. How could such a man, with such a face and such a bearing, go about with such a secret? But perhaps, like me, he did not suffer himself to think about it. For his face was as that of David when he was full of his great mission, or of Apollo the sun-god, or of Adonis whom the Syrian women weep, or of Troilus when he believed that Cressida was true.

To be sure, he never thought of the thing at all. He put it behind him as an evil dream: he would take no steps until he wished to be married, when he would instruct his lawyers, and they would break the bonds—which were no true bonds—asunder. If he thought at all, he would think that he was married—if that was indeed a marriage— to some poor unworthy wretch who might be set aside at pleasure: why should his thoughts ever dwell—so I said to myself with jealous bitterness—on the girl who stood before him for ten minutes, her face muffled in a hood, her eyes cast down, who placed a trembling and wicked hand in his and swore to follow his fortunes for better for worse?

Alas poor Kitty! Her case seemed sad indeed.

Then my lord finished his minuet with Nancy, and other couples advanced into the arena, and the dancing became general. Of course there was nothing but minuets until eight o'clock.

Nancy was merry. She said that her partner was delightful to dance with, partly because he was a lord—and a title, she said, gives an air of grace to any block—partly because he danced well and talked amiably.

"He is a pretty fellow, my dear," she said, "though of position too exalted for one so humble as myself. He had exhausted all his compliments upon the Queen and had none for a simple maid of honour, which I told him at parting, and it made him blush like a girl. How I love to see a man blush; it is a sign that there is yet left some remains of grace. Perhaps Lord Chudleigh is not so hardened as his fellows. Look at Peggy's languid airs: she thinks a minuet should be danced as if you were going to die the very next minute; and she rolls her eyes about as if she were fainting for a man to kiss her. My dear, Lord Chudleigh, I fear, is above us both; yet he is but a man, and all men are made of tinder, and a woman is the spark. I think he may be on fire before long, think not upon him until you find out how his affections are disposed, and whether he is free. A roving lord, at the watering-places, who is young and handsome, is as dangerous to us poor damsels, and plays as much havoc among our hearts, as Samson when he had got that jawbone, among the Philistines. A truly dreadful thing it would be"—it was wonderful that she should be saying all this in ignorance, how every word went home—"to set your affections upon a lord, and to find out afterwards that he was pledged to somebody else. Hateful thing she would be!"

While the minuets were dancing we stood and watched the gay throng. Never had I dreamed of anything so gay and animated. There were three hundred people, at least as many men as women, and all dressed in their very best. As for the ladies, it was the fashion when I was a girl for all to be powdered, but there were many modes of dressing the head. For some wore aigrettes of jewels (who could afford them) some false flowers, and some true flowers, which were pretty and becoming for a young girl: and some had coiffures *à la culbutte*, some *en dorlotte*, some *en papillon*, or *en vergette, en équivoque, en désespoir*, or *en tête de mouton*. The last was the commonest, in which there were curls all over the back of the head. And there were French curls, which looked something like eggs strung on a wire round the head, and Italian curls or scallop-shells. The petticoats were ornamented with falbalas and *pretantailles*; most ladies wore *criardes*, and all had hoops, but some wore hoops *en coupole* and some small hoops, and some looked like a state-bed on castors, and as if they had robbed the valance for the skirt and the tester for the trimmings. But there is no end to the changes of fashion. As for the gentlemen, their vanities were mostly in the wig, for though the full wig was now gone out of fashion, having given place to the neat and elegant tie-wig with a broad black ribbon and a little bag, or a queue, yet there was not wanting the full-bottomed periwig, the large flowing grizzle, and the great wig with three tails. And every kind of face, the vacant, the foolish, the sensual, the envious, the eager, the pert, the dignified, the brave, the anxious, the confident—but none so noble as that face of my lord.

"Is our Queen meditating?"

I started, for he was beside me.

"It is my first ball," I said, "and I am wondering at the pretty sight of so many happy and merry people."

"Their merriment I grant," he replied. "As for their happiness, we had better perhaps agree to take that for granted."

"I suppose we all agree to give ourselves up to the pleasures of the hour," I said. "Can we not be happy, even if we have a care which we try to hide?"

"I hope, at least," he said, "that Miss Pleydell has no cares."

I shook my head, thinking how, if all hearts were opened and all secrets known, there would be wailing instead of laughter, and my lord and myself would start asunder with shame on my part and loathing on his.

"Yes," he said; "an assembly of people to please and to be pleased is a charming sight. For a time we live in an atmosphere of ease and contentment, and bask at the feet of the Queen of Hearts."

"Oh, my lord!" I said, "do not pay me compliments: I am only used to plain truth."

"Surely that is the honest truth," he said. "To be Queen of the Wells is nothing, but to be the Queen of Hearts is everything."

"Nay, then," I returned, blushing, "I see I must put myself under the protection of Mr. Walsingham."

The old beau was hovering round, and gave me his hand with a great air of happiness.

"From me," he said, "Miss Pleydell knows that she will hear nothing but truth. The language of gallantry with a beautiful woman is pure truth."

It was eight o'clock, and country dances began. I danced one with Lord Chudleigh and one with some gentleman of Essex, whose name I forget. But I remember that next day he offered me, by letter, his hand, and eight hundred pounds a year. At nine we had tea and chocolate. Then more country dances, in which my Nancy danced with such enjoyment and happiness as made Sir Robert clap his hands and laugh aloud.

At eleven all was over, mantles, hoods, and capuchins were donned, and we walked home to our lodgings, escorted by the gentlemen. The last face I saw as we entered the house was that of my lord as he bowed farewell.

Cicely was waiting to receive us.

"O madam!" she cried, "I was looking through the door when my lord took out miss for the minuet. Oh! oh! oh! how beautiful! how grand she did it! Sure never was such a handsome pair."

"My dear," said Mrs. Esther to me, when Cicely had left us, "I believe there never was known so great a success for a first appearance. There is no doubt you are the reigning Toast of the season, child. Well, enjoy when you can, and be not spoiled by flattery, Kitty, which is vanity. Such a face, they all declare, such a figure, such eyes, such a carriage, were never before seen at Epsom. Beware of Flatterers, my dear. Where did you get such graces from? Pay no heed to the compliments of the men, child. Sure, it is the prettiest creature ever formed. They would turn thy head, my dear."

In the middle of the night I awoke from an uneasy dream. I thought that I was dancing with my lord before all the people at the assembly: they applauded loudly, and I heard them whispering: "What a noble pair! Sure Heaven hath made them for each other!" Then suddenly Peggy Baker burst through the crowd, leading by the hand my uncle: and crying: "Lord Chudleigh, I congratulate you upon your marriage! Your bride is with you, and here is the Chaplain of the Fleet, who made you happy." Then the people laughed and hissed: the Doctor lifted his great forefinger and shook it at my lord; I saw his face change from love to disgust, and with a cry I hid my shameful cheeks in my hands and fled the place.

The waking was no better than the dreaming. The husband whom I had almost forgotten, and whom to remember gave me no more than a passing pang, was here, with me, in the same town. What was I to do—how treat him—in what words to tell him, if I must tell him, the dreadful, the humiliating truth?

Or, again—a thought which pierced my breast like a knife—suppose I were condemned to see him with my own eyes, falling in love, step by step, with another woman: suppose that I were punished by perceiving that my humble and homely charms would not fix, though they might attract for a single night, his wandering eyes: oh! how could I look on in silence, and endure without a word the worst that a woman can suffer? Ah! happy Esther, whom the king loved above all women: so that he set the royal crown upon her head!

The day broke while I was lying tortured by these dreadful suspicions and fears. My window looked towards the east: I rose, opened the casement, and let in the fresh morning air. The downs rose beyond the house with deep heavy woods of elm and birch. There was already the movement and stir of life which begins with the early dawn: it is as if the wings of the birds are shaking as their pretty owners dream before they wake: as if the insects on the leaves were all together exhorting each other to fly about and enjoy the morning sun, because, haply, life being so uncertain to the insect tribe, and birds so numerous, that hour might be their last: as if the creatures of the underwood, the rabbits, hares, weasels, ferrets, snakes, and the rest were moving in their beds, and rustling the dry leaves on which they lie. Over the tree-tops spread broader and broader the red glow of the morning: the sounds of life grew more distinct; and the great sun sprang up. Then I heard a late-singing thrush break into his sweet song, which means a morning hymn of content. The other birds had mostly done their singing long before July: but near him there sang a turtle with a gentle coo which seemed to say that she had got all she wanted or could look for in life, and was happy. Truly, not the spacious firmament on high alone, but all created things do continually teach man to laud, praise, and glorify the name of the great Creator. "Whoso," says the Psalmist, "is wise and will observe these things"—but alas for our foolishness! I looked, and drank the sweetness of the air, and felt the warmth of the sun, but I thought of nothing but my husband—mine, and yet not mine, nor could he ever be mine save for such confession and shame as made my heart sick to think of. To be already in love with a man whom one had seen but twice! was it not a shame? Yet such a man! and he was already vowed to me and I to him—although he knew it not: and, although in a secret, shameful way, the holy Church had made us one, so that, as the service hath it, GOD Himself hath bound us together. To be in love already! O Kitty! Kitty!

There is a chapter in the Song of Solomon which is, as learned men tell us, written "of Christ and His Church," the poet speaking in such an allegory that, to all but the most spiritual-minded, he seemeth to speak of the simple love of a man and a maid. And surely it may be read without sin by either man or maid in love. "I am," she says, "the rose of Sharon and the lily of the valleys… My beloved spake, and said unto me, Rise up, my love, my fair one, and come away. For lo! the winter is past, the rain is over and gone; the flowers appear on the earth; the time of the singing of birds is come, and the voice of the turtle is heard in the land."

When I had read that chapter and dried my weeping eyes, and perhaps prayed awhile, I lay down upon my bed again, and slept till Cicely came at seven and called me up to dress and walk abroad.

CHAPTER V.

HOW KITTY WORE HER CROWN.

Thus happily began our stay at Epsom Wells.

After our morning walk we returned home, being both fatigued with the excitement and late hours, and one, at least, desirous to sit alone and think about the strange and perilous adventure of the evening. Strange, indeed; since when before did a man dance with his own wife and not recognise her? Perilous, truly, for should that man go away and give no more heed to his wife, then would poor Kitty be lost for ever. For already was her heart engaged in this adventure, and, like a gambler, she had staked her whole upon a single chance. Fortunately for her, the stake was consecrated with tears of repentance, bitterness of shame, and prayers for forgiveness.

Mrs. Esther gently dozed away the morning over "Pamela." I was occupied with needlework. Cicely ran in and out of the room, looking as if she longed to speak, but dared not for fear of waking madam.

After a while she beckoned me to the door, and whispered me that outside was a higgler with ducklings and cherries, should we please to choose them for our dinner. I followed her, and after a bargain, in which the Surrey maiden showed herself as good as if she had been bred in Fleet Market (though without the dreadful language), she began upon the business which she was burning to tell me.

"Sure, Miss Kitty," she said, "all the world is talking this morning about the beautiful Miss Pleydell. The book-shop is full of nothing else, the gentlemen in the coffee-house can talk of nothing but of Miss Pleydell, and up and down the Terrace it is nothing but, 'Oh, madam, did you see the dancing of Miss Pleydell last night?' 'Dear madam, did you remark the dress of Miss Pleydell?' And 'Can you tell me whence she comes, this beautiful Miss Pleydell?' And the men are all sighing as if their hearts would burst, poor fellows! And they say that Lord Chudleigh gave a supper after the ball to the gentlemen of his acquaintance, when he toasted the beautiful Miss Pleydell. Oh the happiness! He is a young nobleman with a great estate, and said to be of a most virtuous and religious disposition. The gentlemen are mounting ribbons in honour of the peerless Kitty, so I hear—and you will not be offended at their venturing so to take your name—and, with a little encouragement, they will all be fighting for a smile from the fair Kitty."

"Silly girl, to repeat such stories!"

"Nay," she replied, "it is all truth, every word. They say that never since the Wells began has there been such a beauty. The oldest dipper, old Mrs. Humphreys, who is past eighty, declares that Miss Pleydell is the loveliest lady that ever came to Epsom. When you go out this afternoon you will be finely beset."

And so on, all the morning, as her occasion brought her into the room, whisking about, duster in hand, and always clatter, clatter, like the mill-wheel. After dinner we received a visit from no other than Lord Chudleigh himself.

He offered a thousand apologies for presenting himself without asking permission, kindly adding, that however he might find Miss Kitty, whether dressed or in dishabille, she could not be otherwise than charming. I know one person who thought Kitty in her morning frock, muslin pinner, and brown hair (which was covered with little curls), looped up loosely, or allowed to flow freely to her waist, prettier than Kitty dressed up in hoop, and patches, and powder. It was the mirror which told that person so, and she never dared to tell it to any other.

He had ventured, he said, still speaking to Mrs. Esther, to present an offering of flowers and fruit sent to him that morning from his country house in Kent; and then Cicely brought upstairs the most beautiful basket ever seen, filled with the finest flowers, peaches, plums, apricots, and cherries. I had seen none such since I said farewell to the old Vicarage garden, where all those things grew better, I believe, than anywhere else in England.

"My lord," said my aunt, quite confused at such a gift, such condescension! "What can we say but that we accept the present most gratefully."

"Indeed, madam," he replied, "there is nothing to say. I am truly pleased that my poor house is able to provide a little pleasure to two ladies. It is the first time, I assure you, that I have experienced the joy of possessing my garden."

Then he went on to congratulate Mrs. Esther on my appearance at the ball.

"I hear," he said, "that on the Terrace and in the coffee-house one hears nothing but the praises of the fair Miss Pleydell."

I blushed, not so much at hearing my name thus mentioned, because I was already (in a single day—fie, Kitty!) accustomed and, so to speak, hardened, but because he smiled as he spoke. My lord's smile was not like some men's, bestowed upon every trifle; but, like his speech, considered. I fear, indeed, that even then, so early in the day, my heart was already thoroughly possessed of his image.

"The child," said Mrs. Esther, "must not have her head turned by flattery. Yet, I own, she looked and moved like one of the three Graces. Yet we who love her must not spoil her. It was her first ball, and she did her best, poor child, to acquit herself with credit."

"Credit," said my lord kindly, "is a poor, cold word to use for such a grace."

"We thank your lordship." Mrs. Esther bowed with dignity. This, surely, was a return to the Pimpernel Manner. "We have been living in seclusion, for reasons which need not be related, for some time. Therefore, Kitty has never been before to any public assembly. To be sure, I do not approve of bringing forward young girls too early; although, for my own part, I had already at her age been present at several entertainments of the most sumptuous and splendid character, not only at Bagnigge Wells and Cupid's Garden, but also at many great city feasts and banquets for the reception of illustrious personages, particularly in the year of grace, 1718, when my lamented father was Lord Mayor of London."

The dear lady could never avoid introducing the fact that she was thus honourably connected.

Lord Chudleigh, however, seemed interested. I learned, later, that some had been putting about, among other idle rumours, that I was the daughter of a tattered country curate.

"Indeed," he said, "I knew not that the late Mr. Pleydell had been the Lord Mayor. It is a most distinguished position."

"Not Mr. Pleydell, my lord. Sir Samuel Pimpernel, Knight, my father, was the Lord Mayor in question. His father was Lord Mayor before him. Kitty Pleydell is not my blood relation, but my niece and ward by adoption. Her father was a most distinguished Cambridge scholar and divine."

"There are Pleydells," said Lord Chudleigh, "in Warwickshire. Perhaps——"

"My father," I said, "was rector of a country parish in Kent, where Sir Robert Levett hath a large estate. He was the younger son of the Warwickshire family of that name, and died in the spring of last year. My relations of that county I have never met. Now, my lord, you have my genealogy complete."

"It is an important thing to know," he said, laughing; "in a place like Epsom, where scandal is the staple of talk, as many freedoms are taken with a lady's family as with her reputation. I am glad to be provided with an answer to those who would enact the part of town-crier or backbiter, a character here greatly aspired to. No doubt the agreeable ladies whose tongues in the next world will surely be converted into two-edged swords, have already furnished Miss Kitty with highwaymen, tallow-chandlers, or attorneys for ancestors, and Wapping, Houndsditch, or the Rules of the Fleet"—it was lucky that Mrs. Esther had a fan—"for their place of residence. In the same way, they have most undoubtedly proved to each other that she has not a feature worth looking at, that her eyes squint—pray pardon me, Miss Kitty—her hair is red, her figure they would have the audacity to call crooked, and her voice they would maliciously say was cracked. It is the joy of these people to detract from merit. You can afford to be charitable, Miss Kitty. The enumeration of impossible disgraces and the distortion of the rarest charms afford these ladies some consolation for their envy and disappointment."

"I hope, my lord," I said, "that it will not afford me a consolation or happiness to believe that my sex is so mean and envious thus to treat a harmless stranger."

He laughed.

"When Miss Kitty grows older," he said to Mrs Esther, "she will learn to place less confidence in her fellows."

"Age," said Mrs. Esther sadly, "brings the knowledge of evil. Let none of us wish to grow older. Not that your lordship hath yet gained the right to boast this knowledge."

Then my lord proceeded to inform us that he purposed presenting some of the ladies of the Wells with an entertainment, such as it seems is expected from gentlemen of his rank.

"But I would not," he said, "invite the rest of the company before I had made sure that the Queen of the Wells would honour me with her presence. I have engaged the music, and if the weather holds fine we will repair to Durdans Park, where we shall find dancing on the grass, with lamps in the trees, supper, and such amusements as ladies love and we can provide."

This was indeed a delightful prospect; we accepted with great joy, and so, with protestations of service, his lordship departed.

"There is," said Mrs. Esther, "about the manners of the great a charming freedom. Good breeding is to manners what Christianity is to religion. It is, if one may reverently say so, a law of perfect liberty. My dear, I think that we are singularly fortunate in having at the Wells so admirable a young nobleman, as well as our friends (also well-bred gentlefolks) Sir Robert and Lady Levett. I hear that the young Lord Eardesley is also at the Wells, and was at last night's assembly; and no doubt there are other members of the aristocracy by whom we shall be shortly known. You observed, Kitty, the interest shown by his lordship, when I delicately alluded to the rank and exalted station of my late father. It is well for people to know, wherever we are, and especially when we are in the society of nobility, that we are not common folk. What ancestors did his lordship say that envious tongues would give us—tallow-chandlers? attorneys? A lying and censorious place, indeed!"

Later on, we put on our best and sallied forth, dressed for the evening in our hoops, patches and powder, but not so fine as for Monday's ball. The Terrace and New Parade were crowded with people, and very soon we were surrounded by gentlemen anxious to establish a reputation for wit or position by exchanging a few words with the

The Chaplain of the Fleet

Reigning Beauty of the season—none other, if you please, than Kitty Pleydell.

But to think in how short a time—only a few hours, a single night—that girl was so changed that she accepted, almost without wondering, all the incense of flattery that was offered up to her! Yet she knew, being a girl of some sense, that it was unreal, and could not mean anything; else a woman so bepraised and flattered would lose her head. The very extravagance of gallantry preserves the sex from that calamity. A woman must be a fool indeed who can really believe that her person is that of a Grace, her smile the smile of Venus, her beauty surpassing that of Helen, and her wit and her understanding that of Sappho. She knows better: she knows that her wit is small and petty beside the wit of a man: her wisdom nothing but to learn a little of what men have said: her very beauty, of which so much is said, but a flower of a few years, whereas the beauty of manhood lasts all a life. Therefore, when all is said and done, the incense burned, the mock prayers said, the hymn of flattery sung, and the Idol bedecked with flowers and gems, she loves to step down from the altar, slip away from the worshippers, and run to a place in the meadows, where waits a swain who will say: "Sweet girl, I love thee—with all thy faults!"

On this day, therefore, began my brief reign as Queen of the Wells. Mr. Walsingham was one of the first to salute me. With courtly grace he bowed low, saying—

"We greet our Queen, and trust her Majesty is in health and spirits."

Then all the gentlemen round formed a lane, down which we walked, my old courtier marching backwards.

The scene, Mrs. Esther said afterwards, reminded her of a certain day long ago, when they crowned a Queen of Beauty at Bagnigge Wells, in the presence of the Lord Mayor, her father.

To be sure, it was a very pretty sight to watch all these gallants making legs and handling their canes with such grace as each could command, some of them having studied in those noble schools of manners, the *salons* of Paris or the reception-rooms of great ladies in London. Yet it was certain to me that not one of them could compare with my lord—my own lord, I mean.

Presently we came upon Lady Levett and her party, when, after a few words of kind greeting from her ladyship, and an admonition not to believe more of what I was told than I knew to be true, we divided, Nancy coming with me and Mrs. Esther remaining with Lady Levett. The music was playing and the sun shining, but a fine air blew from the Downs, and we were beneath the shade of the trees. We sat upon one of the benches, and the gentlemen gathered round us.

"Gentlemen," said Nancy, "I am the Queen's maid of honour. You may all of you do your best to amuse her Majesty—and me. We give you permission to exhaust yourselves in making the court happy."

What were they to do? What had they to offer? There was a bull-baiting in the market at which my maid of honour cried fie! There was a match with quarterstaves on the Downs for the afternoon, but that met with little favour.

"We need not leave home," said Nancy, "to see two stout fellows bang each other about the head with sticks. That amusement may be witnessed any summer evening, with grinning through a horse-collar and fighting with gloves on the village green at home. Pray go on to the next amusement on the list. The cock-pit you can leave out."

One young gentleman proposed that we might play with pantines, a ridiculous fashion of paper doll then in vogue as a toy for ladies with nothing to do: another that we should go hear the ingenious Mr. King lecture on Astronomy: another that we should raffle for chocolate creams: another that we should do nothing at all, "for," said he, "why do we come to the Wells but for rest and quiet? and if Miss Pleydell and her maid of honour do but grant us the privilege of beholding their charms, what need we of anything but rest?

> "'To walk and dine, and walk and sup,
> To fill the leisure moments up,
> Idly enough but to the few
> Who've really nothing else to do.
> Yet here the sports exulting reign,
> And laughing loves, a num'rous train;
> Here Beauty holds her splendid court,
> And flatt'ring pleasures here resort.'"

The Chaplain of the Fleet

I, for one, should have enjoyed the witnessing of a little sport better than the homage of lovers.

"Here is Miss Peggy Baker," cried Nancy, jumping up. "Oh! I *must* speak to my dear friend Miss Peggy."

Miss Baker was walking slowly down the Terrace, accompanied by her little troop of admirers. At sight of us her face clouded for a moment, but she quickly recovered and smiled a languid greeting.

"Dear Miss Peggy," cried Nancy—I knew she was going to say something mischievous—"you come in the nick of time."

"Pray command me," she replied graciously.

"It is a simple question"—Miss Baker looked suspicious. "Oh! a mere trifle"—Miss Baker looked uneasy. "It is only—pray, gentlemen, were any of you in the book-shop this morning?"

All protested that they were not—a denial which confirmed my opinion that impertinence was coming.

"Nay," said Nancy, "we all know the truthfulness of gallants, which is as notorious as their constancy. Had you been there you would not have paid Miss Pleydell those pretty compliments which are as well deserved as they are sincere. But, Miss Peggy, a scandalous report hath got abroad. They say that you said, this morning, at the book-shop, that Kitty Pleydell's eyes squinted."

"Oh! oh!" cried Mr. Walsingham, holding up his hands, and all the rest cried "Oh! oh!" and held up theirs.

"I vow and protest," cried Peggy Baker, blushing very much. "I vow and protest——"

"I said," interrupted Nancy, "that it was the cruellest slander. You are all good-nature. Stand up, Kitty dear. Now tell us, Miss Peggy, before all these gentlemen, do those eyes squint?"

"Certainly not," said poor Peggy, in great confusion.

"Look at them well," continued Nancy. "Brown eyes, full and clear—eyes like an antelope. Saw any one eyes more straight!"

"Never," said Peggy, fanning herself violently.

"Or more beautiful eyes?"

"Never," replied Miss Peggy.

"There," said Nancy, "I knew it. I said that from the lips of Miss Peggy Baker nothing but kind words can fall. You hear, gentlemen; women are sometimes found who can say good things of each other: and if we find the malicious person who dared report that Miss Peggy Baker said such a thing, I hope you will duck her in the horse-pond."

Miss Peggy bowed to us with her most languishing air, and passed on. Nancy held up her hands, while the gentlemen looked at one another and laughed.

"Oh, calumny!" she cried. "To say that Kitty's eyes were askew!"

For there had been a discussion at the book-shop that morning, in which the name of Miss Pleydell was frequently mentioned; and her person, bearing, and face were all particularly dwelt upon. Miss Baker, as usual in their parliaments, spoke oftenest, and with the most animation. She possessed, on such occasions, an insight into the defects of women that was truly remarkable, and a power of representing them to others which, while it was eloquent and persuasive, perhaps erred on the side of exaggeration. She summed up what she had to say in these kind words—

"After all, one could forgive fine clothes worn as if the girl had never had a dress on fit to be seen before, and manners like a hoyden trying to seem a nun, and the way of dancing taught to the cits who go to Sadler's Wells, and a sunburnt complexion, and hands as big as my fan—all these things are rustic, and might be cured—or endured. But I cannot forgive her squint!"

And now she had to recant publicly, and confess that there was no squint at all.

This audacious trick of Nancy's was, you may be sure, immediately spread abroad, so that for that day at least the unfortunate creature found the people looking after and laughing wherever she went. Naturally, she hated me, who really had done her no harm at all, more and more.

The Chaplain of the Fleet

The gentlemen, or one among them, I knew not who, offered this evening a general tea-drinking with the music. It was served under the trees upon the open walk, and was very gay and merry. After the tea, when the day began to decline, we went to the rooms where, though there was no dancing, there was talking and laughing, in one room, and in the other games of cards of every kind—cribbage, whist, quadrille, hazard, and lansquenet. We wandered round the tables, watching the players intent upon the chances of the cards. I thought of poor Sir Miles Lackington, who might, had it not been for his love of gaming, have been now, as he began, a country gentleman with a fine estate. In this room we found Lord Chudleigh. He was not playing, but was looking on at a table where sat a young gentleman and an officer in the army. He did not see us, and, under pretence of watching the play of a party of four ladies playing quadrille, one of whom was Lady Levett, I sat down to watch him. Was he a gambler?

I presently discovered that he was not looking at the game, but the players. Presently he laid his hand upon the shoulder of the younger man, and said, in a quiet voice—

"Now, Eardesley, you have had enough. This gentleman knows the game better than you."

"I hope, my lord," cried the other player, springing to his feet, "that your lordship doth not insinuate——"

"I speak what I mean, sir. Lord Eardesley will, if he takes my advice, play no more with you."

"Your lordship," cried the gentleman in scarlet, "will perhaps remember that you are speaking to a gentleman——"

"Who left Bath, a fortnight ago, under such circumstances as makes it the more necessary for me to warn my friend. No, sir,"—his eye grew hard, and his face stern. "No, sir. Do not bluster or threaten. I will neither play with you, nor suffer my friends to play with you; nor, sir, will I fight with you, unless you happen to attack me upon the road. And, sir, if I see you here to-morrow, the master of the ceremonies will put you to the door by means of his lackeys. Come, Eardesley."

The gamester, thus roundly accused, began to bluster. His honour was at stake; he had been grossly insulted; he would have the satisfaction of a gentleman; he would let his lordship know that his rank should not protect him. With these noble sentiments, he left the room, and the Wells saw him no more.

Then, seeing me alone, for I had escaped from my court, being weary of compliments and speeches, he came to my chair.

"I saw you, my lord," I said, "rescue that young gentleman from the man who, I suppose, would have won his money. Is it prudent to engage in such quarrels?"

"The young gentleman," he replied, "is, in a sense, my ward. The man is a notorious sharper, who hath been lately expelled from Bath, and will now, I think, find it prudent to leave the Wells. I hope, Miss Kitty, that you do not like gaming?"

"Indeed, my lord, I do not know if I should like what I have never tried. 'Tis the first time I have seen card-playing."

"Then you must have been brought up in a nunnery."

"Not quite that, but in a village, where, as I have already told you, my father was vicar. I do not know any games of cards."

"How did you amuse yourself in your village?"

"I read, made puddings, worked samplers, cut out and sewed my dresses, and learned lessons with Nancy Levett."

"The pretty little girl who is always laughing? She should always remain young—never grow old and grave. What else did you do?"

"We had a choir for the Sunday psalms—many people came every Sunday to hear us sing. That was another occupation. Then I used to ride with the boys, or sometimes we would go fishing, or nutting, or black-berrying—oh! there was plenty to do, and the days were never too long."

"A better education than most ladies can show," he replied, with his quiet air of authority.

"And you, my lord. Do you never play cards?"

"No," he replied. "Pray do not question me further on my favourite vices, Miss Kitty. I would not confess all my sins even to so charming and so kind a confessor as yourself."

"I forgive you, my lord," I said, "beforehand. Especially if you promise to abandon them all."

"There are sins," he said slowly, "which sometimes leave behind them consequences which can never be forgotten or undone."

Alas! I knew what he meant. His sin had left him burdened with a wife—a creature who had been so wicked as to take advantage of his wickedness; a woman whom he feared to hear of and already loathed. Poor wife! poor sinner! poor Kitty!

CHAPTER VI.

HOW THE DOCTOR WROTE TO KITTY.

The next morning at dinner, we heard the summons of the post-boy's horn, and Cicely presently ran in with a letter in her hand. It was addressed to me, in a large bold handwriting, and was sealed with red wax. I opened it and found a smaller letter inside it, marked "Private. For my niece's eye alone." So that both letters were from my uncle, the Doctor.

"Your private letter," said Mrs. Esther, "doubtless contains some admonition or advice designed for you alone. Put it in your pocket, child, and read it in your own room. As for the other letter, as it is not marked private, it would be well for you to read it aloud, after dinner, and while we are eating one of my Lord Chudleigh's delicious peaches."

To this I willingly complied, because I greatly feared the private letter would contain some instructions concerning the secret which the Doctor and I possessed between us. Accordingly, the dinner over, I began the perusal of my uncle's letter.

"MY DEAR NIECE,—You will first of all, and before reading any further, convey my dutiful respects to the lady by whose goodness you have been placed in a position as much above what you could have wished, as her benevolence is above the ordinary experience of mortals."

"Oh, the excellent man!" cried Mrs. Esther.

"I have to report that, under Providence, I am well in health, and in all respects doing well; the occupation in which I am now engaged having received a stimulus by the threatening of a new Act for the prevention of (so-called) unlawful marriages. The increase in the number of applicants for marriage hath also (as is natural) caused an increase in the upstarts and pretenders who claim to have received canonical orders, being most of them as ignorant as a butcher's block, and no more ordained than the fellows who bang a cushion in a conventicle. The clergymen of London complain that the parsons of the Fleet take away their parishioners, and deprive them of their fees:

they cannot say that I, who never take less than a guinea, undersell them. You will be glad to learn that Sir Miles Lackington hath left this place. He hath lately received a legacy from a cousin of a small estate, and hath made an arrangement with his creditors, by virtue of which his detainers are now removed. Nevertheless, we expect him back before long, being well assured that the same temptation and vice of gambling, which brought him here before, will again beset him. Yet he promiseth brave things. We gave him a farewell evening, in which his health was toasted, and more punch drunk than was good for the heads of some present, among whom were gentlemen members of the Utter Bar, from the two Temples and Lincoln's Inn, with many others, and honourable company.

"It will also be a pleasure to you to learn that the ingenious Mr. Stallabras is also at large. Probably he, too, will return to us ere long. For the present his sole detaining creditor, who had supplied him for years with such articles of apparel (at second-hand) as were necessary for his decent appearance on the credit of his future glory, agreed to take ten guineas in full discharge of a bill for forty, which the poet could never hope to pay, nor the tradesman to receive. The calling of poet is at best but a poor one, nor should I counsel any one to practise the writing of verse unless he be a man of fortune, like Mr. Alexander Pope (unfortunately a Papist), or a Fellow of some substantial college, such as the Houses of Trinity, Peter, and Christ, at Cambridge, like Mr. Ray. Nor is there any greater unhappiness than to draw a bill, to speak after the manner of merchants, upon your future success and industry, and to be compelled to discount it. He hath now conceived the idea of a tragedy and of an epic poem. The first he will endeavour to produce at Drury Lane as soon as it is written: the second he will immediately get subscribed among his friends and patrons. Unfortunately he has already obtained subscriptions, for a volume of verses, and, having eaten the subscriptions, cannot now find a publisher: in truth, I believe the verses are not yet written. This melancholy accident obliges him to seek for new patrons. I wish him well.

"It is, my dear niece, with the greatest satisfaction that I learn you have, with Mrs. Esther, gone to Epsom. The situation of the place, the purity of the air upon the Downs, the salubrity of the waters, the gaiety of the company, will, I hope, all be conducive to the health of that most excellent lady, your best friend — —"

"Oh, the good man!" cried Mrs. Esther.

"To whom I charge you be dutiful, obedient, and careful in the smallest punctilio. The cheerfulness of the amusements (if Epsom be the same as when I once visited it, when tutor to a young gentleman of quality) should communicate to her spirits something of the joy with which I could now wish her to regard the world. As for yourself, my child, I am under no apprehension but that music, gay companions, and your time of life will together make you as mirthful as is possible for human being. Remember, however, that happiness is but for a season: that mirth must never pass beyond the bound of good manners: and that when a woman is no longer young, the reputation she has earned as a girl remains with her, even to the grave. Wherefore, Kitty, be circumspect. The town news is but little: the (so-styled) young Pretender is said to be moving again, but little importance is now attached to his doings, and for the moment the Protestant dynasty seems firm. But Heaven knows — —"

Here followed a quantity of news about the ministers, the Houses of Parliament, the foreign news, and so forth, which I omit.

"I have seen a sermon, published this year by one Laurence Sterne, on 'Conscience,' which I would commend to Mrs. Pimpernel. I also commend to you Dr. Samuel Johnson's 'Vanity of Human Wishes,' and the first number of the 'Rambler,' of which I hear great things. Mr. Henry Fielding hath produced a novel called 'Tom Jones,' of which the town is talking. I mention it here in order that you may be cautioned against a book whose sole merit is the faithful delineation of scenes and characters shocking to the female moralist. For the same reason I would have thee beware of Mr. Smollett's 'Peregrine Pickle,' in which, as a man who knows — alas! the wickedness of the world, I find a great deal to commend.

"The weather has been strangely hot even for July, and fever is rife in this neighbourhood. I hear that the Bishop of London threatens me with pains and penalties. I have sent word to his lordship, that if he will not allow me to marry, I will *bury*, and that at such prices as will leave his clergy nothing but the fees of the paupers, beggars, and malefactors.

"I think that I have no more news to send. I would that I were able to send thee such tidings as might be looked for in a London letter; but I know not what actor is carrying away all hearts, nor what lady is the reigning toast, nor what is the latest fashion in cardinal, sack, patch, or tie-wig, nor anything at all that is dear to the hearts of an assembly on the Terrace of Epsom. Therefore, with my duty to Mrs. Pimpernel,—I remain, my dear niece, your loving uncle,

"GREGORY SHOVEL, *Doctor of Divinity*.

"*Post Scriptum.*—I enclose herewith a short letter of admonition, which thou mayest read by thyself, as such things are not interesting to Mistress Pimpernel."

"Now," cried Mrs. Esther, "was there ever such a man? Living in such a place, he preserves his virtue: among such dregs and offscourings of mankind he stands still erect, proclaiming and preaching Christian virtue. O Kitty! why was not that man made a bishop? Sure, there is no other position in the world fit for him. With what eloquence would he defend Christian faith? With what righteous indignation would he not expel evil-doers?"

I did not dare to ask, which of course occurred to me, what indignation he would show against such as violated the law by marrying in the Fleet.

"Now," I said, "with your permission, madam, I will retire, in order to read my uncle's private letter of admonition."

I opened the short note in fear; yet there was nothing alarming in it.

"MY DEAR NIECE,—I add a word to say that Lord Chudleigh is going to visit Epsom, and hath either engaged or been offered the mansion of Durdans for the summer: perhaps he is already there. It may be that you will make his acquaintance: in any case you cannot fail of being interested in his doings. Since his visit to the Fleet, I hear that he has been afflicted with a continual melancholy, of which you and I know the cause. He has also led a very regular and almost monastic life, reproaching himself continually for that lapse from temperance which led to what he regards as the curse of his life.

"Child, if he pays you attentions, receive them with such coquettish allurements as your sex knows how to hang out. On this point I cannot advise. But if he is attracted by more showy and more beautiful women"—I looked at the glass and smiled—"then be careful not to exhibit any jealousy or anger. Remember that jealousy and anger have ruined many a *femina furens*, or raging woman. Let things go on, as if nothing of all that you and I wot of had happened. He will be watched, and at the right time will be called upon to acknowledge his wife. Such a return for the evil done me by his father shall be mine. And with such a return of good for evil, a brilliant position for yourself. If he should fall in love, if he hath not already done so, with another woman, you would, in one moment, blast his hopes, trample on all that he held dear, and make him ridiculous, a criminal, and a deceiver. But it is at all times a more Christian thing for a man to fall in love with his own wife.

"Remember, my dear Kitty, I place the utmost reliance on thy good sense. Above all, no woman's jealousies, rages, and fits of madness. These things will only do thee harm.

"Your loving uncle,
"GREGORY SHOVEL, *Doctor of Divinity*."

Were one a stock or a stone; had one no feelings; were one destitute of pity, sympathy, and compassion, these letters might have been useful as guides to conduct. But the thing had happened to me which my uncle, in his worldly wisdom, could never calculate upon: I had fallen in love with Lord Chudleigh: I was passionately anxious that he should fall in love with me. What room, in such a condition of mind as was this man, for advice so cold, so interested as this? Return good for evil? What had I to do with that? I wanted to wreak no vengeance on my lord: I would have surrounded him with love, and been willing to become his servant, his slave, anything, if only he would forgive me, take me for his sweetheart, and make me his wife. But to lay those snares: to look on coldly while he made love to other women: to wait my time, so as to bring shame and remorse upon that noble heart— that, Kitty, was impossible. Yet I could not write to my uncle things which he could not understand. I could not say that I repented and was very sorry: that I loved my lord, and was determined to inflict no harm upon him: and that, if he chose to fall in love with another woman—who was I, indeed, that he should love me?—I was firmly resolved that no act or word of mine should injure him, even though I had to stand in the church and see him with my own eyes married to that other—that happy woman—before the altar.

CHAPTER VII.

HOW KITTY BROKE HER PROMISE.

No one must think that I was sorry, or even embarrassed, when I heard that Harry Temple had joined the company at Epsom; and though the name of coquette was given me by him, and that of jilt, with such other abusive terms as the English tongue provides, by Will Levett, later on, I beg that every one will believe me when I declare that I had no knowledge at all of being betrothed, or under any kind of promise, to either of these two young men. Yet, as will have been perceived by any who have read the second chapter of this narrative, both of them had just grounds for believing me to be their promised wife. In fact, I was at the time so silly and ignorant that I did not understand what they meant; nor had I, being so much tossed about, and seeing so many changes, ever thought upon their words at all, since. And whereas there was no day in which the thought of my dear and fond Nancy did not come into my mind, there never was a day at all in which my memory dwelt upon either Will or Harry, save as companions of Nancy. And although grievous things followed upon this neglect of mine, I cannot possibly charge myself with any blame in the matter. As for Will, indeed, his conduct was such as to relieve me of any necessity for repentance; while Harry, even if he did play the fool for a while, speedily recovered his senses, and found consolation in the arms of another. Lastly, men ought not to go frantic for any woman: they should reflect that there are good wives in plenty to be had for the asking; women virtuously reared, who account it an honour (as they should) to receive the offer of an honest man's faithful service; that no woman is so good as to have no equal among her contemporaries: while as for beauty, that is mostly matter of opinion. I am sure I cannot understand why they made me Queen of the Wells, when Nancy Levett was passed over; and I have since seen many a plain girl honoured as a beauty, while the most lovely faces were neglected.

The first, then, of my two lovers—or promised husbands—who arrived at Epsom was Harry Temple.

We were walking on the New Parade in the afternoon, making a grand display; I in my new purple velvet with purple ribbons, a purple mantle and purple trimmings to my hat, very grand indeed. Mr. Walsingham was talking like a lover in a novel—I mean of the old-fashioned and romantic school of novel, now gone out. The art of saying fine things now too much neglected by the young, was then studied by old and young.

"Ladies," he was saying, "should never be seen save in the splendour of full dress: they should not eat in public, unless it be chocolates and Turkish sweets: nor drink, unless it be a dish of tea: they should not laugh, lest they derange the position of the patch or the nice adjustment of the coiffure: they may smile, however, upon their lovers; all their movements should be trim and evenly balanced, according to rules of grace: in fact, just as a woman was the last and most finished work in Nature, so a lady dressed, taught, and cultivated, should be the last and most finished work in Art. The power of beauty—Miss Pleydell will approve this—should be assisted by the insinuation of polite address: rank should be enhanced by the assumption of a becoming dignity: dishabille should hide at home: nor should she show herself abroad until she has heightened and set off her charms, by silk and satin, ribbons and lace, paint, powder, and patches."

"I suppose, sir," said Nancy, pointing to an absurd creature whose follies were the diversion of the whole company, "the dress of the lady over there in the short sack would please you. Her body a state-bed running upon castors, and her head-dress made up of trimmings taken from the tester. She is, sir, I take it, a finished work of Art."

Then she screamed: "O Kitty! here is Harry Temple." And then she blushed, so that Mr. Walsingham looked at both of us with a meaning smile. He came sauntering along the walk, looking about him carelessly, for as yet he knew none of the company. His manner was improved since last I saw him, a year and more ago: that was doubtless due to a visit to the Continent. He was a handsome fellow certainly, though not so tall or so handsome as Lord Chudleigh: his features were smaller and his air less distinguished; but still a pretty fellow. I thought of Nancy's secret and laughed to myself, as yet never suspecting what he would say. The great difference at first sight between Harry Temple and Lord Chudleigh was that the former looked as if he was ready to take the place which the world would assign to him, while the latter would step to the front and stand there as if in his proper place. It is a grand thing to be a leader of men.

Suddenly he saw us, and stood still with such a look of bewilderment and astonishment as I never saw.

"Nancy!"—he had his eyes upon me all the time—"I knew you were here, but—but——"

Here Nancy burst out laughing.

"Harry does not remember you, Kitty. Oh the inconstancy of men!"

"Kitty?" It was his turn to look confused now. "Is it possible? Kitty Pleydell? Yet, surely——"

"I am sorry that Mr. Temple so easily forgets his old friends," I said.

"No, no. Forget? not at all." He was so disconcerted that he spoke in single words. "But such a change!"

"A year ago," I said, "I was in russet and brown holland, with a straw hat. But this watering-place is not my native village, and I wear brown holland frocks no longer."

"Save in a pastoral," said Mr. Walsingham. "A shepherdess should always wear brown holland, with ribbons and patches, powder and paint; and a crook beautifully wreathed with green ribbons."

"Gentlemen," I said to my followers, "this is my old friend, Mr. Harry Temple, of Wootton Hampstead, Kent, whom you will, I doubt not, welcome among you. But what punishment shall be inflicted upon him for forgetting a lady's face?"

This gave rise to a dispute on an abstract point of gallantry. One held that under no circumstances, and during no time of absence, however prolonged, should a gentleman forget the face of his mistress; another, that if the lady changed, say from a child to a woman, the forgetfulness of her face must not be charged as a crime. We argued the point with great solemnity. Nancy gave it as her opinion that the rest of a woman's face might be forgotten, but not the eyes, because they never change. Mr. Walsingham combated this opinion. He said that the eyes of ladies change when they marry.

"What change?" I asked.

"The eyes of a woman who is fancy free," said he gravely, "are like stars: when she marries, they are planets."

"Nay," said Nancy; "a woman does not wait to be married before her eyes undergo that change. As soon as she falls in love they become planets. For whereas, before that time, they go twinkle, twinkle, upon every pretty fellow who has the good taste to fall in love with her, as mine do when I look upon Lord Eardesley"—the young fellow blushed—"so after she is in love, they burn with a steady light upon the face of the man she loves, as mine do when I turn them upon Mr. Walsingham."

She gazed with so exaggerated an ardour into the old beau's wrinkled and crows'-footed face, that the rest of us laughed. He, for his part, made a profound salute, and declared that the happiness of his life was now achieved, and that he had nothing left to live for.

In the evening, a private ball was given in the Assembly Rooms by some of the gentlemen, Lord Chudleigh among the number, to a circle of the most distinguished ladies at the Wells. In right of my position as Queen, I opened the ball (of course with his lordship). Afterwards, I danced with Harry. When the country dances began, I danced again with Harry, who kept looking in my eyes and squeezing my hand in a ridiculous fashion. At first I set it down to rejoicing and fraternal affection. But he quickly undeceived me when the dance was over, for while we stood aside to let others have their turn, he began about the promise which we know of.

"Little did I think, sweet Kitty," he said, with half-shut eyes, "that when I made that promise to bring you back into Kent, you would grow into so wonderful a beauty."

"Well, Harry," I replied, "it was kindly meant of you, and I thank you for your promise—which I now return you."

"You return me my promise?" he asked, as if surprised, whereas he ought most certainly to have considered what had been my country ignorance and my maidenly innocence when he gave me his promise.

"Certainly," I said; "seeing that I am now under the protection of Mrs. Esther Pimpernel, and have no longer any need for your services."

"My services?" as if still more surprised. I am convinced that he was only acting astonishment, because he must have known the truth had he reflected at all. "Why, Kitty, I do not understand. You are not surely going to throw me over?"

Then I understood at last.

"Harry," I said, "there has been, I fear, some mistake."

"No," he replied; "no mistake—no mistake at all. How could there be a mistake? You promised that you would return with me, never to go away again."

"Why, so I did. But, Harry, I never thought — —"

"You *must* have known what I meant, Kitty! Do not pretend that you did not. Oh! you may open your eyes as wide as you like, but I shall believe it, nevertheless."

"You have made a great mistake," I said; "that is very certain. Now let us have no more talk of such things, Harry."

Lord Chudleigh came at that moment to lead me in to supper. I thought very little of what had passed, being only a little vexed that Harry had made so great a blunder.

The supper was pleasant too, with plenty of wax candles, cold chickens, capons, wheat-ears, ice-creams, and champagne, which is certainly the most delicious wine ever made.

After supper, my lord asked me if there was any friend of mine whom I would especially like to be invited to his party at Durdans?

I named Harry Temple, whom my lord immediately sought out, and invited in my name. Harry bowed sulkily, but accepted.

"Is there any person," Lord Chudleigh asked next, "whom you would like not to be asked?"

"No," I said; "I have no enemies."

"As if the Queen of the Wells could avoid having enemies?" he laughed. "But there are none who can do you harm, even by the venom of spiteful tongues."

He was silent for a minute or two, and then he went on, with hesitation—

"Pardon me, Miss Pleydell: I have no right to speak of these things to you; my interest is greater than my politeness, and I venture to ask you a question."

"Pray speak, my lord."

"A spiteful tongue has whispered it abroad that you have to-day given your plighted lover a cold reception."

"Who is my plighted lover?"

"Mr. Harry Temple. Tell me, Miss Pleydell, if there is any promise between you and this gentleman?"

He looked at me in such a way as made me both rejoice and tremble.

"No, my lord," I said, blushing against my will, and to my great confusion; "I am not promised to Mr. Temple. Will your lordship take me to the dancing-room?"

It was a bright moonlight night when we came away. We walked home, escorted by some of the gentlemen. Lord Chudleigh, as he stooped to take my hand, raised it rapidly to his lips and pressed my fingers. The action was not seen, I think, by the others.

That night I tried to put the case plainly to myself.

I said: "Kitty, my dear, the man you want above all other men to fall in love with you has done it; at least, it seems so. He seeks you perpetually; he talks to you; he singles you out from the rest; he is jealous; his eyes follow you about; he sends fruit and flowers to you; he gives an entertainment, and calls you the Queen of the Feast; he presses your hand and kisses your fingers. What more, Kitty, would you have?"

On the other hand, I thought: "If he falls in love with you, being already married, as he believes, to another woman, he commits a sin against his marriage vows. Yet what sin can there be in breaking vows pronounced in such a state as he was in, and in such a way? Why, they seem to me no vows at all, in spite of the validity of the Doctor's orders and the so-called blessing of the Church. Yet he cannot part from his wife by simply wishing; and, knowing that, he does actually commit the sin of deceit in loving another woman.

"Kitty, what would you have? For, if he doth not love you, then are you miserable above all women; and if he does, then are you grieved, for his own sake, for it is a sin—and ashamed for your own, because your confession will be a bitter thing to say. Yet must it be made, soon or late. Oh! with what face will you say to him: 'My lord, I am that wife of the Fleet wedding'? Or, 'My lord, you need not woo me, for I was won before I was wooed'? Or perhaps, worst thing of all, 'My lord, the girl who caught your fickle fancy for a moment at Epsom, whom you passed over, after a day or two, for another, who was not pretty enough to fix your affections, is your lawful wife'?

"Kitty, I fear that the case is hopeless indeed. For, should he really love you, what forelook or expectancy is there but that the love will turn to hatred when he finds that he has been deceived?"

Then I could not but remember how a great lord, with a long rent-roll, of illustrious descent, might think it pleasant for a day or two to dance attendance upon a pretty girl, by way of sport, meaning nothing further, but that he could not think seriously of so humble a girl as myself in marriage. It would matter little to him that she was descended from a long line of gentlemen, although but a vicars daughter; the Pleydells were only simply country gentlefolk. I was a simple country clergyman's daughter, whose proper place would be in his mother's still-room; a daughter of one of those men whose very vocation, for the most part, awakens a smile of pity or contempt, according as they are the sycophants of the squire whose living they enjoy, or the drudges of their master the rector whose work they do. It was not in reason to think that Lord Chudleigh——Would to Heaven he had not come to Epsom Wells at all! Then, when the Doctor chose the day for revealing the truth, I might have borne the hatred and scorn which now, I thought, would kill me.

Oh, if one could fix him! By what arts do girls draw to themselves the love of men, and then keep that love for ever, so that they never seek to wander elsewhere, and the world is for them like the Garden of

Eden, with but one man and one woman in it? I would have all his heart, and that so firmly and irrevocably given to me, that forgiveness should follow confession, and the heart remain still in my keeping when he knew all my wickedness and shame.

Then a sudden thought struck me.

Long ago, when I was a child, I had learned, or taught myself, a thing which I could fain believe was not altogether superstitious. One day my father, who would still be talking of ancient things, and cared for little of more modern date than the Gospels, told me of a practice among the ancients by which they thought to look into the future. It was an evil practice, he said, because if these oracles were favourable, they advanced with blind confidence; and, if unfavourable, with a heart already prepared for certain defeat and death. Their method was nothing in the world but the opening of a Virgil anywhere, and accepting the first line which offered itself as a prophecy of the event of their undertaking. I was but a little thing when he told me this, but I pondered it in my mind, and I reasoned in this way (nothing doubting that the ancients did really in this manner read the future)—

"If these pagans could tell the event by consulting the words of Virgil, a heathen like unto themselves, how much more readily ought we to learn what is going to happen by consulting the actual Word of God?"

Thereupon, without telling any one, I used to consult this oracle, probably by myself, in every little childish thing which interested me.

It was a thing presumptuous, though in my childhood I did not know that it was a sin. Yet I did it on this very night—a grown-up woman—trying to get a help to soothe my mind.

The moonlight was so bright that I could read at the open window without a candle. I had long since extinguished mine.

I opened the Bible at random, kept my finger on a verse, and took the book to the casement.

There I read—

"Wait on the Lord: be of good courage; and He shall strengthen thy heart. Wait, I say, on the Lord."

Now these words I thankfully accepted as a solemn message from Heaven, an answer to my prayer.

So I laid me down, and presently fell fast asleep.

CHAPTER VIII.

HOW KITTY HAD LETTERS AND VERSES.

Everybody knows that a watering-place in summer is a nest of singing birds. I do not mean the birds of the air, nor the ladies who sing at the concerts, nor the virtuosos, male and female, who gather together to talk of appogiatura, sonata, and—and the rest of the musical jargon. I mean rather those epigrammatists, libellous imitators of Pasquin, and love-verse writers who abound at such places. Mostly they are anonymous, so that one cannot thank them as one would. The verses, this year at Epsom, came down upon us in showers. They were stuck up on the pillars of the porch of the Assembly Rooms, they were laid upon the table of the book-shop, they were handed about on the Terrace. Also they came to me at my lodgings, and to Nancy at hers, and very likely to Peggy Baker at hers. Here, for instance, is one set which were shown round at the Assembly—

"Epsom could boast no reigning Toast:
The Terrace wept for pity.
Kind Fortune said, 'Come, lift your head;
I send you stately Kitty.'

"She came, she reigned, but still disdained
The crowd's applause and fancy;
Quoth Fortune, 'Then, content ye, men,
With pretty, witty Nancy.'"

Every morning lovers were at our feet (on paper). They wrote letters enjoining me "by those soft killing eyes" (which rhymed with "sighs") to take pity on their misery, or to let them die. You would have thought, to read their vows, that all the men in the town were in profound wretchedness. They could not sleep: they could no longer go abroad: they were wasting and pining away: they were the victims of a passion which was rapidly devouring them: Death, they said, would be welcomed as a Deliverer. Yet it will hardly be believed that, in spite of so dreadful an epidemic of low fever, no outward signs of it were visible in the town at all: the gentlemen were certainly fat and in good case: their hearts seemed merry within them: they laughed, made jokes, sang, and were jolly to outward show: their appetites were good: they were making (apparently) no preparations for demise. Their letters and verses were, however, anonymous, so that it was impossible to point with accuracy to any sufferer who thus dissembled. From information conveyed to me by Cicely Crump, I believe that the verses and letters came in great measure from the apprentices and shopmen employed by the mercers, haberdashers, hosiers, and drapers of the town—young men whose employment brings them constantly into the presence of ladies, but whose humble positions in the world forbid them to do anything more than worship at a great distance: yet their hearts are as inflammable as their betters, and their aspirations are sometimes above their rank, as witness the gallant elopement of Joshua Crump, Cicely's father, with Miss Jenny Medlicott, daughter of an alderman: then they find relief and assume a temporary dignity—as they fondly think—in writing anonymous love-letters. I think the letters must have come from these foolish and conceited young men, because I cannot understand how a gentleman who values his self-respect could so far humiliate himself as to write letters which he would be ashamed to sign, declaring himself the foolish victim of a foolish passion, and addressing a fellow-creature, a being like himself, with all the imperfections of humanity upon her, as an angel (which is blasphemous), and a sun of glory (which is nonsense), or a bright particular star (which is copied from the preface to the Bible). I confess that we liked the open compliments and public attentions of the gentlemen: they pleased us, and we took them in sober honesty for what they were worth—the base coin of gallantry rings as pleasantly sometimes as the guinea gold of love—but it is one thing to be called a goddess in the accepted language of exaggeration and mock humility commonly used in polite assemblies, and another to be addressed in a grovelling strain, seriously and humbly, as if one were the Lama of Thibet, or the great Bashaw, or the Pope himself. It is pleasant to see a young fellow dancing along the walk with his hat under his arm, making reverence, with his eyes full of admiration, his face lit with smiles, and compliments upon his tongue, because one knows that it is the natural homage paid by an honest fellow to a pretty girl, and that when years have robbed the beauty, the homage will be paid to some one else. But for these silly boys' letters——

And then we made the sad discovery, by comparing our letters, that they were not even original. Many of them were, word for word, the same, showing that they had been copied from the same model. If it be true that passion makes the most tongue-tied lover eloquent, then this discovery proved that the violence of the passion was as feigned as the letters were false, unless Nancy's supposition was true.

"Fie!" cried she, "the wretch has written the same letters to both of us. Can he be in love with two maids at the same time?"

Then she took both letters and showed them about among the company.

There was another kind of letter which I received: it was filled with slander and abuse, and was written in disguised handwriting. Several of them came to me, and I was foolish enough to be vexed over them, even to shed tears of vexation. My anonymous correspondent gave me, in fact, such information and advice as the following, which was not conveyed to me all at once, but in several letters.

"Your Lord Chudleigh is very well known to be a gambler who hath already dipped more than half his estate; do you think it possible that he should marry the daughter of that poor thing—a country parson—with no more fortune to her back than what a city madam may chance to give her? Be not deceived. Your triumph is to walk the Terrace with him at your elbow: your disgrace will be when he leaves you to lament alone…"

"Do not think that any other gentleman will stoop to pick up the cast-off fancy of Lord Chudleigh. When he leaves you, expect nothing but general desertion and contempt. This advice comes from a well-wisher."

"Lord Chudleigh is, as is very well known, the falsest and the most fickle of men. When he hath added you to the list of women whom he hath deceived, he will go away to Bath or town, there to boast of what he hath done. He belongs to the Seven Devils' Club, whose boast it is to spare no man in play and no woman in love. Be warned in time."

"Poor Kitty Pleydell! Your reputation is now, indeed, cracked, if not broken altogether. Better retire to the obscurity of your town lodging, where, with Mrs. Pimpernel, you may weep over the chances that you think to have lost, but have never really possessed. Better take up, while is yet time, with Harry Temple. All the Wells is talking of your infatuation about Lord Chudleigh. He, for his part, is amused. With his friends he laughs and makes sport."

And so on, and so on: words which, like the buzzing of a fly or the sting of a gnat, annoy for a while and are then forgotten. For the moment one is angry: then one remembers things and words which show how false are these charges: one reflects that the writer is more to be pitied than the receiver: and one forgives. Perhaps I was the readier to forgive because I saw a letter written by no other (from the similarity of the *t*'s and *k*'s) than Miss Peggy Baker, and was fully persuaded that the writer of these unsigned letters was that angry nymph herself.

As for the verses which were left at the door, and brought by boys who delivered them and ran away—Nancy said they had no clothes on except a quiver and a pair of wings, and so ran away for shame lest Cicely should see them—they bore a marvellous resemblance to those which the ingenious Mr. Stallabras was wont to manufacture; they spoke of nymphs and doves and bosky groves; of kids and swains on verdant plains; of shepherds' reeds and flowery meads, of rustic flutes and rural fruits.

"The fashion of verses," said Mrs. Esther, "seems little changed since we were here in 1720. Doubtless the English language has never been able to achieve a greater excellence than that arrived at by Dryden, Pope, Addison, and Steele."

Perhaps the language of love is always the same, and when a man feels that tender emotion he naturally desires to quit the garish town and the artificial restraints of society, and with his *inamorata* to seek the simple delights of the meadows and the fields, there to be together:

"Come, live with me and be my love,
And we will all the pleasures prove — — "

So that to every lover the old language, with its musty tropes and rusty figures, is new and fresh, just as any other delight in life when first tasted. I say nothing for that poor weakling, that hothouse plant, the passion affected by beaux at a watering-place for fashionable beauties, which may use the strong language of real love, and yet is so fragile as to be in danger of perishing with every cold blast and frosty air.

I would not laugh at these simple poets, because I have learned since then that there are youths who, too bashful to speak, may yet conceive such a pure and noble passion for a woman—who certainly does not deserve it—as may serve for them as a stimulus and goad to great actions. For no creature, whether man or woman, can do fit suit and service to another, whether in thought or action, without endeavouring to make himself fit and worthy to be her servant. And if he be but one of a hundred following in a crowd of worshippers, it is good for him to mark and obey the laws of gallantry and knightly service, and to lay aside for a while the talk of barrack, stable, coffee-house, and gaming-room.

"Pretty moralist," said Nancy, "you would like the young fellows at your heel, doing suit and service; and you would like to feel that their attendance is doing good to their innocent souls. Now, for my part, I think only how they may be doing good to myself, and when I see them figuring and capering, hat under arm, one foot valiantly stuck out—so—the ties of their wigs wagging behind them, and their canes bobbing at their wrists. I feel, my dear, as if I was not born in vain. All this posturing, all this capering, like a French dancing-master or a bear with a hurdy-gurdy, is meant for me—that is, except what is meant for you, which is the larger half. It may do good to the men: I am sure I wish from my heart it does, because the poor profligates want so much good done to them; but I rather love to think of the honour it confers upon us women, and the envy, hatred, and malice it awakens in the breast of our sisters. My dear Peggy Baker is turning positively green with this hateful passion of jealousy. To be a Toast, even a second Toast, like me, when your superior charms—I am not a bit jealous, Kitty, my dear—have had their due acknowledgment, is a very great honour. In years to come, say about the beginning of the nineteenth century, if I live so long, I shall say to my grandchildren, who will then be about eighteen or nineteen, and as beautiful as the day, 'My dears,' I shall say, 'your grandmother, though you will find it difficult to believe, was not always toothless, nor did her hands always shake, nor were her cheeks wrinkled, nor were her chin and nose close together. Look in the glass, girls, and you may guess what your poor old grandmother once was, in the days when she was pretty Nancy Levett, a Toast when the beautiful Kitty Pleydell was Queen of the Wells. Kitty Pleydell, who married — —,' no, my dear, I will not say it, because it might bring you bad luck."

I told Nancy about Harry Temple's strange mistake; she grew very serious over it, and reflected what was best to be done. I warned her to say nothing herself, but to leave him to his own reflections. First he sulked, that is to say, he avoided me in public, and did not even pay his respects to Mrs. Pimpernel in private; then he implored me to give him another hearing. I gave him what he asked, I heard him tell his story over again, then I assured him once more that it was impossible. He behaved very strangely, refused to take my answer as final, and vexed us by betraying in public the discontent and anger which, had he possessed any real regard for me, he ought to have kept a secret in his own breast. Some of the backbiters, as Lord Chudleigh told me, put it about that I had thrown over my former lover. Allusion to this calumny was made, as has already been shown, in the anonymous letters.

Lord Chudleigh paid me no compliments and wrote me no verses, nor did he often join in our train upon the Terrace. But he distinguished us by frequently paying a visit to our lodgings in the morning, when he would sit and read, or talk, and sometimes share our simple dinner.

"We who belong to the great City houses," said Mrs. Esther after one of these visits, "are accustomed from infancy to familiarity with Nobility. My father, when Worshipful Master of the Scourers' Company, or in his year of office as Lord Mayor, would sometimes have a peer on one side and a bishop on the other. Baronets and simple knights we hardly valued. Therefore these visits of his lordship, which are no doubt a great distinction for both of us, seem like a return of my childhood."

We learned from Lord Chudleigh that it was his intention (afterwards fully carried out) to take that active part in the administration of state affairs to which his exalted rank naturally called him.

"I am ever of opinion," he said, "that a gentleman in this country owes it to his birth and position to do his utmost for the preservation of our liberties and the maintenance of sound government."

And he once told us, to our astonishment, that had he lived in the days of Charles the First, he should have joined the party of the Parliament.

It seemed to me, who watched him narrowly and with trembling, that he was desirous, in these visits, to find out what manner of person I was, and whether I possessed any virtues, to illustrate that external comeliness which had already taken his fancy. Alas! I thought continually with shame of the time when I should have to throw myself at his feet and implore his mercy and forgiveness.

Then he encouraged me to talk about my childhood and my father, taking pleasure, I thought, in the contemplation of a life given up to heaven and learning, and smiling at the picture of Lady Levett, who ruled us all, the two boys who came home to tease the girls, and little Nancy, so fond and so pretty. I wondered then that he should care to hear about the way I lived, the books I read, the death of my honoured father, and the little things which make up a country maid's life, wherein the ripples and the gentle breezes are as important to her as great storms and gales to men and women of the world. I know, now, that when a man loves a girl there is nothing concerned with her that he does not want to know, so that her image may be present to him from the beginning, and that he may feel that there has been no year of her life, no action of hers at all, that he does not know, with what she thought, what she did, who were her friends, and what she was like.

Thus he told me about his own country house, which was a very fine place indeed, and his gardens, stables, library, pictures, and all the splendid things which he had inherited.

Two things we hid from each other, the one that I was the girl whom he had married: the other, that he was already married.

"Child," said Nancy, "the young lord hath plainly bewitched thee. Remember, my dear, that a woman must not be won too easily. Can we not break his heart a little?"

Lady Levett took occasion to speak to me to the same effect.

"Kitty," she said, "I have eyes in my head and can see. Do not encourage the man too much. Yet it would be a grand match, and I should be well content to see a coronet on that pretty head. Still, be not too ready. But he is a handsome fellow, and I believe as good as we can expect of any man in this profligate age. Nay, child, do not change colour: I know nothing against his character, except that he has a town house and that he has lived much in London. But make him feel a little the pangs of love. Listen, or pretend to listen, to the addresses of another man. When my husband came courting me, do you think I said yes all at once? Not so. There were other suitors in the field, let me tell thee, Kitty, as young and as rich as Sir Robert, and of as good a family. To be sure, there was none so good in my eyes. As for one, he rode to hounds all day, and in the evening slept in his chair. He broke his neck jumping a brook when he was but thirty. Another, he drank October all day long, and at night was carried to bed like a log. When he was forty he was taken with a seizure, being still a bachelor, all for love of me and his brown jug, which I think he loved still more. And a third, he was choleric, and used to beat his grooms. Now, my dear, a man who beats his grooms is just as likely to beat his wife. Wherefore, beware of strikers. And a fourth, he was a gambler, and all night over his cards, so that I would have none of him. He lost his estate and went into the Austrian service. There he was run through the body and killed in a duel by a French chevalier, who had first robbed him at faro. But do not think I let my true love know my resolution. I plagued him first, and teased him until he was humble. Then I bade him be happy, and the good man hath been happy ever since."

Alas! I could not tease my lord or plague him: I could not coquet with other men, even though Peggy went about saying—

"The silly wretch is in love with him: she shows it in her eyes. Oh the impudence!"

CHAPTER IX.

HOW LORD CHUDLEIGH WENT TO LONDON.

Without telling any one of his intention, Lord Chudleigh posted one morning to town. I was acquainted with this news by Miss Peggy Baker, who informed me of it in her kindest manner.

"Dear Miss Pleydell," she said, after morning service, as we were coming out of church, "have you heard the dreadful news?"

"I have heard no news," I replied.

"We have lost the chief ornament of the company. Yes; you may well turn pale"—I am sure I did nothing of the kind—"Lord Chudleigh has left Epsom—some say for the season: some say on account of some distaste he has conceived for the place: some say on account of previous engagements."

"What kind of engagements?"

"I thought you would ask that. It is rumoured that he is shortly to be married to a young lady of good birth and with a fortune equal to his own. It is certain that he will not return."

"Really!" said Nancy, who had now come to my aid, "how shall you be able to exist, dear Miss Peggy, without him?"

"I? Oh, indeed, I am not concerned with Lord Chudleigh."

"I mean, how can you exist when the principal subject for scandalous talk, and the chief cause of anonymous letters, is removed?"

She blushed and bit her lips.

"I think, Miss Levett," she gasped, "that you allow your tongue greater liberties than are consistent with good-breeding."

"Better the tongue than the pen, dear Miss Baker," replied Nancy. "Come, Kitty, we will go weep the absence of this truant lord."

"The Temple still remains—he! he!" said Miss Baker.

This was a conversation at which I could laugh, spiteful though it was. I knew not that my lord was gone away, nor why. But one thing I knew very well. He was not gone to marry any one. If that can be called ease which was mostly shame, I felt easy, because ordinary jealousy was not possible with me. He *could not marry, if he wished.* Poor lad! his fate was sealed with mine.

Yet, thinking over what might happen, I resolved that night upon a thing which would perhaps incense my uncle, the Doctor, beyond all measure. I resolved that should that thing happen which most I dreaded, that my lord should fall in love with another woman, I would myself, without his ever knowing who had done it, release him from his ties. I knew where the Doctor kept his registers: I would subtract the leaf which certified our union, and would send it to my lord; or should the Doctor, as was possible, propose any legal action, I would refuse to appear or to act. Now without me the Doctor was powerless.

Lord Chudleigh went to town, in fact, to see the Doctor. He drove to his town house in St. James's Square, and in the morning he sallied forth and walked to the Fleet Market.

The Reverend Doctor Shovel was doing a great and splendid business. Already there were rumours of the intention of Government to bring in a bill for the suppression of these lawless Fleet marriages. Therefore, in order to stimulate the lagging, he had sent his messengers, touters, and runners abroad in every part of the city, calling on all those who wished to be married secretly, or to avoid wedding expenses, feasts, and junketings, and to be securely married, to make haste, while there was yet time. Therefore there was a throng every day from seven in the morning, of prentices with their masters' daughters, old men with their cooks, tradesmen who would avoid the feasting, sailors home for a few weeks, as eager to marry a wife as if they were to be home for the whole of their natural lives, officers who wanted to secure an heiress, and many honest folk who saw in a Fleet wedding the easiest way of avoiding the expenses of their friends' congratulations, with the foolish charges of music, bells, dancing, and rejoicing which often cripple a young married couple for years. Why, the parents connived with the girls, and when these ran away early in the morning, and came home falling upon their knees to confess the truth, the play had been arranged and rehearsed beforehand, and the forgiveness took the form of money for furniture instead of for

The Chaplain of the Fleet

feasting. But still the parents went about holding up their hands and calling Heaven to witness that they could not have believed their daughter so sly and deceitful a puss.

Hither came Lord Chudleigh, heavy of heart.

The Doctor at eleven in the morning was in the full swing of his work. Two couples of the lower class were being married in the house. Outside, the place was beset with wedding parties, couples coming shyly and timidly, and couples coming openly and without shame. The touters and runners of the rival Fleet parsons were fighting, swearing, cajoling and inviting people to stop with them, holding out offers of cheapness, safe marriage, expedition, secrecy, and rum punch. Strangers to London, who had never heard of Doctor Shovel's greatness, were led away to those pretenders whose canonical orders were so doubtful. I believe the world at large entertains contempt for all Fleet parsons as a body (happily no longer existent), but, for my own part, while I hold the memory of the Doctor in mingled shame and respect, I despise the rest because he himself held them in such low esteem.

Roger, the touter, recognised his lordship, as he made his way slowly through the mob along the side of the market.

"Good morning, my lord," he said—his face was bloody and bruised, his tie-wig was awry, his coat was torn, so fierce had been the struggle of the morning—"good-morning, my lord. We have not seen your lordship this long while. Would your lordship like speech with the Doctor? He is busy now, and six couples wait him. Warm work it is now! But I think he will see your lordship. We should be glad to drink your lordship's health."

The fellow made his way through the crowd, and presently returned, saying that the Doctor was very near the benediction, after which he would give his lordship ten minutes, but no longer, and should lose a guinea for every minute.

The Doctor, in fact, was dismissing a pair of couples with a few words of advice. They were respectable young city people, getting the secret marriage for the reasons which I have already described.

The Chaplain of the Fleet

"You are now," he said, "married according to the rites of holy Mother Church. You are tied to each other for life. I hope you will thank and continually bless my name for tying the knot this morning. Remember what the Church charges her children in the words of the service. Go: be honest in your dealings, thrifty in your habits, cautious in your trusts, careful of small gains; so shall you prosper. Let the husband avoid the tavern in the morning, and the conventicle on the Sunday; let the wife study plain, roast, and boiled, make her own dresses, pretend not to be a fine madam, and have no words with gallants from the west of Temple Bar.

"If, on the other hand," he went on, knitting his brows, "the husband spends his money in clubs, among the freemasons, and in taverns; if he do not stick to business, if he cheat in his transactions; or if the wife go finely dressed, and talk with pretty fellows when she ought to be cleaning the furniture; if they both go not to church regularly and obey the instruction of their rector, vicar, or curate—then, I say, the fate of that couple shall be a signal example. For the husband shall be hanged at Tyburn Tree, and the wife be flogged at Bridewell. Go."

They bowed, being overwhelmed with the terrors of this parting advice, and departed. Outside, they were greeted with a roar of rough congratulation, and were followed by the shouts of the market till they reached Fleet Bridge, where they were quickly lost in the crowd.

Then the Doctor turned to Lord Chudleigh.

"Your lordship has come, I suppose," he asked, "to inquire after the health of her ladyship?"

"I come, Doctor Shovel," replied my lord gravely, "to know from your own lips, before I commit the affair to counsel, how far I am compromised by the disgraceful trick you played upon me about a year ago."

"Your lordship is married," said the Doctor simply. "So far are you compromised, and no further. Nay, we seek no further complication in this business."

He sat down in his wooden arm-chair, and, with his elbow on the table, knitted his bushy eyebrows, frowned and shook his great forefinger in his visitor's face.

"Your lordship is married," he repeated. "Of that have no doubt; no doubt whatever is possible. Tell your lawyer all; refer him to me."

"The story," said Lord Chudleigh, "is this. I come here, out of curiosity, to see you—a man of whom I had heard much, though little to your credit. I am received by you with courtesy and hospitality. There is much drinking, and I (for which I have no defence to offer) drink too much. I awake in the morning still half unconscious. I am taken downstairs by you, and married, while in that condition, to some woman I had never before seen. After this I am again put to bed. When I awake, I am informed by you what has taken place."

"That is a story neatly told," said the Doctor. "If I had to tell it, however, the details would assume another complexion. What brought your lordship to spend the night in such a place as the Liberties of the Fleet? A common parson of the Fleet? Nay, that is improbable; my modesty forbids me to believe so incredible a circumstance. But we may suppose an appointment for the morning; an appointment made and kept; a secret marriage——"

"Would you dare to tell such a story as that?" Lord Chudleigh interrupted the Doctor with vehemence. "Would you dare, sir, to hint that I, Lord Chudleigh, had designed a Fleet marriage?"

"My lord, where a member of your family, where your father's son is concerned, I dare a great deal, I assure you."

"And the woman—who is she? Produce me this wretch, this creature who became an accomplice in the plot."

"All in good time. Be assured, my lord, that we shall produce her in good time—at the right time. Also, be resigned to the inevitable. Nothing can unmarry you now."

"I think," said his lordship, "that thou art the greatest villain in England."

"Ta, ta, ta!" The Doctor lay back in his chair with his arms extended and a genial laugh. "Your lordship is not complimentary. Still, I make allowances. I cannot fight you, because I am a clergyman; you can therefore say what you please. And I own that it certainly is a vexatious thing for a gentleman of your rank and position to have a wife and yet to have no wife: not to know her name and parentage.

Why, she may be in the soap-suds over the family linen in the Fleet Liberties, or selling hot furmety on Fleet Bridge, or keeping a farthing sausage-stall in the Fleet Market, or making the rooms for the gentlemen in the Fleet Prison, or frying beefsteaks in Butcher Row; or she may be picking pockets in St. Paul's Churchyard, or she may be beating hemp in Bridewell, or she may be under the Alderman's rod in Newgate. Nay, my lord, do not swear in this place, which is, as one may say, a chapel-of-ease. Then her parents: your lordship's father and mother-in-law. Roger, my touter—say—may be her parent; or she may come of a dishonest stock in Turnmill Lane; or she may be ignorant of father and mother, and may belong to the numerous family of those who sleep in the baskets of Covent Garden and the ashes of the glass-houses. I repeat, my lord, that to swear in such a place, and before such a man, a reverend divine, is impious. Avoid the habit of swearing altogether; but, if you must swear, let it be outside this house."

"You will not, then, even tell me where she is, this wife of mine?"

"I will not, my lord."

"You will not even let me know the depth of my degradation?"

"My lord, I will tell you nothing. As for her ladyship, I will say not a word. But as I have shown you the possibilities on one side, so I would show them to you on the other. She may be the wretched creature you fear. She may also be a gentlewoman by birth, young, beautiful, accomplished; fit, my lord, to bear your name and to be your wife."

"No," he cried; "that is impossible. What gentlewoman would consent to such a marriage?"

The Doctor laughed.

"There are many things in this world," he said, "that even Lord Chudleigh cannot understand. Now, my lord, if you have nothing more to say, you may leave me. There are already half a dozen expectant brides upon the threshold. One would not, sure, keep the poor things waiting. I am generally at home, my lord, in the evening, and should you feel inclined for another social night with punch, and a song over the bowl, your lordship will be welcome, in spite of hard words."

Lord Chudleigh answered not a word, but walked away.

Small comfort had he got from the Doctor.

Now was he in a sad plight indeed; for his heart was altogether filled with the image of Kitty Pleydell. Yet how hope to win her? And how stand by and let her be won by another man?

To be married in such a way, not to know who or what your wife might be, is, surely, a thing quite beyond any history ever told.

CHAPTER X.

HOW TWO OLD FRIENDS CAME TO EPSOM.

The Doctor's letter had informed us of the liberation of Mr. Stallabras and Sir Miles Lackington; but we were not prepared for their arrival at Epsom. They came, however, travelling together by the coach, their object being not so much, I believe, to visit the watering-place of Epsom or to enjoy its amusements, as to renew certain honourable proposals, formerly made in less happy times, to Kitty Pleydell.

Naturally, we were at first somewhat perturbed, fearing the scandal should certain tongues spread abroad the truth as to our residence in the Fleet.

"My dear," said Mrs. Esther, with a little sigh, "my mind is made up. We will go to Tunbridge out of their way."

This was impossible, because they would follow us. For my own part, I looked upon the Fleet Rules with less shame than poor Mrs. Esther. To her, the memory of the long degradation was infinitely painful. For everybody, certainly, a time of degradation, however unmerited, is never a pleasant thing to remember. I think that the whole army of martyrs must agree together in forgetting the last scenes of their earthly pilgrimage. The buffetings, strippings, scourgings, roastings, burnings, and hangings, the long time of prison, the starvation, the expectancy and fear—the going forth to meet the hungry lion and the ruthless tiger—surely it cannot be comfortable to remember these? No martyr on the roll had ever been more innocent or undeserving of punishment than Mrs. Esther Pimpernel: no sufferer ever complained less: but she loved not to think of the past, nor to be reminded of it by the arrival of one whom she had known there.

Nevertheless, when Sir Miles Lackington presented himself at our lodging, he was received with a gracious friendliness.

His newly recovered liberty made little alteration in the appearance of this prodigal son. His dress was worn in the same easy disorder, the ruffles being limp, his wig tied carelessly, the lace upon his hat torn, as if in some scuffle, and the buckles of his shoes were an odd pair.

His face preserved the same jolly content, as if the gifts of Fortune were to be regarded no more than her buffeting.

"We are always," said my guardian, with a little hesitation, "we are always glad to welcome old friends—even friends in common misfortune. But, Sir Miles, it is not well to remind us—or—or to talk to others of those unhappy days."

He laughed.

"I remember them not," he said. "I never remember any day but the present. Why should we remember disagreeable things? Formerly we borrowed; now we lend: let us go on lending till we have to borrow again. Do you remember Mr. Stallabras the poet?"

Surely, we remembered Solomon.

"He goes abroad now in a silk-lined coat with lace ruffles. He has bought a new wig and started a subscription list for a new poem, having eaten up the last before the poem was written. I subscribed for three copies yesterday, and we pretended, both of us, he that he did not want the money, and I that I had always had it. Without forgetting and pretending, where should we be?"

"Indeed," said Mrs. Esther, "one would not willingly either forget or pretend. But some things are best remembered in silence. The memory of them should keep us humble, Sir Miles."

"I do not wish to be humble," replied the baronet. "Humble people do not sing and drink, nor gamble, nor make love. They go in sadness and with hanging heads. I would still go proud."

While he was with us came Solomon himself, bravely dressed indeed, with about an ell of ribbon tied around his throat, a new and fashionable wig, and bearing himself with all the dignity possible in a poet of five-feet-three. His chin was in the air and his hat under his arm when he marched into the little room.

I shook hands with him, and whispered to him not to mention the word Fleet. Thereupon he advanced to Mrs. Esther with such a bow as would have graced a court, saying—

"Madam, I have had the honour of being presented to you in London, but I know not if I am still distinguished by your recollection."

"Sir," said Mrs. Esther, "that person must indeed be blind to merit who can forget Mr. Stallabras, the favourite of the Muses."

"O madam! this compliment——"

"O sir! our hearts are not so insensible as to forget those delightful verses, which should be the glory of an unthinking age."

I asked him then if he had received a bequest.

"I have found what is better," he said, "a female Mæcenas. The virtues of antiquity linger only in the breasts of the fair. She is a person of singularly cold and calm judgment. Despréaux himself had not a cooler head or a sounder critical faculty. Therefore, when such a lady prophesies immortal renown to a poet, that poet may congratulate himself. I am poet laureate to Lady Tamarind, relict of Sir Joseph Tamarind, brewer and sometime sheriff in the City of London. Her ladyship's taste is considered infallible in all subjects, whether china, tulips, plays, pictures, fans, snuff-boxes, black boys, or poets."

His eyes twinkled so brightly, his turn-up nose seemed so joyfully to sniff the incense of praise, prosperity had already made his cheeks so sleek and fat, that we could hardly recognise our starveling poet.

"The taste," said Mrs. Esther, "of a woman who recognises the merit of your verses, Mr. Stallabras, is beyond a doubt."

He rubbed his hands and laughed.

"I was already out—" he began, but as we all manifested the greatest confusion at the beginning of this confession, he stopped and turned red. "I mean I was—I was——"

"You were beginning, I think," I interrupted, "to open a new subscription."

"Thank you, Miss Kitty," he replied. "I was—as soon as I left the Ru— I mean, as soon as I could, I went round among my patrons with my project. This lady immediately bought all my previous poems, including the translation of 'Lucretius,' which the rascal publisher declared had been his ruin, when he went bankrupt, and presented me with a hundred guineas, with which I was enabled"—here he surveyed his person with satisfaction, and raised one leg to get a better view of his stockings and shoe-buckles—"I was enabled to procure garments more suitable to a personage of ambition, and to present myself to the honourable company assembled at Epsom on a footing of easy equality."

"But a hundred guineas will not last for ever," I said, thinking of the sums of money which I had already spent on frocks and ribbons since we came from London.

"That is not all," he said; "I have my new volume of poems, which has been subscribed by Lady Tamarind and her friends. This is a change, is it not, Miss Kitty? Formerly, when I was in the Ru—I mean, before my good fortune came—a sixpenny ordinary was beyond me: I have lived upon half-a-crown for a week: I have written lines on a 'Christian's Joys' when starving: and I have composed the 'Lamentations of a Sinner' when contemplating suicide as the only relief from my troubles. Now—now—how different! Fortune's wheel has turned—Fame is mine. And as for poems, I can write as many as I please to give the world, and always find a subscription list ready to my hand. This brain, Miss Kitty, like the Fountain of Helicon, will run for ever: that is, while life and Lady Tamarind remain."

"The stream may get muddy sometimes," said Sir Miles, with a smile.

Fate, which condemns poets to poverty, also compensates them with hope. If they are in present sunshine, it will last for ever: if in cold neglect, the future will give what the past has refused: posterity will continue to wave the censing-pot and send up wreaths of spicy smoke, a continual flow, grateful to the blessed Spirit above: so that, fortunate or in neglect, they dwell in a perpetual dream, which keeps them ever happy.

Then the sanguine bard drew forth his new subscription list.

"I call it," he said, "by the modest title of a 'Project for the Publication of a New Collection of Odes and Heroic Pieces,' by Solomon Stallabras, Esquire. I am aware that my birth gives no warrant for the assumption of the rank of Esquire, but Lady Tamarind is good enough to say that the possession of genius lifts a man to the level of the gentry, if not the nobility of the country."

"It does, Solomon; it does," said Sir Miles.

"I venture, ladies, therefore," he said, taking a pencil from his pocket, "to solicit your honoured names as subscribers for this poor effort of a (perhaps) too ambitious brain. The poems, when completed, will be printed in royal quarto, with the portrait of the author as he appears crowned by Fame, while the Graces (draped for the occasion in the modern taste) stand behind him: Cupid will raise aloft the trumpet of Fame: the Muses will be seen admiring from a gentle eminence which represents Parnassus: Apollo will be figured presenting the poet with his own lyre, and the sacred stream will flow at his feet—my own design. In the distance the skin of Marsyas will hang upon a tree, as a warning to the presumption of rivals. The work will be bound in calf, and will be issued at the price of two guineas. For that small sum, ladies, Solomon Stallabras offers a copy of his poems."

"O Mr. Stallabras!" cried Mrs. Esther, "for so charming a picture I would give not two but twenty guineas, to say nothing of the poems. Go on, dear sir; raise our thoughts to virtue, and strengthen our inclinations in the path of duty. Poets, indeed, make the way to heaven a path of roses."

Now here was a change from old times! Solomon flourishing a subscription list in lace and silk, and Mrs. Esther offering guineas by the dozen! Sir Miles, who was leaning by the window just as he had been wont to do in our poor lodging, nodded and laughed, unseen by Mrs. Esther.

"Permit me, sir," she said, "if you will be so good, to put my name down for— —"

"O madam!"

The poet bowed low and brandished his pencil.

"For ten copies of this immortal work, in one of which I would ask you to write your name, in your own hand, for the enrichment of the volume and the admiration of posterity."

"Madam," said Solomon, with emotion, "I will write my name in the whole ten."

"And, dear sir, one copy for Miss Kitty."

"Such generosity! such princessly, noble patronage of the Poetical Art!" he fairly chuckled as he wrote down the names. "Eleven copies! Twenty-two guineas! This is indeed to realise fame."

He received the money, which Mrs. Esther paid him with a countenance all smiles, although he vainly tried to throw into his expression the pride of the poet, to whom money is but filthy lucre.

We then conversed on Epsom and its beauties, and as the gentlemen had as yet seen none of them, I proposed to lead them to the Downs, whence I promised them such a landscape as should infinitely rejoice their eyes. They accepted with expressions of gratitude, and we started. When, however, we came to the doors of the Spread Eagle, Sir Miles recollected that at twelve he always took a tankard of cool October for the good of his health. He therefore left us, promising to follow. But as he did not come, and we saw him no more that day, I suppose he found the society of the tankard more enchanting than that of Kitty Pleydell. We therefore walked up the hill alone, and presently stood upon the open down, which commands so noble a view. The place was quite deserted that day, save for a single group of gentlemen, who were conducting a match, but so far off that we heard not their voices.

I took advantage of this solitude to convey to the poet an instruction that it would be better not to talk freely at Epsom concerning such vicissitudes of fortune as we had experienced. I pointed out to him that until Mrs. Esther's position was securely fixed it might do her injury to have her story garbled by censorious tongues; that, for his own sake, his late connection with the Liberties of the Fleet would be better concealed; and that, for myself, although it mattered less, because I was never a prisoner while yet an inmate of the Rules, I did not wish my story, such as it was, to be passed about the Wells, and mangled in the telling.

Mr. Stallabras declared stoutly that he would not for worlds reveal one word about the past—for my sake.

"Nay," I said, "not for mine, but for the sake of that dear lady to whom you owe so much."

"It is true," he said; "I owe her even life. She hath fed me from her slender stores when I was starving. And when no one would even read my verses she would learn them by heart and repeat them with tears. For her sake, then, if not for yours."

Then his face assumed an expression like unto that with which he had once before made me an offer of his hand, and I knew that he was going to do it again. If such a thing is going to be done, the sooner it is over the better. Therefore I waited with calmness, hoping that the paroxysm would be short and not violent.

"Miss Kitty," he began, turning very red, "some time ago I was penniless, almost starving, and detained in the (absurdly called) Liberties of the Fleet for the amount of forty pounds sixteen shillings and eightpence—a sum so small that it made me blush to confess it, most of my friends in the same place being incarcerated for substantial sums of hundreds and even thousands. In this difficult position, which required the philosophy of a Stoic to endure with resignation, I had the temerity to offer my hand to the most beautiful woman in the world. I have often, since, wondered at my own audacity and her gentleness while she refused so presumptuous a proposal."

"Indeed, Mr. Stallabras," I said, "you conferred great honour upon me."

He bowed.

"The position of affairs," he went on, "is now changed. The poet's brows are crowned with bays by the hand of a lady as skilled in poets as she is in pug-dogs; his pockets are lined with guineas; as for the Fleet Rules—I whistle the memory of the place to the winds. Phew! it is gone, never to return: I see before me a long and great future, when booksellers will compete for the honour of publishing me, and the greatest lords and ladies in the land will rush to subscribe for copies. Like Shakespeare, I shall amass a fortune: like Prior, I shall receive offers of embassies: like Addison and Chaucer, I shall be placed in posts of honour and profit."

"I hope, Mr. Stallabras," I said, "that such will indeed be your future."

"Do you really hope so, Miss Kitty?" His face flushed again, and I was quite sorry for him, knowing the pain I was about to inflict upon him. "Do you hope so? Then that emboldens me to say—Fairest of your sex, divine nymph, accept the homage of a poet: be celebrated for ever in his immortal verse. Be my Laura! Let me be thy Petrarch!"

"I will," I replied. "I accept that offer joyfully. I will be to you what Laura was to Petrarch, if that will content you."

I gave him my hand, which he seized with rapture.

"Oh, beautiful Kitty!" he cried, with such joy in his eyes that I repented having said so much, "fortune has now bestowed upon me all I ask. When, goddess, wilt thou crown my happiness!"

"It is already crowned," I replied. "I have given you, Mr. Stallabras, all you asked for. Let me remind you that you yourself told me the story of Petrarch's love. I will be your Laura, but I must have the liberty of doing what Laura did—namely, the right to marry some one else."

His face fell.

"Oh!" he murmured. "Why did I not say Heloïse?"

"Because she was shut up in a convent. Come, Mr. Stallabras, let us remain friends, which is far better for both of us, and less trying to the temper than being lovers. And I will help you with your subscription-book. As for being married, you would tire of me in a week."

Upon this he fell to protesting that it was impossible for any man to tire of such a paragon among women, and I dare say the poor deluded creature really meant what he said, because men in love are blind. When this failed to move me, he lamented his ill-fortune in having placed his hopes upon the heart of a beautiful statue as cold as Dian. Nor was it until he had prophesied death to himself and prayed for ruin and loss of his fame, both of which, he said, were now useless, or comparatively useless to him, that I succeeded in making him, to a certain extent, reasonable, and calming his anger. He really had thought that so grand an offer of marriage with a poet, whom he placed on about the same level with Homer, would tempt any woman. According to some detractors of the fair sex, every woman believes that every man must fall in love with her: but I am sure that there is no man who does not believe that he is irresistible when once he begins to show a preference or an inclination.

I then persuaded him, with honeyed words, to believe in my sorrow that I was not able to accept his proposals; and I added that as he had by this time sufficiently admired the beauties of the landscape, we might return to the town, when I should have the honour of presenting him to some of the better sort among the visitors.

He came down the hill with me, sighing after the manner of poets in love, and panting a little, because he was fat and short of breath, and I walked fast.

We found the Terrace crowded with people congregated for the morning talk; the breakfasts being all eaten, the tea-drinking over, morning prayers finished, and the music playing merrily.

I presented the poet to Lady Levett as an ingenious gentleman whose verses, known all over town, were doubtless already well known to her ladyship. She had not the hardness of heart to deny knowledge of the poet, and gave him a kindly welcome to Epsom, where, she said, she had no doubt whatever but that he would meet with the reception due to qualities of such distinction.

Then I ventured to suggest that Mr. Stallabras was receiving names for a subscription edition of his new poems. Lady Levett added hers, and begged the poet to visit her at her lodging, where she would discharge her debt.

In the course of an hour I presented Stallabras to young Lord Eardesley, Harry Temple, and half the gentlemen at the Wells, asking of each a subscription to the poems, so that the fortunate poet found himself some fifty guineas the richer by his morning's work.

"Miss Kitty," he said humbly, "I knew not, indeed, that you were so great a lady. The 'Queen of the Wells,' I am told. Not but all who know your worth and kindness must rejoice at this signal triumph. I now plainly see why I must be content with the lot of Petrarch."

Once launched in society, the poet became quickly a kind of celebrity. Just as, in some years, a watering-place would boast of having among its visitors such famous men as Dr. Johnson, Mr. Garrick, or Mr. Richardson, so now it pointed to Mr. Stallabras, and said to strangers, "See! The great Mr. Stallabras! The illustrious poet!"

He, like all men born in London, was equal to the opportunity, and rose on the wave of fashion; his subscription-list kept mounting up; he sent his poems to the press; he received proofs and read them beneath the portico, which he compared to the columns where the Roman poets had been accustomed to read their compositions. We gathered round and listened; we cried, with our handkerchiefs to our eyes: "O Mr. Stallabras, how fine! how wondrous pathetic! how just!" Then would he bow and twist, and wave his hand, and wag his head.

He became an oracle, and, like all oracles in the matter of taste, he quickly learned to give the law. He affected to understand pictures, and talked about the "brio" of one painter, and the "three-lights" rule of another; he was very sarcastic in the matter of poetry, and would allow but two good poets in the century—himself and Mr. Alexander Pope; in the region of romance he would allow little credit to Fielding, but claimed immortality for Richardson.

"Oh, sir, pardon me," he said to one who attributed the greater merit to the former writer. "Pardon me. The characters and the situations of Fielding are so wretchedly low and dirty that I cannot imagine any one being interested in them. There is, I admit, some strength of humour in him, but he hath over-written himself. I doubt he is a strong hulking sort of man."

"But, sir," said Lady Levett, "we ladies like men to be strong and hearty as becomes a man. You surely do not mean that every big man must have low tastes."

"The mind and the body are united," said the little poet, "they influence one another. Thus, in a weak frame we find delicacy, and in a strong frame, bluntness. Softness and tenderness of mind are often remarkable in a body possessed of the same qualities. Tom Jones could get drunk on the night of his uncle's recovery—no doubt Mr. Fielding would manifest his joy in the same manner."

He went on to assure us that Lady Bellaston was an intimate friend of Mr. Fielding's; that Booth was himself; Tom Jones, again, himself; Amelia his first wife; his brawls, gaols, sponging-houses, and quarrels all drawn from his own personal experience.

"He who associates with low companions, ladies," concluded the ex-prisoner of the Fleet, "must needs himself be low. Taste consorts only with tasteful persons."

"Should not a lady be beautiful, Mr. Stallabras?" asked a bystander. "I always supposed so, but since a man is not to be strong, perhaps I was wrong."

"Sir!" Mr. Stallabras drew himself up to his fall height, and his fingers closed upon the roll of proof-sheets as if it had been a sword-hilt. "Sir! all ladies—who have taste—are beautiful. I am ready to be the champion of the sex. Some are more beautiful than others,"—here he raised his eyes to me and sighed. "Some flowers are more beautiful than others. The man of taste loves to let his eyes rest on such a pleasing object,"—here two young gentlemen winked at each other—"she is a credit to her sex. When goodness is joined to such beauty, as is the case with——" Here he looked at me and hesitated.

"Oh!" cried Nancy, "say with *me*, Mr. Stallabras, or Miss Peggy Baker."

"May I say Miss Pleydell?" he asked, with a comprehensive smile. "There, indeed, is all Clarissa, and the heart of sensibility, in contemplating her perfections, reverts to the scenes of our divine Richardson."

CHAPTER XI.

HOW SIR MILES RENEWED HIS OFFER.

Thus did I get rid of one suitor, knowing that there were still two more in the field, and anxious about my lord's absence, which, I doubted not, was concerned in some way with me. Heavens! if he should find out the secret! If the Doctor should communicate to him the thing which I desired to tell at my own time and place.

The Evil One, at this juncture, suggested a temptation of his own.

Suppose a message, which my lord could trust, were to reach him, stating that there would be no attempt to follow up the so-called marriage in the Rules, that he could go his own way, unmolested; that the very certificate and the leaf of the register containing the proof of the marriage would be restored to him—how would that be?

Yet, what sort of happiness could a wife expect who every day had to fear the chance of detection and exposure? Some time or other he would learn that I was the niece of the man who had dealt him this blow; some day he would learn the whole story. Why, there was not only the Doctor, but his man Roger, the villain with the pale face, the scarred cheeks, and the red nose. If the Doctor were dead, what would prevent such a man from telling the story abroad and proclaiming it to all comers?

For poor Kitty there was only one course open; she must work her way to happiness through shame and confession. Yet with all the shame and confession there was no certainty that the happiness would follow. A man vehemently loves and desires a woman, but a woman vehemently desires the love and desire of a man. I desired, with all my strength and with all my might, the affections of my lord. His image, his idea, were with me always. For me there was no other man in the world.

But first I had to deal with my present suitors.

Solomon dismissed, and made happy with praises and guineas (a poet is a creature whose vanity seems always to outweigh all other qualities), I had next to reckon with Sir Miles, who was more reasonable and yet more persistent.

I knew that he had come to Epsom on purpose to seek me out. That was borne in upon me with a force not to be resisted. He always did me the honour of showing me a preference when we lived under the same roof, and when he would lie in wait for me at the foot of the sanded stairs. And, of course, I liked him. He was good-natured, he had the *air noble*; he would not, certainly, beat his wife or treat her unkindly, although he would probably spend all the money in drink and play. And whether he was rich or poor, in the Rules or in the Prison, or wandering free, he would still be the same easy, careless creature, happy in the sunshine, happier by candlelight over a bowl of punch.

On the Terrace, where we met him in the afternoon, he was the same, save that his clothes were newer, as when, just as he lounged now beneath the trees, he had then lounged among the bulkheads and stalls of the market, till evening came with the joys of the day. Always with the carriage of a gentleman. Most of the beaux of Epsom were such gentlemen as claim the title of Esquire by right of their profession as attorneys, barristers, officers, nabobs, rich merchants, and the like. As for their manners, they were easy so long as they were natural, and then they were somewhat barbarous; when they endeavoured to assume the manners of such as Lord Chudleigh, they were awkward. As for the young fellows from the country estates, they were always clowns; they came clowns to the Wells; they put on fine clothes; laughed and grimaced; lost their money at horse-racing and lansquenet, and went home clowns. But Sir Miles was always, even when drunk, a gentleman.

I suppose he had the impudence, at first, to suppose that I was going to seek him out and distinguish him before all the company with my particular regard. When he discovered that it was difficult to get speech with the Queen of the Wells unless you joined her court, he came along with the rest, and was speedily as ready with his compliment, his innuendo, his jest, and his anecdote. He was more ready than most, because he had seen the great world in his youth, and had caught their manner. The general run of gallants were, it seemed to me, afraid of him. To be sure, he was a big, strong man, could have crunched two or three of the slender beaux between his arms; yet he was the most kind-hearted fellow in the world.

Three days after his arrival, Lord Chudleigh having then been away for a week, and I beginning to wonder what business kept him so long from the apron strings of Kitty, he invited me to go with him to the Downs to see a match. I would go with him, though well I knew what he meant; and, of course, when we got to the Downs, the match was over and the people going home.

"Egad, Miss Kitty," he said, "there is always such a plaguy crowd after your ladyship's heels, that a man gets never a chance of a word with you, save edgeways with the pretty little beaux. Well, I have told Solomon to go to the house and take care of Mrs. Esther. There they are, cheek by jowl, and her handkerchief up to her eyes over his sentimental poetry. You and I can have a talk to ourselves. It is only a quarter of a mile from here to your lodging, but, if you like to come with me by way of the old well and Banstead, we can make it half a mile."

"Thank you, Sir Miles," I said; "I am not anxious to double that quarter of a mile. Consider, if you please, that I have to get home, dine, and dress for the day."

"Very good. Have it your own way. That, to be sure, you always will have. I think, for my part, that you never looked so nice as when you wore your hair in curls, and a holland frock. Miss Kitty, do you remember a certain day when a baronet, out at elbows, offered you his hand—with nothing in it?"

"I remember it perfectly." I laughed at the recollection. "And oh, Sir Miles, to think of how you looked when you made that condescending proposal. It was after a most disgraceful evening—you best know where. You had been brought home singing. Your neck-ribbon was untied, your wig awry, your hand shaky, your cheeks red, and in your left hand a brown mug full of old October. What a suitor!"

"Yes," he replied, laughing, without the least appearance of being offended by my picture. "When in the Rules, I behaved according to the custom of the place. I am no longer in the Rules, but at the Wells. I remember that tankard. Considering that the day is sultry, I wish I had one in my hand this very moment."

"I am sure, Sir Miles, that your conduct under these happier circumstances will reflect greater credit upon you."

"Happier circumstances?" he said. "Well, I suppose so. In the Fleet I could borrow of my cousins a guinea a week or thereabout; yet borrowing is uncertain and undignified: the manner of living was cheap, but it was rude. Drink there was—more than one had a right to expect; drink was plentiful, but only the Doctor got good punch; no morals were expected of a Fleet Rules Christian. I know not that things are happier now than then. However, you might think so. Girls never have any philosophy. I have come into a small estate of six hundred pounds a year. It is not so much, by five times six hundred, as what I started with; still, with six hundred a year, one can live. Do you not think so?"

"It seems to me a very handsome provision," I replied, thinking that Mrs. Esther had about the same.

"Yes, it will do."

He fanned his face with his hat, and begged me to sit down on the grass and listen to him for a moment. Men, even the most careless, like Sir Miles, have a way of becoming suddenly solemn when they ask a woman to become their wife. I know not whether their gravity springs from a sense of their own great worth, or from a feeling of unworthiness; whether it is a compliment to the woman they woo, or to themselves. Or it may be a confession of the holiness of the state of matrimony, which one would fain hope to be the case.

Sir Miles then, blushing and confused, offered me, for the second time, his hand.

"You see," he said, "the right hand doth no longer shake, nor doth the left hand hold a pot of October. I no longer am carried home at night." He sighed, as if the reminiscence of past times was pleasing but saddening. "I am not any more the man that once I was. Will you, sweet Kitty—will you be Lady Lackington?"

"I cannot," I said.

"There is an income of six hundred pounds a year," he went on. "I believe there is a small house somewhere; we could live in it rent-free. You were always fond of hens and pigs, and milk, flowers, apples, and all these things. I will keep two hundred pounds for myself, and give you four. With two hundred I shall have to manage, once a week or so, a little hazard, or a trifling lansquenet."

"What?" I asked. "Marry a gamester?"

"What matter as to that, when he will settle his money on his wife? Think of it, Kitty. I am a baronet, though a poor one, and of as good a family as any in Norfolk. Why the Lackingtons, as everybody knows, were on their lands before the Conqueror."

"And if it is not enough to be a gamester, you are also—O Sir Miles! the shame of it——"

"We gentlemen of Norfolk," he replied, without any appearance of shame, "are honest topers all. I deny it not. Yet what matters such a trifle in the habits of a man? Did any gentlemen in the county drink harder than my father? Yet he was hale and tough at sixty, and would have lived to eighty but for a fall he got riding home one night after dinner, having a cask, or thereabouts, of port inside him, by reason of which he mistook an open quarry for the lane which should have led him home, and therefore broke his neck."

"So that, if his wife loved him, as no doubt she did, it was the drink that robbed her of a husband. Your tale hath a useful moral, Sir Miles."

"Come, pretty Puritan, look at me. I am twenty-nine—in my thirtieth year; strong and hearty, if I do get drunk of an evening. What then? Do you want to talk to your husband all night? Better know that he is safe asleep, and likely to remain asleep till the drink is gone out of his head."

"Oh, the delights of wedlock! To have your husband brought home every night by four stout fellows!"

"Evening drink hurts no man. Have I a bottle nose? Do my hands shake? Are my cheeks fat and pale? Look at me, Kitty." He held out his arms and laughed.

"Yes, Sir Miles," I replied; "I think you are a very lusty fellow, and, in a wrestling-bout, I should think few could stand against you. But as a husband, for the reasons I have stated, I say—No!"

"Take the four hundred, Kitty, and make me happy. I love thee, my girl, with all my heart."

"Sir Miles, I cannot do it honestly. Perhaps I wish I could."

"You won't?" He looked me full in the face. "I see you won't. You have such a telltale, straightforward face, Kitty, that it proclaims the truth always. I believe you are truth itself. They pulled you out of a well, down in your country place, in a bucket, and then went about saying you had been born."

"Thank you, Sir Miles."

"Am I, therefore, to go hang myself in my garters, or yours, if you will give them to me?"

"If you do, I shall be the first to run and cut you down."

"Sweet it were," he murmured, "to be even cut down by your fair hand. If one was sure that you would come in time——"

"You will be reasonable, dear sir, and you will neither say nor do anything silly."

"I do not suppose I shall pine away in despair; nor shall I hang my head; nor shall I go about saying that there are as good fish in the sea as ever came out of it, because, when we fished you, we fished the best. And I swear. Kitty"—here he did swear after men's profane way, but he needed not to have sworn so loudly or so long—"that truly, sweet Kitty, thou art the fairest, the loveliest, and the best fish that ever came out of any sea—a bewitching mermaid! I wish thee a good husband.

> "On Stella's lap he laid his head,
> And, looking in her eyes,
> He cried, 'Remember, when I'm dead,
> That I deserved the prize.'"

"Thank you, Sir Miles. A shorter and a less profane oath would surely have better graced the subject."

"It cannot be graced too much," he said, as if to swear lustily was to confer honour upon the woman he thought to love. "For your sake, Kitty, I would ever forswear punch, tobacco, and strong waters; drink nothing but October; and never get drunk save on Saturday nights: for your sake would I go live in the country among the cocks and the hens, the ducks and the pigs; for you would I go religiously to church every Sunday at forenoon, and expect the parson for the beef and pudding after the sermon; for your sake would I gamble no more, save once in a way when quarter-day brought in the rents."

"That would be a mighty reformation indeed, Sir Miles."

"Now, however, since you will not have me, I shall play with four hundred a year out of the six. But I will be careful, all the same: I shall punt low, and never lose more than a guinea a night."

Thus I was rid of my second suitor. Sir Miles ceased to attend the count of followers who attended on the Terrace, but sat all day in the card-room, playing. From time to time he met and saluted me.

"Be not afraid," he would say, "on my behalf. The card-tables are more pleasant than the air under the trees, and I think the players are better company than your priggish popinjays. As for my habits, fair Kitty, pattern of virtue, they have become virtuous. I am never drunk—well, not often—and you have brought me luck. I have won five hundred guineas from a nabob. Think of the joy, when he pays me, of losing it all again!"

CHAPTER XII.

HOW HARRY TEMPLE PROVED HIS VALOUR.

Thus were poet and baronet reduced to submission. The third suitor was harder to manage, because he turned sulky. Sportsmen have said that a fish, or a bird, or a fox, when he sulks, is then most difficult to secure. Thus, to be captured or cajoled, the victim must be in a good temper.

Now Harry Temple went in gloomy indignation, as was visible to all eyes. He walked alone upon the Terrace, or sat alone in the Assembly Room, a Killjoy to behold. That would not have mattered, because no girl feels much sorrow for a man who foolishly sulks because he cannot marry her; but everybody knew, or thought they knew, the cause of his heavy looks. Peggy Baker said I had thrown him over for the sake of a lord, who, she added kindly, would certainly throw me over in turn. Some of the company cried shame on the flinty-hearted woman who could let so pretty a fellow go love-sick.

"Kitty," his melancholy seemed to say, "you left us a simple country girl: you would have been proud of my addresses had you understood my meaning"—this was quite true: "you are now a woman of fashion, and you have ambition: your head is turned with flattery: you aspire to nothing short of a coronet. In those days you were satisfied with the approval of your looking-glass and your conscience: now you would draw all men to your heels, and are not happy unless you make them all miserable." But that was not true at all; I did not wish to make men miserable; and it was nothing to me whether they were miserable or happy. I thought of one man only, as is natural to a woman in love.

"If," I said to him one day, being tired by such exhibition of temper, "if you do not like the place, why make yourself unhappy by staying here? Cambridge, methinks, would be a more fitting abode for you, where there are books and scholars; not a watering-place, where people come together to amuse themselves and be merry."

"I shall stay here," he replied, "until I find there is no hope for me."

"Oh, silly Harry!" I said; "is there no other woman in the world who will make you happy, except poor Kitty Pleydell?"

"No—none," he shook his melancholy wig, the tie at the back of his head wagging sorrowfully.

How was it possible to have any sympathy with so rueful a lover? Why, it made one ridiculous. Everybody said that Harry Temple was in love with me, that I, for the worst of motives, viz., to catch a coronet, refused him, and that he was an excellent match, especially for one who was nothing better than a country parson's daughter.

"I believe only a curate, my dear," Peggy Baker would say. "No doubt she lived on bacon fat and oatmeal, and knitted her own stockings. And yet she refuses Harry Temple, a pretty fellow, though studious, and a man whom any of us, gentlewomen born, would be glad to encourage."

"Oh!" I said to him, "why do you not go? Why do you look reproaches on me?"

"Because," he replied, "I still love you, unworthy as you are."

"Unworthy? Mr. Temple, methinks that a little civility——"

"Yes, unworthy. I say that a girl who throws over her oldest friends with the almost avowed intention of securing a title, without knowing anything of the character of the man who bears it——"

"This is too much!" I said. "First, sir, let me know what there is against Lord Chudleigh's character. Tell me, upon your word, sir, do you know anything at all? Is he not a man of principle and honour?"

"I know nothing against him. I dare say that he is what you think."

"Well, sir; and, in the next place, how dare you accuse me of deliberately trying to attract my lord? Do you know me so well as to read my soul? Do you know me so well as to be justified to yourself when you attribute such a motive to me?"

"What other motive can I attribute to you?" he asked bitterly. "Is he not a peer? Is he not rich?"

"O Harry!" I cried, "you will drive me mad between you. Cannot a peer be a good man? Cannot a girl—I say—may not a girl—Harry, you force me to say it—is it not possible for a girl to fall in love with a man who is even a peer and a rich man? Go sir! you have humbled me, and made me say words of which I am ashamed. Go, if you please, and tell all the world what I have said."

Then he fell to asking my forgiveness. He was, he said, wretched indeed: he had long lost my love.

"Man!" I said, "you never had it!"—and now he was like to lose my friendship.

This talk about friendship between a man and woman when both are young seems to me a mighty foolish thing. For if the woman is in love with some one else her friendship is, to be sure, worth just nothing at all, because she must needs be for ever thinking of the man she loves. There is but one man in all the world for her, and that man not he who would fain be her friend. Therefore she gives not a thought to him. Now if a man be in love with one woman and "in friendship" with another, I think that either his love for one must be a poor lukewarm passion, which I, for one, would not be anxious to receive, or his friendship for the other must be a chilly sort of thing.

However, one must not be angry for ever: Harry Temple had made me say a thing which I could not have said to any woman—not even Nancy—and was ashamed of having said: yet when he begged forgiveness I accorded it to him. Harry, I was sure, would not repeat what I had said.

Somebody about this time wrote another of those little worthless epigrams or poems, and handed it about:

> "Kitty, a fair Dissenter grown,
> Sad pattern doth afford:
> The Temple's laws she will not own,
> Yet still doth love her Lord."

"Do not be angry, Kitty," said Nancy. "This is the penalty of greatness. What would Peggy Baker give to be lampooned? Harry is a fool, my dear. Any woman could tell, with half an eye, that you are not the least in love with him. What are the eyes of men like? Are they so blinded by vanity as not to be able to see, without being told, when they are disagreeable objects for a woman's contemplation?"

"I condole with you, Miss Pleydell," said Peggy Baker. "To be the victim of an irreligious and even impious epigram must be truly distressing to one, like yourself, brought up in the bosom of the Church."

"Thank you, dear Miss Peggy," I replied, returning her smiling courtesy. "The epigram's wound is easily healed. Is it true that you are yourself the author?"

"O Lord, no!" she replied. "I am but a poor poet, and could not for the world write or say anything to wound another woman's feelings."

"She would not, indeed, dear Kitty," cried Nancy, who was with me. "It is not true—though you may hear it so stated—that Miss Peggy said yesterday on the Parade that your father was only a curate, and that you made your own stockings. She is the kindest and most generous of women. We think so, truly, dear Miss Peggy. We would willingly, if we could, send you half-a-dozen or so of our swains to swell your train. But they will not leave us."

Was there ever so saucy a girl?

Miss Peggy bit her lips, and I think she would have liked to box Nancy's ears there and then, had she dared. But a few gentlemen were standing round us, laughing at Nancy's sally. So she refrained.

"O Miss Nancy!" she replied, trying to laugh, "you are indeed kind. But I love not the attentions of men at second-hand. You are welcome to all my cast-off lovers. Pray, Miss Pleydell, may I ask when we may expect his lordship back again?"

"I do not know," I replied. "Lord Chudleigh does not send me letters as to his movements or intentions."

"I said so," she replied, triumphant for the moment. "I said so this morning at the book-shop, when they were asking each other what news of Lord Chudleigh. Some said Miss Pleydell would surely know: I said that I did not think there was anything between his lordship and Miss Pleydell: and I ventured to predict that you knew no more about his movements than myself."

"Indeed," said Nancy, coming to my assistance. "I should have thought you were likely to know more than Kitty."

"Indeed, why?"

"Because," said Nancy, laughing, "his lordship, who is, I believe, one of your cast-off lovers, might perhaps have written to you for old acquaintance' sake."

Miss Peggy had no reason for loving me, who had dethroned her, but she had reason for hating Nancy, who always delighted in bringing her to open shame.

"What have I done to you, Miss Levett?" she asked her once, when they were alone. "You are not the reigning Toast: I am not jealous of you: you have done no harm to me, nor I to you. Yet you delight in saying the most ill-natured things."

"You have done nothing to me, Miss Peggy," Nancy told her. "But you have done a great deal to my poor Kitty, who is innocence itself. You have slandered her: you have traduced her family, which everybody knows is as good as your own, though her father was a country clergyman and a younger son: you have denied her beauty: you have written anonymous letters to her, calumniating a young nobleman who, I verily believe, is a paragon of peers. No doubt, too, you have written letters to him calumniating her character. Truly, with the best intentions, you could not do much to hurt her, for my Kitty is above suspicion."

"Very well, miss," said Miss Peggy; "very well: we understand each other. As for your charges about anonymous letters——"

"We keep them all," said Nancy; "and with them a letter written and signed by yourself. And I think I shall show the letters about on the Terrace."

"If you dare——" but here she checked herself, though in a great rage. "You will do as you please, Miss Levett. I shall know, some day, how to revenge myself for your insults. As for your curate's girl, I warrant her innocence and her being 'above suspicion'—indeed!—to be pretty hypocrisy and pretence. As if any woman was above suspicion!"

"Oh!" said Nancy, as a parting shot, "nobody, I assure you, ever thought Miss Peggy Baker or any of her friends above suspicion. Let us do you, dear miss, so much justice. You shall not find us ungrateful or unmindful of the benefits you have conferred, or are about to confer, upon us. Malice and spite, when they are impotent, are amusing, like the tricks of a monkey in a cage, or a bear dancing at a stake."

Such angry passions as these disturbed the peaceful atmosphere of the Wells. What use was it for Mr. Nash of Bath, to deprive the gentlemen of their swords when he left the ladies their tongues? "The tongue can no man tame: it is an unruly evil, full of deadly poison."

The accident which followed, a day or two after this, may or may not have been instigated by an enemy. Nancy always declared it was, but then she may have been prejudiced, and we never got at the truth.

Every Friday or Saturday there came down from London a coach full of gentlemen from the City or the Inns of Court, to spend two or three days at the Wells. These were our most noisy visitors: they pushed into the coteries, and endeavoured to form parts of the trains of the beauties in vogue: they drank too much wine: gambled fiercely for small sums; and turned the quiet decorum of the assembly into a babel of riot, noise, loud laughter, coarse jokes, and ill-breeding. The Sunday was thus spoiled: those of us who loved quiet stayed, for the most part, at home when we were not in church, or wandered on the quiet Downs, where we were undisturbed. Solomon Stallabras attended us on these occasions, and we turned our conversation on grave matters. I exhorted him, for instance, to direct his splendid genius to the creation of a sacred epic, which should be to the eighteenth century what Milton's "Paradise Lost" was to the seventeenth. He promised to think of it, and we talked over various plans. The Deluge, St. Paul, the Apocalypse, were discussed in turn; for my own part, I thought that the Book of Revelation would prove a subject too sublime for our poet's strength, and recommended, as a fitter subject for his easy and graceful verses, the life and travels of St. Paul. In these considerations we forgot, for awhile, the calumnies of our enemy, and each put aside, for a time, his own private anxieties.

One Saturday evening, while Lord Chudleigh was still away, a noisier party than usual were in the Assembly Rooms, and although there was no dancing, the talk and quarrelling of the gamblers were incessant, while lights were hung out among the trees, and the walk was crowded with people. Neither Nancy nor I was present, having

The Chaplain of the Fleet

little desire to be stared at by ill-bred young citizens or pushing templars. Unfortunately, Harry Temple was among them.

While he was idling among the trees there passed him a group of three young fellows, all talking together noisily. I suppose they had been drinking. One of them, unfortunately, caught sight of Harry, and began to laugh. Then they stopped, and then one stepped forward and made Harry a profound bow.

"We welcome," he said, "the Knight of the Rueful Countenance. We condole with your misfortune.

"'Her Temple's rule she doth not own,
Though still she loves her Lord.'"

Harry was not only melancholy, but also, as some such men are, he was choleric; and he was strong, being bred and brought up to country pursuits. In a moment his cane was in one hand and his assailant's cravat was in his other. Then he began to beat the man with his cane.

The others stood stupid with amazement. Sir Miles, who was on his way to the tables, and had seen the beginning of the fray, stepped to the front.

"Who interferes with Mr. Temple has to do with me," he shouted. "Fair play, gentlemen. Let them fight it out with fists like men, first—and stick each other afterwards with rapiers like Frenchmen, if they like. Gentlemen, I am Sir Miles Lackington, Baronet, at your service, if any one wants a little breathing."

He held his cane in readiness, but the other gentlemen kept aloof. When Harry had spent his rage, because, so far as I can learn, there was no resistance, he shook off his opponent, adjusted his wig, which was a little deranged, and turned quietly to Sir Miles—

"You will oblige me, Sir Miles? Thank you, gentlemen all—your servant."

He resumed his walk, lounging among the trees, the women looking after him with a mixture of fright and admiration, as calm as if nothing had happened.

The man who was beaten was followed off the field by his friends. Nor could Sir Miles get speech of them that evening. In the morning, when he went to make his murderous appointment, he found they were gone. Fighting, it would seem, was not to their liking; though an insult to a harmless gentleman was quite in their way.

"I am sorry, Harry," I said honestly, because a woman cannot help respecting a man who is brave and strong, "that the taking of my name has caused you this trouble."

"I am sorry, too," he said sadly. "Yet I blame them not, Kitty."

"But you do blame me," I replied. "Harry, if, in a little while—somehow—I am able to show that I could not, even if I wished, grant the thing you want—if—I say—I can make that quite clear and plain to you—will you promise to be reconciled to what cannot—cannot be avoided?"

"If, Kitty—what an if? But you ask the impossible. There is no reason—there cannot be. Why, such a thing is impossible."

"But again—if—Harry, promise me so much."

He laughed grimly.

"Well, I promise."

"Give me your hand upon it," I said. "Now we shall be friends indeed. Why, you silly Harry, you let the days go by, and you neglect the most beautiful girls who could perhaps make you a hundred times as happy as Kitty, all because you deck her out with imaginary virtues which she doth not possess. Foolish Harry! Open your eyes and look about you. What do you see?"

I, for my part, saw pretty Nancy running along the walk to meet us. Love was in her eyes, grace in her action; youth, beauty, sweetness in her comely shape, her rosy cheeks, her pretty smile, her winning tongue, her curly locks. She was in morning dress, without hoop or patch. Through the leaves of the trees the sun shone softly upon her, covering her with a soft light which might have been that in which Venus stole along the shore in a golden mist to meet her son—of which my father had read to me. She was pretty, she was sweet; far prettier than I, who was so tall; far sweeter than I, who was full of evil passions and shame, being a great sinner.

"Foolish Harry!" I said. "What do you see?"

He only looked me in the face and replied—

"I see nothing but the beautiful Kitty."

"Oh, blind, blind!"

CHAPTER XIII.

HOW DURDANS WAS ILLUMINATED.

While these things were proceeding, Lord Chudleigh being still absent from Durdans, I received a second letter from the Doctor.

After the usual compliments to Mrs. Esther, he proceeded to the important part of his communication—

"For your private eye only.

"I have to tell you that yesterday I saw and conversed with Lord Chudleigh. He sought me in order to find out, if possible, the name, character, and condition of a certain person. I refused to grant him that information; I also assured him that he would find it impossible to break the alliance with which I had provided him. This I did with the greater pleasure, having heard from a sure source that he hath lately paid addresses to you of so particular a kind as to make the whole company at Epsom Wells believe that they mean honourable proposals. I presume, therefore, that could he destroy the evidence of his former marriage he would be prepared to offer his hand. This is every way better than I could expect or wish, because when the moment arrives for informing him of the truth, I can point out to his lordship that his opinion and mine of what a wife should be exactly agree. Our triumph will then be complete."

Our triumph! This was what he called it. I was to be the consenting party to inflict shame and humiliation upon my lord. This was too much. Humiliation for him? Why, it was for myself, and my whole thoughts were how to save him, how to set him free. The Doctor expected me to triumph over him. Why, what did he know of a woman in love? To triumph over a man for whose dear sake she would lay down her life to save him from humiliation!

It was certain to my heart that my lord already felt for me that warmth of affection which impels a man to make a woman his wife. I was sure of this. I was so sure that I already gave myself in imagination entirely to him, and placed his interests above my own.

In short, before I ventured to confess the fact to myself, and before he spoke to me—for as yet he had said no word except in compliment and common gallantry—I loved him. There was, for me, but one thing wanting to make me happy; there was, for me, nothing to think of, to hope for, to pray for, but the welfare of that one man. And to such a woman did the Doctor send such a letter, proposing that I should join him in covering him with shame and indignation. Would I thus let him choose the moment to confess my shameful sin? Would I assist in covering the man I loved with confusion, who would have clothed him in purple and placed a chain about his neck, and helped him to ride forth in bravery and triumph? Forbid the thought, kind Heaven! Oh, that a man should have such a mind, so thick and cloudy as not to perceive that no woman but the basest and worst could join a conspiracy so hateful! Unhappy girl, to be made the victim of a plot in which the punishment would fall upon herself, while the wickedness would rest with the man who devised it, and he against whom the plot was designed would be its sole avenger!

I resolved to be beforehand with the Doctor. I would myself choose the time: I would tell him all: I would assure him that, innocent as I had been in intention, I would never, never seek to assert any rights over him; that he was free, and could go seek a wife where he pleased. Ah! should he please to go elsewhere, it were better had I never been born.

Then, whatever moment I might choose for the confession, I could think of none which could be chosen as favourable to myself. I might write to him. That would be best; I would write: for how could a girl bear to see that face, which had always looked upon her with kindness and affection, suddenly grow hard and stern, and reproach her for her great wickedness with looks of horror and indignation? It seemed better to write. But, for reasons which will presently appear, that letter was never written.

My lord returned. He called upon us next forenoon, and informed us, looking grave and downcast, that he proposed to hold his garden-party in Durdans Park on the next day. People had come from Vauxhall to decorate the trees, and there would be fireworks, with supper, and concert of horns.

I asked him, deceitfully, if his business in London had prospered. He replied that it had not turned out so favourably as he hoped: and then he checked himself and added that, to be sure, his affairs were of no interest to us.

Said Mrs. Esther—

"Your lordship will not, I hope, believe that anything which contributes to your happiness is so indifferent to us."

He bowed, and we began to talk again about his *fête*.

His invitations included all the visitors of respectability at Epsom. Nancy, out of pure kindness, had gone about inquiring of every one if he was invited; and, if not, she got him an invitation at once. We did not, indeed, include the tallow-chandlers and hosiers of London, who frequented Epsom that year in great numbers, but took up their own end of the Assembly Rooms, and mostly walked on the New Parade. But we included all who could claim to belong to the polite world, because nothing is more humiliating than to be omitted from such a festivity at a watering-place. I have known a lady of fashion retire from Bath in mortification, being forgotten at a public tea, and never again show her face at that modish but giddy town.

The company were to assemble at five o'clock, the place of meeting being fixed in that part of Durdans Park most remote from the mansion, where the great trees of birch and elm make such an agreeable wilderness that one might fancy one's self in some vast forest. We were escorted by Sir Miles Lackington, who came because all his brother gamblers had deserted the card-room for the day; and Mr. Stallabras—Solomon—was dressed in another new coat (of purple), and wore a sword with a surprisingly fine hilt. He also had a pair of shoe-buckles in gold, given him by his female Mæcenas, the widow of the brewer, in return for a copy of verses. He was greatly elated, never before having received an invitation from a person of such exalted rank.

"Now, indeed," he said, "I feel the full sweetness of fame. This it is, Miss Kitty, to be a poet. His society is eagerly sought by the Great: he stands serene upon the giddy height of fashion, ennobled by the Muses (who possess, like our own august sovereign, the right of conferring rank): he takes his place as an equal among those who are ennobled by birth. No longer do I deplore that obscurity of origin which once seemed to shut me out of the circles of the polite. Fetter Lane may not be concealed in my biography: it should rather be held up to fame as the place in which the sunshine of Apollo's favour (Apollo, Miss Kitty, was the sun-god as well as the god of poets, which makes the image appropriate)—the sunshine of Apollo has once rested during the birth of an humble child. It was at number forty-one in the second pair back, a commodious garret, that the child destined to immortality first saw the light. No bees (so far as I can learn) played about his cradle, nor did any miracles of precocious genius foreshadow his future greatness. But, with maternal prescience, his mother named him Solomon."

All this because Nancy made Lord Chudleigh send him an invitation! Yet I doubt whether his lordship had ever read one of his poems.

"It is a great blessing for a man to be a poet," said Sir Miles, smiling. "If I were a poet I dare say I should believe that my acres were my own again. If I were a poet I should believe that luck would last."

"Does the name of Kitty cease to charm?" I asked.

Yes, it was true: Sir Miles had lost his five hundred guineas, won of the nabob, and was now reduced to punt at a guinea a night. This hardship made him melancholy.

"Yet," he said, plucking up, "if I cannot play, I can drink. Why, my jolly poet," slapping Solomon on the shoulder, "we will presently toast Miss Kitty as long as his lordship's champagne lasts."

Mrs. Esther said that she saw no reason why, because one vice was no longer possible, another should take its place.

"Madam," said the baronet, "it is not that I love one more than the other. When the purse is full, Hazard is my only queen. When the purse is empty, I call for the bowl."

In such converse we entered the park, and followed in the procession of visitors, who flocked to the place of meeting, where, under the trees, like another Robin Hood, Lord Chudleigh stood to receive his guests.

Kind fortune has taken me to many feasts and rejoicings since that day, but there are none to which my memory more fondly and tenderly reverts; for here, amid the sweet scent of woodland flowers, under the umbrageous trees, while the air of the Downs, fragrant and fresh, fanned our cheeks, my lord became my lover, and I knew that he was mine for ever, in that sweet bond of union which shall only be exchanged by death for another of more perfect love, through God's sweet grace. Ah, day of days! whose every moment lives eternally in our hearts! Sometimes I think that there will hereafter be no past at all, but that the sinner shall be punished by the ever-present shame of his sins, and the saints rewarded by the continual presence of great and noble thoughts.

Horns were stationed at various parts of the park, and while we drank tea, served to us at rustic tables beneath the trees, these answered one another in lively or plaintive strains. The tea finished, we danced to the music of violins, on a natural lawn, as level as a bowling-green, which seemed made for the feet of fairies. After an hour of minuets, the country dances began, and were carried on until sunset. Then for a while we roamed beneath the trees, and watched the twilight grow darker, and presently rose the great yellow harvest moon.

"In such a scene," said Solomon, who was discoursing to a bevy of ladies, "man shrinks from speaking; he is mute: his tongue cleaves to his palate"—at all events, the poet was not mute—"here nature proclaims the handiwork of the Creator." He tapped his forehead reflectively.

"Great Nature speaks: confused the sceptic flies;
Rocks, woods, and stars sing truth to all the skies."

All the while the concert of the horns charmed the ear, while the romantic aspect of the woods by night elevated the soul. When we returned to our lawn we were delighted and surprised to find coloured lamps hanging from the trees, already lit, imparting a look most magical and wonderful, so that we cried aloud for joy. Nor was this all: the tables were laid for supper with every delicacy that our noble host could think of or provide.

Everybody was happy that evening. I think that even Peggy Baker forgot her jealousies, and forgave me for the moment when Lord Chudleigh gave as a toast "The Queen of the Wells," and all the gentlemen drained a bumper in honour of Kitty Pleydell.

While the supper went on, a choir of voices sang glees and madrigals. Never was party more enchanting: never was an evening more balmy: never were guests more pleased or host more careful for them.

After supper more lamps were lit and hung upon the trees: the violins began again, and country dances set in.

Now while I looked on, being more delighted to see than to dance—besides, my heart was strangely moved with what I now know was a presentiment of happiness—Lord Chudleigh joined me, and we began to talk, not indifferently, but, from the first, gravely and seriously.

"You will not dance, Miss Kitty?" he asked.

"No, my lord," I replied; "I would rather watch the scene, which is more beautiful than anything I have ever dreamed of."

"Come with me," he said, offering me his hand, "to a place more retired, whence we can see the gaiety, without hearing too much the laughter."

They should have been happy without laughing: the cries of merriment consorted not with the scene around us.

Outside the circle of the lamps the woods were quite dark, but for the light of the solemn moon. We wandered away from the noise of the dancers, and presently came to a rustic bench beneath a tree, where my lord invited me to rest.

It was not so dark but that I could see his face, which was grave and unlike the face of an eager lover. There was sadness in it and shame, as belongs to one who has a thing to confess. Alas! what ought to have been the shame and sadness of my face?

"While they are dancing and laughing," he said, "let us talk seriously, you and I, Miss Kitty."

"Pray go on, my lord," I said, trembling.

He began, not speaking of love, but of general things: of the ambition which is becoming to a man of rank: of the serious charge and duties of his life: of the plans which he had formed in his own mind worthily to pass through the years allotted to him, and to prepare for the eternity which waits us all beyond.

The Chaplain of the Fleet

"But," he said sadly, "we wander in the dark, not knowing which way to turn: and if we take a wrong step, whether from inadvertence or design, the fairest plan may be ruined, the most careful schemes destroyed."

"But we have a guide," I said, "and a light."

"We follow not our leader, and we hide the light. Addison hath represented life under the image of a bridge, over which men are perpetually passing. But the bridge is set everywhere with hidden holes and pitfalls, so that he who steps into one straightway falls through and is drowned. We are not always drowned by the pitfalls of life, but, which is as bad, we are maimed and broken, so that for the rest of our course we go halt."

"I pray, my lord," I said, "that you may escape these pitfalls, and press on with the light before you to the goal of your most honourable ambition."

"It is too late," he said sadly. "Miss Kitty, you see in me the most wretched of mortals, who might, I would sometimes venture to think, have become the most happy."

"You wretched, Lord Chudleigh?"—oh, beating heart!—"you wretched? Of all men you should be the most happy."

"I have tried," he said, "to escape from the consequences of a folly—nay, a crime. But it is impossible. I am fast bound and tied." He took my hand and held it, while he added: "I may not say what I would: I may not even think, or hope, or dream of what might have been."

"Might have been, my lord?"

"Which cannot, now, ever be. Kitty, I thought after I discovered that it was impossible that I would not return any more to Epsom Wells; in the country, or away on foreign travel, I might in time forget your face, your voice, your eyes—the virtues and graces which sit so well in a form so charming—the elevated soul——"

"My lord! my lord!" I cried, "spare me——Yet," I added, "tell me all that is in your mind. If I cannot rid you of your burden, at least I may soothe your sorrow."

"The matter," he replied, "lies in a few words, Kitty. I love you, and I may not ask you to be my wife."

I was silent for a while. He stood before me, his face bent over mine.

"Why not?" I asked.

"Because I have been a fool—nay, worse than a fool, a knave; because I am tied by bonds which I cannot break: and I am unworthy of so much goodness and virtue."

"Oh!" I cried, "you know not. How can you know? I am none of the things which you imagine in me. I am a poor and weak girl; if you knew me you would surely think so too. I cannot bear that you should think me other than what I am."

"Why, my angel, your very modesty and your tears are the proof that you are all I think, and more."

"No," I cried. "If I told you all: if I could lay bare my very soul to you, I think that you could"—I was going to add, "love me no longer," but I caught myself up in time—"that you could no longer think of me as better, but rather as worse, than other girls."

"You know," he said, "that I love you, Kitty. You have known that for some time—have you not?"

"Yes, my lord," I replied humbly; "I have known it, and have felt my own unworthiness. Oh, so unworthy, so unworthy am I that I have wept tears of shame."

"Nay—nay," he said. "It is I who am unworthy. My dear, there is nothing you could tell me which would make me love you less."

I shook my head. There was one thing which I had to tell. Could any man be found to forgive that?

"I came back here resolved to tell you all. If I could not ask for your love, Kitty, I might, at the very least, win your pity."

"What have you to tell me, my lord?"

It was well that the night was so dark that my face could not be seen. Oh, telltale cheeks, aglow with fear and joy!

"What have you to tell me?" I repeated.

"It is a story which I trust to your eyes alone," he said. "I have written it down. Before we part to-night I will give it to you. Come"—he took my hand again, but his was cold—"come, we must not stay longer. Let me lead you from this slippery and dangerous place."

"One moment"—I would have lingered there all night to listen to the accents of his dear voice. "If you, my lord, have a secret to tell to me, I also have one to tell you."

"Nay," he replied. "I can hear none of your pretty secrets. My peace is already destroyed. Besides," he added desperately, "when you have read what I have written you will see that it would be idle to waste another thought upon me."

"I will read it," I said, "to-night. But, my lord, on one promise."

"And that is?"

"That you will not leave Epsom without my knowledge. Let me speak with you once more after I have read it, if it is only to weep with you and to say farewell."

"I promise."

"And—oh, my lord! if I may say it—since your lordship may not marry me, then I, for your sake, will never marry any other man."

"Kitty!"

"That is my promise, my lord. And perhaps—sometimes—you will give a thought to your poor—fond Kitty."

He caught me in his arms and showered kisses upon my cheeks and lips, calling me his angel and a thousand other names, until I gently pushed him from me and begged him to take me back to the company. He knelt at my feet and took my hand in his, holding it in silence. I knew that he was praying for the blessing of Heaven upon my unworthy head.

Then he led me back to the circle of lights, when the first person we met was Miss Peggy Baker.

"Why, here," she cried, looking sharply from one to the other, "are my lord and Miss Pleydell. Strange that the two people we have most missed should be found at the same time—and together, which is stranger still."

Nancy left her swains and ran to greet me.

"My dear," she whispered, "you have been crying. Is all well?"

"I am the happiest woman and the most unhappy in the world," I said. "I wish I were in my bed alone and crying on my pillow;" and she squeezed my hand and ran back to her lovers.

My lord himself walked home with us. We left before the party broke up. At parting he placed in my hand a roll of paper.

"Remember," I whispered; "you have promised."

He made no answer, but stooped and kissed my fingers.

CHAPTER XIV.

HOW MY LORD MADE HIS CONFESSION.

It was not a long manuscript. I kissed the dear handwriting before I began.

"To the Queen of my Heart," it began.

"Dearest Girl,—Since I first had the happiness of worshipping at your shrine I have learned from watching your movements, listening to your voice, and looking at your face, something of what that heavenly beauty must have been like which, we are told, captivated and drove mad the ancients, even by mere meditation and thought upon it."

Did ever girl read more beautiful language?

"And by conversations with you, even in the gay assembly or on the crowded Terrace, I have learned to admire and to love that goodness of heart which God hath bestowed upon the most virtuous among women. I say this in no flattery or desire to pay an empty compliment, but sincerely, and out of the respect and admiration, as well as the love, which I have conceived for one who is, I dare maintain, all goodness."

O Kitty, Kitty! to read this with blushing cheeks and biting conscience! Surely it must make people good to be believed good; so that, by a little faith, we might raise and purify all mankind!

"It is my purpose to-night, if I find an opportunity, to tell you that I am the most wretched man in the world, because by a fatal accident, of which I must presently force myself to speak, I am for ever shut out from the happiness which it was, I believe, the intention of a merciful Providence to confer upon me. Yet am I also fortunate, and esteem myself happy in this respect, that I have for once in my life been in the presence of as much female beauty and virtue as was ever, I believe, found together in one human soul. To tell you these things, to speak of my love, is an alleviation of suffering. To tell the cause of this unhappiness is worse than to plunge a knife into my heart. Yet must it be told to your ear alone.

The Chaplain of the Fleet

"Last year, about the early summer, a rumour began to run through the coffee-houses that there was a man of extraordinary wit, genius, and humour to be met with in the Liberties, or Rules, of the Fleet Prison. These Rules, of which you know nothing"—oh, Kitty! nothing!—"are houses, or lodgings, lying in certain streets adjacent to the Fleet Market, where prisoners for debt are allowed, on payment of certain fees, and on finding security, to reside outside the prison. In fact they are free, and yet being, in the eyes of the law, still prisoners, they cannot any more be arrested for debt. Among these prisoners of the Rules was a certain Reverend Gregory Shovel, a man of great learning, and a Doctor of Divinity of Cambridge, a divine of eloquence and repute, once a fashionable preacher, who, being of extravagant and luxurious habits, which brought him into expenditure above his means, at last found himself a prisoner in the Fleet; and presently, through the influence of friends, was placed in the enjoyment of the Rules.

"Here, whether because he had exhausted the generosity of his friends, or because he craved for action, or for the baser purposes of gain, he became that most unworthy thing, a Fleet parson—one of a most pestilent crew who go through the form of marriage for all comers, and illegally bind together for life those whom Heaven, in mercy and knowledge, had designed to be kept asunder.

"I believe that, by his extraordinary ability and impudence, coupled with the fact that he really was, what his rivals chiefly pretended to be, a clergyman of the Established Church of England and Ireland, he has managed to secure the principal part of this nefarious trade to himself, and has become what he has named himself, 'the Chaplain of the Fleet.'

"This person attracted to himself, little by little, a great gathering of followers, admirers, or friends. No one, I suppose, could be the friend of one who had so fallen; therefore the men who thronged to his lodgings, nearly every night in the week, were drawn thither by the fashion of running after a man who talked, sang, told stories, and kept open house in so desperate a quarter as the Fleet Market, and who yet had the manners of a gentleman, the learning of a scholar, and the experience of a traveller.

"It was for this reason, solely for curiosity, that on one fatal evening last year I entreated Sir Miles Lackington, a former friend of my father's and myself, to present me to the Doctor. You have made the acquaintance of Sir Miles. He was once, though perhaps the fact has not been made known to you by him, also a prisoner of the Rules. To this had he been brought by his inordinate love of gambling, by which he had stripped himself, in six months, of as fine an estate as ever fell to the lot of an English gentleman, and brought himself to a debtor's prison. Sir Miles, who, when he could no longer gamble, showed signs of possessing virtues hitherto unsuspected in him, offered, on the occasion of borrowing a few guineas of me, to conduct me, if I wished to spend an evening with the Doctor, as he is called, to the house which this Doctor either owns or frequents.

"I am not a lover of that low humour and those coarse scenes depicted by Mr. Fielding and Dr. Smollet. I do not delight in seeing drunken men sprawl in the gutter, nor women fight upon Fleet Bridge, nor bears baited, nor pickpockets and rogues pilloried or flogged. But I was promised something very different from these scenes. I was to meet, Sir Miles told me, a remarkable man, who could narrate, declaim, preach, or sing a drinking song, just as he was in the vein.

"I accepted the invitation, the strangeness of which affected my curiosity rather than excited my hopes. I was to witness, I thought, the spectacle of a degraded wretch who lived by breaking the law, for each offence being liable to a penalty of not less than a hundred pounds. It would be, I expected, such a sight as that which the drunken Helot once presented to the virtuous Spartan youth.

"We made our way through a mean and filthy neighbourhood, by the side of a market heaped with cabbage-stalks, past houses where, through the common panes of green glass set in leaden frames, one might see a rushlight or a tallow candle feebly glimmering, for a crew of drunken men to shout songs and drink beside.

"The room into which I was led opened off the street, and was of fair proportions, but low. In it was a table, at the head of which, in a vast wooden chair, sat a man who looked, though perhaps he was not, the biggest man I had ever seen. Some tall men have small hands, or narrow shoulders, or small heads; Doctor Shovel is great all over, with a large and red face, a silk cassock, a full and flowing wig, clean bands, and a flowered morning-gown very large and comfortable.

"He seemed struck with some astonishment on hearing my name, but presently recovered, and invited me to sit at his right hand. Sir Miles sat at his left. The room was pretty full, and we found that the evening had already begun by the exhaustion of the first bowl of punch. The guests consisted of gentlemen who came, like myself, to see and converse with the famous Doctor: and of prisoners who, like Sir Miles, were living in the Rules.

"As the punch went round, the talk grew more jovial. That is to say, the talk of the Doctor, because no one else said anything. He talked continuously; he talked of everything. He seemed to know everything, and to have been everywhere. When he was not talking he was singing. At intervals he smoked a pipe of tobacco, which did not interrupt his talk; and he never ceased sending round the punch. I found that the visitors were expected to provide this part of the entertainment.

"I am sure that the kindest-hearted of women will believe me when I tell her that I am no drunkard. Yet there are times when, owing to the foolish custom of calling for toasts, no heeltaps, and a brimming glass, the most careful head may be affected. Nor can I plead inexperience in the dangers of the bottle, after three years at St. John's, Cambridge, where the Fellows of the Society, and the noblemen and gentlemen commoners on the Foundation, drank freely at every college feast of the college port and the punch sent up from the butteries. I had been like other young men, but I trust that your imagination will not picture Lord Chudleigh carried away from the combination-room and put to bed by a couple of the college gyps. Yet, worse still, I have to present that spectacle before your eyes, not at a grave and reverend college feast, but in the dissolute Liberties of the Fleet.

"The atmosphere of the room was close and hot, with the smell of the tobacco and the fumes of the punch bowl. Presently I found that my eyes were beginning to swim and my head to reel. I half rose to go, but the Doctor, laying his hand upon me, cried, with a great oath, that we should not part yet.

"By this time Sir Miles was lying with his head on the table. Some of the guests were lying on the floor; some were singing, some crying; some kissing each other. It was, in short, one of those scenes of debauchery which may be witnessed whenever a party of men meet together to drink. I sat down; it was plain that I could not escape from these hogs without myself becoming a hog. I sat still, therefore, while the Doctor still talked, still laughed, still waved his monstrous great hand in the air as he talked, and the punch still went briskly round among the few who sat upright.

"In the morning I was awakened by no other than my host of the preceding evening, in whose bed I had spent the rest of the night unconscious.

"He stood over me with grave face, and, in reproachful accents, asked me how I fared, and for what purpose I had come to him? I was still half-drunk; I could not remember for what purpose. He assisted me to dress; and then, because I could not stand, he gave me a mug of small ale with which to clear my brain.

"Being thus partly restored to my senses, I listened while he answered his own question, and told me why I had come to him.

"'You came,' he said, 'to be married.'

"I stared. He repeated the words—

"'You came to be married.'

"It seems incredible that a man should hear a statement so utterly false and not cry out upon the liar. Yet I did not. My brain was confused, that is my excuse. Also, this great man seemed to hold me like a wizard, while he held up his forefinger and, with wrinkled brow, shook it in my face.

"'You came to be married.'

"Good heavens! What did this mean? I was drunk, horribly drunk the night before—I could not remember—so drunk was I—how I came to the house, with whom, with what intent.

"'She waits below,' he told me.

"She? Who?

"He gave me his arm to support me down the stairs. I descended, curious and agitated. I remember a figure with a hood. While I looked, this Chaplain of the Devil began the marriage service, his eyes still fixed on me while he recited, and seemed to read.

"When he had finished, I was married.

"After we had signed a book, he gave me another great mug of ale, which I drank to the bottom.

"Then, I suppose, I rolled over, and was carried upstairs, for I remember nothing more until the evening, when I was again awakened by this rogue and common cheat, who, sitting by my bedside, congratulated me calmly on the day's work.

"I will not go on to tell you all the things he said. I discovered that in some way, I know not how, but can guess, my father had once done this man an injury. This conspiracy was his revenge.

"Who was my wife?

"He would not tell me.

"What was her position, her birth, her name? Was she some wretched creature who could be bought off to keep silence while she lived, although she was a thing to be ashamed of and to hide? Was she some person who would trade on her title, parade her infamy, and declare herself to the world as Lady Chudleigh by her lord's marriage in the Fleet? A hundred things I asked. He gave me no reply.

"Her name? I had forgotten it. The register? it had been put away. I seemed to know the name, somehow; yet it escaped me. In the night it came back to me in a dream; yet in the morning it was gone again. Once, after my first evening with you, the name came to me once more in a dream; yet it was gone when I awoke, and could remember no other name than yours. It is nearly a year ago. I know not yet whom I married. She hath made no sign. Yet I know full well that the day will come when she will confess herself and demand acknowledgment.

"One hope remains: that the marriage is not valid. It is a slender hope, for the man is an ordained clergyman of the Established Church. I am going to London to see him, to implore his pity, to humble myself if necessary.

"It is of no avail. I have gone. I have humbled myself, and then, flying into the opposite extreme, I have cursed him. He enjoyed both the wrath and the humility.

"I have no longer any hope; I have taken the advice of my lawyers, who tell me that an Act of Parliament alone can set me free; this Act—how can it be got when I do not know the name of the woman?

"Even if there were any reasonable chance that so dreadful a place could produce a woman of virtue and honour, which there is not, I could never look upon that woman with any but feelings of loathing and horror. For not only is her idea black beyond compare, but my heart is full, and will remain for ever full of Kitty Pleydell.

"Strange to say, as I wrote the words, it seemed as if I had touched at last the chord of memory. The name was on my lips. No—it was an illusion; I have forgotten it again, and can only murmur Kitty Pleydell, sweet Kitty, divine Kitty, on whom may all the blessings of Heaven rest for ever!"

CHAPTER XV.

HOW NANCY HAD A QUICK TONGUE.

This was at once a sad and yet most joyful confession. For while the girl who read it was full of shame and terror in thinking of his righteous wrath and loathing, yet the tender love which filled the pages and fired her soul with wonder and rejoicing forbade her to believe that love was not stronger than wrath. She was so ignorant and inexperienced, the girl who joined in this treacherous deed; she was so dominated by the will of that masterful man, her uncle; she was so taken by surprise—surely, when he learned these things, he would forgive the past.

But should she tell him at once?

It would be better to tell him than that he should find it out. There were many ways in which he could find it out. Oh, the shame of being found out, the meanness of taking all his secrets and giving none! Roger, the Doctor's man, might for a bribe, were the bribe heavy enough to outweigh his fear of the Doctor, tell the name of the bride; the Doctor might think the time had come when he should step forward and reveal the secret; even there was danger that his lordship might remember the name which he had seen but once, and ask me sternly if there were upon the earth two Kitty Pleydells, of the same age, the same height, and the same face. And what should I say then?

Stimulated by this thought, as by the touch of a sharp spur, I procured an inkstand and paper, and began to write a letter of confession.

"MY LORD,"

What to say next?

"MY LORD,"

In what words to clothe a most shameful story?

We cheat ourselves; we do one thing and call it another; we stop the voice of conscience by misrepresenting our actions; and whereas we ought to be weighed down by the burden of our sins, we carry ourselves confidently, with light hearts, as if we had done nothing to be ashamed of. It is only when our crimes are set forth in plain English that we know them for the shameful things they are. What was I to tell my lord?

A girl, brought up in the fear of God and His commandments, can be so weak as to obey a man who ordered her to do a wicked thing. Could she be, afterwards, so cowardly as not to tell the man whom she had thus injured, even when she knew that he loved her? A wicked crime and a course of deceit! How could I frame the words so as to disarm that righteous wrath!

"My Lord,—It has been for a long time upon my conscience to tell you a thing which you ought to know before you waste one more thought upon the unworthy person to whom you addressed a confession. That confession, indeed, depicted your lordship with such fidelity as to make me the more ashamed to unburden my conscience. Know, then, that——"

Here I stopped, with trembling fingers, which refused to move.

"Know that"—what? That I was his wicked and unworthy wife, the creature whom most of all he must hate and despise.

I could not tell him—not then. No; it must be told by word of mouth, with such extenuating phrases and softening of details as might present themselves to my troubled mind.

I tore the letter into a thousand fragments. Was girl ever so bested? That sacred bond of union which brings happy lovers together, the crown of courtship, the end of wooing, the marriage service itself, was the thing which kept us asunder.

I would tell him—later on. There would come an opportunity. I would make the opportunity, somewhere, at some time. Yes; the best way would be to wait till we were alone; and it should be in the evening, when my face and his would be partly veiled by the night; then I could whisper the story, and ask his forgiveness.

But that opportunity never came, as will be presently seen.

After morning prayers, that day, we walked upon the Terrace, where the company were, as usual, assembled, and all talking together below the trees. I held in my hand the manuscript of my lord's confession.

Presently we saw him slowly advancing to meet us, wearing a grave and melancholy look. But then he was never one of those who think that the duties of life are to be met with a reckless laugh.

"Even in laughter," said the Wise Man, "the heart is sorrowful: and the end of that mirth is heaviness."

"Dear Miss Pleydell," whispered Peggy Baker, as he appeared, "can his lordship have repented already of what he said beneath the trees last night? The poor young gentleman wears a heavy countenance this morning."

It was best to make no answer to this raillery. Let her say what she would; I cared nothing, and was too heavy myself to made reply. I would neither help nor hinder. Then, leaving Mrs. Esther with the party, I advanced boldly and met my lord, returning him his manuscripts before the eyes of all.

Everybody stared, wondering what could be in the packet I placed in his hands; he, however, received it with a low bow, and accompanied me to my party, saying nothing for the moment.

The music was playing its loudest, and as we walked, my lord beside me, and Mrs. Esther with Lady Levett—Nancy remaining behind to exchange insinuations and pert speeches (in which the saucy damsel took great delight) with Peggy Baker. I looked back and saw their heads wagging, while the bystanders smiled, and presently Peggy fanned herself, with agitation in her face, by which it was easy to conclude that Nancy had said something more than usually biting, to which her opponent had, for the moment, no reply ready.

"You have read these papers?" asked my lord, and that in as careless a tone as if they contained nothing of importance.

"Yes," I said, "I have read the sad story. But I pity the poor woman who was persuaded to do your lordship this grievous wrong."

"I think she needs and deserves little of our pity," he replied. "And as for persuasion, it could have wanted but little with a woman so designing as to join in such a plot."

A designing woman! Poor Kitty!

The Chaplain of the Fleet

Then I tried, beating about the bush, to bring his mind round to see the possibility of a more charitable view.

"Remember, my lord, two things. This Doctor Shovel could not have known of your coming. The plot, therefore, was swiftly conceived, and as quickly carried into execution. You have told me in your paper—I entreat you, my lord, burn it with all speed—that this man's influence over you was so great as to coerce you (because your brain was not in its natural clearness) into doing and suffering what, at ordinary times, you would have rejected with scorn. Bethink you, then, with charity, that this Doctor Shovel, this so-called Chaplain of the Fleet, may have found some poor girl, over whom he had authority, and in like manner coerced and forced her to join with him in this most wicked plot."

"You would make excuses," he said, "for the greatest of sinners. I doubt not that. But this story is too improbable. I cannot think that any woman could be so coerced against her will."

I sighed.

"My lord, I beg you to remember your promise to me. You will not leave Epsom without first telling me: you will not seek out this man, this Doctor Shovel, or quarrel with him, or do aught to increase his malice. Meantime, I am feeble, being only a woman, and bound in obedience and duty to my guardian and protectress. Yet I bethink me of an old fable. The lion was one day caught in the coils of a net, and released by the teeth of a——"

He started.

"What does this mean! O Kitty! what can you do?"

"I do not know. Yet, perhaps I may be able to release you from the coils of this net. Have patience, my lord."

"Kitty!"

"Let us speak no more about it for the moment," I replied. "Perhaps, my lord, if my inquiries lead to the result you desire—it is Christian to forgive your enemies——"

"I cannot understand you," he replied. "How should you—how should any one—release me? Truly, if deliverance came, forgiveness were a small thing to give."

CHAPTER XVI.

HOW SPED THE MASQUERADE.

It was at this time that the company at Epsom held their masquerade, the greatest assembly of the season, to which not only the visitors at the Wells, but also the gentry from the country around, and many from London, came; so that the inns and lodging-houses overflowed, and some were fain to be content to find a bed over shops and in the mean houses of the lower sort. Nay, there were even many who put up tents on the Downs, and slept in them like soldiers on a campaign.

At other times my head would have been full of the coming festivity, but the confession of my lord and the uncertainty into which it threw my spirits, prevented my paying that attention to the subject which its importance demanded.

"Kitty," cried Nancy, "I have talked to you for half an hour, and you have not heard one word. Oh, how a girl is spoiled the moment she falls in love! Don't start, my dear, nor blush, unless you like, because there is no one here but ourselves. As for that, all the place knows that you and Lord Chudleigh are in love with each other, though Peggy Baker will have it that it is mostly on one side. 'My dear,' she said at the book-shop yesterday, 'the woman shows her passion in a manner which makes a heart of sensibility blush for her sex.' Don't get angry, Kitty, because I was there, and set her down as she deserved. 'Dear me!' I said, 'we have not all of us the sensibility of Miss Peggy Baker, who, if all reports are true, has had time to get over the passion she once exhibited for the handsome Lord Chudleigh.' Why, my dear, how can any one help seeing that the women are monstrous jealous, and my lord in so deep a quagmire of love, that nothing but the marriage-ring (which cures the worst cases) can pull him out?"

I had, in verity, been thinking of my troubles, while Nancy was thinking over her frocks. Now I roused myself and listened.

"My mother will go as the Queen of Sheba. She will wear a train over her hoop, a paper crown, a sceptre, and have two black boys to walk behind her. That will show who she is. I am to go as Joan of Arc, with a sword in my hand, but not to wear it dangling at my side, lest it cause me to fall down: Peggy Baker will be Venus, the Goddess of Love. She will have a golden belt, and a little Cupid is to follow her with bow and arrows, which he is to shoot, or pretend to shoot, at the company. She will sprawl and languish in her most bewitching manner, the dear creature; but since she has failed with Lord Eardesley there is nobody at Epsom good enough for her. I hear she goes very shortly to Bath, where no doubt she will catch a nabob. I hope his liver and temper will be good. Oh! and Mr. Stallabras will go as a Greek pastoral poet, Theo something—I forget his name—with a lyre in one hand and a shepherd's crook in the other. Harry Temple is to go as Vulcan: you will know him by his limp and by the hammer upon his shoulder. Sir Miles wants to go as the God of Cards, but no one seems to know who that Deity was. My father says he shall go as a plain English country gentleman, because he sees so few among the company that the sight may do them good."

I was going as the Goddess of Night, because I wanted to have an excuse for wearing a domino all the evening, most of the ladies throwing them aside early in the night. My dress was a long black velvet hood, covering me from head to foot, without hoops, and my hair dressed low, so that the hood could cover the head and be even pulled down over the face. At first I wanted my lord to find out by himself the *incognita* who had resolved to address him; but he asked me to tell him beforehand, and to be sure I could refuse him nothing.

The splendour of the lights was even greater than that at Lord Chudleigh's entertainment, when he lit up the lawn among the trees with coloured oil lamps. Yet the scene lacked the awful contrast of the dark and gloomy wood behind, in which, as one retired to talk, the music seemed out of place, and the laughter of the gay throng impertinent. Here was there no dark wood or shade of venerable trees to distract the thoughts from the gaiety of the moment, or sadden by a contrast of the long-lived forest with the transitory crowd who danced beneath the branches, as careless as a cloud of midges on the river-bank, born to buzz away their little hour, know hope, fear, and love, feel pain, be cut off prematurely at their twentieth minute, or wear on to a green old age and die at the protracted term of sixty minutes.

The Terrace and the New Parade were hung with festoons of coloured lamps. There must have been thousands of them in graceful arches from branch to branch: the doors of the Assembly Rooms had columns and arches of coloured lamps set up beside and over them: there were porches of coloured lamps; a temple of coloured lamps beside the watch-house at the edge of the pond, where horns were stationed to play while the music rested: in the Rooms was, of course, to be dancing: and, which was the greatest attraction, there were amusements of various kinds, almost as if one was at a country fair, without the crowding of the rustics, the fighting with quarterstaves, the grinning through horse-collars, the climbing of greasy poles, and the shouting. I have always, since that evening, longed for the impossible, namely, a country fair without the country people. Why can we not have, all to ourselves, and away from a noisy mob of ill-bred and rough people, the amusements of the fair, the stalls with the gingerbread, Richardson's Theatre, with a piece addressed to eyes and ears of sensibility, a wax-work, dancing and riding people, and clowns?

Here the presenters of the masquerade had not, it is true, provided all these amusements; but there were some: an Italian came to exhibit dancing puppets, called fantoccini; a conjurer promised to perform tricks, and swallow red-hot coals, which is truly a most wonderful feat, and makes one believe in the power of magic, else how could the tender throat sustain the violence of the fire? a girl was to dance upon the tight-rope: and a sorcerer or magician or astrologer was to be seated in a grotto to tell the fortunes of all who chose to search into the future.

Nothing could be gayer or more beautiful than the assemblage gathered together beneath these lighted lamps or in the Assembly Rooms in the evening. Mrs. Esther was the only lady without some disguise; Sir Robert, whose dress has been already sufficiently indicated, gave her his arm for the evening. All the dresses were as Nancy told me. I knew Venus by her golden cestus and her Cupid armed (he was, indeed, the milk-boy); and beneath the domino I could guess, without having been told, that no other than Peggy Baker swam and languished. Surely it is great presumption for a woman to call herself the Goddess of Beauty. Harry Temple was fine as Vulcan,

The Chaplain of the Fleet

though he generally forgot to go lame: he bore a real blacksmith's hammer on his shoulder; but I am certain that Vulcan never wore so modish a wig with so gallant a tie behind. And his scowls, meant for me, were not out of keeping with his character. Nancy Levett was the sweetest Joan of Arc ever seen, and skipped about, to the admiration of everybody, with a cuirass and a sword, although the real Joan, who was, I believe, a village maid, probably wore a stuff frock instead of Nancy's silk, and I dare say hoops were not in fashion in her days. Nor would she have lace mittens or silk shoes, but bare hands and wooden sandals. Nor would she powder her hair and dress it up two feet high, but rather wear it plain, blown about by the winds, washed by the rain, and curling as nature pleased. As for Mr. Stallabras, it did one good to see him as Theocritus, nose in air, shepherd's crook on shoulder, lyre in hand, in a splendid purple coat and wig newly combed and tied behind, illustrating the dignity and grandeur of genius. The Queen of Sheba's black pages (they were a loan from a lady in London) attracted general attention. You knew her for a queen by her crown. There were, however, other queens, all of whom wore crowns; and it was difficult sometimes to know which queen was designed if you failed to notice the symbol which distinguished one from the other. Thus Queen Elizabeth of England, who bore on a little flag the motto "*Dux fæmina facti,*" was greatly indignant when Harry Temple mistook her for Cleopatra, whose asp was for the moment hidden. Yet so good a scholar ought to have known, because Cleopatra ran away at Actium, and therefore could not carry such a motto, while Elizabeth conquered in the Channel. Then it was hard at first sight to distinguish between Julius Cæsar, Hannibal, Timour the Tartar, Luther, Alfred, and Caractacus, because they were all dressed very much alike, save that Luther carried a book, Alfred a sceptre, Cæsar a short sword, Timour a pike, Hannibal a marshal's *bâton,* and Caractacus a bludgeon. The difficulties and mistakes, however, mattered little, because, when the first excitement of guessing a character was over, one forgot about the masquerade and remembered the ball. Yet it was vexatious when a man had dressed carefully for, say, Charles the First, to be mistaken for Don Quixote or Euripides, who wore the same wigs.

I say nothing of the grotesque dresses with masks and artificial heads, introduced by some of the young Templars. They amused as such things do, for a while, and until one became accustomed to them. Then their pranks ceased to amuse. It is a power peculiar to man that he can continue to laugh at horse-play, buffoonery, and low humour for hours, while a woman is content to laugh for five minutes if she laughs at all. I believe that the admirers of those coarse and unfeeling books, "Tom Jones" and "Humphrey Clinker," are entirely men.

All the ladies began by wearing masks, and a few of the men. One of them personated a shepherd in lamentation for the loss of his mistress; that is to say, he wore ribbons of black and crimson tied in bows about his sleeve, and carried a pastoral hook decorated with the same colours. In this character some of the company easily recognised Lord Chudleigh; and when he led out for the first minuet a tall, hooded figure, in black velvet, some thought they recognised Kitty Pleydell.

"But why is he in mourning?" asked Peggy Baker, who understood what was meant. "She cannot have denied him. He must have another mistress for whom he has put on the black ribbons. Poor Kitty! we are all of us sorry for her. Yet pride still goes before a fall."

No one knew what was meant except Lord Chudleigh's partner, the figure in black velvet.

"I suppose," continued Peggy, alluding to the absence of my hoops, "that she wants to show how a woman would look without the aid of art. I call it, for my part, odious!"

After the minuet we left the dancers and walked beneath the lighted lamps on the Terrace. Presently the music ceased for a while, and the horns outside began to play.

"Kitty," whispered my lord, "you used strange words the other night. Were they anything but a kind hope for the impossible? Could they mean anything beyond an attempt to console a despairing man?"

"No," I replied. "They were more than a hope. But as yet I cannot say more. Oh, my lord! let me enjoy a brief hour of happiness, if it should die away and come to nothing."

I have said that part of the entertainment was a magician's cave. We found ourselves opposite the entrance of this place. People were going in and coming out—or, more correctly, people were waiting outside for their turn to go in; and those who came out appeared either elated beyond measure with the prophecies they had heard, or depressed beyond measure. Some of the girls had tears in their eyes—they were those to whom he had denied a lover; some came out bounding and leaping with joy—they were the maidens to whom he had promised a husband and children dear. Some of the young men came out with head erect and smiling lips: I suppose the wizard had told them of fortune, honour, long life, health and love—things which every young man must greatly desire. Some came out with angry frowns and lips set sternly, as if resolved to meet adverse fortune with undaunted courage—which is, of course, the only true method. But I fear the evening's happiness was destroyed for these luckless swains and nymphs: the lamps would grow dim, the music lose its gladness, the wine its sparkle.

"Let us, my lord," I said, little thinking of what was to happen within the cave—"Let us, too, consult the oracle, and learn the future."

At first he refused, saying, gravely, that to inquire of wise men or wise women was the sin of Saul with the witch of Endor; that whatever might have happened in olden time, as in the case of the Delphic oracles or the High Places, where they came to inquire of Baal or Moloch, there was now no voice from the outer world nor any communication from the stars, or from good spirits or from evil.

"Therefore," he said, "we waste our time, sweet Kitty, in idly asking questions of this man, who knows no more than we know ourselves."

"Then," I asked, "let us go in curiosity, because I have never seen a wizard, and I know not what he is like. You, I am sure, will keep me safe from harm, whatever frightful creature he may be."

So, without thinking, I led the way to the Wizard's Cave.

It stood in the Parade, beneath the trees; at the door were assembled a crowd of the masqueraders, either waiting their turn or discussing the reply of the oracle; the entrance, before which was a heavy curtain, double, was guarded by a negro, armed with an immense cutlass, which he ever and anon whirled round his head, the light falling on the bright steel, so that it seemed like a ring of fire, behind which gleamed his two eyes, as bright as a panther's eyes, and his teeth, as white as polished ivory. The sight of him made some of the women retreat, and refuse to go in at all.

The wise man received only one couple at a time: but when the pair then with him emerged, the negro stepped forward and beckoned to us, though it was not our turn to enter the cave. I observed that the last pair came out with downcast eyes. I think I am as free from superstition as any woman, yet I needs must remark, in spite of my lord's disbelief in magic or astrology, that the unhappy young man whose fortune this wizard told (an evil fortune, as was apparent from his face) ran away with the girl who was with him (an honest city merchant's daughter), and having got through his whole stock, took to the road, and was presently caught, tried, sentenced, and hanged in chains on Bagshot Heath, where those who please may go and see him. With such examples before one it is hard not to believe in the conjurer and the wise woman, just as a thousand instances might be alleged from any woman's experience to prove that it is unlucky to spill salt (without throwing some over your left shoulder), or to dream of crying children, or to cross two knives upon a plate—with many other things which are better not learned, would one wish to live a tranquil life.

What they called the Wizard's Cave was a little building constructed specially for the occasion, of rude trunks of trees, laid one upon the other, the interstices filled up with moss, to imitate a hermitage or monkish cell; a gloomy abode, consecrated to superstition and horrid rites. The roof seemed to be made of thatch, but I think that was only an illusion produced by the red light of an oil-lamp, which hung in the middle, and gave a soft and flickering, yet lurid light, around the hut. There also hung up beside the lamp, and on the right hand, the skin of a grisly crocodile, stuffed, the sight of which filled me with a dreadful apprehension, and made me, ever after, reflect on the signal advantages possessed by those who dwell in a land where such monsters are unknown. A table stood in the middle, on which, to my horror, were three grinning skulls in a row; and in each they had placed a lamp of different colours, so that through the eye-holes of one there came a green, of another a red, and of the third a blue light, very horrible and diabolical to behold.

There was also a great book—doubtless the book of Fate—upon the table. Behind it sat the Sage himself. He was a man with a big head covered with grey hair, which hung down upon his shoulders long and unkempt, and with a tall mitre, which had mysterious characters engraved over it, and between the letters what seemed in the dim light to be flames and devils—the fit occupant of this abominable place. He wore spectacles and a great Turkish beard, frightful and Saracenic of aspect.

I thought of the witch of Endor, of those who practised divinations, and of the idolatrous practices on High Places and in groves, and I trembled lest the fate of the Prophets of Baal might also be that of the profane inquirers. Outside, the music played and the couples were dancing.

The Wizard looked up as we stood before him. Behind the blue spectacles and the great beard, even in the enormous head, I recognised nothing and suspected nothing; but when he spoke, and in deep sonorous tones called my companion by his name— —

"Lord Chudleigh, what wilt thou inquire of the oracle?"— —

Then indeed I turned giddy and faint, and should have fallen, but my lord caught me by the waist.

"Be soothed, Kitty," he whispered. "Here is nothing to fright us but the mummery of a foolish masquerade or the roguery of a rascal quack. Calm yourself."

Alas! I feared no more the crocodile, nor the horrid death's heads, nor the Turkish beard, nor the mitre painted with devils—if they were devils. They disquieted me at first sight, it is true: but now was I in deadly terror, for I knew and feared the voice. It was no other than the voice of the Doctor, the Chaplain of the Fleet. For what trouble, what mischief, was he here?

Then I recovered, saying to myself: "Kitty, be firm. Resolve by neither act nor word to do harm to thy lover. Consent not to any snare. Be resolute and alert."

Lord Chudleigh, seeing me thus composed, stepped forward to the table and said—

"Sir Magician, Wizard, Conjurer, or whatever name best befits you, for you and your pretended science I care not one jot, nor do I believe but that it is imposture and falsehood. Perhaps, however, you are but acting a part in the masquerade. But the young lady hath a desire to see what you do, and to ask you a question or two."

"Your lordship must own that I know your name, in spite of your domino."

"Tut, tut! everybody here knows my name, whether I wear a domino or take it off. That is nothing. You are probably one of the company in disguise."

"You doubt my power? Then, without your leave, my lord, permit me to tell you a secret known to me, yourself, and one or two others only. It is a secret which no one has yet whispered about; none of the company at the Wells know it; it is a great secret: an important secret"—all this time his voice kept growing deeper and deeper. "It is a secret of the darkest. Stay—this young lady, I think, knows it."

"For Heaven's sake——" I cried, but was interrupted by my lord.

"Tell me your secret," he said calmly. "Let us know this wonderful secret."

The Doctor leaned forward over the table and whispered in his ear a few words. Lord Chudleigh started back and gazed at him with dismay.

"So!" he cried; "it is already becoming town talk, is it?"

The Magician shook his head.

"Not so, my lord. No one knows it yet except the persons concerned in it. No one will ever know it if your lordship so pleases. I told you but to show the power of the Black Art."

"I wonder, then, how you know."

"The Wizard, by his Art, learns as much of the past as he desires to know; he reads the present around him, still by aid of this great Art; he can foretell the future, not by the gift of prophecy, but by studying the stars."

"Tell me, then," said Lord Chudleigh, as if in desperation, "the future. Yet this is idle folly and imposture."

"That which is done"—the Sage opened the book and turned over the pages, speaking in low, deep tones—"cannot be undone, whatever your lordship might ignorantly wish. That which is loved may still be loved. That which is hoped may yet come to pass."

"Is that all you have to say to me?"

"Is it not enough, my lord? Would any king's counsel or learned serjeant give you greater comfort? Good-night. Leave, now, this young lady with me, alone."

"First read me the oracle of her future, as you have told me mine; though still, I say, this is folly and imposture."

The Magician gravely turned over his pages, without resenting this imputation, and read, or seemed to read—

"Love shall arise from ashes of buried scorn:
Joy from a hate in a summer morning born;
When heart with heart and pulse with pulse shall beat,
Farewell to the pain of the storm and the fear of the Fleet."

"Good heavens!" cried Lord Chudleigh, pressing his hand to his forehead. "Am I dreaming? Are we mad?"

"Now, my lord," said the pretended Wizard, "go to the door; leave this young lady with me. I have more to tell her for her own ears. She is quite safe. She is not the least afraid. At the smallest fright she will cry aloud for your help. You will remain without the door, within earshot."

"Yes," I murmured, terrified, yet resolute. "Leave me a few moments alone. Let me hear what he has to say to me."

Then my lord left me alone with the Doctor.

When the heavy curtain fell before the door, the Wizard took off the great mitre and laughed silently and long, though I felt no cause for merriment.

"Confess, child," he said, "that I am an oracle of Dodona, a sacred oak. Lord Chudleigh is well and properly deceived. But we have little time for speech. I came here, Kitty, to see you, and no one else. By special messengers and information gained from letters, I learned, as I wrote to you (to my great joy), that this young lord is deeply enamoured. You are already, it is true, in some sort—nay, in reality, his bride, though he knows it not. Yet I might waive my own dignity in the matter, for the sake of thy happiness; and, if you like to wed him, why, nothing is easier than to let him know that his Fleet wife is dead. They die of drink daily. Roger, my man, will swear what I tell him to swear. This I have the less compunction in persuading him to do, because, in consequence of his horrid thieving, robbing, fighting, and blaspheming, his soul is already irretrievably lost, his conscience seared with a hot iron, and his heart impenitent as the nether millstone. Also the evidence of the marriage, the register, is in my hands, and may be kept or destroyed, as I please. Therefore it matters nothing what this rogue may swear. I think, child, the best thing would be to accept my lord's proposals; to let him know, through me, that his former wife, whose name he knows not, is dead; he may be told, so that he may remain ashamed of himself, and anxious to bury the thing in silence, that she died of gin. He would then be free to marry you; and, should he not redeem his promise and give you honourable marriage, it will be time to reduce him to submission—with the register."

Shall I confess that, at the first blush, this proposal was welcome to me? It seemed so easy a relief from all our troubles. The supposed death of his wife, the destruction of the register—what could be better?

"Be under no fear," continued the Doctor, "of my fellow Roger. He dares not speak. By Heaven! I have plenty to hang him with a dozen times over, if I wished. He would murder me, if he dared, and would carry me up to Holborn Bridge, where I could be safely dropped into the Fleet Ditch; but he dares not try. Why, if he proclaimed this marriage on Fleet Bridge (but that he dares not do), no one would believe it on his word, such a reputation has he, while I have the register safely locked up. Whereas, did they come forward to give evidence for me, at my bidding, so clear is my case, and so abundant my proofs, that no counsel could shake them."

This speech afforded me a little space wherein to collect my thoughts. Love makes a woman strong. Time was when I should have trembled before the Doctor's eyes, and obeyed him in the least particular. But now I had to consider another beside myself.

What I thought was this. Suppose the plot carried out, and myself married to my lord again. There would be this dreadful story on my mind. I should not dare to own my relationship with this famous Doctor; I should be afraid lest my husband should find it out. I should be afraid of his getting on the scent, as children say; therefore I should be obliged to hide all that part of my life which was spent in the Fleet. Yet there were many persons—Mrs. Esther, Sir Miles, Solomon Stallabras, beside my uncle—who knew all of it, except that one story. Why, any day, any moment, a chance word, an idle recollection, might make my husband suspicious and jealous. Then farewell to all my happiness! Better none at all than to have it snatched from me in that way.

"There is a second plan," he went on. "We may tell him exactly who and what you are."

"Oh, sir!" I cried, "do nothing yet. Leave it all with me for a little—I beg, I implore you! I love him, and he loves me. Should I harm him, therefore, by deceiving him and marrying him, while I hid the shameful story of the past? You cannot ask me to do that. I will not do it. And should you, against my will, acquaint him with what has happened, I swear that, out of the love I bear him, I will refuse and deny all your allegations—yea, the very fact itself, with the register and the evidence of those two rogues. Sir, which would the court believe? the daughter of the Rev. Lawrence Pleydell, or the rascal runner of a—of yourself?"

He said nothing. He looked surprised.

"No," I went on; "I will have no more deception. Every day I suffer remorse from my sin. There shall be no more. My mind, sir, is made up. I will confess to him everything. Not to-night; I cannot, to-night. And then, if he sends me away with hatred, I will never—never—stand in his way; I will be as one dead."

"This," said the Doctor, "it is to be young and to be in love. I was once like that myself. Go, child; thou shalt hear from me again."

He put on his mitre and beckoned me to the door. I went out without another word. Without stood a crowd, including Peggy Baker.

"Oh!" she cried. "She looks frightened, yet exulting. Dear Miss Pleydell, I hope he prophesied great things for you! A title perhaps, an estate in the country, a young and handsome lover, as generous as he is constant. But we know the course of true love never——"

Here my lord took my hand and led me away from the throng. Another pair went in, and the great negro before the door began again to flash his cutlass in the lights, to show his white teeth, and to turn those white eyes about which looked so fierce and terrible.

CHAPTER XVII.

HOW KITTY PREVENTED A DUEL.

The agitation of spirits into which I was thrown by this interview with the Doctor, blinded me for the moment to the fact that Harry Temple, of whose pretensions I thought I had disposed, was still an angry and rejected suitor. Indeed, for a few days he had ceased to persecute me. But to-night he manifested a jealousy which was inexcusable, after all I had said to him. No one, as I had gone so far as almost to explain to him, had a better right to give me his hand for the evening than my lord; yet this young man, as jealous as the blacksmith god whom he personated, must needs cross our steps at every turn, throwing angry glances both upon me and my partner. He danced with no one; he threw away his hammer, left off limping, consorted with none of the gay company, but nursed his wrath in silence.

Now the last dance of the evening, which took place at two o'clock in the morning, was to be one in which all the ladies threw their fans upon the table, and the gentlemen danced each with her whose fan he picked from the pile. My lord whispered to me that I was first to let him see my fan, whereupon, when the fans lay upon the table, he deliberately chose my own and brought it to me.

I took off my domino, which was now useless, because all the company knew the disguise. Everybody laughed, and we took our places to lead off the country-dance.

It was three o'clock when we finished dancing and prepared to go home.

Harry Temple here came up to me and asked if he might have the honour of escorting me to my lodgings. I answered that I had already promised that favour to Lord Chudleigh.

"Every dance, the whole evening: the supper, the promenade: all given to this happy gentleman! Surely, Kitty, the Queen of the Wells might dispense her favours more generously."

"The Queen," said Lord Chudleigh, "is the fountain of honour. We have only to accept and be grateful."

The Chaplain of the Fleet

I laughed and bade Harry good-night, and offered him my hand, which he refused sullenly; and murmuring something about pride and old friends, turned aside and let us go.

Everybody, it seems, noticed the black looks of Harry Temple all the evening, and expected, though in my happiness I thought not of such a thing, that high words would pass between this sulky young gentleman and his favoured rival, to whom he was so rude and unmannerly. Now, by the laws of the Wells, as laid down strictly in the rules of the great Mr. Nash for Tunbridge Wells and Bath, and adopted at all watering-places, the gentlemen wore no swords on the Parade and in the card-rooms; yet it was impossible to prevent altogether the quarrels of hot-blooded men, and the green grass of the Downs had been stained with the blood of more than one poor fellow, run through as the consequence of a foolish brawl. When will men cease to fight duels, and seek to kill each other for a trifling disagreement, or a quarrel?

Generally, it takes two to make a quarrel, and few men are so perverse as deliberately to force a duel upon another against his will. Yet this was what Harry Temple, my old schoolfellow, my old friend, of whom I once held so high an opinion, so great a respect, actually did with Lord Chudleigh. He forced the quarrel upon him. My lord was always a gentleman of singular patience, forbearance, and sweetness, and one who would take, unprovoked, a great deal of provocation, never showing the usual sign of resentment or anger, although he might be forced to take up the quarrel. He held, indeed, the maxim that a man should always think so well of himself as to make an insult impossible, unless it be deliberate, open, and clearly intended. As for his courage, he went on to say that it was a matter of self-respect: if a man's own conscience approve (which is the ultimate judge for all but those whose consciences are deadened by an evil life), let him fear not what men say, knowing full well that if they dare say more than the customs of the polite world allow, it is easy for every man to prove that he is no coward.

Lord Chudleigh, then, having led us to the door of our own lodging, unfortunately returned to the Assembly Rooms, where—and outside upon the Terrace—some of the gentlemen yet lingered. I say unfortunately, because, as for what followed, I cannot believe but that poor Harry, whose disposition was not naturally quarrelsome, might have been inflamed by drinking wine with them when he ought to have gone to bed. Now wine, to one who is jealous, is like oil upon fire. And had my lord, for his part, retired to Durdans—as he might very properly have done, seeing the lateness of the hour—the morning's reflection would, I am sure, have persuaded Harry that he had been a fool, and had no reasonable ground for quarrel with his lordship or with me.

The sun was already rising, for it was nearly four o'clock in the morning; the ladies were all gone off to bed; those who lay about the benches yawned and stretched themselves; some were for bed, some for another bottle; some were talking of an early gallop on the Downs; the lamps yet glimmered in their sockets; the Terrace looked, with its oil lamps still burning in the brightness of the morning sunshine, with the odds and ends of finery, the tattered bravery of torn dresses, gold and silver lace, tinfoil, broken paper crowns and helmets, as sad as a theatre the morning after a performance; the stalls of the Wizard, the Italian performers, and the dancing girl, were empty and open; their hangings were already torn down, the stand for the horses beside the pond was broken in parts.

When Lord Chudleigh came back he found waiting for him, among the latest of the revellers, Harry Temple, his face pale, his lips set, his manner agitated, as of one who contemplates a rash act.

My lord threw himself upon a bench under the trees, his head upon his hand, pensive, thinking to calm the agitation of his spirits by the freshness of the morning air. Harry began walking up and down in front of him, casting angry glances at him, but as yet speaking not. Now, within the deserted card-room when the lights had all burned out, and the windows were wide open, sat all by himself Sir Miles Lackington, turning over a pack of cards at one of the empty tables, and thinking over the last night's play, at which he had won some money, and regretted to have been stopped just when he was in luck. There were now only a few gentlemen left, and these were one by one dropping off.

Presently, with an effort, Harry Temple stopped in front of his lordship and spoke to him.

I declare that up to this time poor Harry had always been the most peaceful of creatures, though strong, and well accustomed to hold bouts with Will, in which he proved almost equal to that stalwart competitor, at wrestling, singlestick, quarterstaff, or boxing. Also, as was proved by the affray of the Saturday evening, already related, not unready on occasion. But a bookish youth, and not one who sought to fix quarrels upon any man, or to commit murder in the name of honour. And this shows how dangerous a passion is thwarted love, which can produce in a peaceful man's bosom jealousy, hatred, rage, and forgetfulness of that most sacred commandment which enjoins us not to slay.

"I trust, my lord," he said, laughing and blushing, as if uncertain of himself, "that your lordship hath passed a pleasant evening with the Queen of the Wells."

Lord Chudleigh looked up, surprised. Then he rose, for there was a look in Harry's eyes which meant mischief. The unlucky love-sick swain went on—

"Lord Chudleigh and Miss Kitty Pleydell. The very names seem made for one another; no doubt his lordship is as fine a gentleman as the lady is beautiful."

"Sir!" said Lord Chudleigh quietly, "you have perhaps been drinking. This is the only excuse for such an association of my name with that young lady's in a public assembly."

"Oh!" he said, "I want no excuse for addressing your lordship. The Temples were gentlefolk before the Chudleighs were heard of."

"Well, Mr. Temple, so be it. Enjoy that superiority. Shall we close this discussion?"

"No, my lord; there is more to be said."

He spoke hotly, and with an anger which ought surely to have been simulated, such small provocation as he had received.

"Then, sir, in Heaven's name, let us say it and have done with it."

"You have offended me, my lord—you best know how."

"I believe I know, Mr. Temple. You also know what grounds you have for believing that to be an offence."

"I say, my lord," his voice rose and his eyes flashed, "that you have offended me."

"Had I done so wittingly," returned Lord Chudleigh, "I should willingly ask pardon. But I deny your right to take offence."

"You have offended me highly," he repeated, "and that in a manner which makes an apology only a deeper insult. You have offended me in a manner which only one thing can satisfy."

"Before we go any farther, Mr. Temple," said my lord, sitting down again calmly and without heat, "I would know exactly the nature of my offence, and your reasonable right to regard it as such."

"It needs not, my lord. You know well enough what I mean."

"I know that, of course; I would wish to know, as well, your right to be offended."

"I say, my lord, that it is enough."

Harry, being in the wrong, spoke still more loudly, and those who were left drew near to see the quarrel.

"You need not raise your voice, sir," said Lord Chudleigh; "I like any altercation in which I may be unhappily engaged to be conducted like the rest of my business in life, namely, with the decorum and quietness which become gentlemen like the Temples, and those of that younger family the Chudleighs. You have, I believe, travelled. You have, therefore, without doubt, had opportunities of observing the well-bred and charming quietness with which gentlemen in France arrange these little matters, particularly when, as now, the dispute threatens to involve the name of a lady. Now, sir, that we understand each other, I must inform you that unless I know the exact nature of my offence to you, which I have the right to demand, this affair will proceed no further. I would as soon accept a quarrel from a mad Malay running amuck at all he meets."

"My lord!" cried Harry, with red face and trembling fingers.

"Of course I do not pretend to be unable to form a guess," Lord Chudleigh went on gravely; "but I must beg you to instruct me exactly what you mean. You will observe, sir, that I am here, as a visitor, previously unknown to yourself. It is therefore strange to learn that one has offended a gentleman towards whom my behaviour has been neither less nor more guarded than towards others."

"My lord, you have offended me by the attentions you have paid to a young lady."

"Indeed, sir! So I believed. But permit me to ask if the young lady is connected with you or with your house by any ties of relationship or otherwise?"

"She is not, my lord."

"Further: have you any right of guardianship over this young lady?"

"None, my lord. But yet you have offended me."

"The young lady is free to accept the attention of any man she may prefer; to show her preference as openly as she considers proper. I conclude this to be the case. And, if so, I am unable to perceive in what way I can wilfully have offended you."

"Your lordship," said Harry Temple, enraged by his adversary's calmness, but yet with sufficient self-command to speak in lower tones, "has offended me in this: that if you had not paid those attentions to Miss Pleydell, she might have accepted those courtesies which I was prepared to offer her."

"Indeed, sir! that is a circumstance with which I am wholly unconcerned. No doubt the same thing might be said by other gentlemen in this company."

"I knew that young lady, my lord, long before you did. It was my deliberate purpose, long ago, to make her my wife when the opportunity arrived——"

"The time has come," resumed Lord Chudleigh, "but not the man——"

"I say, it was my fixed intention to marry Miss Pleydell. I did not, my lord, form these resolutions lightly, nor abandon them without sufficient reason. It is still my resolution. I say that you shall not stand between me and my future wife!"

"Indeed! But suppose Miss Pleydell refuses to give her consent to this arrangement? Surely such a resolve, however laudable, demands the consent of the other party."

"Miss Pleydell will not refuse my hand when you have left her. Abandon a field, my lord, which never belonged to yourself——"

"Tut, tut!" said Lord Chudleigh. "This, sir, is idle talk. You cannot seriously imagine——"

"I seriously imagine that, if necessary, I will make my way to that young lady over your lordship's body, if you stand in my way."

Lord Chudleigh took off his hat and bowed low.

"Then, sir, the sooner you take the first step in the pursuance of your resolution the better. I will bar your way upon the Downs at any time you may appoint."

Harry returned the obeisance.

"I wait your lordship's convenience," he said.

"My convenience shall be yours, Mr. Temple. For it is you who desire to run me through, not I you. Have your own way."

"It is late to-night," said Harry, now quite calm, though with a hot flush upon his cheek. "Your lordship would like to rest. Perhaps to-morrow, after breakfast, while the ladies are at morning prayer."

Oh, the bloodthirsty wretch!

Lord Chudleigh bowed again.

"That time, Mr. Temple, will I dare say suit the convenience of my second."

The code of honour, be it observed, does not allow the exhibition of any emotion of horror, remorse, or repugnance, when you arrange to commit that private murder which gentlemen call a duel.

Lord Chudleigh bowed once more, and left his adversary. He walked across the Terrace to the card-room, where Sir Miles was alone with the scattered packs of cards. When he came out, he bowed a third time, and walked slowly away. I hope that, in his own chamber, he reflected on the wickedness of the appointment he had made, and on its possible consequences.

Sir Miles threw away the cards, and came out rubbing his eyes.

"Ods my life, sir!" he said, addressing Harry Temple, who, now that the mischief was done, looked somewhat sheepish, though dignified.

The few gentlemen who were left drew nearer, anxious to lose nothing of what might happen. English people of all ranks love above all things to watch a quarrel or a fight, whatever be the weapons.

"Ods my life, sir!" repeated Sir Miles. "This is a pretty kettle of fish! Here we have all spent a pleasant night—dancing, playing, and making love, every one happy, even though some gentlemen did lose their mistresses or their money, and here you spoil sport by quarrelling at the end of it. What the Devil, sir, does it concern you whether my lord talks gallantry with one young lady or another?"

"That, Sir Miles, allow me to tell you, is my business. If you are his lordship's second, let us arrange accordingly. If a principal, let us fight afterwards."

"No, sir," replied the baronet. "It is everybody's business. It concerns the cheerfulness, the security, the happiness of all this honourable company. What! if I amuse myself, and a young lady too, by writing poems on her dainty fingers, must I needs go out and measure swords with every young hot-head who would fain be doing the same? Seconds and principals? Have we nothing to do but to fight duels? Mr. Temple, I thought better things from a gentleman of your rank and family. What! any jackanapes lawyer—any pert young haberdasher— might think it fine thus to insult and challenge a harmless nobleman of great name and excellent qualities! But for *you*, Mr. Temple! you, sir, a gentleman of your county, and of ancient and most honourable stock——Fie, sir, fie!"

"I think, Sir Miles," said Harry, who wished now to have the preliminaries settled without more ado, "that things having so far advanced, these reproaches may be spared. Let us proceed to business."

"A girl can choose, I suppose," Sir Miles went on, "without the interference or the objection of a man who is neither her father, her guardian, her brother, nor her cousin? Why, as for this young lady, whose name, I say, it is not respectful to name in this business—I myself, sir, I myself paid her attentions till she bade me go about my business. What, sir! do you think I should have suffered any man to question my right to make a Lady Lackington where I choose, and where I could! She laughed in my face. Mighty pretty laughing lips she has, and teeth as white as pearls; and a roguish eye when she chooses, for all she goes so grave. Did I, then, go snivelling in the dumps? Did I take it ill that she showed a liking for Lord Chudleigh, who is worth ten of me, and a dozen of you? Did I hang my chops and wipe my eyes? Did I, therefore, insult his Lordship, and call him out?"

"All this, Sir Miles," Harry replied impatiently, "has nothing to do with the question which lies between Lord Chudleigh and myself."

"What I argued, for my own comfort, when sweet Kitty said me nay, was this: that the marriage condition hath many drawbacks, as is abundantly evident from history and poetry, while freedom hath many sweets—that a man may tire of a Beauty and a Toast in a month, but he never tired of liberty—that children often come after matrimony, and they are expensive—that, as for the lady's good looks, why, as many pretty women are in the sea as ever came out of it. And as for my wounded feelings, why, what is it but so much vanity? Granted that she is the Toast this year: prithee who will be the Toast next? Last year, they tell me, it was Peggy Baker—and a monstrous pretty woman, too, though not to compare with Kitty. Now her nose is out of joint. Who next? Some little miss now getting rapped over the knuckles in the nursery, Mr. Temple; and she will be, in her turn, quite as fine a woman as we shall live to see. That is to say, as I shall live to see, because you, of course, will be no more. At eleven o'clock upon the Downs you will get your quietus; when my lord's sword has once made daylight through your fine waistcoat. 'Tis pity, but yet what help? Mighty little looking after pretty women where you are going to, Mr. Temple. I advise you to consider your earthly concerns before you go out. Well, 'tis a shame, it is, a well-set-up man like you, with a likely face and pretty fortune, to throw all away because a woman says nay:

'Shall I wasting in despair,
Die because a woman's fair?'

Tilly vally! A pretty reason why two tall fellows should stick swords into each other. I have a great mind, sir, not to allow my principal to go out on such a provocation."

"I can easily give him more, Sir Miles," said Harry hotly, "or you either, as soon as you have finished your sermon."

"Oh, sir!" Sir Miles laughed and bowed. "Pray do not think that I desire to fight on that or any other provocation. We gentlemen of Norfolk sometimes try conclusions with the cudgel before the rapier comes into play. Therefore, sir, having given you my mind on the matter, and having nothing more to say at this moment, you may as well refer me at once to your friend."

Harry turned to the group of lookers-on.

"Gentlemen," he said, "an unhappy difference, as some of you have witnessed, has arisen between the Lord Chudleigh and myself. May I request the good offices of one among you in this affair?"

One of them, an officer in the king's scarlet, stepped forward and offered his services. Harry thanked him, briefly told him where he lodged, introduced him formally to Sir Miles, and walked away. A few minutes' whispered consultations between Sir Miles and this officer concluded the affair. The principals were to fight on the Downs at eleven o'clock, when there are generally, unless a match is going on, but few people up there. This arranged, Sir Miles walked away to tell Lord Chudleigh; and Harry, with his second, left the Terrace.

Thus the affair, as gentlemen call an engagement in which their own lives and the happiness of helpless women are concerned, was quietly arranged on the well-known laws of "honour," just as if it were nothing more than the purchase of a horse, a carriage, or a house; we at home sleeping meanwhile without suspicion, dreaming, very likely, of love and joy, even when death was threatening those dearest to us. Sometimes when I think of this uncertain life, how it is surrounded by nature with unknown dangers—how thoughtless and wicked men may in a moment destroy all that most we love—how in a moment the strongest fortune is over-thrown—how our plans may be frustrated—how the houses of cards (which we have thought so stable) tumble down without a warning, and all our happiness with them—when, I say, I think of these things I wonder how any one can laugh and be merry, save the insensate wretches whose whole thought is of their own enjoyment for the moment. Yet the Lord, our Father, is above all; in whose hand is the ordering of the smallest thing—the meanest life. Moreover, He hath purposed that youth should be a time of joy, and so hath wisely hidden away the sources of evil.

Cicely Crump was stirring betimes in the morning, and before six was in the market buying the provisions for the day. And as she passed the door of the Assembly Rooms, she looked in to see the dipper, a friend of hers, who sat at the distribution of the water, though but few of the visitors took it regularly. This good woman, Phœbe Game by name, had kept the secret for more than an hour, having heard it, under promise of strictest secrecy, from one of the late revellers when she took her place among the glasses at five o'clock in the morning. She was a good woman and discreet according to her lights; but this dreadful secret was too much for her, and if she had not told it to Cicely, must have told it to some one else. At sight of her visitor, therefore, discretion abandoned this good woman, and she babbled all she knew. Yet not in a hurry, but little by little, as becomes a woman with such a piece of intelligence, the parting of which is as the parting with power.

"Cicely," she said, shaking her forefinger in an awful and threatening way, "I have heard this very morning—ah! only an hour or so since—news which would make your poor young lady jump out of her pretty shoes for fright. I have—I have."

"Goodness!" cried Cicely. "Oh, Phœbe! whatever in the world is it?"

"I dare not tell," she replied. "It is as much as my place is worth to tell. We dippers are not like common folk. We must have no ears to hear and no tongue to speak. We must listen and make no sign. The quality says what they like and they does what they like. It isn't for a humble dipper to speak, nor to tell, nor to spoil sport—even if it is murder."

"Oh, tell me!" cried Cicely. "Why, Phœbe, your tongue can run twenty to the dozen if you like. And if I knew, why there isn't a mouse in all Epsom can be muter, or a guinea-pig dumber. Only you tell me."

Thus appealed to, Mrs. Game proceeded (as she had from the first intended) to transfer her secret to Cicely, with many interjections, reflections, sighs, prayers, and injunctions to tell no one, but to go home and pray on her bended knees that Lord Chudleigh's hand might be strengthened and his eye directed, so that this meddlesome young gentleman might be run through in some vital part.

Cicely received the intelligence with dismay. The good girl had more of my confidence than most ladies give to maids: but she was above the common run and quick of apprehension. Besides, she loved me.

"What use," she asked bitterly, "for Mr. Nash to prohibit the gentlemen from wearing their swords when they have got them at home ready for using when they want? Mr. Temple, indeed! To think that my young lady would look at him when my lord is about!"

"Well—go, child," said the dipper. "You and me, being two poor women with little but our characters, which are, thank the Lord, good so far as we have got, cannot meddle nor make in this pie. I am glad I told you, though. I felt before you came as if the top of my head was being lifted off with the force of it like a loaf with the yeast. Oh, the wickedness of gentlefolk!"

Cicely walked slowly back, thinking what she had best do—whether to keep the secret, or to tell me. Finally she resolved on telling me.

Accordingly she woke me up, for I was still asleep, and communicated the dreadful intelligence. There could be no doubt of its truth. Sir Miles, she told me, had expostulated with Harry Temple, who would hear no reason. They would meet to kill each other at eleven o'clock, when the ladies were at prayers, on the Downs behind Durdans.

I thanked her, and told her to leave me while I dressed; but not to awaken Mrs. Pimpernel, who would be the better for a long sleep after her late night, while I thought over what was to be done.

First of all I was in a mighty great rage with Harry; the rage I was in prevented me from doing what I ought to have done—viz., had I been in my right mind, I should have gone to him instantly, and then and there I should have ordered him to withdraw from the Wells. Should he refuse, I would have gone to Sir Robert, a Justice of the Peace, and caused the duel to be prevented.

I could find no excuse for Harry. Even supposing that his passion was so violent (which is a thing one ought to be ashamed of rather than to make a boast of it), was that any reason why my happiness was to be destroyed? Men, I believe, would like to carry off their wives as the Romans carried off the Sabine women, and no marriage feast would be more acceptable to their barbarous hearts than the one in which these rude soldiers celebrated this enforced union.

Cicely and I looked at each other. It was seven o'clock. The duel was to take place at eleven. Could I seek out Lord Chudleigh? No; his honour was concerned. Or Sir Miles? But the honest baronet looked on a duel as a necessity of life, which might happen at any time to a gentleman, though he himself preferred a bout with cudgels.

Presently Cicely spoke.

"I once heard," she said, "a story."

"Child, this is no time for telling stories."

"Let me tell it first, Miss Kitty. Nay, it is not a silly story. A gentleman once had planned to carry off a great heiress."

"What has that to do with Lord Chudleigh? He does not want to carry me off."

"The gentleman was a wicked man and an adventurer. He only wanted the lady's money. One of her friends, a woman it was, found out the plot. She wanted to prevent it without bloodshed, or murder, or duelling, which would have happened if it had been prevented by any stupid interference of clumsy men — —"

"O Cicely! get on with the story."

"She did prevent it. And how do you think?"

"How?"

Cicely ran and shut the door, which was ajar. Then she looked all about the room and under the bed.

"It was a most dreadful wicked thing to do. Yet to save a friend or a lover, I would even do it."

"What was it, Cicely?"

"I must whisper."

"Quick! give me my hood, child."

She put it on and tied it with trembling fingers, because we were really going to do a most desperate thing.

"Is the house on the road, Cicely? Cannot he go by another way?"

"No; he cannot go by any other way."

"Say not a word, Cicely. Let not madam think or suspect anything."

On the road which leads from the town by a gentle ascent to the Downs, there stood (on the left-hand side going up) a large square house in red brick, surrounded by a high wall on which were iron spikes. The door of the wall opened into a sort of small lodge, and the great gates were strong, high, and also protected by iron spikes. I had often observed this house; but being full of my own thoughts, and not a curious person always wanting to discover the business of others, I had not inquired into the reason of these fortifications. Yet I knew that the house was the residence of a certain learned physician, Dr. Jonathan Powlett by name, who daily walked upon the Terrace dressed in black, with a great gold-headed cane and an immense full periwig. He had a room in one of the houses of the Terrace in which he received his patients, and he made it his business to accost every stranger on his arrival with the view of getting his custom. Thus he would, after inquiring after the stranger's health, branch off upon a dissertation on the merits of the Epsom waters and an account of the various diseases, with their symptoms (so that timid men often fancied they had contracted these disorders, and ran to the doctor in terror), which the waters would cure. Mrs. Esther was pleased to converse with him, and I believe spent several guineas in consultations on the state of her health, now excellent.

I had never spoken to him except once, when he saluted me with a finely pompous compliment about youth and beauty, the twin stars of such a company as was gathered together at Epsom. "Yet," he said, "while even the physician cannot arrest the first of these, the second may be long preserved by yearly visits to this invigorating spot, not forgetting consultations with scientific and medical men, provided they are properly qualified and hold the license of the College of Physicians, without which a so-called doctor is but a common apothecary, chirurgeon, or leech, fit only to blister and to bleed."

I made my way to his house, hoping to catch him before he sallied forth in the morning. The place was, as I have said, hidden by high brick walls, and the gate was guarded by a lodge in which, after ringing a great bell, I found a man of rough and strong appearance, who asked me rudely what was my business.

I told him my business was with his master.

After a little demur, he bade me wait in the lodge while he went away, and presently returned with the doctor.

"My dear young lady," he cried. "I trust there is nothing wrong with that most estimable lady, Mrs. Pimpernel?"

"Indeed, doctor," I replied, "I come on quite a different errand. And my business is for your ear alone."

Upon this he bade the fellow retire, and we were left alone in the little room of the lodge.

Then I exposed my business.

He looked very serious when he quite understood what I wanted him to do.

"It is very dangerous," he said.

I then told him how it might be so managed as that there should be no danger in it at all. He thought for a little, and then he laughed to himself.

"But, madam," he said, "suppose I do this for you safely and snugly. What reward am I to have for my trouble and risk?"

"What do you think the business is worth?"

He looked curiously in my face as if wondering how much he could safely say. Then he replied—

"I believe it is worth exactly twenty guineas."

"I can spare no more than ten," I replied.

"Well," he said, "ten guineas is a trifle indeed for so great a risk and so great a service. Still, if no more is to be had, and to oblige so sweet a young lady——"

Here he held out a fat white hand, the fingers of which were curled as if from long habit in clutching guineas.

I gave him five as an instalment, promising him the other five when the job was done.

All being safely in train, I returned home to breakfast; but after breakfast I returned to the physician's house, and sat down in the lodge, so placed that I could see without being seen, and looked down the road.

After the bell for morning prayers had stopped, I began to expect my friends. Sure enough the first who came into sight were my lord and Sir Miles, the former looking grave and earnest. A little while after them came a gentleman whom I knew to be one of the company at Epsom. He was alone. Now this was the most fortunate accident, because had the gentleman, who was none other than Harry's second, accompanied his principal, my plot had failed. But fortunately (as I learned afterwards) they missed each other in the town, and so set off alone. This, at the time, I knew not, being ignorant of the laws of the duello. And last there came along Harry himself, walking quickly as if afraid of being late.

I gave a signal which had been agreed upon, and as he approached the house, the great gates were thrown open, and two strapping tall fellows, stepping quickly into the road, caught poor Harry (the would-be murderer) by the arms, ran a thick rope round him before he had time to cry out, and dragged him into the gates, so quickly, so strongly, and so resolutely, that he had not the least chance of making any resistance. Indeed, it was done in so workmanlike a fashion that it seemed as if the rogues had done the same thing dozens of times before.

Heavens! To think that a man brought up so virtuously as Harry Temple, a young man of such excellent promise, so great a scholar, and one who had actually studied Theology, and attended the lectures of a Lady Margaret Professor, should, under any circumstances of life, abandon himself to language so wicked and a rage so overwhelming. Nothing ever surprised me so much as to hear that gentle scholar use such dreadful language, as bad as any that I had ever heard in the Fleet Market.

Caught up in this unexpected way, with his arms tied to his sides, carried by two stout ruffians, Harry had, to be sure, some excuse for wrath. His wig had fallen to the ground, his face was red and distorted by passion, so that even I hardly knew him, when Doctor Powlett came out of his house and slowly advanced to meet him.

"Ay, ay, ay!" he asked slowly, wagging his head and stroking his long chin deliberately, in the manner of a physician who considereth what best treatment to recommend. "So this is the unfortunate young gentleman, is it? Ay, he looks very far gone. Nothing less, I fear, than *Dementia acuta cum rabie violentâ*. Resolute treatment in such cases is the best kindness. You will take him, keepers, to the blue-room, and chain him carefully. Your promptitude in making the capture shall be rewarded. As for you, sir"—he shook his forefinger at the unlucky Harry as if he was a schoolmaster admonishing a boy—"as for you, sir, it is lucky, indeed, that you have been caught. You were traced to this town, where, I suppose, you arrived early this morning. Ha! I *have* known madmen to be run through their vitals by some gentlemen whom they have accosted; or smothered between mattresses—a reprehensible custom, because it deprives the physician of his dues—or brained with a cudgel. You are fortunate, sir. But have a care; this house is remarkable for its kindness to the victims of mania! but have a care."

Here Harry burst into a fit of imprecations most dreadful to listen to.

"Anybody," said the Doctor, "may swear in this house; a good many do: that often relieves a congested brain, and does no harm to me and my attendants. But disobedience or violence is punished by cold-water baths, by being held under the pump, by bread and water, and by other methods with which I hope you will not make yourself better acquainted. Now, keepers!"

For the truth is that the doctor kept a house for the reception of madmen and unhappy lunatics, and I had persuaded him to kidnap Harry—by mistake. In four-and-twenty hours, I thought, he would have time to repent. It was sad, however, to see a man of breeding and learning so easily give way to profane swearing, and it shows the necessity of praying against temptation. Women, fortunately, do not *know* how to swear. It was, I confess, impossible to pity him. Why, he was going up the hill and on to the Downs with no other object than to kill my lover!

CHAPTER XVIII.

HOW HARRY GOT RELEASED.

"He is now," said Dr. Powlett, returning to the lodge where I awaited him, "safely chained up in a strait-waistcoat. A strong young gentleman, indeed, and took four of my fellows to reduce him. Almost a pity," he went on, thinking of the case from a professional point of view, "that so valiant a fellow is in his right mind."

"Doctor, what may that mean?"

"Nay, I was but thinking—a physician must needs consider these things—that a county gentleman, with so great an estate, would be indeed a windfall in such an establishment as mine."

"Why, doctor, would you have all the world mad?"

"They are already," he replied; "as mad as March hares—all of them. I would only have them in establishments, with strait-waistcoats on, and an experienced and humane physician to reduce them by means of—those measures which are never known to fail."

"I hope," I said seriously, because I began to fear that some violence might have been used, "that my poor friend has been treated gently."

"We never," replied the doctor, "treat them otherwise than gently. My fellows understand that this—ahem!—unfortunate escaped sufferer from lunacy or dementia (because I have not yet had time to diagnose his case with precision) is to be treated with singular forbearance. One or two cuffs on the head, an admonition by means of a keeper's boot, he hath doubtless received. These things are absolutely necessary: but no collar-bones put out or ribs broken. In the case of violent patients, ribs, as a rule, do get broken, and give trouble in the setting. Your friend, young lady, has all his bones whole. No discipline, so far, has been administered beyond a few buckets of water, which it was absolutely necessary to pour over his head, out of common humanity, and in order to calm the excessive rage into which the poor gentleman fell. He is quite calm now, and has neither been put under the pump nor in the tank. I have expressly ordered that there is to be no cudgelling. And I have promised my fellows half-a-guinea apiece"—

here he looked at me with a meaning smile—"if they are gentle with him. I have told them that there is a young lady interested in his welfare. My keepers, I assure you, madam, have rough work to do, but they are the most tender-hearted of men. Otherwise, they would be sent packing. And at the sight of half-a-guinea, their hearts yearn with affection towards the patients."

I smiled, and promised the half-guineas on the liberation of the prisoner. Cuffs and kicks! a few buckets of cold water! a strait-waistcoat! My poor Harry! surely this would be enough to cure any man of his passion. And what a fitting end to a journey commenced with the intention of killing and murdering your old playfellow's lover! Yet, to be sure, it was a wicked thing I had done, and I resolved to lose no time (as soon as there was no longer any fear of a duel) in beginning to repent.

All this accomplished, which was, after all, only a beginning, I left the house and walked up the hill, intending to find the three gentlemen waiting for their duel. These meetings generally took place, I knew, on the way to the old well. I left Durdans on the right, and struck across the turf to the left. Presently I saw before me a group of three gentlemen, standing together and talking. That is to say, two were talking, and one, Lord Chudleigh, was standing apart. They saw me presently, and I heard Sir Miles, in his loud and hearty voice, crying out: "Gad so! It is pretty Kitty herself."

"You look, gentlemen," I said, "as if you were expecting quite another person. But pray, Sir Miles, why on the Downs so early? There is no race to-day, nor any bull-baiting. The card-room is open, and I believe the inns are not shut."

"We are here," he replied, unblushingly, "to take the air. It is bracing: it is good for the complexion: it expands the chest and opens the breathing pipes: it is as good as a draught of the waters: and as stimulating as a bottle of port."

"Indeed! Then I am surprised you do not use the fresh air oftener. For surely it is cheaper than drinking wine."

"In future," he said, "I intend to do so."

"But why these swords, Sir Miles? You know the rule of the Wells."

"They wanted sharpening," he replied. "The air of the Downs is so keen, that it sets an edge on sword-blades."

"You looked—fie, gentlemen!—for Mr. Temple to help sharpen the blades, as a butcher sharpens his knife, by putting steel to steel. Sir Miles, you are a wicked and bloodthirsty man."

He laughed, and so did the officer. Lord Chudleigh changed colour.

"Gentlemen," I went on, "I have to tell you—I have come here to tell you—that an accident has happened to Mr. Temple, which will prevent his keeping the appointment made for him at this hour. I am sure, if he knew that I was coming here, he would ask me to express his great regret at keeping you waiting. Now, however, you may all go home again, and put off killing each other for another day."

They looked at each other, astonished.

"My lord," I said, "I am sure you will let me ask you what injury my poor friend Harry Temple has done you that you desire to compass his death."

"Nay," he replied, "I desire not to compass any man's death. I am here against my will. I have no quarrel with him."

"What do you say, Sir Miles?" I asked. "Are you determined that blood should be spilt?"

"Not I," he replied. "But as the affair concerns the honour of two gentlemen, I think, with respect to so fair a lady, that it had better be left in the hands of gentlemen."

"But," I said, "it concerns me too now, partly because I have brought you the reason of Mr. Temple's absence, and partly because he is one of my oldest friends and a gentleman for whom I have a very great regard. And methinks, Sir Miles, with submission, because a woman cannot understand the laws of the duello or the scruples of what gentlemen call honour—that honour which allows a man to drink and gamble, but not to take a hasty word, that if I can persuade Lord Chudleigh that Mr. Temple does not desire the duel, and is unfeignedly ashamed of himself, and if I can assure Mr. Temple that Lord Chudleigh would not be any the happier for killing Mr. Temple, why then this dreadful encounter need not take place, and we may all go home again in peace."

Upon this they looked at each other doubtfully, and Sir Miles burst out laughing. When Sir Miles laughed I thought it would all end well at once. But then Harry's second spoke up gravely, and threatened to trouble the waters.

"I represent Mr. Temple in this affair. I cannot allow my principal to leave the field without satisfaction. We have been insulted. We demand reparation to our honour. We cannot be set aside in this unbecoming manner by a young lady."

"Pray, sir," I asked, "does your scarlet coat and your commission"—I have said he was an officer—"enjoin you to set folks by the ears, and to promote that method of murder which men call duelling? What advantage will it be to you, provided these two gentlemen fight and kill each other?"

"Why, as for advantage—none," he said. "But who ever heard——"

"Then, sir, as it will be of infinite advantage to many of their friends, and a subject of great joy and thankfulness that they should not fight, be pleased not to embroil matters further. And, indeed, sir, I am quite sure that you have breathed the bracing air of the Downs quite long enough, and had better leave us here, and go back to the town. You may else want me to fight in the place of Mr. Temple. That would be a fine way of getting reparation to your wounded honour."

At this he became very red in the face, and spoke more about honour, laws among gentlemen, and fooling away his time among people who, it seemed, either did not know their own minds, or contrived accidents to happen in the nick of time.

"Hark ye, brother," said Sir Miles upon this, "the young lady is right in her way, because, say what we will, our men were going out on a fool's errand. Why, in the devil's name, should they fight? What occasion has Mr. Temple to quarrel with my lord?"

"If Mr. Temple likes..." said his second, shrugging his shoulders. "After all it is his business, not mine. If, in the army, a man pulls another man's nose, why——"

"Will you please to understand, sir," I broke in, "that Mr. Temple is really delayed by an accident—it happened to him on his way here, and was entirely unforeseen by him, and was one which he could neither prevent nor expect? If a woman had any honour, in your sense, I would give you my word of honour that this is so."

"Under these circumstances," the gallant officer said, "I do not see why we are waiting here. Mr. Temple will, of course, tell his own story in his own way, and unless the fight takes place on the original quarrel, why, he may find another second. Such a lame ending I never experienced."

"And that," interposed Sir Miles, who surely was the most good-natured of men, "that reminds me, my good sir, that in this matter, unless we would make bad worse, we all of us had better make up our minds to tell no story at all, but leave it to Mr. Temple. Wherefore, if it please you, I will walk to the town in your company, there to contradict any idle gossip we may hear, and to lay upon the back of the rightful person, either with cudgels or rapiers, any calumny which may be attached to Mr. Temple's name. But, no doubt, he is strong enough to defend himself."

"Really, Sir Miles," said the officer with a sneer, "I wonder you do not fight for him yourself. Here is your principal, Lord Chudleigh, ready for you."

"Sir, he is not my friend, but the friend of Miss Pleydell. He is, as I believe you or any other person who may quarrel with him would find, perfectly well able to fight his own battles. Meantime I am ready to fight my own, as is already pretty well known."

With that they both walked off the field, not together, but near each other, the officer in a great huff and Sir Miles rolling along beside him, big and good-tempered, yet, like a bull-dog, an ugly dog to tackle.

Lord Chudleigh and I were left alone upon the Downs.

"Kitty," he cried, "what does this mean?"

"That there is to be no fighting between you and Harry Temple. That is what it means, my lord. Oh, the wickedness of men!"

"But where is he? what is the accident? What does your presence mean? Did he send you?"

I laughed, but could not tell him. Then I reflected that the errand on which he had come was no laughing matter, and I became grave again.

"My lord," I said, "is it well to tell a girl one day that you love her, and the next to come out to fight with swords about a trifle? Do you think nothing of a broken heart?"

"My dear," he replied, "it was forced upon me, believe me. A man must fight if he is insulted openly. There is no help for it till customs change."

"Oh!" I cried; "can that man be in his senses who hopes to win a woman's heart by insulting and trying to kill—her—her lover?"

"Yes, Kitty." He caught my hand and kissed it. "Your lover—your most unhappy lover! who can do no more than say he loves you, and yet can never hope to marry you. How did I dare to open my heart to you, my dear, with such a shameful story to tell?"

"My lord," I said, "promise me, if you sincerely love me, which I cannot doubt, not to fight with this hot-headed young man."

"I promise," he replied, "to do all that a man of honour may, in order to avoid a duel with him."

"Then, my lord, I promise, once more in return—if you would care to have such a promise from so poor a creature as myself——"

"Kitty! Divine angel!"

"I swear, even though you never wed me, to remain single for your sake. And even should you change your mind, and bestow your affections upon another woman, and scorn and loathe me, never to think upon another man."

He seized me in his arms, though we were on the open Downs (only there was not a soul within sight, so far as I could see around), and kissed me on the cheeks and lips.

"My love!" he murmured; "my sweet and gracious lady!"

Next, I had to consider what best to do about my prisoner. I begged my lord to go home through the Durdans, while I returned by the road. On the way I resolved to liberate Harry at once, but to make conditions with him. I therefore returned to the doctor's, and asked that I might be allowed to see the prisoner.

Dr. Powlett was at first very unwilling. He pointed out, with some justice, that there had not, as yet, been time enough to allow of a colourable pretence at discovering the supposed mistake; a few days, say a fortnight, should elapse, during which the search might be supposed to be a-making; in that interval Harry was to sit chained in his cell, with a strait-waistcoat on.

"And believe me," said this kind physician, "he will learn from his imprisonment to admire the many kindnesses and great humanity shown to unhappy persons who are afflicted with the loss of their wits. Besides this, he will have an opportunity of discovering for what moderate charges such persons are received, entertained, and treated with the highest medical skill, at Epsom, by the learned physician, Jonathan Powlett, *Medicinæ Doctor*. He will swallow my pills, drink my potions (which are sovereign in all diseases of the brain), be nourished on my gruel (compounded scientifically with the Epsom water), will be tenderly handled by my keepers, and all for the low charge of four guineas a week, paid in advance, including servants. And he will, when cured (if Providence assist), come out——"

"Twice as mad as he went in. No, doctor; that, if you please, was not what I intended. The mischief is averted for the present, and, if you will conduct me to your prisoner, I think I can manage to avert it altogether."

Well, finding that there was nothing more to be got out of the case—I am quite sure that he was ready to treat poor Harry as really mad, and to keep him there as long as any money could be got out of him—the doctor gave way, and led me to the room in which lay prisoner Harry.

It was a room apart from the great common rooms in which idiots and imbecile persons are chained at regular intervals to the wall, never leaving their places, night or day, until they die. I was thus spared the pain of seeing what I am told is one of the most truly awful and terrifying spectacles in the world. The doctor, who measured his kindness by the guineas which he could extract from his patients' friends, kept certain private chambers, where, if the poor creatures were chained, they were not exposed to the sights and sounds of the common rooms.

In one of these, therefore, he had bestowed Harry.

"Let me," I said, "go in first, and speak with him. Do you come presently."

I think if I had known, beforehand, what they were going to do, I might have relented—but no: anything was better than that those two men should stand, sword in hand, face to face, trying to kill each other for the sake of an unworthy girl.

Yet the poor lad, whom I had ever loved like a brother, looked in piteous case; for they had put the strait-waistcoat over him, which pinned his arms to his sides, and a chain about his waist which was fastened to the wall behind him; his wig was lying on the floor; he seemed wet through, which was the natural effect of those savage keepers' buckets; his face wore a look of rage and despair sad to behold: his eyes glared like the eyes of a bull at a baiting.

"You here, Kitty?" he cried. "You? What is the meaning of you in this house?"

"Harry, there has been, it seems a very terrible blunder committed by Dr. Powlett's servants; they were told you were a certain escaped madman, and they arrested you in the discharge of their duty. It is most fortunate that the fact has been brought to my ears, because I could hasten— —"

"Then quick, Kitty, quick!" he cried. "Go, call the doctor, and set me free. It may not yet be too late. Quick, Kitty! They are waiting for me."

He forgot, I suppose, what this "waiting" might mean to me.

"Who are waiting, Harry?"

He did not reply.

"What were you going to do on the Downs this morning, Harry, when they made a prisoner of you?"

"That is nothing to do with you," he replied. "Go, call the rascally doctor, whose ribs I will break, and his men, whom I will murder, for this job."

"Nothing to do with me, Harry! Are you quite sure?"

"You look, Kitty, as if you knew. Did Lord Chud — — No; he would not. Did Sir Miles go sneaking to you with the news? Gad! I feel inclined to try conclusions with the Norfolk baronet with his cudgel about which he makes such a coil."

"Never mind who told me. I know the whole wicked, disgraceful, murderous story!"

"Disgraceful! You talk like a woman. Shall a man sit down idly, and see his wife snatched out of his arms?"

"What wife? O Harry! you have gone mad about this business. Cannot you understand that I was never engaged to marry you — that I never thought of such a thing? I could never have been your wife, whether there was any rival or no. And did you think that you would make me think the more kindly of you, should you kill the man who, as you foolishly think, had supplanted you? Or was it out of revenge, and in the hope of making me miserable, that you designed to fight this duel?"

He was silent at this. When a man is in a strait-waistcoat, and chained to a wall, it is difficult to look dignified. But Harry's look of shame and confusion, under the circumstances of having no arms, was truly pitiful.

"You can talk about that afterwards," he said doggedly. "Go, call the scoundrel doctor."

"Presently. I want to tell you, first, what I think about it. Was it kind to the woman you pretended to love to bring upon her the risk of this great unhappiness? Remember, Harry, I told you all. I told you what I could not have told even to Nancy, in the hope of breaking you of this mad passion. I trusted that you were good and true of heart; and this is the return."

"It is done now," he replied gloomily. "Do not reproach me, Kitty. Let Lord Chudleigh run me through the body, and so an end. Now, fetch the doctor fellow and his men."

"That would have been indeed an end," I said. "But, Harry, I have done better than that for you. I have stayed the duel altogether. You will not have to fight."

With that I told him how I had gone to the Downs, and what I had said to the gentlemen. Only, be sure that I left out what passed in the road between his lordship and myself.

Well, Master Harry flew into a mighty rage upon hearing this, and, being still in the strait-waistcoat and in chains, his wrath was increased because he could not move: he talked wildly about his injured honour, swore that he would go and offer Lord Chudleigh first, and Sir Miles later, such an open and public affront as must be washed out with the blood of one; declared that I might have destroyed his reputation for courage for good, but that he was resolved the world should judge to the contrary. As for the company at the Wells, he would challenge every man at Epsom, if necessary, if he should dare to asperse his bravery. More he said to the same effect, but I interrupted him.

First, I promised to go with him upon the Terrace, there to meet the people and give him such countenance as a woman could. Next I promised him that Lord Chudleigh should meet him in a friendly spirit; that Sir Miles should be the first to proclaim Mr. Temple's courage. I assured him that he might be quite certain of finding many other opportunities of proving his valiancy, should he continue in his present bloodthirsty frame of mind. I congratulated him on his Christian readiness to throw away a life which had hitherto been surrounded by so many blessings. Lastly, I advised him to consider how far his present attitude and sentiments corresponded with the divine philosophy of the ancients, whom he had once been so fond of quoting.

He refused to make any promise whatever.

Then I bade him remember—first, where he was; second, under what circumstances he came there; third, that he was surrounded by raving madmen, chained to the wall as one of them, put in a strait-waistcoat like one of them, and about to be reduced to a diet of bread and water; that no one knew where he was except myself and Dr. Powlett; that neither of us would tell anything about him; and that, in point of fact, unless he promised what I asked, he might remain where he was until all danger was past.

"And that, Harry, may be I know not when. For be very well assured that, as I have obtained from Lord Chudleigh a promise to seek no quarrel with you, I will not let you go from this place until I am assured that you will seek no quarrel with him, either on my account or under any other pretext whatever. You are in great misery (which you richly deserve for your wicked and murderous design); you are wet and hungry: if I go away without your promise, you will continue in greater misery until I return. Bethink thee, Harry."

Still he was obdurate. Strange that a man will face almost anything rather than possible ridicule.

What, after long persuasion, made him give way, was a plain threat that if he would not promise what I required I would release him at once, but tell his story to all the town, so that, for very ridicule's sake, it would be impossible for the duel to take place.

"It will tell very prettily, Harry," I said. "Nancy will dress it up for me, and will relate it in her best and liveliest way; how you tried to get a little country girl of sixteen to engage herself to you; how, when you found her a year later turned into a lady, you thought that you could terrify her into accepting your proposals, on the plea that she had already promised; how you turned sulky; how you quarrelled with Lord Chudleigh, and made him accept your duel; how you were taken prisoner by mistake, and kicked, cuffed — —"

"I was not kicked!" he cried.

"You were. Dr. Powlett's patients are always kicked. Then you had buckets of cold water thrown over you; you were put into a strait-waistcoat and chained to the wall: while I came and asked you whether you preferred remaining in the madhouse or promising to behave like an honourable gentleman, and abstain from insulting persons who have done no harm to you or yours."

"I believe," he said, "that it is none other than yourself who has had me captured and treated in this manner, *femina furens*!"

"A mere mistake, Harry," I replied, "of this good physician's zealous servants. Why, it might have happened in any such establishment. But for me to order it—oh! impossible—though, when one comes to think of it, there are few things a woman—*Femina furens*, the English of which, Master Harry, I know—would not do to save two friends from hacking and slashing each other."

Upon this he gave way.

"I must," he said, "get away from this place with what speed I may, even if I have to pink half the men in Epsom to prove I am no coward. Kitty, call the doctor. I believe, mad nymph, thou hast a devil!"

"Nay, Harry, all this was planned but to lay the devil, believe me. But promise first."

"Well, then. It is a hard pill to swallow, Kitty."

"Promise."

"I promise."

"Not to pick any quarrel, or to revive any old quarrel, with Lord Chudleigh or Sir Miles Lackington."

He repeated the words after me.

"And to remain good friends with Kitty Pleydell and all who are her friends and followers."

He repeated these words as well, though with some appearance of swallowing distasteful food.

"I cannot shake hands with you, Harry, because, poor boy, your hands are hidden away beneath that strait-waistcoat. But I know you to be an honourable gentleman, as becomes a man of your birth and so great a scholar, and I accept your word. Wherefore, my dear old friend and schoolfellow, seeing that there is to be no more pretence of love between us, but only of friendship and good wishes, I will call—Dr. Powlett."

That good man was waiting in the corridor or passage while Harry and I held this long conversation. He came as soon as I called him.

"Sir," said I, as soon as he came in (I noticed that he looked anxiously behind him to see that his four varlets were at hand, ready to defend him if necessary)—"Sir, here is a most grievous mischance indeed. For this gentleman is no other than Mr. Harry Temple, Justice of the Peace, Bachelor of Arts of the University of Cambridge, Fellow Commoner of his College, Member of the Honourable Society of Lincoln's Inn, and a country gentleman, with a great estate of East Kent. He is, in truth, doctor, no more mad than you or I, or any one else in the world."

The doctor affected the greatest surprise and indignation. First he expressed his inability to believe my statement, although it pained him deeply to differ from a lady; then he called upon one of his men to bring him the *Hue and Cry*, and read out a description of a runaway madman which so perfectly answered the appearance of Harry, that it would deceive any one, except myself, because I was sure he had himself written it—*after the capture*. He then asked me, solemnly and gravely, if I did not think, having heard the description, that the men were justified in their action.

I replied that the paper so exactly tallied with Harry's appearance that such a mistake was most easy to account for, and must at once, when explained, command forgiveness. Nevertheless, Harry's face looked far from forgiving.

"Varlets," said Dr. Powlett, who in some respects reminded me of a certain Doctor of Divinity, because his voice was deep and his manner stately, "go, instantly, every man Jack, upon his bended knees and ask the pardon of Mr. Temple for an offence committed by pure inadvertence and excess of honourable zeal in the extirpation—I mean the comfortable and kindly confinement—of the lunatic, insane, and persons demented."

They all four fell upon their knees and asked forgiveness.

Harry replied briefly, that as for pardoning them, he would wait until he was free, when he would break all their ribs and wring their necks.

"Sir," said the doctor, "you are doubtless in the right, and are naturally, for the moment, annoyed at this little misadventure, at which you will laugh when you consider it at leisure. It will perhaps be of use to you as showing you on what humane, kindly, and gentle a system such establishments as ours are conducted. As regards the pardon which you will extend to these honest fellows, time is no object to them. They would as soon receive their pardon to-morrow, or a week hence, or a year, or twenty years hence, as to-day, because their consciences are at rest, having done their duty; therefore, good sir, they will wait to release you until you are ready with their pardon."

Harry, after thinking for a few moments over this statement, said, that so far as he was concerned, the four men might go to the devil, and that he pardoned them.

"There remains only," said the doctor, "one person who infinitely regrets the temporary annoyance your honour has been subjected to. It is myself. I have to ask of you, for the sake of my establishment and my reputation, two or three conditions. The first of them is your forgiveness, without which I feel that my self-respect as a true Christian and man of science would suffer; the second, absolute secrecy as regards these proceedings, a knowledge of which might be prejudicial to me; and the third——" here he hesitated and glanced sideways at me. "The third is, of course"—he plucked up courage and spoke confidently—"a reimbursement of the expenses I have been put to, as, for instance"—here he drew out a long roll, and read from it—"services of four men in watching for the escaped lunatic for five hours, at five shillings an hour for each man, five pounds; to the capture of the same, being done in expeditious and workmanlike fashion, without confusion, scandal, cracking of crowns or breaking of ribs, two guineas; to bringing him in, and receiving many cuffs, blows, kicks, &c., on the way, three guineas; to use of private room for one month at one guinea a week (we never let our private and comfortable chambers for less than one month), four guineas; to wear and tear of bucket, strait-waistcoat, and chain, used in confining and bringing to reason the prisoner, two guineas; to board and lodging of the patient for one month at two guineas a week (we never receive a patient for less than one month), eight guineas; to attendants' fees for the same time, two guineas for entrance and three guineas for departure: to my own professional attendance at two guineas a week (I never undertake a case for less than one month certain), eight guineas. The total, good sir, I find to amount to a mere trifle of thirty-eight pounds twelve shillings."

Heavens! did one ever hear of such an extortionate charge? And all for two hours in a strait-waistcoat!

Harry stormed and swore. But the most he could get was a reduction of the bill by which certain items, including the three guineas for giving and receiving kicks and cuffs, and the two guineas for wear and tear of the bucket which had been emptied over him, were to be remitted. Finally he accepted the conditions, with the promise to pay thirty guineas in full discharge. And really I think that Dr. Powlett had done a good morning's work, having taken ten guineas out of me and thirty out of Harry. But then, as he said, it was a delicate and dangerous business, and might, in less skilful hands (meaning perhaps mine, perhaps his own), have led to very awkward results.

The Terrace was full of people, for it was now half-past twelve. As Harry and I made our way slowly under the trees they parted for us left and right, staring at us as we passed them with curious eyes. For the rumour had spread abroad that there was to have been a duel that morning between Lord Chudleigh and Mr. Temple, and that it was stopped—no one knew how—by some accident which prevented Mr. Temple from keeping his appointment. Now at the other end of the Terrace we met Lord Chudleigh himself, who, after saluting me, held out his hand before all the world to Harry, who took it with a bow and a blush.

There was a great sigh of disappointment. No duel, then, would be fought at all, and the two gentlemen who were to have fought it were shaking hands like ordinary mortals, and the lady for whom they were going to fight was walking between them, and all three were smiling and talking together like excellent friends.

Thus, then, did I heal up the quarrel between Harry Temple and my lord. It would have grieved me sore had poor Harry, almost my brother, been wounded or killed; but what would have been my lot had my lover fallen?

Three suitors had I rejected in a month, and a lover had I gained, who was also, though this I never ventured to confess, my husband. But there was one man whom I had forgotten quite, and he was destined to be the cause of the greatest trouble of all. Who would have believed that Will Levett would have dared to call himself my accepted lover?

Who would have believed that this sot, this stable and kennel haunter, would have remembered me for a whole year, and would have come to Epsom in the full confidence that he was coming to claim a bride?

CHAPTER XIX.

HOW WILL LEVETT WAS DISAPPOINTED.

Thus was Harry Temple at last pacified and brought to reason. In the course of a short time he was so far recovered from his passion as to declare his love for another woman whom he married. This shows how fickle and fleeting are the affections of most men compared with those of women; for I am truly of opinion that no woman can love more than one man in her life, while a man appears capable of loving as many as he pleases all at once or in turn, as the fancy seizes him. Could Solomon have loved in very truth the whole seven hundred?

When I was no longer harassed by Harry's gloomy face and jealous reproaches, I thought that the time was come when I ought to consider how I should impart to my lord a knowledge of the truth, and I said to myself, day after day: "To-morrow morning I will do it;" and in the morning I said: "Nay, but in the evening." And sometimes I thought to write it and sometimes to tell it him by word of mouth. Yet the days passed and I did not tell him, being a coward, and rejoicing in the sunshine of his love and kindness, which I could not bear to lose or put in any danger.

And now you shall hear how this delay was the cause of a most dreadful accident, which had well-nigh ruined and lost us altogether.

I could not but remember, when Harry Temple reproached me with falsehood and faithlessness, that Will Levett had made use of nearly the same words, making allowance for Will's rusticity. The suspicion did certainly cross my mind, more than once, that Will may have meant (though I understood him not) the same thing as Harry. And I remembered how he pulled a sixpence out of his pocket and gave me the half, which I threw upon the table unheeding, though every girl knows that a broken sixpence is a pledge of betrothal. But I was in such great trouble and anxiety, that I thought nothing of it and remembered nothing for long afterwards. Yet if Harry came to claim a supposed promise at my hands, why should not Will? which would be a thing much worse to meet, because Harry was now amenable to reason, and by means of the strait-waistcoat and bucket of cold water, with a little talk, I had persuaded him to adopt a wiser course. But no reason ever availed anything with Will, save the reason of desire or the opposition of superior force. As a boy, he took everything he wanted, unless he could be prevented by a hearty flogging; and he bullied every other boy save those who could by superior strength compel him to behave properly. I have already shown how he treated us when we were children and when we had grown up to be great girls. So that, with this suspicion, and remembering Will's dreadful temper and his masterfulness, I felt uneasy indeed when Nancy told me that her brother was coming to Epsom.

"We shall be horribly ashamed of him," she said, laughing, though vexed. "Indeed, I doubt if we shall be able to show our faces on the Terrace, after Will has been here a day or two. Because, my dear, he will thrash the men-servants, kiss the girls, insult the company—some of whom will certainly run him through the body, while some he will beat with his cudgel—get drunk in the taverns, and run an Indian muck through the dance at the Assembly Rooms. I have told my father that the best thing for him to do is to pretend that Will is no relation of ours at all, only a rustic from our parish bearing the same name; or perhaps we might go on a visit to London for a fortnight, so as to get out of his way; and that, I think, would be the best. Kitty! think of Will marching up and down the Terrace, a dozen dogs after him, his wig uncombed, his hunting-coat stained with mud, halloing and bawling as he goes, carrying an enormous club like Hercules—he certainly is very much like Hercules—his mouth full of countrified oaths. However, he does not like fine folks, and will not often show among us. And while we are dancing in the rooms, he will be sitting at the door of a tavern mostly, smoking a pipe of tobacco and taking a mug of October with any who will sit beside him and hear his tales of badgers, ferrets, and dogs. Well, fortunately, no one can deny the good blood of the Levetts, which will, we hope, come out again in Will's children; and my father is a baronet of James the First's creation, otherwise it would go hard with our gentility."

"When do you expect him to come?"

"He sends word that he may come to-night or to-morrow, bringing with him a horse which he proposes to match upon the Downs with any horse at Epsom for thirty guineas a side. One match has been already fixed, and will be run the next day, provided both horses are fresh. I hope Will will not cheat, as he was accused of doing at Maidstone. I suppose we shall all have to go to the Downs to see. Why do men like horse-racing, I wonder? Crack goes the whip, the horses rush past, the people shout, the race is over. Give me enjoyment which lasts a little longer, such as a good country dance, or a few words with Peggy Baker on the Terrace."

"Does Will know that I am here?" I asked.

"I suppose not," she replied. "Why, my dear, how is Will to know anything? My father laid out large sums upon his education. Yet the end of all is that he never reads anything, not even books on Farriery. As for letters, he is well known not to read those which my mother sometimes sends him; and as for sending any himself, I believe he has forgotten the art of writing. He does everything by word of mouth, like the savages. Perhaps he remembers how to read, because he cannot forget his sufferings over the criss-cross-row and horn-book. Will, Kitty, is an early Briton; he should be dressed in wool and painted with woad; he lives by preference in a stable or a kennel; he ought to have the body and tail and legs of a horse, then he could stay in the stable altogether and be happy."

Perhaps, I thought, he would not know me again. But in this I was deceived, as shall be presently shown.

Well, then, knowing that Nancy would help me in this possible trouble, I told her exactly what happened between Will and myself, just as I had told her about Harry, and asked her advice.

It might be that Will had clean forgotten his words, or it might be that he had changed his mind; he might have fallen in love with some girl of the village, or he might find me changed and no longer care for pressing his suit.

Nancy looked grave.

"My brother Will," she said, "is as obstinate as he is pig-headed. I am afraid he will expect you to fulfil the engagement which he may think he has made. Never mind, my dear; do not think of it to distress yourself. If he is obstinate, so are you. He cannot marry you against your will."

He came the next morning, riding into town, followed by two servants, one of whom led the famous horse which was to ride the race.

"There," whispered Nancy, "is my brother Will."

We were standing in the church porch after morning prayers, when he came clattering down the street. He was really a handsome man for those who like a man to be like Hercules for strength, to have full rosy cheeks which later in life become fat and purple, a resolute eye, and a strong, straight chin which means obstinacy.

"Oh, how strong he is!" said Nancy, looking after him. "He could crush together half-a-dozen of our beaux and fribbles between his fingers, and break all their ribs with a single flourish of his cudgel. Well, Will!" she added, as her brother rode out of sight, "we shall meet at dinner, I dare say. Do you remember, Kitty, how he would tease and torment us, and make us cry? There ought to be no brothers and sisters at all—the girls should grow up in one house, and the boys in another—they should never meet till they are old enough to be lovers, and never be together when they are too old to be lovers. Fancy the stupidity of philosophers in putting men and women under the same name, and calling us all humanity, or mankind, as their impudent way is of putting it. What have they in common? Man drinks, and gambles, and fights—woman sits at home and loves peace and moderation: man wastes—woman saves: man loves to admire—we love to be admired. What single quality have we in common except a desire to be amiable and seem pleasing to the other sex?"

"Very likely," I replied, thinking of something else. "No doubt he has long since forgotten the sixpence. No doubt he thinks no more of me or the sixpence either."

I saw nothing of him that day, because he had so much to do with his stable, and so much to attend to in the matter of his race, that he did not appear upon the Terrace or at the Assembly Room. Harry Temple shrugged his shoulders when I asked him if he had seen Will.

"I saw him," he said, "engaged in his usual occupations. He had just cudgelled a stable-boy, was swearing at a groom, rubbing down his racehorse with his own hands, and superintending the preparation of a warm mash for his hack. He seems perfectly happy."

It was agreed, in spite of my fears, that we should make a party to see this race the next morning. Nowadays it is no longer the *mode* to seek health at Epsom Wells and on Banstead Downs. The votaries of fashion go to Bath and Tunbridge; the old Wells are deserted, I hear that the Assembly Rooms have fallen into decay, and there are no longer the Monday public breakfast, the card-table, the music, the dancing, which made the place a little heaven for the young in those times when I myself was young. But in one respect Epsom has grown more frequented and more renowned every year:

"On Epsom Downs, when racing does begin,
Large companies from every part come in."

The spring races were in April, and the summer races in June; but there was a constant racing all the year round with the horses of country gentlemen. They would bring them to make matches with all comers, at such stakes as they could afford to venture on the horses; and in the morning the company would crowd upon the Downs in goodly numbers to bet upon the race, and shout to the winner. Sometimes ladies would go too; not out of any love for the sport, or interest in horses, but to please their lovers—a desire which is the cause of many a pretty maid's sudden liking for some manly sport. I have known them even show an interest in such rough sports as badger-drawing and otter-hunting: they have been seen to ride after hounds in the midst of the hallos and horns of the hunters: they have even gone with the gentlemen on shooting-parties. Thus there were plenty of girls at Epsom ready to please their gallants by standing about on the Downs (where the wind plays havoc with powder and paint, and destroys irretrievably the fabric of a head), while the panting horses were spurred over the long course by the jockeys, and the backers cried and shouted.

Lord Chudleigh took little joy in this kind of sport, which, perhaps, is a reason why I also disliked the sight. Nancy, also, as well as myself, cared but little to see this famous Epsom sport; nor, indeed, did any of the ladies who formed part of our more intimate company. But on this occasion, as Will was to run a three-year-old of his own training, and as he was going to ride the horse himself, and had staked thirty guineas (beside bets) upon the event, it was judged a duty owed to him by the family that all should go. Mrs. Esther went out of respect

The Chaplain of the Fleet

to Lady Levett; Mr. Stallabras, because he remembered how Pindar had sung of the Olympian Games, and was suddenly fired with the desire of writing a Pindaric Ode upon the Epsom contests. Now, it behoves a poet who sings of a horse-race, first to witness one. Therefore he came to see how it would lend itself to modern metaphor. Sir Miles came because he could get the chance of a few bets upon the race, and because, when there were no cards to the fore, he liked, he said, to hear me talk. Harry Temple came, grumbling and protesting that for men of learning and fashion nothing was more barbarous and tedious than this sport. Could we have had chariot-racing, with athletic games after the manner of the ancients, he would have been pleased. As it was, he hoped that Will would win, but feared that a clown and his money were soon parted; with other remarks equally good-natured.

The race was to be run at half-past eleven. We had chairs for such as preferred being carried, but the younger ladies walked. We made a gallant procession as we came upon the course, all the ladies wearing Will's colours, which were red and blue. They had railed off a piece of ground where the better sort could stand without being molested by the crowd which always congregates when a great race is to be run. Indeed, on this occasion, it seemed as if all the idle fellows for twenty miles round had gathered together on the Downs with one consent, and with them half the rustics of the villages, the tradesmen and workmen of Epsom, Leatherhead, and Dorking, and the greater part of the company at the Wells. There were gipsies to tell our fortunes or steal our poultry—but I, for one, had had enough already of fortune-telling from the tent of the pretended Wizard of the masquerade: there were Italians leading a bear: there were a couple of rough men with a bull which was presently to be baited: a canvas enclosure was run up on poles, within which the Cornish giant would wrestle all comers at sixpence a throw: another, where a prize-fight would be held, admittance one shilling, with twopence each for the defeated man: a puppet play was shown for a penny: for twopence you might see a rare piece of art, the subject of which I know not: and in wax, the histories of Fair Rosamond and Susanna. Other amusements there were. I, at first, took all in honour of Will and his race, but presently learned that a fair had been held at Leatherhead the day before, and that these people, hearing of what was forward, came over to get what could be picked up. And, as one fool makes many, the knowledge of their coming, with the race for an excuse, brought out all the country people, mouth agape, as is their wont.

The horses presently rode out of the paddock—a place where they weigh, dress, put on the saddles, and adjust the preliminaries. Will in his cap pulled over his ears like a nightcap (because a jockey wears no wig), and in silk jacket, striped with blue and red, riding as if he was part of the animal he sat, looked in his true place. Ever after I have thought of the gallant show he made, while with left hand holding the whip, he bridled the beautiful creature, which but for his control would have been bounding and galloping over the plain. But they explained to us that racehorses know when racing is meant, and behave accordingly, save that they cannot always be refrained from starting before the time.

Will's rival and competitor, whose name I forget (but I had never seen him before), was a man of slighter figure, who rode equally well, but did not at the same time appear to such advantage on horseback. Lord Chudleigh explained to us that while Will rode naturally, sitting his horse as if he understood what the creature wished to do, and where he wanted to go; the other man sat him by rule of thumb, as if the horse was to understand his master and not the master his horse. I have ridden a great deal since then, and I know, now, the justice of my lord's remarks, though I own that this perfect understanding between horse and rider is not commonly found; and for my own part I remember but one horse, three parts Arabian, with which I ever arrived at a complete understanding. Even with him the understanding was onesided, and ended in his always going whithersoever he pleased.

The adversary's colours were white and green; pretty colours, though bad for the complexion of women; so that I was glad Will's were suited to the roses of our cheeks.

They began by riding up and down for a quarter of an hour, Will looking mighty important, stroking his horse, patting his neck, talking to him, checking him when he broke into a canter or a gallop. The other man (he in white and green) had trouble to keep his horse from fairly bolting with him, which he did for a little distance more than once.

Then the starters took their places, and the judge his, in front of the winning-post, and the horses started.

White and green led for a quarter of a mile; but Will was close behind: it was pretty to see the eagerness of the horses—how they pressed forward with straining necks.

"Will is holding back," cried Harry, with flashing eyes. "Wait till they are over the hill."

"I feel like Pindar," cried Mr. Stallabras. "Would that Mr. Levett was Hiero of Syracuse!"

"O Will!" exclaimed Nancy, as if he could hear. "Spur up your horse! If you lose the race I will never forgive you."

We all stood with parted lips and beating hearts. Yes; we understood the joy of horse-racing: the uncertainty of the struggle: the ambition of the noble creatures: the eagerness of the riders: their skill: their coolness: the shouts of the people—ah! the race is over.

Just before the finish, say two hundred yards the other side of the winning-post, Will rose in his saddle, plied whip, and cried to his horse. It answered with a rush, as if struck by a sudden determination to be first: the other horse, a little tired perhaps, bounded onward as well; but Will took the lead and kept it. In a moment the race was finished, and Will rode gallantly past us, ahead by a whole length, amid the cheers and applause of the people.

When the race was finished the visitors ran backward and forwards, congratulating or condoling with each other. Many a long face was pulled as the bets were paid: many a jolly face broadened and became more jolly as the money went into pocket. And then I saw what is meant by the old saying about money made over the devil's back. For those who lost, lost outright, which cannot be denied: but those who won immediately took their friends to the booths where beer and wine and rum were sold, and straightway got rid of a portion of their winnings. No doubt the rest went in the course of the day in debauchery. So that the money won upon the race benefited no one except the people who sold drink. And they, to my mind, are the last persons whom one would wish to benefit, considering what a dreadful thing in this country is the curse of drink.

The Chaplain of the Fleet

If Will looked a gallant rider on horseback, he cut but a sorry figure among the gentlemen when he came forth from the paddock, having taken off his jacket and put on again his wig, coat, and waistcoat. For he walked heavily, rolling in his gait (as a ploughboy not a sailor), and his clothes were muddy and disordered, while his wig was awry. Lady Levett beckoned to him, and he came towards us sheepishly bold, as is the way with rustic gentlemen.

"So, Will," shouted his father heartily, "thou hast won the match. Well rode, my boy!"

"Well rode!" cried all. "Well rode!"

He received our congratulations with a grin of satisfaction, saluting the company with a grin, and his knuckles to his forehead like a jockey. On recovering, he examined us all leisurely.

"Ay," he said. "There you are, Harry, talking to the women about books and poetry and stuff. What good is that when a race is on? Might as well have stayed at Cambridge. Well, Nancy—oh! I warrant you, so fine as no one in the country would know you. Fine feathers make fine birds, and——" here he saw me, and stared hard with his mouth open. "Gad so!—it's Kitty! Hoop! Hollo!" Upon this he put both hands to his mouth and raised such a shout that we all stopped our ears, and the dogs barked and ran about furiously, as if in search of a fox. "Found again! Kitty, I am right glad to see thee. Did I ride well? Were you proud to see me coming in by a neck? Thinks I, 'I don't care who's looking on, but I'll show them Will Levett knows how to ride.' If I'd known it was you I would have landed the stakes by three clear lengths, I would. Let me look at thee, Kitty. Now, gentlemen, by your leave." He shoved aside Lord Chudleigh, and Harry, and pushed between them. "Let me look at thee well—ay! more fine feathers—but"—here he swore great oaths—"there never was anything beneath them but the finest of birds ever hatched."

"Thank you, Will, for the compliment," I began.

"Why, if any one should compliment you, Kitty, who but I?"

I thought of the broken sixpence and trembled.

"A most pretty speech indeed," said Peggy Baker. "Another of Miss Pleydell's swains, I suppose?"

"My brother," said Nancy, "has been Kitty's swain since he was old enough to walk; that is, about the time when Kitty was born. He is as old a swain as Mr. Temple here."

"I don't know naught about swains," said Will, "but I'm Kitty's sweetheart. And if any man says nay to that, why let him step to the front, and we'll have that business settled on the grass, and no time wasted."

"Brother," cried Nancy, greatly incensed by a remark of such low breeding, "remember that you are here among gentlemen, who do not fight with cudgels and fists for the favours of ladies."

"Nay, dear Miss Levett," said Peggy, laughing; "I find Mr. William vastly amusing. No doubt we might have a contest, a tournament after the manner of the ancients, with Miss Pleydell as the Queen of Beauty, to give her favours to the conquering knight. I believe we can often witness a battle with swords and pistols, if we get up early enough, in Hyde Park; but a duel with fists and cudgels would be much more entertaining."

"Thank you, miss," said Will. "I should like to see the man who would stand up against me."

"I think," Lord Chudleigh interposed, "that as no one is likely to gratify this gentleman's strange invitation, we may return to the town. Miss Pleydell, we wait your orders."

Will was about to say something rude, when his sister seized him by the arm and whispered in his ear.

"O Lord! a lord!" he cried. "I beg your lordship's pardon. There, that is just like you, Nancy, not to tell me at the beginning. Well, Kitty, I am going to look after the horse. Then I will come to see thee."

"Your admirer is a bucolic of an order not often found among the sons of such country gentlemen as Sir Robert Levett," said Lord Chudleigh presently.

"He is addicted to horses and dogs, and he seems to consider that he may claim—or show—some sort of equal attachment to me," I answered.

Then I told him the story of the broken sixpence, and how I became engaged, without knowing it, to both Harry Temple and Will Levett on the same day.

My lord laughed, and then became grave.

"I do not wonder," he said, "that all classes of men have fallen in love with the sweetest and most charming of her sex. That does not surprise me. Still, though we have disposed of Mr. Temple, who is, I am bound to say, a gentleman open to reason, there may be more trouble with this headstrong country lad, who is evidently in sober earnest, as I saw from his eyes. What shall we do, Kitty?"

"My lord," I whispered, "let me advise for your safety. Withdraw yourself for a while from Epsom. Give up Durdans and go to London. I could not bear to see you embroiled with this rude and boisterous clown. Oh, how could such a woman as Lady Levett have such a son? Leave me to deal with him as best I can."

But he laughed at this. To be sure, fear had no part in the composition of this noble, this incomparable man.

"Should I run away because a rustic says he loves my Kitty?" But then his forehead clouded again. "Yet, alas! for my folly and my crime, I may not call her my Kitty."

"Oh yes, my lord! Call me always thine. Indeed, I am all thine own, if only I could think myself worthy."

We were walking together, the others a little distance behind us, and he could do no more than touch my fingers with his own. Alas! the very touch of his fingers caused a delightful tremor to run through my veins—so helplessly, so deeply was I in love with him.

Thus we walked, not hand-in-hand, yet from time to time our hands met: and thus we talked, not as betrothed lovers, yet as lovers: thus my lord spoke to me, confiding to me his most secret affairs, his projects, and his ambitions, as no man can tell them save to a woman he loves. Truly, it was a sweet and delicious time. I fondly turn to it now, after so many years, not, Heaven knows! with regret, any more than September, rich in golden harvest and laden orchards, regrets the sweet and tender April, when all the gardens were white and pink with the blossoms of plum and pear and apple, and the fields were green with the springing barley, oats, and wheat. Yet a dear, delightful time, only spoiled by that skeleton in the cupboard, that consciousness that the only person who stood between my lord and his happiness was—the woman he loved. Heard man ever so strange, so pitiful a case?

At the foot of the hill Lord Chudleigh left us, and turned in the direction of Durdans, where he remained all that day, coming not to the Assembly in the evening. Mrs. Esther and I went home together to dinner, and I know not who was the better pleased with the sport and the gaiety of the morning, my kind madam or Cicely, the maid, who had been upon the Downs and had her fortune told by the gipsies, and it was a good one.

"But, my dear," said Mrs. Esther, "it is strange indeed that so loutish and countrified a bumpkin should be the son of parents so well-bred as Sir Robert and Lady Levett."

"Yet," I said, "the loutish bumpkin would have me marry him. Dear lady, would you wish your Kitty to be the wife of a man who loves the stable first, the kennel next, and his wife after his horses and his dogs?"

After dinner, as I expected, Will Levett called in person. He had been drinking strong ale with his dinner, and his speech was thick.

"Your servant, madam," he said to Mrs. Esther. "I want speech, if I may have it, with Miss Kitty, alone by herself, for all she sits with her finger in her mouth yonder, as if she was not jumping with joy to see me again."

"Sir!" I cried.

"Oh! I know your ways and tricks. No use pretending with me. Yet I like them to be skittish. It is their nature to. For all your fine frocks, you're none of you any better than Molly the blacksmith's girl, or Sukey at the Mill. Never mind, my girl. Be as fresh and frolic as you please. I like you the better for it—before we are married."

"Kitty dear," cried Mrs. Esther in alarm, "what does this gentleman mean?"

"I do not know, dear madam. Pray, Will, if you can, explain what you mean?"

"Explain? explain? Why— —" here he swore again, but I will not write down his profane and wicked language. Suffice it to say that he called heaven and earth to witness his astonishment. "Why, you mean to look me in the face and tell me you don't know?"

"We are old friends, Will," I said, "and I should like, for Nancy's sake, and because Lady Levett has been almost a mother to me, out of her extreme kindness, that we should remain friends. But when a gentleman salutes me before a company of gentlemen and ladies as his sweetheart, when he talks of fighting other gentlemen—like a rustic on a village green— —"

"Wouldst have me fight with swords and likely as not get killed, then?" he asked.

"When he assumes these rights over me, I can ask, I think, for an explanation."

"Certainly," said Mrs. Esther. "We are grieved, sir, to have even a moment's disagreement with the son of so honourable a gentleman and so gracious a lady as your respected father and worthy mother, but you will acknowledge that your behaviour on the Downs was startling to a young woman of such strict propriety as my dear Kitty."

He looked from one to the other as if in a dream.

Then he put his hand into his pocket and dragged out the half sixpence.

"What's that?" he asked me furiously.

"A broken sixpence, Will," I replied.

"Where is the other half?"

"Perhaps where it was left, on the table in the parlour of the Vicarage."

"What!" he cried; "do you mean to say that you didn't break the sixpence with me?"

"Do you mean to say, Will, that I did? As for you breaking it, I do not deny that: I remember that you snapped it between your fingers without asking me anything about it; but to say that I broke it, or assented to your breaking it, or carried away the other half—Fie, Will, fie!"

"This wench," he said, "is enough to drive a man mad. Yet, for all your fine clothes and your paint and powder, Mistress Kitty, I've promised to marry you. And marry you I will. Put that in your pipe, now."

"Marry me against my consent, Will? That can hardly be."

"Is it possible," cried Mrs. Esther, seriously displeased, "that we have in this rude and discourteous person a son of Sir Robert Levett?"

"I never was crossed by woman or man or puppy yet," cried Will doggedly, and taking no notice whatever of Mrs. Esther's rebuke; "and I never will be! Why, for a whole year and more I've been making preparations for it. I've broke in the colt out of Rosamund by Samson and called him Kit, for you to ride. I've told the people round, so as anybody knows there's no pride in me, that I'm going to marry a parson's girl, without a farden, thof a baronet to be——"

Will easily dropped into rustic language, where I do not always follow him.

"Oh, thank you, Will. That is kind indeed. But I would rather see you show the pride due to your rank and birth. You ought to refuse to marry a parson's girl. Or, if you are resolved to cast away your pride, there's many a farmer's girl—there's Jenny of the Mill, or the blacksmith's Sue: more proper persons for you, I am sure, and more congenial to your tastes than the parson's girl."

"I don't mind your sneering—not a whit, I don't," he replied. "Wait till we're married, and I warrant you shall see who's got the upper hand! There'll be mighty little sneering then, I promise you."

This brutal and barbarous speech made me angry.

"Now, Will," I said, "get up and go away. We have had enough of your rustic insolence. Why, sir, it is a disgrace that a gentleman should be such a clown. Go away from Epsom: leave a company for which your rudeness and ill-temper do not fit you: go back to your mug-house, your pipe, your stables, and your kennels. If you think of marrying, wed with one of your own rank. Do you hear, sir? one of your own rank! Gentle born though you are, clown and churl is your nature. As for me, I was never promised to you; and if I had been, the spectacle of this amazing insolence would break a thousand promises."

He answered by an oath. But his eyes were full of dogged determination which I knew of old; and I was terrified, wondering what he would do.

"I remember, when you were a boy, your self-will and heedlessness of your sister and myself. But we are grown up now, sir, as well as yourself, and you shall find that we are no longer your servants. What! am I to marry this clown— —"

"You shall pay for this!" said Will. "Wait a bit; you shall pay!"

"Am I to obey the command of this rude barbarian, and become his wife; not to cross him, but to obey him in all his moods, because he wills it? Are you, pray, the Great Bashaw?"

"Mr. Levett," said Mrs. Esther, "I think you had better go. The Kitty you knew was a young and tender child; she is now a grown woman, with, I am happy to say, a resolution of her own. Nor is she the penniless girl that you suppose, but my heiress; though not a Pimpernel by blood, yet a member of as good and honourable a house as yourself."

He swore again in his clumsy country fashion that he never yet was baulked by woman, and would yet have his way; whereas, so far as he was a prophet (I am translating his rustic language into polite English) those who attempted to say him nay would in the long-run find reason to repent with bitterness their own mistaken action. All his friends, he said, knew Will Levett. No white-handed, slobbering, tea-drinking hanger-on to petticoats was he; not so: he was very well known to entertain that contempt for women which is due to a man who values his self-respect and scorns lies, finery, and make-believe fine speeches. And it was also very well known to all the country-side that, give him but a fleer and a flout, he was ready with a cuff side o' the head; and if more was wanted, with a yard of tough ash, or a fist that weighed more than most. As for drink, he could toss it off with the best, and carry as much; as for racing, we had seen what he could do and how gallant a rider he was; and for hunting, shooting, badger-baiting, bull-baiting, dog-fighting, and cocking, there was not, he was ready to assure us, his match in all the country. Why, then, should a man, of whom his country was proud—no mealy-mouthed, Frenchified, fine gentleman, of whom he would fight a dozen at once, so great was his courage—be sent about his business by a couple of women? He would let us know! He pitied our want of discernment, and was sorry for the sufferings which it would bring upon one of us, meaning Kitty; of which sufferings he was himself to be the instrument.

When he had finished this harangue he banged out of the room furiously, and we heard him swearing on the stairs and in the passage, insomuch that Cicely and her mother came up from the kitchen, and the former threatened to bring up her mop if he did not instantly withdraw or cease from terrifying the ladies by such dreadful words.

"My dear," said Mrs. Esther, "we have heard, alas! so many oaths that we do not greatly fear them. Yet this young man is violent, and I will to Lady Levett, there to complain about her son."

She put on her hat, and instantly walked to Sir Robert's lodgings, when before the baronet, Lady Levett, and Nancy she laid her tale.

"I know not," said Lady Levett, weeping, "what hath made our son so self-willed and so rustical. From a child he has chosen the kennel rather than the hall, and stable-boys for companions rather than gentlemen."

"Will is rough," said his father, "but I cannot believe that he would do any hurt to Kitty, whom he hath known (and perhaps in his way loved) for so long."

"Will is obstinate," said Nancy, "and he is proud and revengeful. He has told all his friends that he was about to marry Kitty. When he goes home again he will have to confess that he has been sent away."

"Yet it would be a great match for Kitty," said Will's mother.

"No, madam, with submission," said Mrs. Esther. "The disparity of rank is not so great, as your ladyship will own, and Kitty will have all my money. The real disparity is incompatibility of sentiment."

"Father," said Nancy, "you must talk to Will. And, Mrs. Pimpernel, take care that Kitty be well guarded."

Sir Robert remonstrated with his son. He pointed out, in plain terms, that the language he had used and the threats he had made were such as to show him to be entirely unfitted to be the husband of any gentlewoman: that Kitty was, he had reason to believe, promised to another man: that it was absurd of him to suppose that a claim could be founded on words addressed to a child overcome with grief at the death of her father. He spoke gravely and seriously, but he might have preached to the pigs for all the good he did.

Will replied that he meant to marry Kitty, and he would marry her: that he would brain any man who stood in his way: that he never yet was crossed by a woman, and he never would; with more to the same effect, forgetting the respect due to his father.

Sir Robert, not losing his patience, as he would have been perfectly justified in doing, went on to remonstrate with his son upon the position which he was born to illustrate, and the duties which that involved. Foremost among these, he said, were respect and deference to the weaker sex. Savages and barbarous men, he reminded him, use women with as little consideration as they use slaves; indeed, because women are weak, they are, among wild tribes, slaves by birth. "But," he said, "for a gentleman in this age of politeness to speak of forcing a lady to marry him against her will is a thing unheard of."

"Why, lad," he continued, "when I was at thy years, I would have scorned to think of a woman whose affections were otherwise bestowed. It would have been a thing due to my own dignity, if not to the laws of society, to leave her and look elsewhere. And what hath poor Kitty done, I pray? Mistaken an offer of marriage (being then a mere child and chit of sixteen) for an offer of friendship. Will, Will, turn thy heart to a better mood."

Will said that it was no use talking, because his mind was made up: that he was a true Kentishman, and a British bull-dog. Holdfast was his name: when he made up his mind that he was going to get anything, that thing he would have: that, as for Kitty, he could no more show himself back upon the village-green, or in the village inn, or at any cock-fighting, bull-baiting, badger-drawing, or horse-race in the country-side, unless he had brought home Kitty as his wife. Wherefore, he wanted no more ado, but let the girl come to her right mind, and follow to heel, when she would find him (give him his own way, and no cursed contrariness) the best husband in the world. But, if not— —

Then Sir Robert spoke to other purpose. If, he told his son, he molested Kitty in any way whatever, he would, in his capacity as justice of the peace, have him instantly turned out of the town; if he offered her any insult, or showed the least violence to her friends, he promised him, upon his honour, to disinherit him.

"You may drink and smoke tobacco with your grooms and stable-boys at home," he said. "I have long been resigned to that. But if you disgrace your name in this place, as sure as you bear that name, you shall no longer be heir to aught but a barren title."

Will answered not, but walked away with dogged looks.

CHAPTER XX.

HOW WILL WOULD NOT BE CROSSED.

I know not what Will proposed to himself when his father at first admonished him; perhaps, one knows not, he even tried to set before himself the reasonableness of his father's rebuke; perhaps, as the sequel seems to show, he kept silence, resolving to have his own way somehow.

However that might be, Will ceased to molest me for the time, and I was even in hopes that he had seen the hopelessness of his desires. Our days went on without any other visits from him, and he did not seek me out upon the Terrace or in the Assembly Rooms.

Poor Nancy's predictions were, however, entirely fulfilled. For Will could not, by any persuasion of hers, be induced at first to abstain from showing himself in public. To be sure, he did not "run an Indian muck" among the dancers, but he became the terror of the whole company for a rough boorishness which was certainly unknown before in any polite assembly. He did not try to be even decently polite: he was boorish, not like a boor, but like a Czar of Russia, with a proud sense of his own position; he behaved as if he were, at Epsom Wells, the young squire among the villagers who looked up to him as their hero and natural king. If he walked upon the Terrace he pushed and elbowed the men, he jolted the ladies, he stepped upon trains, pushed aside dangling canes and deranged wigs, as if nobody was to be considered when he was present. Sometimes he went into the cardroom and took a hand; then, if he was tempted to give his antagonist the lie direct, he gave it; or if he lost, he said rude things about honesty; and he was so strong, and carried so big a cudgel, that for a time nobody dared to check him. Because, you see, by Nash's orders, the gentlemen wore no swords. Now, although it is possible to challenge a man and run him through, what are you to do with one who perhaps would refuse a challenge, yet would, on provocation, being horribly strong, cudgel his adversary on the spot? Of course, this kind of thing could not last; it went on just as long as the forbearance of the gentlemen allowed, and then was brought to an end. As for Will, during the first few days he had not the least consideration for any one; all was to give way to his caprice.

I have already remarked upon the very singular love which young men of all ranks seem to have for chucking under the chin young women of the lower classes. It was very well known at Epsom Wells that many gentlemen rose early in the morning in order to enjoy this pastime upon the chins of the higglers who brought the fruit, eggs, fowls, and vegetables from the farmhouses. From six to nine chin-chucking, not actually upon the Parade and the Terrace, but close by, among the trees, on the steps of houses, beside the pond, was an amusement in full flow. Many of the higglers were comely red-cheeked damsels who thought it fine thus to be noticed by the quality, and I suppose no harm came of it all, save a little pampering of the conceit and vanity of young girls, so that they might dream of gentlemen instead of yeomen, and aspire beyond their rank instead of remembering the words of the Catechism to "learn and labour to do their duty in their own station of life." To attract the attention of a dozen young fellows: to have them following one about, even though one carried a basket full of eggs for sale: to listen to their compliments: to endure that chin-chucking—I suppose these things were to the taste of the girls, because, as Cicely told me, there was great competition among them who should carry the basket to the Wells. Now Master Will was quite at home, from his village experiences, with this pastime, and speedily fell in with it, to the annoyance and discomfiture of the London beaux and fribbles. For, still acting upon the principles that Epsom was his own parish, the village where he was Sultan, Great Bashaw, Heyduc, or Grand Seigneur, he at once took upon himself the right of paying these attentions to any or all of the damsels, without reference to previous preferences. This, which exasperated the fair higglers, drove the beaux nearly mad. Yet, because he was so strong and his cudgel was so thick, none durst interfere.

I have since thought, in reflecting over poor Will's history, that there are very few positions in life more dangerous to a young man than that of the only son of a country squire, to have no tastes for learning and polite society, and to live constantly on the estate. For among the rough farmers and labourers there can be no opposition or public feeling upon the conduct, however foolish and ungoverned, of such a young man; the rustics and clowns are his very humble servants, nay, almost his slaves; they tremble at his frown; if he lifts his stick they expect a cudgelling; as for the women and girls of the village, the poor things are simply honoured by a nod and a word; the estate will be his, the fields will be his, the cottages his; the hares, rabbits, partridges, pheasants will be his; even the very men and women will be his, nay, are his already. Wherever he goes he is saluted; even in the church, the people rise to do him reverence: hats are doffed and reverence paid if he walks the fields, or rides upon the roads; every day, supposing he is so unhappy as to remain always upon his own estate, he is made to feel his greatness until he comes to believe, like King Louis XV. himself, that there is no one in the world but must bow to his order, nothing that he desires but he must have. And, speaking with the respect due to my benefactors, I think that Sir Robert, a man himself of singular good feeling and high breeding, was greatly to blame in not sending his son to travel, or in some way to make him mix with his equals and superiors. For such a character as Will's is formed insensibly. A man does not become selfish and boorish all at once. Therefore, his parents did not notice, until it was forced upon them, what all the world deplored—the self-will and boorishness of their only son. To the last I think that Lady Levett looked upon him as a young man of excellent heart, though stubborn.

"You *shall* marry me," he had said. Therefore it was war to the death, because, as you all know, I could not possibly marry him.

It was no secret at Epsom that this young autocrat had said those words; in fact, he used them in public, insulting Harry Temple upon the very Terrace before all the company.

"I warn you," he said, "keep away from Kitty. She's going to be my wife. I've told her so. Therefore, hands off."

"Why, Will," Harry replied good-naturedly, "what if she refuses?"

"She shan't refuse. I've said she shall marry me, and she shall," he replied. "Refuse? It's only her whimsical tricks. All fillies are alike. Hands off, Master Harry."

"Why," cried Peggy Baker, "what a pretty, genteel speech, to be sure! Oh, Mr. Levett, happy is the woman who will be your wife! Such kindness of disposition! such sweetness! such gallantry! such sensibility!"

"I know what you mean," said Will, swearing a big oath; "and I don't value your words nor your opinion—no—not a brass farden, no more than I value your powder, and your paint, and your patches. You're all alike; blacksmith's Sue is worth a hundred of ye."

Peggy burst out laughing, and Will strode away. He did not like to be laughed at, yet could not help being intolerably rude.

When I found that Will, although he made himself the laughing-stock—and the terror—of the place, ceased to molest me, I was more easy in my mind; certainly, it would not have been pleasant to walk on the Terrace, or even to go to the Assembly, if one had feared to meet this rough and bearish inamorato, who might have insulted one, or a gentleman with one, in the most intolerable manner. However, the evening was generally a safe time, because then he loved to sit in a tavern playing all-fours over a pipe and a tankard with any country parson, or even any town tradesman, who would share his beer and be complaisant with his moods.

This was worse than the case of Harry Temple, because, as I have said before, I could not hope, whatever I did, to bring him to reason. Sometimes I thought, but wildly, of Dr. Powlett's establishment. Suppose that the whole force of the house had succeeded in putting him into chains and a strait-waistcoat, which was certainly doubtful—besides, so wicked a thing could not be done twice—what assurance had I of good behaviour on release? He would promise—Will was always ready to promise, having no more regard to truth than an ourang-outang; but when he was free, with his cudgel in his hand, what would he not do?

I have said that he was prodigiously strong, besides being fierce and masterful of aspect. This made men give way to him; also he got a reputation for being stronger than perhaps he really was. For when, as continually happened, booths were put on the Downs for wrestling, singlestick, quarterstaff, boxing, and other trials of skill and strength, Will would always go, sit out the whole games, and then challenge the victor, whom he always conquered, coming off the hero of the day. To be sure, it was whispered that the contest was generally arranged—

by promise of half-a-crown—to be decided in favour of Will. It seems strange, but I suppose there are men who, for half-a-crown, will not only sell a fight—on which bets have been made—but also take a sound drubbing as well.

And if he had a dispute with a gentleman—it was impossible for him to exchange two words without causing a dispute—he would immediately propose to settle the affair with cudgels or fists. Now a gentleman should be ready to fight a street bully or a light porter in London with any weapons, if necessary; but what sort of society would that be in which the gentlemen would take off coat and wig and engage with fists or clubs on the smallest quarrel?

He was so rude and overbearing that the company began to be positively afraid of going to the Terrace or the Assembly Rooms, and indeed I think he would have driven the whole of the visitors away in a body but for the timely interference of Lord Chudleigh and Sir Miles Lackington. It was the day after his open insult to Harry Temple, who could not call out the son of his former guardian and his old playfellow. Therefore these two resolved that there should be an end of this behaviour.

It was bruited abroad that some steps of a serious nature were going to be taken; there had been found a man, it was said, to bell the cat; it was even whispered that a prize-fighter of stupendous strength, dexterity, and resolution had been brought down expressly from London in order to insult Will Levett, receive a challenge for singlestick, or fists, or quarterstaff, instantly accept it, and thereupon give the village bantam-cock so mighty a drubbing that he would not dare again to show his face among the company. Indeed, I think that was the best thing which could have been done, and I sincerely wish they had done it.

But Lord Chudleigh and Sir Miles would not treat a gentleman, even so great a cub and clown, with other than the treatment due to a gentleman. Therefore, they resolved upon an open and public expostulation and admonition. And, mindful of the big cudgel, they broke the laws of the Wells, and put on their swords before they came together on the Terrace, looking grave and stern, as becomes those who have duties of a disagreeable kind to perform. But to see the excitement of the company. They expected, I believe, nothing short of a battle between Lord Chudleigh and Sir Miles on the one hand, armed with swords, and Will on the other, grasping his trusty cudgel. The cudgel, in his hands, against any two combatants, would have been a mighty awkward weapon, but, fortunately, gentlemen of Will's kind entertain a healthy repugnance to cold steel.

It was about twelve o'clock in the forenoon when Will the Masterful, forcing his way, shoulders first, among the crowd, found himself brought up short by these two gentlemen. Round them were gathered a circle of bystanders, which increased rapidly till it was twenty or thirty deep.

"Now then," he cried, "what is the meaning of this? Let's pass, will ye, lord or no lord?"

As Lord Chudleigh made no reply, Will, growling that a freeborn Englishman was as good as a lord or a baronet in the public way, tried to pass through them. Then he was seized by the coat-collar by Sir Miles, whose arm was as strong as his own.

"Hark ye," said the baronet. "We want a few words with you, young cub!"

Will lifted his head in amazement. Here was a man quite as strong as himself who dared to address him as a cub.

"We find that you go about the Wells," continued the baronet, "which is a place of entertainment for ladies and gentlemen, insulting, pushing, and behaving with no more courtesy than if you were in your own stableyard. Now, sirrah, were it not for the respect we have for your father, we should make short work of you."

"Make short work of ME!" cried Will, red in the face, and brandishing his cudgel. "Make short work of ME!"

"Certainly. Do not think we shall fight you with sticks; and if you make the least gesture with that club of yours, I shall have the pleasure of running you through with my sword." Contrary to the rules of the Wells, both gentlemen, as I have said, wore their swords on this occasion, and here Sir Miles touched his sword-hilt. "And now, sir, take a word of advice. Try to behave like a gentleman, or, upon my word of honour, you shall be driven out of the Wells with a horsewhip by the hands of the common grooms of the place, your proper companions."

Will swore prodigiously, but he refrained from using his cudgel. Indeed, the prospect of cold steel mightily cooled his courage.

"And a word from me, sir," said Lord Chudleigh, speaking low. "You have dared to make public use of a certain young lady's name. I assure you, upon the honour of a peer, that if you presume to repeat this offence, or if you in any way assert a claim to that lady's favour, I will make you meet me as one gentleman should meet another."

Will looked from one to the other. Both men showed that they meant what they promised. Sir Miles, with a careless smile, had in his eye a look of determination. Lord Chudleigh, with grave face and set lip, seemed a man quite certain to carry out his promise. Will had nothing to say; he was like one dumbfounded: therefore he swore. This is the common refuge of many men for all kinds of difficulties, doubts, and dangers. Some rogues go swearing to the gallows. Men call them insensible and callous, whereas I believe that these wretches are simply incapable of expressing emotion in any other way. Swearing, with them, stands for every emotion. The divine gift of speech, by which it was designed that men should express their thoughts, and so continually lead upwards their fellow-creatures, become in their case a vehicle for profane ejaculation, so that they are little better than the monkeys on the branches.

Will, therefore, swore vehemently. This made no impression upon his assailants. He therefore swore again. He then asked what sort of treatment this was for a gentleman to receive. Sir Miles reminded him that he had offended against the good manners expected of gentlemen at a watering-place, and that he could no longer fairly be treated as belonging to the polite class.

"Indeed," he explained, "we have gravely considered the matter, my lord and myself, and have come to the conclusion that although, for the sake of your most worthy father, we were ready to admonish as a gentleman (though in this open and public manner, as the offence required), yet we cannot consider your case to be deserving of any better treatment than that of a common, unruly porter, carter, or labouring man, who must be brought to his senses by reason of blows, cuffs, and kicks. Know, then, that although this Terrace is open to all who comport themselves with civility, decency, and consideration for others, it is no place for brawlers, strikers, and disturbers of the peace. Wherefore, four stout men, or if that is not enough, six, will be told off to drive you from the Terrace whenever you appear again upon it armed with that great stick, or upon the least offer to fight any gentleman of the company. I believe, sir, that you are no fool, and that you perfectly understand what we mean, and that we do mean it. Wherefore, be advised in time, and if you do not retreat altogether from the Wells, be persuaded to study the customs of polite society."

This was a long speech for Sir Miles, but it was delivered with an authority and dignity which made me regret that such good abilities should have been thrown away at the gaming-table.

Will swore again at this. Then, observing that many of the bystanders were laughing, he brandished his cudgel, and talked of knocking out brains, breaking of necks, and so forth, until he was again reminded by Sir Miles, who significantly tapped the hilt of his sword, that Signor Stick was not to be allowed to reign at the Wells. Then he hung his head and swore again.

"It will be best, sir," said Lord Chudleigh, "that you come no more to the Terrace or the Assembly Rooms, with or without your cudgel. The Downs are wide and open; there you will doubtless find room for walking, and an audience in the birds for these profane oaths, to which our ladies are by no means accustomed."

"Let me go then," he said sulkily. "Od rot it—get out of my way, some of you!"

He walked straight down the Terrace, the people making way for him on either hand, with furious looks and angry gestures. He went straight to his stable, where he thrashed a groom for some imaginary offence. Thence he went to the King's Head, where he called for a tankard and offered to fight the best man in the company or for ten miles round, for fifty pounds a side, with quarterstaff, singlestick, or fists. Then he drank more beer; sat down and called for a pipe: smoked tobacco all the afternoon; and got drunk early in the evening.

But he came no more to the Terrace.

"And now," said Peggy Baker, "I hope that we shall see Miss Nancy back again. Doubtless, my lord, the return of that lady, and the more frequent appearance of Miss Pleydell with her, will bring your lordship oftener from Durdans."

I have already mentioned our poets at Epsom, and their biting epigrams. Here is another, which was sent to me at this time:

> "Kitty, a nymph who fain would climb,
> But yet may tumble down,
> Her charms she tries with voice and eyes
> First on a rustic clown.
>
> "But bumpkin squire won't serve her turn
> When gentle Harry woos her,
> So farewell Will, for Kitty still
> Will laugh, although you lose her.
>
> "Yet higher still than Hal or Will
> Her thoughts, ambitious, soar'd:
> 'Go, Will and Hal: my promise shall
> Be transferred to my Lord.'"

I suppose the verses were written at the request of Peggy Baker; but after all they did me very little harm, and, indeed, nothing could do me either good or harm at Epsom any more, because my visit was brought to a sudden close by an event which, as will be seen, might have been most disastrous for us all.

The selfishness and boorish behaviour of Will Levett not only kept us from walking on the Terrace in the afternoon, but also kept poor Nancy at home altogether. She would either come to our lodgings and sit with me lamenting over her bumpkin brother, or she would sit at home when Sir Robert was testy and her ladyship querulous, throwing the blame of her son's rudeness sometimes upon her husband, who, she said, had never whipped the boy as he ought to have been whipped, in accordance with expressed Scripture orders strictly laid down; or upon Nancy, whose pert tongue and saucy ways had driven him from the Hall to the kennel; or upon myself, who was so ungrateful, after all that had been done for me, as to refuse her son, in spite of all his protestations of affection. It was hard upon poor

Nancy, the ordinary butt and victim of her brother's ill-temper, that she should be taunted with being the cause of it; and one could not but think that had madam been more severe with her son at the beginning, things might have gone better. When a mother allows her son from the very beginning to have all his own way, it is weak in the father to suffer it: but she must not then turn round when the mischief is done, and reproach her daughter, who took no part in the first mischief, with being the cause of it; nor should she call a girl ungrateful for refusing to marry a man whose vices are so prominent and conspicuous that they actually prevent his virtues from being discerned. Beneath that smock-frock, so to speak, that village rusticity, behind that blunt speech and rough manner, there may have been the sound kind heart of a gentleman, but the girl could not take that for granted. The sequel proved indeed that she was right in refusing, even had she been free; for Will died, as he lived, a profligate and a drunkard of the village kind. So that even his poor mother was at last fain to acknowledge that he was a bad and wicked man, and but for some hope derived from his deathbed, would have gone in sorrow to her dying day.

"I must say, Kitty," said Lady Levett to me, "that I think a little kindness from you might work wonders with our Will. And he a boy of such a good heart!"

"He wants so much of me, madam," I replied. "With all respect, I cannot give him what he asks, because I cannot love him."

"He says, child, that you promised him."

"Indeed, madam, I did not. I was in sorrow and lamentation over my fathers death and my departure from kind friends, when first Harry and then Will came, and one after the other said words of which I took no heed. Yet when I saw them again, they both declared that I was promised to them. Now, madam, could a girl promise to two men within half an hour?"

"I know not. Girls will do anything," said Lady Levett bitterly. "Yet it passes my understanding to know how the two boys could be so mistaken. And yet you will take neither. What! would nothing serve you short of a coronet?"

I made no reply.

"Tell me, then, girl, will Lord Chudleigh marry thee? It is a great condescension of him, and a great thing for a penniless young woman."

"He will marry me, madam," I replied, blushing, and thinking of what I had first to tell him.

She sighed.

"Well, I would he had cast his eyes on Nancy! Yet I say not, Kitty, that a coronet will be too heavy for thy head to wear. Some women are born to be great ladies. My Nancy must content herself with some simple gentleman. Go, my dear. I must try to persuade this headstrong boy to reason."

"Persuade him, if you can, madam," I said, "to leave Epsom and go home. He will come to harm in this place. Two or three of the gentlemen have declared that they will follow the example of Lord Chudleigh and Sir Miles Lackington, and wear swords, although that is against the rules of the Wells, in order to punish him for his rudeness should he venture again to shake his cudgel in the faces of the visitors, which he has done already to their great discomfiture."

I know not if his mother tried to persuade him, but I do know that he did not leave Epsom, and that the evil thing which I had prophesied, not knowing how true my words might be, did actually fall upon him. This shows how careful one should be in foretelling disasters, even if they seem imminent. And indeed, having before one the experiences of maturity, it seems as if it would be well did a new order of prophets and prophetesses arise with a message of joy and comfort, instead of disaster and misery, such as the message which poor Cassandra had to deliver.

Now, when my lord had given poor Will the warning of which I have told, he retired ashamed and angry, but impenitent, to those obscure haunts where tobacco is continually offered as incense to the gods of rusticity. Here he continued to sit, smoked pipes, drank beer, and cudgelled stable-boys to his heart's content; while we, being happily quit of him, came forth again without fear.

Nancy, however, assured me that something would happen before her brother, whose stubbornness and masterful disposition were well known to her, relinquished his pursuit and persecution of the woman on whom he had set his heart.

"My dear," she said, "I know Will, as you do, of old. Was there ever a single thing which he desired that he did not obtain? Why, when he was a child and cried for the moon they brought him a piece of green cheese, which they told him was cut from the moon on purpose for him to eat. Was he ever crossed in anything? Has there ever been a single occasion on which he gave up any enjoyment or desire out of consideration for another person? Rather, when he has gone among his equals has he not become an object of scorn and hatred? He made no friends at school, nor any at Cambridge, from which place of learning he was, as you know, disgracefully expelled; the gentlemen of the county will not associate with him except on the hunting-field — you know all this, Kitty. Think, then, since he has made up his mind to marry a girl; since he has bragged about his condescension, as he considers it; since he has promised his pot-companions to bring home a wife, how great must be his rage and disappointment. He will *do something*, Kitty. He is desperate."

What, however, could he do? He came not near our lodgings; he made no sign of any evil intention; but he did not go away.

"He is desperate," repeated Nancy. "He cares little about you, but he thinks of his own reputation. And, my dear, do not think because Will, poor boy, is a sot and a clown that he does not think of his reputation. His hobby is to be thought a man who can and will have his own way. He has openly bragged about the country, and even among his boozing companions at Epsom, that he will marry you. Therefore, oh! my dear, be careful. Go not forth alone, or without a gentleman or two, after dark. For I believe that Will would do anything, anything, for the sake of what he calls his honour. For, Kitty, to be laughed at would be the death-blow to his vanity. He knows that he is ignorant and boorish, but he consoles himself with the thought that he is strong."

What, I repeated, being uneasy more than a little, could he do?

At first I thought of asking Harry Temple quietly to watch over Will and bring me news if anything was in the wind; but that would not do either, because one could not ask Harry to act the part of a spy. Next, I thought that I had only to ask for a bodyguard of the young men at the Wells to get a troop for my protection; but what a presumption would this be! Finally, I spoke my fears to Sir Robert, begging him not to tell madam what I had said.

"Courage, Kitty!" said Sir Robert Levett. "Will is a clown, for which we have to thank our own indulgence. Better had it been to break a thousand good ash-saplings over his back, than to see him as he is. Well, the wise man says: 'The father of a fool hath no joy,' Yet Will is of gentle blood, and I cannot doubt that he will presently yield and go away patiently."

"Have you asked him, sir?"

"Child, I ask him daily, for his mother's sake and for Nancy's, to go away and leave us in peace. But I have no control over him. He doth but swear and call for more ale. His mother also daily visits him, and gets small comfort thereby. His heart is hard and against us all."

"Then, sir, if Mrs. Esther will consent, one cause of his discontent shall be removed, for we will go away to London where he will not be able to find us."

"Yes, Kitty," he replied. "That will be best. Yet who would ever have thought I could wish our sweet tall Kitty to go away from us!"

The sweet tall Kitty could not but burst out crying at such tenderness from her old friend and protector.

"Forgive me, sir," I said, while he kissed me and patted my cheek as if I was a child again. "Forgive me, sir, that I cannot marry Will, as he would wish."

"Child!" he exclaimed, starting to his feet in a paroxysm of passion. "God forgive me for saying so, but I would rather see a girl I loved in her grave than married to my son!"

We then held a consultation, Lord Chudleigh being of the party; and it was resolved that we should return to London without delay, and without acquainting any at the Wells with our intention, which was to be carried into effect as soon as we could get our things put together; in fact, in two days' time.

So secret were our preparations that we did not even tell Nancy, and were most careful to let no suspicion enter the head of Cicely Crump, a town-crier of the busiest and loudest, who was, besides, continually beset by the young gallants, seeking through her to convey letters, poems, and little gifts to me. Yet so faithful was the girl, as I afterwards found out, and so fond of me, that I might safely have trusted her with any secret.

(Soon after the event which I am now to relate, I took Cicely into my service as still-room maid. She remained with me for four years, being ever the same merry, faithful, and talkative wench. She then, by my advice, married the curate of the parish, to whom she made as good a wife as she had been a servant, and brought up eleven children, four of them being twins, in the fear of God and the love of duty.)

We were to depart on Friday, the evening being chosen so that Master Will should not be able to see us go. Lord Chudleigh and Sir Miles promised to ride with our coach all the way to London for protection. I have often remembered since that Friday is ever an unlucky day to begin upon. Had we made the day Thursday, for instance, we should have gotten safely away without the thing which happened.

On Thursday afternoon we repaired to the Terrace as usual, I rather sad at thinking that my reign as Queen of the Wells would soon be over, and wondering whether the future could have any days in store for me so happy as those which a kind Providence had already bestowed upon me. There was to be a dance at six, and a tea at five. About four o'clock, Nancy and I, accompanied only by Mr. Stallabras, sauntered away from the Terrace and took the road leading to the Downs. Nancy afterwards told me that she had noticed a carriage with four horses waiting under the trees between the Terrace and the King's Head, which, on our leaving the crowd, slowly followed us along the road; but she thought nothing of this at the time.

Mr. Stallabras, with gallant and consequential air, ambled beside us, his hat under his arm, his snuff box in his left hand, and his cane dangling from his right wrist. He was, as usual, occupied with his own poetry, which, indeed, through the interest of the brewers widow (whom he subsequently married), seemed about to become the fashion. I thought, then, that it was splendid poetry, but I fear, now, that it must have been what Dr. Johnson once called a certain man's writing, "terrible skimble skamble stuff;" in other words, poor Solomon Stallabras had the power of imitation, and would run you off rhymes as glibly as monkey can peel cocoa-nuts (according to the reports of travellers), quite in the style of Pope. Yet the curious might look in vain for any thought above the common, or any image which had not been used again and again. Such poets, though they hand down the lamp, do not, I suppose, greatly increase the poetic reputation of their country.

"It seems a pity, Mr. Stallabras," I was saying, "that you, who are so fond of singing about the purling stream and the turtles cooing in the grove, do not know more about the familiar objects of the country. Here is this little flower" — only a humble crane's-bill, yet a beautiful flower — "you do not, I engage, know its name?"

He did not.

"Observe, again, the spreading leaves of yonder great tree. You do not, I suppose, know its name?"

He did not. A common beech it was, yet as stately as any of those which may be seen near Farnham Royal, or in Windsor Forest.

"And listen! there is a bird whose note, I dare swear, you do not know?"

He did not. Would you believe that it was actually the voice of the very turtle-dove of which he was so fond?

"The Poet," he explained, not at all abashed by the display of so much ignorance — "the Poet should not fetter his mind with the little details of nature: he dwells in his thought remote from their consideration: a flower is to him a flower, which is associated with the grove and the purling stream: a shepherd gathers a posy of flowers for his nymph: a tree is a tree which stands beside the stream to shelter the swain and his goddess: the song of one bird is as good as the song of another, provided it melodiously echoes the sighs of the shepherd. As for — — "

Here we were interrupted. The post-chaise drove rapidly up the road and overtook us. As we turned to look, it stopped, and two men jumped out of it, armed with cudgels. Nancy seized my arm: "Kitty! Will is in the carriage!" I will do Solomon Stallabras justice. He showed himself, though small of stature and puny of limb, as courageous as a lion. He was armed with nothing but his cane, but with this he flew upon the ruffians who rushed to seize me, and beat, struck, clung, and kicked in my defence. Nancy threw herself upon me and shrieked, crying, that if they carried me away they should drag her too. While we struggled, I saw the evil face of Will looking out of the carriage: it was distorted by every evil passion: he cried to the men to murder Solomon: he threatened his sister to kill her unless she let go: he called to me that it would be the worse for me unless I came quiet. Then he sprang from the carriage himself, having originally purposed, I suppose, to take no part in the fray, and with his cudgel dealt Solomon such a blow upon his head that he fell senseless in the road. After this he seized Nancy, his own sister, dragged her from me, swore at the men for being cowardly lubbers, and while they threw me into the carriage, he hurled his sister shrieking and crying on the prostrate form of the poor poet, and sprang into the carriage after me.

"Run!" he cried to the two men; "off with you both, different ways. If you get caught, it will be the worse for you."

We were half-way up the hill which leads from the town to the Downs; in fact, we were not very far above the doctor's house, but there was a wind in the road, so that had his men been looking out of his doors they could not have seen what was being done, though they might have heard almost on the Terrace the cries, the dreadful imprecations, and the shrieks of Nancy and myself.

They had thrown me upon the seat with such violence that I was breathless for a few moments, as well as sick and giddy with the dreadful scene—it lasted but half a minute—which I had witnessed. Yet as Will leaped in after me and gave the word to drive on, I saw lying in the dust of the road the prostrate and insensible form of poor Solomon and my faithful, tender Nancy, who had so fought and wrestled with the villains, not with any hope that she could beat them off, but in order to gain time, lying half over the body of the poet, half on the open road. Alas! the road at this time was generally deserted; there was no one to rescue, though beyond the tall elms upon the right lay the gardens and park of Durdans, where my lord was walking at that moment, perhaps, meditating upon his wretched Kitty.

As for my companion, his face resembled that of some angry devil, moved by every evil passion at once. If I were asked to depict the worst face I ever saw, I should try to draw the visage of this poor boy. He could not speak for passion. He was in such a rage that his tongue clave to the roof of his mouth. He could not even swear. He could only splutter. For a while he sat beside me ejaculating at intervals disjointed words, while his angry eyes glared about the coach, and his red cheeks flamed with wrath.

The Downs were quite deserted: not even a shepherd was in sight. We drove along a road which I knew well, a mere track across the grass: the smooth turf was easy for the horses, and we were travelling at such a pace that it seemed impossible for any one to overtake us.

My heart sank, yet I bade myself keep up courage. With this wild beast at my side it behoved me to show no sign of terror.

Every woman has got two weapons, one provided by Nature, the other by Art. The first is the one which King Solomon had ever in his mind when he wrote the Book of Proverbs (which should be the guide and companion of every young man). Certainly he had so many wives that he had more opportunities than fall to the lot of most husbands (who have only the experience of one) of knowing the power of a woman's tongue. He says he would rather dwell in the wilderness than with an angry woman: in the corner of the house-top than with a brawling woman. (Yet the last chapter of the book is in praise of the wise woman.) I had, therefore, my tongue. Next I had a pair of scissors, so that if my fine gentleman attempted the least liberty, I could, and would, give him such a stab with the sharp points as would admonish him to good purpose. But mostly I relied upon my tongue, knowing of old that with this weapon Will was easily discomfited.

Presently, the cool air of the Downs blowing upon his cheeks, Will became somewhat soothed, and his ejaculations became less like angry words used as interjections. I sat silent, taking no notice of what he said, and answering nothing to any of his wild speeches. But be sure that I kept one eye upon the window, ready to shriek if any passer-by appeared.

The angry interjections settled down into sentences, and Will at last became able to put some of his thoughts into words.

The Chaplain of the Fleet

He began a strange, wild, rambling speech, during which I felt somewhat sorry for him. It was such a speech as an Indian savage might have made when roused to wrath by the loss of his squaw.

He bade me remember that he had known me from infancy, that he had always been brought up with me. I had therefore a first duty to perform in the shape of gratitude to him (for being a child with him in the same village). Next he informed me that having made up his mind to marry me, nothing should stop him, because nothing ever did stop him in anything he proposed to do, and if any one tried to stop him, he always knocked down that man first, and when he had left him for dead, he then went and did the thing. This, he said, was well known. Very well, then. Did I dare, then, he asked, knowing as I did full well this character of his for resolution, to fly in the face of that knowledge and throw him over? What made the matter, he argued, a case of the blackest ingratitude, was that I had thrown him over for a lord: a poor, chicken-hearted, painted lord, whom he, for his own part, could knock down at a single blow. He would now, therefore, show me what my new friends were worth. Here I was, boxed up in the carriage with him, safe and sound, not a soul within hail, being driven merrily across country to a place he knew of, where I should find a house, a parson, and a prayer-book. With these before me I might, if I pleased, yelp and cry for my lord and his precious friend, Sir Miles Lackington. They would be far enough away, with their swords and their mincing ways. When I was married they might come and — what was I laughing at?

I laughed, in fact, because I remembered another weapon. As a last resource I could proclaim to the clergyman that I was already a wife, the wife of Lord Chudleigh. I knew enough of the clergy to be certain that although a man might be here and there found among them capable of marrying a woman against her will, just as men are found among them who, to please their patrons, will drink with them, go cock-fighting with them, and in every other way forget the sacred duties of their calling, yet not one among them all, however bad, would dare to marry again a woman already married. Therefore I laughed.

A London profligate would, perhaps, have got a man to personate a clergyman; but this wickedness, I was sure, would not enter into the head of simple Will Levett. It was as much as he could devise—and that was surely a good deal—to bribe some wretched country curate to be waiting for us at our journey's end, to marry us on the spot. When I understood this I laughed again, thinking what a fool Will would look when he was thwarted again.

"Zounds, madam! I see no cause for laughing."

"I laugh, Will," I said, "because you are such a fool. As for you, unless you order your horses' heads to be turned round, and drive me instantly back to Epsom, you will not laugh, but cry."

To this he made no reply, but whistled. Now to whistle when a person gives you serious advice, is in Kent considered a contemptuous reply.

"Ah!" he went on, "sly as you were, I have been too many for you. It was you who set the two bullies, your great lord and your baronet, on me with their swords—made all the people laugh at me. You shall pay for it all. It was you set Nancy crying and scolding upon me enough to give a man a fit; it was you, I know, set my father on to me. Says if he cannot cut me off with a shilling, he will sell the timber, ruin the estate, and let me starve so long as he lives. Let 'un! let 'un! let 'un, I say! All of you do your worst. Honest Will Levett will do what he likes, and have what he likes. Bull-dog Will! Holdfast Will! Tear-'em Will! By the Lord! there isn't a man in the country can get the better of him. Oh, I know your ways! Wait till I've married you. Then butter wont melt in your mouth. Then it will be, 'Dear Will! kind Will! sweet Will! best of husbands and of men!'—oh! I know what you are well enough. Why—after all—what is one woman that she should set herself above other women? Take off your powder and your patches and your hoops, how are you better than Blacksmith's Sue? Answer me that. And why do I take all this trouble about you, to anger my father and spite my mother, when Blacksmith's Sue would make as good a wife—ay! a thousand times better—because she can bake and brew, and shoe a horse, and mend a cracked crown, and fight a game-cock, and teach a ferret, and train a terrier or a bull-pup, whereas you—what are you good for, but to sit about and look grand, and come over the fellows with your make-pretence, false, lying, whimsy-flimsy ways, your smilin' looks when a lord is at your heels, and your 'Oh, fie! Will,' if it's only an old friend. Why, I say? Because I've told my friends that I'm going to bring you home my wife, and my honour's at stake. Because I am one as will have his will, spite of 'em all. Because I don't love you, not one bit, since I found you out for what you are, a false, jiltin' jade; and I value the little finger of Sue more than your whole body, tall as you are, and fine as you think yourself. Oh! by the Lord — —"

I am sorry I cannot give the whole of his speech, which was too coarse and profane to be written down for polite eyes to read. Suffice it to say that it included every form of wicked word or speech known to the rustics of Kent, and that he threatened me, in the course of it, with every kind of cruelty that he could think of, counting as nothing a horsewhipping every day until I became cheerful. Now, to horsewhip your wife every day, in order to make her cheerful, seems like starving your horse in order to make him more spirited; or to flog an ignorant boy in order to make him learned; or to kick your dog in order to make him love you. Perhaps he did not mean quite all that he said; but one cannot tell, because his friends were chiefly in that rank of life where it is considered a right and honourable thing to beat a wife, cuff a son, and kick a daughter, and even the coarsest boor of a village will have obedience from the wretched woman at his beck and call. I think that Will would have belaboured his wife with the greatest contentment, and as a pious duty, in order to make her satisfied with her lot, cheerful over her duties, and merry at heart at the contemplation of so good a husband. "A wife, a dog, and a walnut-tree, the harder you flog them, the better they be." There are plenty of Solomon's Proverbs in favour of flogging a child, but none, that I know of, which recommend the flogging of a wife.

Blacksmith Sam, Will said, in his own village, the father of the incomparable Sue, used this method to tame his wife, with satisfactory results; and Pharaoh, his own keeper, was at that very time engaged upon a similar course of discipline with his partner. What, he explained, is good for such as those women is good for all. "Beat 'em and thrash 'em till they follow to heel like a well-bred retriever. Keep the stick over 'em till such times as they become as meek as an old cow, and as obedient as a sheep-dog."

While he was still pouring forth these maxims for my information and encouragement my heart began to beat violently, because I heard (distantly at first) the hoofs of horses behind us. Will went on, hearing and suspecting nothing, growing louder and louder in his denunciation of women, and the proper treatment of them.

The hoofs drew nearer. Presently they came alongside. I looked out. One on each side of our carriage, there rode Lord Chudleigh and Sir Miles Lackington.

But I laughed no longer, for I saw before me the advent of some terrible thing, and a dreadful trembling seized me. My lord's face was stern, and Sir Miles, for the first time in my recollection, was grave and serious, as one who hath a hard duty to perform. So mad was poor headstrong Will that he neither heard them nor, for a while, saw them, but continued his swearing and raving.

They called aloud to the postillions to stop the horses. This it was that roused Will, and he sprang to his feet with a yell of rage, and thrusting his head out of the window, bawled to the boys to drive faster, faster! They whipped and spurred their horses. My lord said nothing, but rode on, keeping up with the carriage.

"Stop!" cried Sir Miles.

"Go on!" cried Will.

Sir Miles drew a pistol and deliberately cocked it.

"If you will not stop," he cried, holding his pistol to the post-boy's head, "I will fire!"

"Go on!" cried Will. "Go on; he dares not fire."

The fellow—I knew him for a stable-boy whose life at the Hall had been one long series of kicks, cuffs, abuse, and horsewhippings at the hands of his young master—ducked his head between his shoulders, and put up his elbows, as if that which had so often protected him when Will was enforcing discipline by the help of Father Stick, would avail him against a pistol-shot. But he obeyed his master, mostly from force of habit, and spurred his horse.

Sir Miles changed the direction of the pistol, and leaning forward, discharged the contents in the head of the horse which the boy was riding. The poor creature bounded forward and fell dead.

There was a moment of confusion; the flying horses stumbled and fell, the boys were thrown from their saddles: the carriage was stopped suddenly.

Then, what followed happened all in a moment. Yet it is a moment which to me is longer than any day of my life, because the terror of it has never left me, and because in dreams it often comes back to me. Ah! what a prophetess was Nancy when she said that some dreadful thing would happen before all was over, unless Will went away.

Sir Miles and my lord sprang to their feet. Will, with a terrible oath, leaped forth from the carriage. For a moment he stood glaring from one to the other like a wild beast brought to bay. He *was* a wild beast. Then he raised his great cudgel and rushed at my lord.

"You!" he cried; "you are the cause of it. I will beat out your brains!"

Lord Chudleigh leaped lightly aside, and avoided the blow which would have killed him had it struck his head. Then I saw the bright blade in his hand glisten for a moment in the sunlight, and then Will fell backwards with a cry, and lay lifeless on the green turf, while my lord stood above him, drops of red blood trickling down his sword.

"I fear, my lord," said Sir Miles, "that you have killed him. Fortunately, I am witness that it was in self-defence."

"You have killed him! You have killed my master!" cried the stable boy, whose left arm, which was broken by his fall from the horse, hung helpless at his side. "You have killed the best master in all the world! Lord or no lord, you shall hang!"

He rushed with his one hand to seize the slayer of his master, this poor faithful slave, whose affections had only grown firmer with every beating. Sir Miles caught him by the coat-collar and dragged him back.

"Quiet, fool! Attend to your master. He is not dead—yet."

He looked dead. The rage was gone out of his eyes, which were closed, and the blood had left the cheeks, which were pallid. Poor Will never looked so handsome as when he lay, to all seeming, dead.

Lord Chudleigh looked on his prostrate form with a kind of stern sadness. The taking of life, even in such a cause and in self-defence, is a dreadful thing. Like Lamech (who also might have been defending his own life), he had slain a man to his wounding, and a young man to his hurt.

"Kitty," he said, in a low voice, taking my hand, "this is a grievous day's work. Yet I regret it not, since I have saved your honour!"

"My lord," I replied, "I had the saving of that in my own hands. But you have rescued me from a wild beast, whose end I grieve over because I knew him when he was yet an innocent boy."

"Come," said Sir Miles, "we must take measures. Here, fellows! come, lift your master."

The two boys, with his help, lifted Will, who, as they moved him, groaned heavily, into the carriage.

"Now," said Sir Miles, "one of you get inside. Lift his head. If—but that is impossible—you come across water, pour a little into his mouth. The other mount, and drive home as quickly as you can."

I bethought me of my friend the mad doctor, and bade them take their master to his house, which was, as I have said, on the road between the town and the Downs, so that he might be carried there quietly, without causing an immediate scandal in the town.

The fellows were now quite obedient and subdued. Sir Miles, who seemed to know what was to be done, made some sort of splint with a piece of poor Will's cudgel, for the broken arm, which he tied up roughly, and bade the boy be careful to get attended to as soon as his master was served. In that class of life, as is well known, wounds, broken bones, and even the most cruel surgical operations, are often endured with patience which would equal the most heroic courage, if it were not due to a stupid insensibility. The most sensitive of men are often the most courageous, because they know what it is they are about to suffer.

However, they did as they were told, and presently drove back, the third horse following with a rope.

Then we were left alone, with the blood upon the grass and the dead horse lying beside us.

Sir Miles took my lord's sword from him, wiped it on the turf, and restored it to him.

"Come," he said, "we must consider what to do."

"There is nothing to do," said Lord Chudleigh, "except to take Miss Pleydell home again."

"Pardon me, my lord," Sir Miles interposed; "if ever I saw mischief written on any man's face, it was written on the face of that boy. A brave lad, too, and would have driven to the death at his master's command."

"How can he do harm?" I asked. "Why, Sir Miles, you are witness; you saw Will Levett with his cudgel rush upon his lordship, who but drew in self-defence. I am another witness. I hope the simple words of such as you and I would be believed before the oath of a stable-lad."

"I suppose they would," he replied. "Meantime, there is the fact, known to all the company at the Wells, that both you and I, Lord Chudleigh, had publicly informed this unhappy young man, that, under certain circumstances, we would run him through. The circumstances *have* happened, and we *have* run him through. This complication may be unfortunate as regards the minds of that pig-headed institution, a coroner's inquest."

"Sir!" cried my lord, "do you suppose—would you have me believe—that this affair might be construed into anything but an act of self-defence?"

"I do indeed," he replied gravely; "and so deeply do I feel it, that I would counsel a retreat into some place where we shall not be suspected, for such a time as may be necessary. If the worst happens, and the man dies, your lordship may surrender yourself—but in London—not to a country bench. If the man recovers, well and good; you can go abroad again."

At first my lord would hear nothing of such a plan. Why should he run away? Was it becoming for a man to fly from the laws of his country? Then I put in a word, pointing out that it was one thing for a case to be tried before a jury of ignorant, prejudiced men upon an inquest, and another thing altogether for the case to be tried by a dispassionate and unprejudiced jury. I said, too, that away from this place, the circumstances of the case, the brutal assault upon Solomon Stallabras, whose ribs, it appeared, were broken, as well as his collar-bone, the ferocious treatment of Nancy by her own brother, and my forcible abduction in open daylight, would certainly be considered provocation enough for anything, and a justification (combined with the other circumstances) of the homicide, if unhappily Will should die.

This moved my lord somewhat.

Where, he asked, could he go, so as to lie *perdu* for a few days, or a few weeks, if necessary?

"I have thought upon that," replied Sir Miles, looking at me with a meaning eye (but I blushed and turned pale, and reddened again). "I have just now thought of a plan. Your lordship has been there once already; I mean the Rules of the Fleet. Here will I find you lodgings, where no one will look for you; where, if you please to lie hidden for awhile, you may do so in perfect safety; where you may have any society you please, from a baronet out at elbows to a baker in rags, or no society at all, if you please to lie quiet."

"I like not the place," said his lordship. "I have been there it is true once, and it was once too often. Find me another place."

"I know no other," Sir Miles replied. "You must be in London; you must be in some place where no one will suspect you. As for me, I will stay near you, but not with you. There will be some noise over this affair; it will be well for us to be separated, yet not so far but that I can work for you. Come, my lord, be reasonable. The place is dirty and noisy; but what signify dirt and noise when safety is concerned?"

He wavered. The recollection of the place was odious to him. Yet the case was pressing.

He gave way.

"Have it," he said, "your own way. Kitty," he took my hand, "hopeless as is my case, desperate as is my condition, I am happy in having rescued you, no matter at what cost."

"Your lordship's case is not so hopeless as mine," said Sir Miles; "yet I, too, am happy in having helped to rescue this, the noblest creature in the world."

The tears were in my eyes as these two men spoke of me in such terms. How could I deserve this worship? By what act, or thought, or prayer, could I raise myself to the level where my lord's imagination had planted me? O Love divine, since it makes men and women long to be angels!

"I mean," Sir Miles continued bluntly, "that since your lordship has found favour in her eyes, your case cannot be hopeless."

Lord Chudleigh raised my hand to his lips, with a sadness in his eyes of which I alone could discern the cause.

"Gentlemen," I cried, "we waste the time in idle compliments. Mount and ride off as quickly as you may. As for me, it is but three miles across the Downs. I have no fear. I shall meet no one. Mount, I say, and ride to London without more ado."

They obeyed; they left me standing alone. As my eyes turned from following them, they lighted on the pool of blood—Will's blood, which reddened the turf—and upon the poor dead horse. Then I hastened back across the Downs.

It was a clear, bright evening, the sun yet pretty high. The time was about half-past five; before long the minuets would be beginning in the Assembly Rooms; yet Lady Levett would know—I hoped that she already knew—the dreadful wickedness of her son. Would not, indeed, all the company know it? Would not the assault on Mr. Stallabras and on Nancy be noised abroad?

Indeed, the news had already sped abroad.

Long before I reached the edge of the Downs. I became aware of a crowd of people. They consisted of the whole company, all the visitors at Epsom, who came forth, leaving the public tea and the dance, to meet the girl who had been thus carried away by force.

Harry Temple came forward as soon as I was in sight to meet me. He was very grave.

"Kitty," he said, "this is a bad day's work."

"How is Will? You have seen Will?"

"I fear he is already dead. The doctor to whom you sent him declares that he is dying fast. His mother is with him."

"O Harry!" I sighed; "I gave him no encouragement. There was not the least encouragement to believe that I would marry him."

"No one thinks you did, Kitty; not even his mother. Yet others have been carried away by admiration of your charms to think— —"

"Oh! my charms, my charms! Harry, with poor Will at death's door, let us at least be spared the language of compliment."

By this time we had reached the stream of people. Among them, I am happy to say, was not Peggy Baker. She, at least, did not come out to gaze upon her unhappy rival, for whose sake one gallant gentleman lay bleeding to death, and two others were riding away to hide themselves until the first storm should be blown over. The rest parted, right and left, and made a lane through which we passed in silence. As I went through, I heard voices whispering: "Where is Lord Chudleigh? where is Sir Miles? How pale she looks!" and so forth; comments of the crowd which has no heart, no pity, no sympathy. It came out to-day to look upon a woman to whom a great insult had been offered with as little pity as to-morrow it would go to see a criminal flogged from Newgate to Tyburn, or a woman whipped at Bridewell, or a wretched thief beaten before the Alderman, or a batch of rogues hanged. They came to be amused. Amusement, to most people, is the contemplation of other folks' sufferings. If tortures were to be introduced again, if, as happened, we are told, in the time of Nero, Christians could be wrapped in pitch and then set fire to, thus becoming living candles, I verily believe the crowd would rush to see, and would enjoy the spectacle the more, the longer the sufferings of the poor creatures were prolonged.

Solomon Stallabras, Harry told me, was comfortably put into bed, his ribs being set and his collar-bone properly put in place: there was no doubt that he would do well. Nancy, too, was in bed, sick with the fright she had received, but not otherwise much hurt. Mrs. Esther was wringing her hands and crying at home, with Cicely to look after her. Sir Robert and Lady Levett were at the doctor's. It was, I have said, the same doctor who had undertaken the temporary charge of Harry Temple. As we drew near the house—I observed that most of the people remained behind upon the Downs in hopes of seeing the return of Lord Chudleigh, in which hope they were disappointed—Harry became silent.

"Come, Harry," I said, reading his thoughts, "you must forgive me for saving your life or from preventing you from killing Lord Chudleigh. Be reasonable, dear Harry."

He smiled.

"I have forgiven you long since," he replied. "You acted like a woman; that is, you did just what you thought best at the moment. But I cannot, and will not, forgive the man with his impudent smile and his buckets of water."

"Nay, Harry," I said, "he acted according to his profession. Come with me to the house. I cannot even go to Mrs. Esther until I have seen or heard about poor Will."

The doctor was coming from the sick man's chamber when we came to the house. They had placed Will in one of the private rooms, away from the dreadful gallery where the madmen were chained to the wall. With him were Lady Levett and Sir Robert.

The doctor coughed in his most important manner.

"Your obedient servant, Miss Pleydell. Sir, your most obedient, humble servant. You are come, no doubt, to inquire after the victim of this most unhappy affair. Poor Mr. William Levett, I grieve to say, is in a most precarious condition."

"Can nothing save him? O doctor!"

"Nothing can save him, young lady," he replied, "but a miracle. That miracle—I call it nothing short—is sometimes granted by beneficent Providence to youth and strength only when—I say only when—their possession is aided by the very highest medical skill that the country can produce. I say the very highest; no mere pretender will avail."

"Indeed, doctor, we have that skill, I doubt not, in yourself."

"I say nothing,"—he bowed and spread his hands—"I say nothing. It is not for me to speak."

"And, sir," said Harry, "you are doubtless aware that Sir Robert is a gentleman of a considerable estate, and that—in fact—you may expect——"

"Sir Robert," he replied, with a smile which speedily, in spite of all his efforts, broadened into a grin of satisfaction, "has already promised that no expense shall be spared, no honorarium be considered too large if I give him back his son. Yet we can but do our best. Science is strong, but a poke of cold steel in the inwards is, if you please, stronger still."

"Will you let me see Sir Robert?" I asked.

The doctor stole back to the room, and presently Sir Robert came forth.

He kissed me on the forehead while his tears fell upon my head.

"My dear," he said, "I ask your pardon in the name of my headstrong son. We have held an honourable name for five hundred years and more: in all that time no deed so dastardly has been attempted by any one of our house. Yet the poor wretch hath paid dearly for his wickedness."

"Oh, sir!" I cried, "there is no reason why you should speak of forgiveness, who have ever been so kind to me. Poor Will will repent and be very good when he recovers."

"I think," said his father sadly, "that he will not recover. Go, child. Ask not to see the boy's mother, because women are unreasonable in their grief, and she might perchance say things of which she would afterwards be ashamed. Go to Mrs. Pimpernel, and tell her of thy safety."

This was, indeed, all that could be done. Yet after allaying the terrors and soothing the agitated spirits of Mrs. Esther, whose imagination had conjured up, already, the fate of Clarissa, and who saw in headstrong Will another Lovelace, without, to be sure, the graces and attractions of that dreadful monster, I went to inquire after my gallant little Poet.

He was lying on his bed, with orders not to move, and wrapped up like a baby.

I thanked him for his brave defence, which I said would have been certainly efficacious, had it not been for the cowardly blow on the back of his head. I further added, that no man in the world could have behaved more resolutely, or with greater courage.

"This day," he said, "has been the reward for a Poet's devotion. In those bowers, Miss Kitty, when first we met"—the bower was the Fleet Market—"beside that stream"—the Fleet Ditch—"where the woodland choir was held"—the clack of the poultry about to be killed—"and the playful lambs frisked"—on their way to the butchers of Newgate Street—"I dared to love a goddess who was as much too high for me as ever Beatrice was for her Italian worshipper. I refer not to the disparity of birth, because (though brought up in a hosier's shop) the Muse, you have acknowledged, confers nobility. An attorney is by right of his calling styled a gentleman; but a Poet, by right of his genius, is equal of—ay, even of Lord Chudleigh."

"Surely, dear sir," I replied, "no one can refuse the highest title of distinction to a gentleman of merit and genius."

"But I think," he went on, "of that disparity which consists in virtue and goodness. That can never be removed. How happy, therefore, ought I to be in feeling that I have helped to preserve an angel from the hands of those barbarous monsters who would have violated such a sanctuary. What are these wounds!—a broken rib—a cracked collar bone—a bump on the back of the head? I wish they had been broken legs and arms in your service."

I laughed—but this devotion, more than half of it being real, touched my heart. The little Poet, conceited, vain, sometimes foolish, was ennobled, not by his genius, of which he thought so much, but by his great belief in goodness and virtue. Women should be humble when they remember, that if a good man loves them it is not in very truth, the woman (who is a poor creature full of imperfections) that they love, but the soul—the noble, pure, exalted soul, as high as their own grandest conception of goodness and piety, which they believe to be in her. How can we rise to so great a height? How can we, without abasement, pretend to such virtue? How can we be so wicked and so cruel as, after marriage, to betray to our husbands the real littleness of our souls? As my lord believed me to be, so might I (then I prayed) rise to heaven in very truth, and even soar to higher flights.

Now, when I reached home, a happy thought came to me. I knew the name of Solomon's latest patron, the brewer's widow. I sat down and wrote her a letter. I said that I thought it my simple duty to inform her, although I had not the honour of her friendship, that the Poet whom she had distinguished with her special favour and patronage, was not in a position to pay her his respects, either by letter, or by verse, or in person, being at that time ill in bed with ribs and other bones broken in defence of a lady. And to this I added, so that she might not grow jealous, which one must always guard against in dealing with women, that he was walking with two ladies, not one, and that the gallantry he showed in defence of her who was attacked was so great that not even a lover could have displayed more courage for his mistress than he did for this lady (myself), who was promised to another gentleman. Nor was it, I added, until he was laid senseless on the field that the ravishers were able to carry off the lady, who was immediately afterwards rescued by two friends of the Poet, Lord Chudleigh and Sir Miles Lackington.

This crafty letter, which was all true, and yet designedly exaggerated, as when I called my lord Solomon's friend, produced more than the effect which I desired. For the widow, who was in London, came down to Epsom the next day, in a carriage and four, to see the hero. Now, she was still young, and comely as well as rich. Therefore, when she declared to him that no woman could resist such a combination of genius and heroic courage, Solomon could only reply that he would rush into her arms with all a lover's rapture, as soon as his ribs permitted an embrace. In short, within a month they were married at Epsom Church, and Solomon, though he wrote less poetry in after years than his friends desired, lived in great comfort and happiness, having a wife of sweet temper, who thought him the noblest and most richly endowed of men, and a brewery whose vats produced him an income far beyond his wants, though these expanded as time went on.

As for Nancy, she was little hurt, save for the fright and the shame of it. Yet her brother, the cause of all, was lying dangerously wounded, and she could not for very pity speak her mind upon his wickedness.

The company, I learned from Cicely, were greatly moved about it: the public Tea had been broken up in confusion, while all sallied forth to the scene of the outrage; nor was the assembly resumed when it was discovered that Will Levett had been run through the body by Lord Chudleigh, and was now lying at the point of death.

In the morning Cicely went early to inquire at the Doctor's. Alas! Will was in a high fever; Lady Levett had been sitting with him all night; it was not thought that he would live through the day. I put on my hood and went to see Nancy.

"Oh, my dear, dear Kitty!" she cried, "sure we shall all go distracted. You have heard what they say. Poor Will is in a bad way indeed; the fever is so high that the doctor declares his life to be in hourly danger. He is delirious, and in his dreams he knows not what he says, so that you would fancy him among his dogs or in his stables—where, indeed, it hath been his chief delight to dwell—or with the rustics with whom he would drink. It is terrible, my father says, that one so near his end, who must shortly appear before his Maker, should thus blaspheme and swear such horrid oaths. If we could only ensure him half an hour of sense, even with pain, so that the clergyman might exhort him. Alas! our Will hath led so shocking a life—my dear, I know more of his ways than he thinks—that I doubt his conscience and his heart are hardened. O Kitty! to think that yesterday we were happy, and that this evil thing had not befallen us! And now I can never go abroad again without thinking that the folk are saying: 'There goes the sister of the man who was killed while trying to carry off the beautiful Miss Pleydell.'"

No comfort can be found for one who sits expectant of a brothers death. I bade poor Nancy keep up her heart and hope for the best.

The fever increased during the day, we heard, and the delirium. We stirred not out of the house save for morning prayers, sending Cicely from time to time to ask the news. And all the company gathered together on the Terrace, not to talk scandal or tell idle stories of each other, but to whisper that Will Levett was certainly dying, and that it would go hard with Lord Chudleigh, who would without doubt be tried for murder, the two grooms protesting stoutly that their master had not struck a blow.

In the evening Sir Robert Levett came to our lodging. He was heavily afflicted with the prospect of losing his only son, albeit not a son of whom a parent could be proud. Yet a child cannot be replaced, and the line of the Levetts would be extinguished.

"My dear," he said, "I come to say a thing which has been greatly on my mind. My son was run through by Lord Chudleigh. Tell me, first, what there is between you and my lord? Doth he propose to marry you?"

"Dear sir," I replied, "Lord Chudleigh has offered me his hand."

"And you have taken it?"

"Unworthy as I am, dear sir, I have promised, should certain obstacles be removed, to marry him."

"His sword has caused my Will's death. Yet the act was done in defence of the woman he loved, the woman whom Will designed to ruin— —"

"And in self-defence as well. Had he not drawn, Will would have beaten out his brains."

"Tell him, from Will's father, my dear, that I forgive him. Let not such a homicide dwell upon his conscience. Where is he?"

"He has gone away with Sir Miles Lackington to await the finding of an inquest, if— —"

"Tell him that I will not sanction any proceedings, and if there is to be an inquest my evidence shall be, though it bring my grey hairs with sorrow to the grave, that my lord is innocent, and drew his sword to defend his own life."

He left me—poor man!—to return to the sick bedside.

He had been gone but a short time when a post-boy rode to the door, blowing a horn. It was a special messenger, who had ridden from Temple Bar with a letter from Sir Miles.

"Sweet Kitty," wrote the Baronet, "I write this to tell thee that we have taken up quarters in London. I have bestowed my lord in certain lodgings, which you know, above the room where once I lay."

Heavens! my lord was in my own old lodging beside the Fleet Market.

"He is downhearted, thinking of the life he has taken. I tell him that he should think no more of running through such a madman in defence of his own life than of killing a pig. Pig, and worse than pig, was the creature who dared to carry off the lovely Kitty. To think that such a rustic clown should be brother of pretty Nancy! I have sent to my lord's lodging an agreeable dinner and a bottle of good wine, with which I hope my lord will comfort his heart. Meantime, they know not, in the house, the rank and quality of their guest. I suppose the fellow is dead by this time. If there is an inquest, I shall attend to give my evidence, and the verdict can be none other than justifiable homicide or even *felo-de-se*, for if ever man rushed upon his death it was Will Levett. I have also sent him paper and pens with which to write to you, and some books and a pack of cards. Here is enough to make a lonely man happy. If he wants more he can look out of the window and see the porters and fishwives of the market fight, which was a spectacle daily delighted me for two years and more. The doctor is well. I have informed him privately of the circumstances of the case, and Lord Chudleigh's arrival. He seemed pleased, but I took the liberty of warning him against betraying to my lord a relationship, the knowledge of which might be prejudicial to your interests."

Prejudicial to my interests!

Sir Miles was in league, with me, to hide this thing from a man who believed, like Solomon Stallabras, that I was all truth and goodness.

I had borne so much from this wicked concealment that I was resolved to bear it no longer. I said to myself, almost in the words of the Prayer-book: "I will arise and go unto my lord. I will say, Forgive me, for thus and thus have I done, and so am I guilty."

Oh, my noble lord! Oh, great heart and true! what am I, wicked and deceitful woman, that I should hope to keep thy love? Let it go; tell me that you can never love again one who has played this wicked part; let hatred and loathing take the place of love; let all go, and leave me a despairing wretch—so that I have confessed my sin and humbled myself even to the ground before him whom I have so deeply wronged.

CHAPTER XXI.

HOW KITTY WENT TO LONDON.

Oppressed with this determination, which left no room for any other thought, I urged upon Mrs. Esther the necessity of going to London at once, as we had resolved to do before the accident. I pointed out to her that, after the dreadful calamity which had befallen us—for which most certainly no one could blame us—we could take no more pleasure in the gaieties of Epsom: that we could enjoy no longer the light talk, the music, and the dancing; that the shadow of Death had fallen over the place, so far as we were concerned: that we could not laugh while Nancy was weeping; and that—in short, my lord was in London and I must needs go too.

"There are a hundred good reasons," said Mrs. Esther, "why we should go away at once: and you have named the very best of all. But, dear child, I would not seem to be pursuing his lordship."

"Indeed," I replied, "there will be no pursuing of him. Oh, dear madam, I should be"—and here I burst into tears—"the happiest of women if I were not the most anxious."

She thought I meant that I was anxious about Will's recovery; but this was no longer the foremost thing in my thoughts, much as I hoped that he would get better—which seemed now hopeless.

"Let us go, dear madam, and at once. Let us leave this place, which will always be remembered by me as the scene of so much delight as well as so much pain. I must see my lord as soon as I can. For oh! there are obstacles in the way which I must try to remove, or be a wretched woman for ever."

"Child," said Mrs. Esther severely, "we must not stake all our happiness on one thing."

"But I have so staked it," I replied. "Dear madam, you do not understand. If I get not Lord Chudleigh for my husband, I will never have any man. If I cannot be his slave, then will I be no man's queen. For oh! I love the ground he walks upon; the place where he lodges is my palace, his kind looks are my paradise; I want no heaven unless I can hold his hand in mine."

I refrain from setting down all I said, because I think I was like a mad thing, having in my mind at once my overweening love, my repentance and shame, and my terror in thinking of what my lord would say when he heard the truth.

Had my case been that of more happy women, who have nothing to conceal or to confess, such a fit of passion would have been without excuse, but I set it down here, though with some shame, yet no self-reproach, because the events of the last day or two had been more than I could bear, and I must needs weep and cry, even though my tears and lamentations went to the heart of my gentle lady, who could not bear to see me suffer. For consider, the son of my kindest friends, to be lying, like to die, run through the body by my lover: I could not be suffered to see his mother, who had been almost my own mother: I could never more bear to meet my pretty Nancy without thinking how, unwittingly, I had enchanted this poor boy, and so lured him to his death: that merry, saucy girl would be merry no more: all our ways of kindly mirth and innocent happiness were gone, never to return: even if Will recovered, how could there, any more, be friendship between him and me? For the memory of his villainous attempt could never be effaced. There are some things which we forgive, because we forget: but this thing, though I might forgive, none of us would ever forget. And at the back of all this trouble was my secret, which I was now, in some words, I knew not what, to confess to my lord.

Poor Mrs. Esther gave way to all I wanted. She would leave Epsom on Monday: indeed, her boxes should be packed in a couple of hours. She kissed and soothed me, while I wept and exclaimed, in terms which she could not understand, upon woman's perfidy and man's fond trust. When I was recovered from this fit, which surely deserved no other name, in which passion got the better of reason, and reason and modesty were abandoned for the time (if Solomon Stallabras had seen me then, how would he have been ashamed for his blind infatuation!), we were able calmly to begin our preparation.

First we told Cicely to go order us a post-chaise for Monday morning, for we must go to London without delay; then I folded and packed away Mrs. Esther's things, while she laid her down to rest awhile, for her spirits had been greatly agitated by my unreasonable behaviour. Then Cicely came to my room to help me, and presently I saw her tears falling upon the linen which she folded and laid in the trunk.

"Foolish Cicely!" I said, thinking of my own foolishness, "why do you cry?"

"O Miss Kitty," she sobbed, "who would not cry to see you going away, never to come back again? For I know you never, never could come here any more after that dreadful carrying away, enough to frighten a maid into her grave. And besides, they say that Epsom is going to be given up, and the Assembly Rooms pulled down; and we should not have had this gay season unless it had been for my lord and his party at the Durdans. And what we shall do, mother and me, I can't even think."

Why, here was another trouble.

"Miss Kitty"—this silly girl threw herself on her knees to me and caught my hand—"take me into your service when you marry my lord."

"How do you know I am to marry my lord, Cicely? There are many things which may happen to prevent it."

"Oh, I know you will, because you are so beautiful and so good." I snatched my hand away. "I haven't offended you, Miss Kitty, have I? All the world cries out that you are as good as you are beautiful; and haven't I seen you, for near two months, always considerate, and never out of temper with anybody, not even with me, or your hairdresser, or your dressmaker? Whereas, Miss Peggy Baker slaps her maid, and sticks pins into her milliner."

"That is enough, Cicely," I said. "I have no power to take anybody into my service, being as penniless as yourself. But if—if—that event *should* happen which you hope for—why—then—I do not—say——"

"It *will* happen. Oh, I know that it will happen. I have dreamed of it three times running, and always before midnight. I threw a piece of apple-peel yesterday, and called it to name your husband. It first made a G., which is Geoffrey, and then a C., which is Chudleigh. And mother says that everything in the house points to a wedding as true as she can read the signs. O Miss Kitty! may I be in your service?"

I laughed and cried. I know not which, for the tears were very near my eyes all that time.

But oh! that thing did happen which she prophesied and I longed for—I will quickly tell you how. And, as I have said before, I took Cicely into my service, and a good and faithful maid she proved, and married the curate. I forgot to say that when young Lord Eardesley heard the story of her father's elopement with Jenny Medlicott, he laughed, because his mother, Jenny's friend and far-off cousin, had taken her away to Virginia with her, where, after (I hope) the death of Joshua Crump, she had married again. Jenny, it appeared, was the daughter of the same alderman whose fall in 1720 ruined my poor ladies. And it was for this reason that his lordship afterwards, when Cicely had a houseful of babies, took a fancy to them, and would have them, when they were big enough, out to Virginia. Here he made them overseers, and, in course of time, settled them on estates of their own, where some of them prospered, and some, as happens in all large families, wasted their substance and fell into poverty.

The next day, being Sunday, we spent chiefly over our devotions. It was moving to hear the congregation invited to pray for one in grievous danger—meaning poor Will, who would have been better at this moment had he sometimes prayed for himself. Nancy sat beside me in our pew, and caught my hand at the words. One could not choose but weep, poor child! for there was no improvement in Will's fever: all night long the doctor had sat beside his bed, while the lad, in his delirium, fancied himself riding races, wrestling, boxing, and drinking with his boon companions. A pitiful contrast! The pleasures of the world in his mind, and eternity in prospect. Yet, for a man in delirium, allowance must be made. The fever was now, in fact, at its height, and four men were necessary to hold him down in his ravings.

We spent a gloomy Sunday indeed, Mrs. Esther being so saddened by the anxieties of our friends that she resumed her reading of "Drelincourt on Death," a book she had laid aside since we left the Rules. And we observed a fast, not so much from religious motives, as because, in the words of Mrs. Esther, roast veal and stuffing is certain to disagree when a heart of sensibility is moved by the woes of those we love. In the evening we had it cold, when Nancy came to sit with us, her eyes red with her weeping, and we were fain to own that we were hungry after crying together all day long.

"Hot meat," said Mrs. Esther, "at such a juncture, would have choked us."

Nancy said, that after what had happened, it would certainly be impossible for us to stay longer at Epsom, and that for herself, all she hoped and expected now was shame and disgrace for the rest of her life. She wished that there were convents in the country to which she could repair for the rest of her days; go with her hair cut short, get up in the middle of the night for service, and eat nothing but bread and water. "For," she said, "I shall never cease to think that my own brother tried to do such a wicked thing."

Nancy as a nun made us all laugh, and so with spirits raised a little, we kissed, and said farewell. Nancy promised to let me know every other day by post, whatever the letter should cost, how things went. It seemed to me, indeed, as if, seeing that Will had not died in the first twenty-four hours, the chance was somewhat in favour of his recovery. And he was so strong a man, and so young. I sent a message of duty and respect to Sir Robert—I dared not ask to have my name so much as mentioned to Will's mother—and left Nancy in her trouble, full of mine own.

Before we started next morning, Cicely went for news, but there was no improvement. The stable-boy, she told me, was going about the town, his arm bandaged up, saying that if ever a man was murdered in cold blood it was his master, because he had never a sword, and only a stick to defend himself with. Also, it was reported that among the lower classes, the servants, grooms, footmen, and such, the feeling was strong that the poor gentleman had met with foul play. Asked whether they understood rightly what Mr. Will Levett was doing, Cicely replied that they knew very well, and that they considered he was doing a fine and gallant thing, one which would confer as much honour upon the lady as upon himself, which shows that in this world there is no opinion too monstrous to be held by rough and uneducated people; wherefore we ought the more carefully to guard the constitution and prevent the rabble from having any share in public business, or the control of affairs.

The Chaplain of the Fleet

Our carriage took us to London in three hours, the road being tolerably good, and so well frequented, after the first three miles, that there was little fear of highway robbers or footpads. And so we came back to our lodgings in Red Lion Street, after such a two months as I believe never before fell to the lot of any girl.

Remember that I was a wife, yet a maiden; married to a man whom I had never seen except for a brief quarter of an hour, who knew not my name, and had never seen me at all—making allowance for the state of drunkenness in which he was married; that I knew this man's name, but he knew not mine; that I met him at Epsom, and that he had fallen in love with me, and I, God help me! with him. Yet that there was no way out of it, no escape but that before he could marry me (again) I must needs confess the deceit of which I had been guilty. No Heaven, say the Roman Catholics, without Purgatory. Yet suppose, after going through Purgatory, one were to miss one's Heaven!

How could I best go to my lord and tell him?

He was in hiding, in the Rules of the Fleet, and in our old lodging looking over the Fleet Market by one window, and over Fleet Lane by the other—a pleasant lodging for so great a lord. Could I go down to him, in hoops and satin, to tell him in that squalid place the whole truth? Yet go I must.

Now, while we drove rapidly along the road, which is smooth and even between Epsom, or at least between Streatham and London, a thought came into my mind which wanted, after a little, nothing but the consent of Mrs. Esther. A dozen times was I upon the point of telling her all, and as many times did I refrain, because I reflected that, although she knew all about the carrying away of girls from the romances which she read, a secret marriage in the Fleet, although she had lived so long in the Rules, and even knew my uncle and thought him the greatest of men, was a thing outside her experience, and would therefore only terrify her and confuse her. Therefore I resolved to tell her no more than I was obliged.

But then my plans made it necessary that I should leave her for a while—two or three days, perhaps, or even more.

So soon, therefore, as we had unpacked our trunks, and Mrs. Esther was seated in an arm-chair to rest after the fatigues of the rapid journey, I began upon the subject of getting away from her, hypocritically pleading my duty towards the Doctor, my uncle. I said that I thought I ought to pay him a visit, and that after my return to London he would certainly take it unkindly if I did not; that, considering the character of the place in which he unhappily resided, it was not to be thought that a person of Mrs. Esther's sensibility could be exposed to its rudeness; and that, with her permission, I would the next day take a coach, and, unless the Doctor detained me, I would return in the afternoon.

We had so firmly maintained our resolution to forget the past, that Mrs. Esther only smiled when I spoke of the rudeness of the market, and said that no doubt it was desirable for a gentlewoman to keep away from rude and unpolished people, so that the elevation of her mind might not be disturbed by unpleasant or harassing scenes. At the same time, she added, there were reasons, doubtless, why I should from time to time seek out that great and good man (now in misfortune) to whom we all owed a debt of gratitude which never could be repaid. She therefore gave me permission to go there, it being understood that I was to be conveyed thither, and back again, in a coach.

In the morning, after breakfast, I dressed myself for the journey, and, because I thought it likely that I might remain for one night at least, and perhaps more, I took with me a bag containing my oldest and poorest clothes, those, namely, in which I was dressed while in the market. Then I wrapped myself in a hood which I could pull, if necessary, over my face, and, so disguised, I stole down the stairs.

London streets are safe for a young woman in the morning, when the throng of people to and fro keeps rogues honest. I walked through Fetter Lane, remembering that here Solomon Stallabras was born — indeed, I passed a little shop over which the name was painted on a swinging sign of the Silver Garter, so that one of his relatives still carried on the business. Then I walked along Fleet Street, crowded with chairs, carriages, waggons, and porters. The Templars were lounging about the gates of their Inns; the windows of the many vintners' houses were wide open, and within them were gentlemen, drinking wine, early as it was; the coffee-houses were full of tradesmen who would have been better at home behind their counters; ladies were crowding into the shops, having things turned over for them; 'prentices jostled each other behind the posts; grave gentlemen walked slowly along, carrying their canes before them, like wands of office; swaggering young fellows took the wall of every one, except of each other; the street was full of the shouting, noise, and quarrelling which I remembered so well. At the end was the bridge with its quacks bawling their wares which they warranted to cure everything, and its women selling hot furmety, oysters, and fish. Beyond the bridge rose before me the old gate of Lud, which has since been pulled down, and on the left was the Fleet Market, at sight of which, as of an old friend, I could have burst into tears.

The touters and runners for the Fleet parsons were driving their trade as merrily as ever. Among them I recognised my old friend Roger, who did not see me. By the blackness of one eye, and the brown paper sticking to his forehead, one could guess that competition among the brethren of his craft had been more than usually severe of late.

Prosperity, I thought to myself, works speedy changes with us. Was it really possible that I had spent six long months and more in this stinking, noisy, and intolerable place? Why, could I have had one moment of happiness when not only was I surrounded by infamy in every shape, but I had no hope or prospect of being rescued? In eight short months these things had grown to seem impossible. Death itself, I thought, would be preferable to living among such people and in the midst of such scenes.

I recognised them all: it gave me pain to feel how familiar they were: the mean, scowling faces, stamped with the seal of wicked lives and wicked thoughts—such faces must those souls wear who are lost beyond redemption: and the deformed men and boys who seemed to select this market as their favourite haunt. There are many more deformed among the poor than with the better sort, by reason of the accidents which befall their neglected children and maim them for life. That would account for the presence of many of these monsters, but not of all; I suppose some of them come to the market because the labour of handling and carrying the fruit and vegetables is light, though poorly paid.

There were hunchbacks in great plenty; those whose feet were clubbed, whose legs were knock-kneed, whose feet were turned inward, whose eyes squinted. I looked about me for—but did not see—a certain dreadful woman whom I remembered, who sold shell-fish at a stall and had fingers webbed like a duck; but there was the other dreadful woman still in her place, whose upper lip was horrid to look at for hair; there was the cobbler who refused to shave because he said it was unscriptural, and so sat like one of the ancients with a long white beard; there were, alas! the little children, pale, hungry-looking, with eager, sharp eyes, in training for the whip, the gallows, or the plantation. They ran about among the baskets; they sat or stood among the stalls waiting for odd jobs, messages and parcels to carry; they prowled about looking for a chance to steal: it was all as I remembered it, yet had forgotten so quickly. On the right the long wall of the Fleet Prison; beyond that, the Doctor's house, his name painted on the door. I pulled my hood closer over my face and passed it by, because before paying my respects to my uncle I was going to make inquiries about the man I loved.

He was, as I knew, in our old lodgings. He slept, unconscious, in my room; he sat where I had so often sat; the place ought to have reminded him of me. But he knew nothing; the name of Kitty Pleydell was not yet associated in his mind with the Rules of the Fleet.

When we went away, one of those who bade us God-speed and shed tears over our departure was Mrs. Dunquerque, who, as I have told, lived above us with her husband, Captain Dunquerque, and her two little girls. The captain, who was not a good man or a kind man, drank and gambled when he got any money, and left his poor wife and children to starve. It was to her that I meant to go. She was a kind-hearted woman, and fond of me for certain favours I had been able to show her little girls. I was sure to find her in the same lodgings, because in the Rules no one ever changes.

I came to the house: I pulled the hood so close about my face that had my lord met me he would not have known me. The door was standing wide open, as usual. I entered and mounted the stairs. The door of the room—our old room, on the first-floor—was half open. Within—oh, my heart!—I saw my lord sitting at the table, with paper before him, pen in hand. I dared not wait, lest he might discover me, but hastened upstairs to Mrs. Dunquerque's room.

I was fortunate enough to find her at home. The captain was gone abroad, and had taken the children with him for a morning's walk. She sat at home, as usual, darning, mending, and making. But oh! the cry of pleasure and surprise when she saw me, and the kisses she gave me, and the praise at my appearance, and the questions after Mrs. Esther! I told her of all, including Sir Miles Lackington and Solomon Stallabras's good fortune. Then she began to tell me of herself. They were as poor as when we went away; but their circumstances had improved in one important particular; for though the captain was no more considerate (as I guessed from a word she dropped), and drank and gambled whenever he could, they had a friend who sent them without fail what was more useful to them than money—food and clothes for the children and their mother. She did not know who the friend was, but the supplies never failed, being as regular as those brought by the prophet's ravens.

I did not need to be told the name of this friend, for, in truth, I had myself begged the Doctor to extend his charity to this poor family, and asked him to send them beef and pudding, which the children could eat, rather than money, which the captain would drink. This he promised to do. Truly, charity, in his case, ought to have covered a multitude of sins, for he had a hand ever open to give, and a heart to pity; moreover, he gave in secret, and never did his right hand know what his left hand was doing.

Then I opened my business to Mrs. Dunquerque, but only partially.

I told her that on the first-floor, in the rooms formerly occupied by ourselves, there was a young gentleman, well known to Sir Miles Lackington, who had reason to be out of sight for a short time; that he was also known to myself—here I blushed, and my friend nodded and laughed, being interested, as all women are, in the discovery of a love secret; that I was anxious for his welfare; that I had made the excuse of paying a visit to the Doctor in order to be near him: that, in fact, I would be about him, wait upon him, and watch over him, without his knowledge of my presence.

"But he will most certainly know thee, child," she cried. "Tell me, my dear, is he in love with thee?"

"He says so," I replied. "Perhaps he tells the truth."

"And you? O Kitty! to think of you only a year ago!"

"There is no doubt about me," I said; "for, oh! dear Mrs. Dunquerque, I am head over ears in love with him. Yet I will so contrive that he shall not know me, if you will help."

"And what can I do?"

"Make his acquaintance; go and see him; tell him that he must want some one to do for him; offer to send him your maid Phœbe—yes, Phœbe. Then I will go, and, if he speaks to me, which is not likely, I will answer in a feigned voice. Go, now, Mrs. Dunquerque. I will dress for Phœbe."

She laughed and went away.

My lord lifted his head as she knocked at the door.

"I ask your pardon, sir," she said, "for this intrusion. I live above you, upon the second-floor, with my husband and children. I suppose, sir, that, like the rest of us in this place, you come here because you cannot help it, and a pity it is to find so young a gentleman thus early shipwrecked."

"I thank you, madam," said my lord, bowing, "for this goodwill."

"The will is nothing, sir, because people in misfortune ought to help each other when they can. Therefore, sir, and because I perceive that your room is not what a gentleman's should be, being inch thick with dust, I will, with your permission, send down my maid when you go out, who may make you clean and tidy."

"I shall not go out," replied my lord; "but I thank you for the offer of the girl. I dare say the place might be cleaner."

"She is a girl, sir," replied Mrs. Dunquerque, "who will not disturb you by any idle chatter. Phœbe!" Here she stepped out upon the stairs. "Phœbe! Come downstairs this minute, and bring a duster."

When Phœbe came, she was a girl whose hair was pulled over her eyes, and she had the corner of her apron in her mouth; she wore a brown stuff frock, not down to her ankles; her hands where whiter than is generally found in a servant; her apron was of the kind which servant-maids use to protect their frocks, and she wore a great cap tied under the chin and awry, as happens to maids in the course of their work; in one respect, beside her hands, Phœbe was different from the ordinary run of maidservants—her shoes and stockings were so fine that she feared his lordship would notice them.

But he noticed her not at all—neither shoes, nor hands, nor cap, nor apron, which, though it was foolish, made this servant-girl feel a little pained.

"Phœbe," said Mrs. Dunquerque, "you will wait upon this gentleman, and fetch him what he wants. And now do but look at the dust everywhere. Saw one ever such untidiness? Quick, girl, with the duster, and make things clean. Dear me! to think of this poor gentleman sitting up to his eyes, as one may say, in a peck of dust!"

She stood in the room, with her work in her hand, rattling on about the furniture and the fineness of the day, and the brightness of the room, which had two windows, and the noise of the market, which, she said, the young gentleman would mind, more than nothing at all, after a while. As for the dreadful language of the porters and fishwives, that, she said, was not pleasant at first, but after a little one got, so to say, used to it, and you no more expected that one of these wretches should speak without breaking the third commandment and shocking ears used to words of purity and piety, than you would expect his Grace the Archbishop of Canterbury himself to use the language of the market. She advised the young gentleman, further, for his own good, not to sit alone and mope, but to go abroad and ruffle it with the rest, to keep a stout heart, to remember that Fortune frowns one day and smiles the next, being a deity quite capricious and untrustworthy; therefore that it behoved a young man to have hope; and she exhorted him in this end to seek out cheerful company, such as that of the great Doctor Shovel, the only Chaplain of the Fleet, as learned as a bishop and as merry as a monk: or even to repair to the prison and play tennis and racquets with the gentlemen therein confined: but, above all, not to sit alone and brood. Why, had he never a sweetheart to whom he could write, and send sweet words of love, whereby the heart of the poor thing would be lightened, and her affections fixed?

So she rattled on, while I, nothing loth, plied duster, and cleaned up furniture with a zeal surpassing that of any housemaid. Yet, because men never observe what is under their eyes, he observed nothing of all this activity. If I had crawled as slowly as possible over the work, it would have been all one to him.

Presently I came to the table at which he was sitting. This, too, was covered with dust. (It had been our table formerly, and had grown old in the service of the Pimpernel ladies.) I brushed away the dust with great care, and in so doing, I saw that he had a letter before him, just begun. It commenced with these enchanting words—

"Love of my soul! My goddess Kitty——"

Oh that I could have fallen at his feet, then and there, and told him all! But I could not; I was afraid.

He had, as yet, written nothing more. But on a piece of paper beside the letter he had traced the outlines of a woman's head. Whose head should it be, I ask you, but Kitty's?

I was amazed at the sight. My colour came and went.

"Phœbe," cried Mrs. Dunquerque warningly, "be careful how you touch the papers! There, sir, we have your room straight for you. It looks a little cleaner than it did awhile since."

"Surely," he replied, without looking around. "Yes, I am truly obliged to you, madam. As for this girl"—still he would not look at me—"perhaps——"

He placed a whole crown-piece in my hand. A crown-piece for such a simple piece of work! Enough to make the best of housemaids grasping! This is how men spoil servants.

"Can I get you anything, sir?" I asked, in a feigned voice.

"Nothing, child, nothing. Stay—yes. One must eat a little, sometimes. Get me some dinner by-and-by."

This was all for that time. We went away, and we spent the rest of the morning in making him such a little dinner as we thought must please him. First we got from the market a breast of veal, which we roasted with a little stuffing, and dished with a slice or two of bacon, nicely broiled, some melted butter made with care, and a lemon. This, to my mind, forms a dish fit for a prince. We added to this some haricot beans, with butter and sweet herbs, and a dish of young potatoes. Then we made a little fruit pudding and a custard, nicely browned, and, at two o'clock, put all upon a tray, and I carried it downstairs, still with my hair over my eyes, my cap still awry, and the corner of the apron still in my teeth.

I set the food before him and waited to serve him. But he would not let me.

Ah! had he known how I longed to do something for him, and what a happiness it was simply to make his dinner, to prepare his vegetables for him, and to boil his pudding! But how should he guess?

I found Sir Miles's bottle of wine untouched in the cupboard, and placed it on the table. Then I left him to his meal. When I returned, I found he had eaten next to nothing. One could have cried with vexation.

"Lord, sir," I said, still in my feigned voice, "if you do not eat you will be ill. Is there never a body that loves you?"

He started, but hardly looked at me.

"A trick of voice," he said. "Yet it reminded me—Is there anybody who loves me, child? I think there is. To be sure, there is some one whom I love."

"Then, sir, you ought to eat, if only to please her, by keeping well and strong."

"Well, well! I dare say I shall be hungry to-morrow. You can take away the things, Phœbe, if that is what they call you."

I could say no more, but was fain to obey. Then as I could do no more for him, I took up the tray and resolved to go and see the Doctor, with whom I had much to say. Therefore I put off my servant's garb, with the apron and cap, and drew the hood over my face again.

The Doctor's busy time was in the morning. In the afternoon, after dinner, he mostly slept in his arm-chair, over a pipe of tobacco. I found him alone thus enjoying himself. I know not whether he slept or meditated, for the tobacco was still burning, though his eyes were closed.

There is this peculiarity about noise in London, that people who live in it and sleep in it do not notice it. Thus while there was a horrible altercation outside his very windows—a thing which happened every day, and all day long—the Doctor regarded it not at all. Yet he heard me open and shut the door, and was awake instantly.

"Kitty!" he cried. "Why, child, what dost thou here?"

"I hope, sir," I said, "that I find you in good health and spirits."

"Reasonable good, Kitty. A man of my years, be he never so temperate and regular in his habits, finds the slow tooth of time gnawing upon him. Let me look at thy face. Humph! one would say that the air of Epsom is good for young maids' cheeks. But why in Fleet Market, child?"

"Partly, sir, I came to see you, and partly— —"

"To see some one else, of whose lodging in the Rules I have been told by Sir Miles Lackington. Tell me—the young man whom he wounded, is he dead?"

"Nay, sir, not dead, but grievously wounded, and in a high fever."

"So. A man in early manhood, who has been wounded by a sword running through his vitals, who four days after the event is still living, though in a high fever—that man, methinks, is likely to recover, unless his physician, as is generally the case, is an ass. For, my dear, there are as many incompetent physicians as there are incapable preachers. Their name is Legion. Well, Kitty, you came about Lord Chudleigh. Have you seen him?"

"Yes; but, sir, he does not know that I am here. I saw him"—here I blushed again—"in disguise as a housemaid."

"Ho! ho! ho!" laughed the Doctor. "Why, girl, thou hast more spirit than I gave thee credit for. Thou deservest him, and shalt have him, too. The time is come." He rose and folded his gown about him, and put on his wig, which for coolness' sake he had laid aside. "I will go to him and say, 'My lord, the person to whom you were married is no other than— —'"

"Oh! no, sir. I pray you do not speak to him in such fashion. Pray hear me first."

"Well—well. Let us hear this little baggage." The Doctor was in very good spirits, and eager to unfold this tale. He sat down again, however, and took up his pipe. "Go on, then, Kitty; go on—I am listening."

This was, indeed, a very critical moment of my life. For on this moment depended, I foresaw, all my happiness. I therefore hesitated a little, thinking what to say and how to say it. Then I began.

I reminded my uncle that, when I first came under his protection, I was a young girl fresh from the country, who knew but little evil, suspected none, and in all things had been taught to respect and fear my betters. I then reminded him how, while in this discipline of mind, I was one morning called away by him, and ordered to go through a certain form which (granting that I well knew it to be the English form of marriage service) I could not really believe to mean that I was married. And though my uncle assured me afterwards that such was the case, I so little comprehended that it could be possible, that I had almost forgotten the whole event. Then, I said, we had gone away from the Rules of the Fleet, and found ourselves under happier circumstances, where new duties made me still more forget this strange thing. Presently we went to Epsom, whither, in the strangest way, repaired the very man I had married.

After this, I told him, the most wonderful thing in the world happened to me. For not only did my lord fall in love with me, his legal wife, but he gave me to understand that the only obstacle to his marrying me was that business in the Fleet, of which he informed me at length.

"Very good," said the Doctor. "Things could not go better. If the man has fallen in love with the girl, he ought to be pleased that she is his wife."

Nay: that would not do either; for here another thing of which the Doctor had no experience, being a man. For when a woman falls in love with a man she must needs make herself as virtuous and pure in mind as she is brave in her dress, in order the more to please him and fix his affection. And what sort of love would that be where a woman should glory, as it were, in deception?

Why, his love would be changed, if not into loathing, then into a lower kind of love, in which admiration of a woman's beauty forms the whole part. Now, if beauty is everything, even Helen of Troy would be a miserable woman, a month after marriage, when her husband would grow tired of her.

"Alas!" I cried, "I love him. If you tell him, as he must now be told, that I was the woman who took a part in that shameful business—yes, sir, even to your face I must needs call it shameful—you may tell him at once that I release him so far as I can. I will not acknowledge the marriage. I will go into no court of law, nor will I give any evidence to establish my rights— —"

"Whom God hath joined— —" the Doctor began.

"Oh! I know—I know. And you are a clergyman of the Church, with power and authority by laying on of hands. Yet I cannot think, I cannot feel that any blessing of heaven could rest upon a union performed in such a place. Is this room, nightly desecrated by revellers, a church? Is your profligate wretch Roger a clerk? Where were the banns put up? What bells were rung?"

"Banns are no longer fashionable," he replied. "But let me think." He was not angry with my plainness of speech, but rather the contrary. "Let me think." He went to his cupboard, took out his great register, and turned over the leaves. "Ay! here it is, having a page to itself: Geoffrey Lord Chudleigh to Catherine Pleydell. Your ladyship is as truly Lady Chudleigh as his mother was before him. But if you *will* give up that title and dignity"—here he smiled and tore out the page, but carefully—"I will not baulk thee, child. Here is the register, and here the certificate of the wedding." He put both together, and laid them carefully aside. "Come to me to-morrow, and I will then go with you to his lordship and give him these papers to deal with as he pleases."

CHAPTER THE LAST.

HOW LORD CHUDLEIGH RECEIVED HIS FREEDOM.

I returned to my lodging, there to await the event of the next morning. My lord would learn that he was free—so far good. But with his freedom would come the news that the woman who restored it to him was the same who had taken it away, and the same whom he had professed to love. Alas! poor Kitty!

Now was I like unto a man sentenced to death, yet allowed to choose the form of his execution, whether he would be hanged, poisoned, beheaded, stabbed, shot, drowned, or pushed violently and suddenly out of life in some other manner which he might prefer. As the time approaches, his anxiety grows the greater until the fatal moment arrives when he must choose at once; then, in trouble and confusion, he very likely chooses that very method which is most painful in the contemplation and the endurance. So with me. I might choose the manner of telling my lover all, but tell him I must. "Pray Heaven," I said, "to direct me into the best way." In the afternoon I became once more Phœbe.

Phœbe carried a dish of tea; would the gentleman choose to taste it? He took it from Phœbe's hand, drank it, and returned to his writing, which was, I believe, a continuation of that letter, the commencement of which I had seen.

In the evening Sir Miles paid him a visit of consolation. He drank up what was left of the bottle, and, after staying an hour or so, went away, noisily promising himself a jovial night with the Doctor.

At eight o'clock Phœbe brought a tray with cold meat upon it, but my lord would take none, only bidding her to set it down and leave him.

"Can I do nothing more for you, sir?" asked the maid.

He started again.

"Your voice, child," he said (although I had disguised my voice), "reminds of one whose voice——"

"La, sir!" she asked. "Is it the voice of your sweetheart?"

He only sighed and sat down again. Phœbe lingered as long as she could, and then she went away.

Then we all went to bed. Captain Dunquerque had by this time brought home the little girls and gone to the Doctor's, where, with Sir Miles and the rest, he was making a night of it.

It was a hot night; the window was open; the noise of the brawling and fighting below was intolerable; the smell from the market was worse than anything I remembered, and the bed was a strange one. Added to all this, my cares were so great that I could not sleep. Presently I arose and looked out, just as I had done a year before when first I came to my uncle for protection. Everything was the same; there was light enough to see the groups of those who talked and the forms of those who slept. I remembered the old and the young, as I had seen them in the bright light of a July dawn: poor wretches, destined from their birth to be soldiers of the devil; elected for disgrace and shame; born for Newgate and Bridewell; brought into the world for the whipping post, the cart-tail, and the gallows. Just the same; and I alone changed. For beneath me, all unconscious, was one whom I might call my husband. Then my thoughts went wholly out to him; then I could neither sit nor rest, nor stand still with thinking of the next day, and what I had to say and how to say it. Oh, my love—my dear—could I bear to give him up? could I bear to see him turn away those eyes which had never looked upon me save with kindness and affection? Could I endure to think that his love was gone from me altogether? Death was better, if death would come.

Then, crazed, I think, with trouble, I crept slowly from the room, and went down the stair till I reached the door of the room where my lord was lying. And here I went on like a mad thing, having just enough sense to keep silence, yet weeping without restraint, wringing my hands, praying, offering to Heaven the sacrifice of my life, if only my lover would not harden his heart to me, and kissing the while the very senseless wood of the door.

Within the room he was sleeping unconscious; without I was silently crying and weeping, full of shame and anxiety, not daring to hope, yet knowing full well his noble heart. Why, had I, weeks before, dared to tell him all, forgiveness would have been mine; I knew it well. Yet now, in such a place, when he was reminded of the companions, or at least the creatures, who had surrounded her, would he not harden his heart and refuse to believe that any virtue, any purity, could survive?

All this was of no avail. When I was calmed a little I returned to my own room and sat upon the bed, wondering whether any woman was so miserable in her shame as myself.

The long minutes crept on slowly: the daylight was dawning: the night had passed away: Captain Dunquerque had rolled up the stairs noisily, singing a drunken song: the revellers below were quiet, but the morning carts had begun when I fell asleep for weariness, and when I awoke the sun was high. So I arose, dressed, and hastened downstairs, hoping to see the Doctor before he sallied forth.

There had been, Roger told me with a smile, a great night. He meant that the Doctor's guests had been many, and their calls for punch numerous. Sir Miles had been carried away to some place in the neighbourhood. The Doctor was still abed.

While we talked he appeared, no whit the worse for his night's potations. Yet I thought his face was of a deeper purple than of old, and his neck thicker. That was very likely an idle fancy, because a few months could make but little difference in a man of his fixed habits.

"Well, Kitty"—he was in good humour, and apparently satisfied with the position of things—"I have thought over thy discourse of yesterday, which, I confess, greatly moved me: first, because I did not know thee to be a girl of such spirit, courage, and dignity; and second, because I now perceive that the marriage, performed in thy interest, was perhaps, as things have now turned out (which is surely providential), a mistake. Yet was it done for the best, and I repent me not. Come, then, to my lord, and let me talk to him."

"First, sir," I begged, "tell him not my name."

He promised this; though, as he said, the name was on the register; and it was agreed between us that we should speak to my lord privately, and then that he was to call me, when I should play my part as best I could.

The Doctor led the way. When he entered the room I ran upstairs, and with trembling hands made myself as fine as I could; that is, I was but in morning dishabille, but I dressed my hair, and put those little touches to my frock and ribbons which every woman understands. And then I put on my hood, which I pulled quite over my face, and waited.

My lord rose angrily when he saw the Doctor.

"Sir," he said, "this visit is an intrusion. I have no business with you; I do not desire to see you. Leave the room immediately!"

"First," said Doctor Shovel, "I have business with your lordship."

"I can have no business with you," replied Lord Chudleigh. "I have already had too much business with you. Go, sir: your intrusion is an insult."

"Dear, dear!" the Doctor replied. "This it is to be young and hot-headed and to jump at conclusions. Whereas, did the young gentleman know the things I have to say, he would welcome me with open arms."

"You come, I suppose, to remind me of a thing of which you ought to be truly ashamed, so wicked was it."

"Nay, nay; not so wicked as your lordship thinks." The Doctor would not be put out of temper. "What a benefactor is he who makes young people happy, with the blessing of the Church!"

"I cannot, I suppose, use violence to this man," said the other. "He is a clergyman, and, for the sake of his cloth, must be tolerated. Would you kindly, sir, proceed at once to the business you have in hand and then begone? If you come to laugh over the misfortune caused by yourself, laugh and go your way. If you come for money for the wretched accomplice in your conspiracy, ask it and go. In any case, sir, make haste."

"My lord," the Doctor replied, "I am a messenger—from one who conceives that she hath done you grievous wrong, is very sorry for the past, which she alone can undo, and begs your forgiveness."

"Who is that person, then?" His curiosity was roused, and he waited in patience to hear what the Doctor might have to say.

"It is, my lord, the lady who may, if she chooses, call herself your wife."

My lord stood confused.

"Does she wish to see me?"

"She wishes to place in your hands"—here the Doctor's voice became deeper and more musical, like the low notes of a great organ—"the proofs of her marriage with you. Does your lordship comprehend? She will stand before you, bringing with her the only papers which exist to prove the fact. She will put them in your own hands, if you wish; she will destroy them before your eyes if you wish; and she will then retire from your presence, and you shall never know, unless you wish it, the name of the woman you married."

"But… This is wonderful… How shall I know that the papers are the only proof of the ceremony?"

"Your lordship has my word—my word of a Christian priest. I break the laws of God and of man daily. I am, however, a sinner who still guards those rags and tatters of a conscience which most sinners hasten to throw away—wherefore must my repentance be some day greater. Yet, my lord, my word I never brake, nor ever looked to hear it questioned. You shall have all the proofs. You shall be free if you please, from this moment. You shall never be molested, reproached, threatened, or reminded of the past."

"Free!" my lord repeated, looking the Doctor in the face. "I cannot but believe, sir, what you solemnly aver to be the truth. Yet what am I to think of this generosity? how interpret it? By what acts have I deserved it? What am I to do in return? Is there any pitfall or snare for me?"

"In return, you will grant her your forgiveness. That is a pitfall, if you please. You will also expect a surprise."

"Strange!" said Lord Chudleigh. "Kitty asked me, too, to forgive this woman. My forgiveness! Does she ask for no money?"

"My lord, you are utterly deceived in your belief as to this woman and her conduct. By your leave I will tell you the exact truth.

"You know, because I told you, that the wrong inflicted upon me by your father was my justification, from a worldly point of view, for the advantage which I took of your condition. You think, I suppose, that some miserable drab was brought in from the market to play the part of dummy wife, and threaten you and persecute you for money. You are wrong.

"There was living in this place at the time, with a lady of ruined fortunes, a young woman of gentle birth (by her father's side), though penniless. She was beautiful exceedingly, well educated, a God-fearing damsel, and a good girl. By her mother's side she was my niece, that branch of her family being of obscure origin. On the death of her father she became for a time my ward, which was the reason why she lived here—no fit place for a girl of good reputation, I own, though at the time I could do no better for her. She was not only all that I have described her in appearance, carriage, and virtues, but she was, as well, very much afraid of me, her guardian. She had been brought up to obey without questioning her spiritual pastors and masters and all who might be placed in authority over her. This girl it was whom you married."

The Doctor paused, to let his words have due effect.

"When I designed the treachery, you being then sound asleep, it first seemed to me that the fitting person for such a revenge as I at first proposed to myself would be one of those women who are confined to the Fleet for life, unless by hook or crook they can get them a husband. Such a one I sent for. I did not disclose the name of the man I proposed, because I found her only too eager to marry any one upon whom she could saddle her debts, and so make him either pay them or change places with her. But while I talked with the woman I thought how cruel a thing it would be for your lordship to be mated with such a wife, and I resolved, if I did give you a wife against your knowledge, that she should be worthy to bear your name. Accordingly I despatched this person, who is still, I suppose, languishing in the prison hard by, and sent for the young lady.

"She came unsuspiciously. I told her with a frown which made her tremble, that she was to obey me in all that I ordered her to do; and I bade her, then, take her place at the table, and repeat such words as I should command. She obeyed. Your lordship knows the rest."

"But she knew—she must have known—that she was actually married?"

The Chaplain of the Fleet

"She could not understand. She had seen marriages performed; but then it was in a church, with regular forms. She did not know until I told her. Besides, I ordered her; and, had my command been to throw herself from a high tower, she would have obeyed. She was not yet seventeen; she was country-bred, and she was innocence itself."

"Poor child," said my lord.

"She has left the Rules of the Fleet for some time. She knows that at any time she might claim the name and the honours of your wife, but she has refrained, though she has had hundreds of opportunities. Now, however, she declares that she will be no longer a party to the conspiracy, and she is desirous of restoring, into your own hands, the papers of the marriage. Will your lordship, first, forgive her?"

"Tell her," said my lord, "that I forgive her freely. Where is she?"

"She waits without."

Then he called me, but not by name.

My knees trembled and shook beneath me as I rose, pulled the hood tighter over my face, and followed the Doctor into the room. In my hand I held the papers.

"This," said the Doctor, "is the young gentlewoman of whom we spoke. The papers are in her hands. Child, give his lordship the papers."

I held them out, and he took them. All this time he never ceased gazing at me; but he could see nothing, not even my eyes.

"Are we playing a comedy?" he asked. "Doctor Shovel, are we dreaming, all of us?"

"Everything, my lord is real. You hold in your hands the certificate of marriage and the register. Not copies—the actual documents. Before you read the papers and learn the lady's name, tell her, in my hearing, that you forgive her. She bids me tell you, for her, that since she learned the thing that she had done, what it meant, and whose happiness it threatened, she has had no happy day."

"Forgiveness!" said my lord, in a voice strangely moved, while his eyes softened. "Forgiveness, madam, is a poor word to express what

I feel in return for this most generous deed. It is a thing for which I can find no word sufficient to let you know how great is my gratitude. Learn, madam, that my heart is bestowed upon a woman whose perfections, to my mind, are such that no man is worthy of her; but she hath graciously been pleased to accept, and even to return my affection. Now by this act, because I cannot think that we are bound together in the eyes of the Church by that form of marriage service——"

"It is a question," said the Doctor, "which it would task the learning of the whole country to decide. By ecclesiastical law—but let us leave this question unconsidered. Nothing need ever be said about the matter. Your lordship is free."

"Then"—he still held the papers in his hand, and seemed in no way anxious to satisfy his curiosity as to the name of the woman who had caused so much anxiety—"before we part, perhaps never to meet again, may I ask to be allowed to see the face of the lady who has performed this wonderful act of generosity?"

I trembled, but made no answer.

"Stay a moment," he said. "Remember that you have given up a goodly estate, with a large fortune and an ancient name—things which all women rightly prize. These things you have given away. Do you repent?"

I shook my head.

"Then let me never know"—he tore the papers into a thousand fragments—"let me never know the name of the woman to whom I owe this gift. Let me think of her as of an angel!"

The Doctor took me by the arm as if to lead me away.

"Since you do not want to know her name, my lord, I do not see any reason why you should. Let us go, child."

"May I only see her face?" he asked.

"Come, child," urged the Doctor; "come away. There is no need, my lord."

But those words about myself, his nobleness, had touched me to the heart. I could deceive him no longer. I threw back the hood, put up my hands to my face, and fell at his feet, crying and sobbing.

"It is I, my lord! It was Kitty Pleydell herself—the woman whom you thought so good. Oh, forgive me! forgive me! Have pity!"

Now I seem to have no words to tell how he raised me in his strong arms, how he held me by the waist and kissed me, crying that indeed there was nothing in his heart towards me but love and tenderness.

Would it not be a sin to write down those words of love and endearment with which, when the Doctor left us alone, he consoled and soothed me? I hid nothing from him. I told him how I had well-nigh forgotten the dreadful thing I had done until I saw him again at the Assembly; how from day to day my conscience smote me more and more, and yet I dared not tell him all—for fear of losing his respect.

Let us pass this over.

The story of Kitty is nearly told.

We forgot all about poor Will and the reason why my lord should for a while lie close. We agreed that we would be married quietly, in due form, and of course at church, as soon as arrangements could be made. And then nothing would do but my lord must carry me to Mrs. Esther, and formally ask her permission to the engagement.

You may think how happy was I to step into the coach which brought me back to my dear lady, with such a companion.

He led me into her presence with a stately bow.

"Madam," he said, "I have the honour to ask your permission to take the hand of your ward, Miss Kitty, who hath been pleased to lend a favourable ear to my proposals. Be assured, dear madam, that we have seriously weighed and considered the gravity of the step which we propose to take, and the inclination of our hearts. And I beg you, madam, to believe that my whole life, whether it be long or short, shall be devoted to making this dear girl as happy as it is in the power of one human creature to make another."

Mrs. Esther was perfectly equal to the proper ceremonies demanded for the occasion, although, as she confessed, she was a great deal surprised at the suddenness of the thing, which, notwithstanding that she had expected it for many weeks, came upon her with a shock. She said that his lordship's proposal was one which the world would no doubt consider a great condescension, seeing that her dear Kitty, though of good family, had no other prospects than the inheritance of the few hundreds which made her own income: but, for her own part, knowing this child as she did—and here she spoke in terms of unmerited praise of beauty and goodness and such qualities as I could lay but small claim to possess, yet resolved to aim at them.

Finally, she held out her own hand to his lordship, saying—

"Therefore, my lord, as I consider Kitty my daughter, so henceforth will I consider you my son. And may God keep and bless you both, and give you all that the heart of a good man may desire, with children good and dutiful, long and peaceful lives, and in the end, to sit together for ever in happy heaven."

Whereupon she wept, falling on my neck.

Now, while we were thus weeping and crying, came Sir Miles, who immediately guessed the cause, and wished my lord joy, shaking him by the hand. Then he must needs kiss my hand.

"The Doctor," he explained, "told me where I should most likely find you. The Doctor's knowledge of the human heart is most extensive. I would I had the Doctor's head for punch. My lord, this is a lucky day. Will Levett is out of his fever, and hath signed a written confession that your sword was drawn in self-defence, and that had he not been run through, his cudgel would have beaten out your brains. Therefore there is no more to keep us in hiding, and we may go about joyfully in the open, as gentlemen should. And as for Will, he may die or live, as seemeth him best."

"Nay, Sir Miles," I said. "Pray that the poor lad live and lead a better life."

This is the story of Kitty Pleydell: how she came to London, and lived in the Rules of the Fleet: how she was made to go through the form of a marriage: how she left the dreadful, noisy, wicked place: how she went to Epsom: how Lord Chudleigh fell in love with her, to her unspeakable happiness; and how she told him her great secret. The rest, which is the history of a great and noble man married to a wife whose weakness was guided and led by him in the paths of virtue, discretion and godliness, cannot be told.

I have told what befell some of the actors in this story—Solomon Stallabras, I have explained, married the brewer's widow: Will Levett recovered and did not repent, but lived a worse life after his narrow escape than before. As for the rest, Mrs. Esther remained with us, either at Chudleigh Court or our town house: Harry Temple was wise enough to give up pining after what he could not get, and married Nancy, so that she, too, had her heart's desire: Sir Miles went on alternately gaming and drinking, till he died of an apoplexy at forty.

There remains to be told the fate of the Chaplain of the Fleet. When they passed the Marriage Act of 1753, the Fleet weddings were suddenly stopped. They had been a scandal to the town for more than forty years, so that it was high time they should be ended. But when the end actually came, the Doctor, who had saved no money, was penniless. Nor could he earn money in any way whatever, nor had he any friends, although there were hundreds of grateful hearts among the poor creatures around him. Who could contribute to his support except ourselves?

Mrs. Esther, on learning his sad condition, instantly wrote to offer him half her income. My husband, for his part, sent a lawyer among his creditors, found out for what sum he could effect a release, paid this money, which was no great amount, and sent him his discharge. Then, because the Doctor would have been unhappy out of London, he made him a weekly allowance of five guineas, reckoning that he would live on one guinea, drink two guineas, and give away two. He lived to enjoy this allowance for ten years more, going every night to a coffee-house, where he met his friends, drank punch, told stories, sang songs, and was the oracle of the company. He took great pride in the position which he had once occupied in the Rules of the Fleet, and was never tired of boasting how many couples he had made into man and wife.

The Chaplain of the Fleet

I know that his life was disreputable and his pleasures coarse, yet when I think of the Doctor and of his many acts of kindness and charity, I remember certain texts, and I think we have reasonable ground for a Christian's hope as regards his deathbed repentance, which was as sincere as it was edifying.

PRINTED BY BALLANTYNE, HANSON AND CO.
EDINBURGH AND LONDON.

Copyright © 2023 Esprios Digital Publishing. All Rights Reserved.